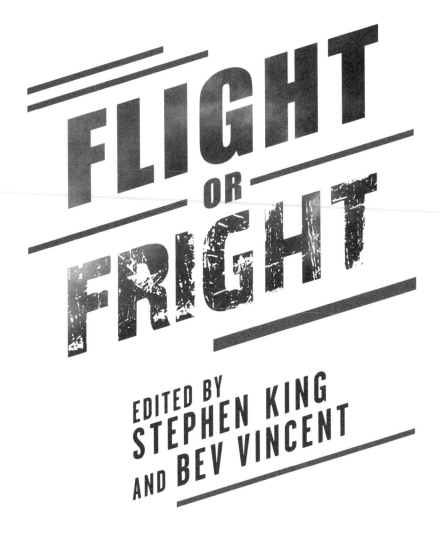

FLIGHT OR FRIGHT

EDITED BY
STEPHEN KING
AND BEV VINCENT

Cemetery Dance Publications
Baltimore
2018

Cemetery Dance Publications
132B Industry Lane, Unit #7
Forest Hill, MD 21050
www.cemeterydance.com

First Cemetery Dance Printing

ISBN: 978-1-58767-679-6

Trade Hardcover Artwork © 2018 by Francois Vaillancourt
Artist Edition artwork © 2018 Cortney Skinner
Cover and Interior Design © 2018 by Desert Isle Design, LLC

This anthology is dedicated to all the pilots, real and fictional, who landed their planes after a harrowing flight and brought their passengers home safely. The list includes:

Wilbur Wright
Chesley Sullenberger
Tammie Jo Shults
Vernon Demerest
Robert Pearson
Eric Gennotte
Tim Lancaster
Min-Huan Ho
Eric Moody
Peter Burkill
Bryce McCormick
Robert Schornstheimer
Richard Champion de Crespigny
Robert Piché
Brian Engle
Ted Striker

 # CONTENTS

INTRODUCTION

STEPHEN KING

Are there people in this modern, technology-driven world who enjoy flying? Hard as it might be to believe, I'm sure there are. Pilots do, most children do (although not babies; the changes in air pressure messes them up), assorted aeronautical enthusiasts do, but that's about it. For the rest of us, commercial air travel has all the charm and excitement of a colorectal exam. Modern airports tend to be overcrowded zoos where patience and ordinary courtesy are tested to the breaking point. Flights are delayed, flights are canceled, luggage is tossed around like beanbags, and on many occasions does not arrive with passengers who desperately desire clean shirts or even *just one* set of fresh underwear.

If you have an early morning flight, God help you. It means rolling out of bed at four in the morning so you can go through a check-in and boarding process as convoluted and tension-inducing as getting out of a small and corrupt South American country in 1954. Do you have a photo ID? Have you made sure your shampoo and conditioner are in small plastic see-thru bottles? Are you prepared to lose your shoes and have your various electronic gadgets irradiated? Are you sure nobody else packed your luggage, or had access to it? Are you ready to undergo a full body scan, and perhaps a pat-down of your naughty bits for good measure? Yes? Good. But you still may discover that your flight has been overbooked, delayed by mechanical or weather issues, perhaps canceled because of a computer meltdown. Also, heaven help you if you're flying standby; you might have better luck buying a lottery scratch ticket.

You surmount these hurdles so you can enter what one of the contributors to this anthology refers to as "a howling shell of death." Isn't that a bit over the top, you might ask, not to mention contrary to fact? Granted. Airliners rarely flame out (although we've all seen unsettling cell phone footage of engines belching fire at 30,000 feet), and flying rarely results in death (statistics say you're more likely to be killed crossing the street, especially if you're a damn fool peering at your cell phone while you do it). Yet you *are* entering what is basically a tube filled with oxygen and sitting atop tons of highly flammable jet fuel.

Once your tube of metal and plastic is sealed up (like—gulp!—a coffin) and leaving the runway, trailing its dwindling shadow behind it, only one thing is sure, a thing so positive it is beyond statistics: you *will* come down. Gravity demands it. The only question is where and why and in how many pieces, one being the ideal. If the reunion with mother earth is on a mile of concrete (hopefully at your destination, but any mile of paved surface will do in a pinch), all is well. If not, your statistical chances of survival plummet rapidly. That, too, is a statistical fact, and one even the most seasoned air travelers must contemplate when their flight runs into clear air turbulence at 30,000 feet.

You're completely out of control at such moments. You can do nothing constructive except double-check your seatbelt as the plates and bottles rattle in the galley and overhead bins pop open and babies wail and your deodorant gives up and the flight attendant comes on the overhead speakers, saying "The captain asks that you remain seated." While your overcrowded tube rocks and rolls and judders and creaks, you have time to reflect on the fragility of your body and that one irrefutable fact: you *will* come down.

Having thus prepared you with food for thought on your next trip through the sky, let me ask the appropriate question: is there any human activity, any at all, more suited to an anthology of horror and suspense stories like the one you now hold in your hands? I think not, ladies and gentlemen. You have it all: claustrophobia, acrophobia, loss of volition. Our lives always hang by a thread, but that is never more clear than when descending into LaGuardia through thick clouds and heavy rain.

On a personal note, your editor is a much better flier than he used to be. Thanks to my career as a novelist, I have flown a great deal over the last forty years, and until 1985 or so, I was a very frightened flier indeed. I understood the theory of flight, and I understood all the safety stats, but neither of those things helped. Part of my problem came from a desire (which I still have) to be in control of every situation. I feel safe when I'm behind the wheel, because I trust myself. When you're behind the wheel...not quite so much (sorry about that). When you enter an airplane and sit down, you are surrendering control to people you don't know; people you may never even see.

Worse, for me, is the fact that I have honed my imagination to a keen edge over the years. That's fine when I'm sitting at my desk and concocting tales where terrible things may happen to very nice people, not so fine when I'm being held hostage in an airplane that turns onto the runway, hesitates, then bolts forward at speeds that would be considered beyond suicidal in the family car.

Imagination is a double-edged blade, and in those early days when I began doing a great deal of flying for my work, it was all too easy to cut myself with it. All too easy to fall into thoughts of all the moving parts in the engine outside my window, so many parts it seemed almost inevitable for them to fall into disharmony. Easy to wonder—impossible not to, really—what every little change in the sound of those engines might mean, or why the plane suddenly tilted in a new direction, the surface of my Pepsi tilting with it (alarmingly!) in its little plastic glass.

If the pilot walked back to have a little chinwag with the passengers, I wondered if the co-pilot was competent (surely he couldn't be *as* competent, or he wouldn't be the redundancy feature). Maybe the plane was on autopilot, but suppose the autopilot suddenly kicked off while the pilot was discussing the chances of the Yankees with someone, and the plane went into a sudden dive? What if the luggage bay latches let go? What if the landing gear froze? What if a window, defective but passed by a quality control employee dreaming about his honey back home, blew out? For that matter, what if a meteor hit us, and the cabin depressurized?

Then, in the mid-eighties, most of those fears subsided, thanks to having a near-death experience while climbing out of Farmingdale Airport in New York, on my way to Bangor, Maine. I'm sure there are plenty of people out there—some perhaps reading this book right now—who have had their own air-scares, everything from collapsing nose gear to planes sliding off icy runways, but this was as close to death as it is possible to come and still live to tell about it.

It was late afternoon. The weather was as clear as a bell. I had chartered a Lear 35, which on takeoff was like having a rocket strapped to your ass. I had been on this particular Lear many times. I knew and trusted the pilots, and why not? The one in the left-hand seat had started flying jets in Korea, had survived scores of combat missions there, and had been flying ever since. He had tens of thousands of hours. I got out my paperback novel and my book of crosswords, anticipating a smooth flight and a pleasant reunion with my wife, kids, and the family dog.

We climbed through 7000 feet and I was wondering if I could persuade my family to go see a movie that night, when the Lear seemed to run into a brick wall. In that instant I felt sure we'd had a midair collision and that the three of us on the plane—both pilots and me—were going to die. The little galley flew open and vomited its contents. The cushions of the unoccupied seats shot into the air. The little jet tilted…tilted some more…then rolled completely over. I felt that part, but didn't see it. I had closed my eyes. My life didn't flash before me. I didn't think *But I had so much more to do.* There was no sense of acceptance (or non-acceptance, for that matter). There was just the surety that my time had come.

Then the plane leveled out. From the cockpit, the co-pilot was yelling, "Steve! Steve! All okay back there?"

I said it was. I looked at the litter in the aisle, which included sandwiches, a salad, and a piece of cheesecake with strawberry topping. I looked at the yellow oxygen masks hanging down. I asked—in an admirably calm voice—what had happened. My two-man flight crew didn't know then, although they suspected and later confirmed that we had had a near miss with a Delta 747, had been caught in its exhaust, and tossed like a paper airplane in a gale.

In the twenty-five years since, I have been a good deal more sanguine about air travel, having had a first-hand experience of just how much trauma modern aircraft can withstand, and how calm and efficient good pilots (which is most of them) can be when the chips are down. One told me, "You train and re-train, so that when six hours of absolute boredom become twelve seconds of maximum danger, you know exactly what to do."

⚑ FLIGHT OR FRIGHT

In the stories that follow, you will encounter everything from a gremlin perched on the wing of a 727 to transparent monsters that live far above the clouds. You will encounter time travel and ghost planes. Most of all, you will experience those twelve seconds of maximum danger, when the worst things that can go wrong high in the air *do* go wrong. You will encounter claustrophobia, cowardice, terror, and moments of bravery. If you are planning a trip on Delta, American, Southwest, or one of the other airlines, you would be well advised to pack a John Grisham or Nora Roberts book instead of this one. Even if you are safe on the ground, you might want to buckle up nice and tight.

Because the ride is going to get rough.

Stephen King
November 2, 2017

CARGO

E. MICHAEL LEWIS

E. Michael Lewis, who will be piloting our maiden flight, studied creative writing at the University of Puget Sound and lives in the Pacific Northwest. Let his Loadmaster usher you aboard a Lockheed C-141A StarLifter (like the one on display at McChord Air Museum that is said to be haunted) about to take off from Panama on a delivery mission to the United States. The StarLifter is a workhorse plane capable of transporting loads up to 70,000 pounds over short distances. It can carry a hundred paratroopers, a hundred and fifty combat troops, trucks and Jeeps, even Minuteman ICBMs. Or smaller loads. Coffins, for instance. Some stories chill your blood; here is one that will creep up your spine, inch by inch, and linger in your brain for a long, long time.

Welcome aboard.

November 1978

dreamt of cargo. Thousands of crates filled the airplane's hold, all made of unfinished pine, the kind that drives slivers through work gloves. They were stamped with unknowable numbers and bizarre acronyms that glowed fiercely with dim red light. They were supposed to be jeep tires, but some were as large as a house, others as small as a spark plug, all of them secured to pallets with binding like straitjacket straps. I tried to check them all, but there were too many. There was a low shuffling as the boxes shifted, then

17

the cargo fell on me. I couldn't reach the interphone to warn the pilot. The cargo pressed down on me with a thousand sharp little fingers as the plane rolled, crushing the life out of me even as we dived, even as we crashed, the interphone ringing now like a scream. But there was another sound too, from inside the crate next to my ear. Something struggled inside the box, something sodden and defiled, something that I didn't want to see, something that wanted *out*.

It changed into the sound of a clipboard being rapped on the metal frame of my crew house bunk. My eyes shot open. The airman—new in-country, by the sweat lining his collar—stood over me holding the clipboard between us, trying to decide if I was the type to rip his head off just for doing his job. "Tech Sergeant Davis," he said, "they need you on the flight line right away."

I sat up and stretched. He handed me the clipboard and attached manifest: a knocked-down HU-53 with flight crew, mechanics, and medical support personnel bound for…somewhere new.

"Timehri Airport?"

"It's outside Georgetown, Guyana." When I looked blank, he went on, "It's a former British colony. Timehri used to be Atkinson Air Force Base."

"What's the mission?"

"It's some kind of mass med-evac of ex-pats from somewhere called Jonestown."

Americans in trouble. I'd spent a good part of my Air Force career flying Americans out of trouble. That being said, flying Americans out of trouble was a hell of a lot more satisfying than hauling jeep tires. I thanked him and hurried into a clean flight suit.

I was looking forward to another Panamanian Thanksgiving at Howard Air Force Base—eighty-five degrees, turkey and stuffing from the mess hall, football on Armed Forces Radio, and enough time out of flight rotation to get good and drunk. The in-bound hop from the Philippines went by the numbers and both the passengers and cargo were free and easy. Now this.

Interruption was something you grew accustomed to as a Loadmaster. The C-141 StarLifter was the largest freighter and troop carrier in the Military Air Command, capable of carrying seventy thousand pounds of cargo or two hundred battle-ready troops and flying them anywhere in the world. Half as long as a football field, the high-set, swept-back wings drooped bat-like over the tarmac. With an upswept T-tail, petal-doors, and a built-in cargo ramp, the StarLifter was unmatched when it came to moving cargo. Part stewardess and part moving man, my job as a Loadmaster was to pack it as tight and as safe as possible.

With everything onboard and my weight and balance sheets complete, the same airman found me cussing up the Panamanian ground crew for leaving a scuffmark on the airframe.

"Sergeant Davis! Change in plans," he yelled over the whine of the forklift. He handed me another manifest.

"More passengers?"

"New passengers. Med crew is staying here." He said something unintelligible about a change of mission.

"Who are these people?"

Again, I strained to hear him. Or maybe I heard him fine and with the sinking in my gut, I wanted him to repeat it. I wanted to hear him wrong.

"Graves registration," he cried.

That's what I'd thought he'd said.

FLIGHT OR FRIGHT

TIMEHRI was your typical third world airport—large enough to squeeze down a 747, but strewn with potholes and sprawling with rusted Quonset huts. The low line of jungle surrounding the field looked as if it had been beaten back only an hour before. Helicopters buzzed up and down and US servicemen swarmed the tarmac. I knew then that things must be bad.

Outside the bird, the heat rising from the asphalt threatened to melt the soles of my boots even before I had the wheel chocks in place. A ground crew of American GIs approached, anxious to unload and assemble the chopper. One of them, bare chested with his shirt tied around his waist, handed me a manifest.

"Don't get comfy," he said. "As soon as the chopper's clear, we're loading you up." He nodded over his shoulder.

I looked out over the shimmering taxiway. Coffins. Rows and rows of dull aluminum funerary boxes gleamed in the unforgiving tropical sun. I recognized them from my flights out of Saigon six years ago, my first as Loadmaster. Maybe my insides did a little flip because I'd had no rest, or maybe because I hadn't carried a stiff in a few years. Still, I swallowed hard. I looked at the destination: Dover, Delaware.

THE ground crew loaded a fresh comfort pallet when I learned we'd have two passengers on the outbound flight.

The first was a kid, right out of high school by the look of it, with bristle-black hair, and too-large jungle fatigues that were starched, clean, and showed the rank of Airman First Class. I told him, "Welcome aboard," and went to help him through the crew door, but he jerked away, nearly hitting his head against the low entrance. I think he would have leapt back if there had been room. His scent hit me, strong and medicinal—Vicks VapoRub.

Behind him a flight nurse, crisp and professional in step, dress, and gesture, also boarded without assistance. I regarded her evenly. I recognized her as one of a batch I had flown regularly from Clark in the Philippines to Da Nang and back again in my early days. A steel-eyed, silver-haired lieutenant. She had been very specific—more than once—in pointing out how any numbskull high school dropout could do my job better. The name on her uniform read Pembry. She touched the kid on his back and guided him to the seats, but if she recognized me, she said nothing.

"Take a seat anywhere," I told them. "I'm Tech Sergeant Davis. We'll be wheels up in less than a half hour so make yourself comfortable."

The kid stopped short. "You didn't tell me," he said to the nurse.

The hold of a StarLifter is most like the inside of a boiler room, with all the heat, cooling, and pressure ducts exposed rather than hidden away like on an airliner. The coffins formed two rows down the length of the hold, leaving a center aisle clear. Stacked four high, there were one hundred and sixty of them. Yellow cargo nets held them in place. Looking past them, we watched the sunlight disappear as the cargo hatch closed, leaving us in an awkward semidarkness.

"It's the fastest way to get you home," she said to him, her voice neutral. "You want to go home, don't you?"

His voice dripped with fearful outrage. "I don't want to see them. I want a forward facing seat."

If the kid would have looked around, he could have seen that there were no forward facing seats.

"It's okay," she said, tugging on his arm again. "They're going home, too."

"I don't want to look at them," he said as she pushed him to a seat nearest one of the small windows. When he didn't move to strap himself in, Pembry bent and did it for him. He gripped the handrails like the oh-shit bar on a roller coaster. "I don't want to think about them."

"I got it." I went forward and shut down the cabin lights. Now only the twin red jump lights illuminated the long metal containers. When I returned, I brought him a pillow.

The ID label on the kid's loose jacket read "Hernandez." He said, "Thank you," but did not let go of the armrests.

Pembry strapped herself in next to him. I stowed their gear and went through my final checklist.

ONCE in the air, I brewed coffee on the electric stove in the comfort pallet. Nurse Pembry declined, but Hernandez took some. The plastic cup shook in his hands.

"Afraid of flying?" I asked. It wasn't so unusual for the Air Force. "I have some Dramamine…"

"I'm not afraid of flying," he said through clenched teeth. All the while he looked past me to the boxes lining the hold.

Next the crew. No one bird was assigned the same crew, like in the old days. The MAC took great pride in having men be so interchangeable that a flight crew who had never met before could assemble at a flight line and fly any StarLifter to the ends of the Earth. Each man knew my job, like I knew theirs, inside and out.

I went to the cockpit and found everyone on stations. The second engineer sat closest to the cockpit door, hunched over instrumentation. "Four is evening out now, keep the throttle low," he said. I recognized his hangdog face and his Arkansas drawl, but I could not tell from where. I figured after seven years of flying StarLifters, I had flown with just about everybody at one time or another. He thanked me as I set the black coffee on his table. His flight suit named him Hadley.

The first engineer sat in the bitchseat, the one usually reserved for a "Black Hatter"—mission inspectors were the bane of all MAC aircrews. He asked for two lumps and then stood and looked out the navigator's dome at the blue rushing past.

"Throttle low on four, got it," replied the pilot. He was the designated Aircraft Commander, but both he and the co-pilot were such typical flight jocks that they could have been the same person. They took their coffee with two creams each. "We're trying to outfly some clear air turbulence, but it won't be easy. Tell your passengers to expect some weather."

"Will do, sir. Anything else?"

"Thank you, Load Davis, that's all."

"Yes, sir."

Finally time to relax. As I went to have a horizontal moment in the crew berth, I saw Pembry snooping around the comfort pallet. "Anything I can help you find?"

"An extra blanket?"

I pulled one from the storage cabinet between the cooking station and the latrine and gritted my teeth. "Anything else?"

"No," she said, pulling a piece of imaginary lint from the wool. "We've flown together before, you know."

"Have we?"

She raised an eyebrow. "I probably ought to apologize."

"No need, ma'am," I said. I dodged around her and opened the fridge. "I could serve an in-flight meal later if you are…"

She placed her hand on my shoulder, like she had on Hernandez, and it commanded my attention. "You do remember me."

"Yes, ma'am."

"I was pretty hard on you during those evac flights."

I wished she'd stop being so direct. "You were speaking your mind, ma'am. It made me a better Loadmaster."

"Still…"

"Ma'am, there's no need." Why can't women figure out that apologies only make things worse?

"Very well." The hardness of her face melted into sincerity, and suddenly it occurred to me that she wanted to talk.

"How's your patient?"

"Resting." Pembry tried to act casual, but I knew she wanted to say more.

"What's his problem?"

"He was one of the first to arrive," she said, "and the first to leave."

"Jonestown? Was it that bad?"

Flashback to our earlier evac flights. The old look, hard and cool, returned instantly. "We flew out of Dover on White House orders five hours after they got the call. He's a Medical Records Specialist, six months in the service, he's never been anywhere before, never saw a day of trauma in his life. Next thing he knows, he's in a South American jungle with a thousand dead bodies."

"A thousand?"

"Count's not in yet, but it's headed that way." She brushed the back of her hand against her cheek. "So many kids."

"Kids?"

"Whole families. They all drank poison. Some kind of cult, they said. Someone told me the parents killed their children first. I don't know what could make a person do that to their own family." She shook her head. "I stayed at Timehri to organize triage. Hernandez said the smell was unimaginable. They had to spray the bodies with insecticide and defend them from hungry giant rats. He said they made him bayonet the bodies to release the pressure. He burned his uniform." She shuffled to keep her balance as the bird jolted.

Something nasty crept down the back of my throat as I tried not to visualize what she said. I struggled not to grimace. "The AC says it may get rough. You better strap in." I walked her back to her seat. Hernandez's mouth gaped as he sprawled across his seat, looking for all the world like he'd lost a bar fight—bad. Then I went to my bunk and fell asleep.

ASK any Loadmaster: after so much time in the air, the roar of engines is something you ignore. You find you can sleep through just about anything. Still, your mind tunes in and wakes up at the sound of anything unusual, like the flight from Yakota to Elmendorf when a jeep came loose and rolled into a crate of MREs. Chipped beef everywhere. You can bet the ground crew heard from me on that one. So it should not come as a shock that I started at the sound of a scream.

On my feet, out of the bunk, past the comfort pallet before I could think. Then I saw Pembry. She was out of her seat and in front of Hernandez, dodging his flailing arms, speaking calmly and below the engine noise. Not him, though.

"I heard them! I heard them! They're in there! All those kids! All those kids!"

I put my hand on him—hard. "Calm down!"

He stopped flailing. A shamed expression came over him. His eyes riveted mine. "I heard them singing."

"Who?"

"The children! All the…" He gave a helpless gesture to the unlighted coffins.

"You had a dream," Pembry said. Her voice shook a little. "I was with you the whole time. You were asleep. You couldn't have heard anything."

"All the children are dead," he said. "All of them. They didn't know. How could they have known they were drinking poison? Who would give their own child poison to drink?" I let go of his arm and he looked at me. "Do you have kids?"

"No," I said.

"My daughter," he said, "is a year-and-a-half old. My son is three months. You have to be careful with them, patient with them. My wife is really good at it, y'know?" I noticed for the first time how sweat crawled across his forehead, the backs of his hands. "But I'm okay too, I mean, I don't really know what the fuck I'm doing, but I wouldn't hurt them. I hold them and I sing to them and—and if anyone else tried to hurt them…" He grabbed me on the arm that had held him. "Who would give their child poison?"

"It isn't your fault," I told him.

"They didn't know it was poison. They still don't." He pulled me closer and said into my ear, "I heard them singing." I'll be damned if the words he spoke didn't make my spine shiver.

"I'll go check it out," I told him as I grabbed a flashlight off the wall and started down the center aisle.

There was a practical reason for checking out the noise. As a Loadmaster, I knew that an unusual sound meant trouble. I had heard a story about how an aircrew kept hearing the sound of a cat meowing from somewhere in the hold. The Loadmaster couldn't find it, but figured it'd turn up when they off-loaded the cargo. Turns out the "meowing" was a weakened load brace that buckled when the wheels touched runway, freeing three tons of explosive ordnance and making the landing very interesting. Strange noises meant trouble, and I'd have been a fool not to look into it.

I checked all the buckles and netting as I went, stooping and listening, checking for signs of shifting, fraying straps, anything out of the ordinary. I went up one side and down the other, even checking the cargo doors. Nothing. Everything was sound, my usual best work.

I walked up the aisle to face them. Hernandez wept, head in his hands. Pembry rubbed his back with one hand as she sat next to him, like my mother had done to me.

"All clear, Hernandez." I put the flashlight back on the wall.

"Thanks," Pembry replied for him, then said to me, "I gave him a Valium, he should quiet down now."

"Just a safety check," I told her. "Now, both of you get some rest."

I went back to my bunk to find it occupied by Hadley, the second engineer. I took the one below him but couldn't fall asleep right away. I tried to keep my mind far away from the reason that the coffins were in my bird in the first place.

Cargo was the euphemism. From blood plasma to high explosives to secret service limousines to gold bullion, you packed it and hauled it because it was your job, that was all, and anything that could be done to speed you on your way was important.

Just cargo, I thought. But whole families that killed themselves...I was glad to get them the hell out of the jungle, back home to their families—but the medics who got there first, all those guys on the ground, even my crew, we were too late to do any more than that. I was interested in having kids in a vague, unsettled sort of way, and it pissed me off to hear about anyone harming them. But these parents did it willingly, didn't they?

I couldn't relax. I found an old copy of the New York Times folded into the bunk. Peace in the Middle East in our lifetimes, it read. Next to the article was a picture of President Carter and Anwar Sadat shaking hands. I was just about to drift off when I thought I heard Hernandez cry out again.

I dragged my ass up. Pembry stood with her hands clutched over her mouth. I thought Hernandez had hit her, so I went to her and peeled her hands away, looking for damage.

There was none. Looking over her shoulder, I could see Hernandez riveted to his seat, eyes glued to the darkness like a reverse color television.

"What happened? Did he hit you?"

"He—he heard it again," she stammered as one hand rose to her face again. "You—you ought to go check again. You ought to go check…"

The pitch of the plane shifted and she fell into me a little, and as I steadied myself by grabbing her elbow she collapsed against me. I met her gaze matter-of-factly. She looked away. "What happened?" I asked again.

"I heard it too," Pembry said.

My eyes went to the aisle of shadow. "Just now?"

"Yes."

"Was it like he said? Children singing?" I realized I was on the verge of shaking her. Were they both going crazy?

"Children playing," she said. "Like—playground noise, y'know? Kids playing."

I wracked my brain for some object, or some collection of objects, that when stuffed into a C-141 StarLifter and flown thirty-nine thousand feet over the Caribbean, would make a sound like children playing.

Hernandez shifted his position and we both brought our attention to bear on him. He smiled a defeated smile and said to us, "I told you."

"I'll go check it out," I told them.

"Let them play," said Hernandez. "They just want to play. Isn't that what you wanted to do as a kid?"

I remembered my childhood like a jolt, endless summers and bike rides and skinned knees and coming home at dusk to my mother saying, "Look how dirty you are." I wondered if the recovery crews washed the bodies before they put them in the coffins.

"I'll find out what it is," I told them. I went and got the flashlight again. "Stay put."

I used the darkness to close off my sight, give me more to hear. The turbulence had subsided by then, and I used my flashlight only to avoid tripping on the cargo netting. I listened for anything new or unusual. It wasn't one thing—it had to be a combination—noises like that just don't stop and start again. Fuel leak? Stowaway? The thought of a snake or some other jungle beast lurking inside those metal boxes heightened my whole state of being and brought back my dream.

Near the cargo doors, I shut off my light and listened. Pressurized air. Four Pratt and Whitney turbofan engines. Fracture rattles. Cargo straps flapping.

And then, something. Something came in sharp after a moment, at first dull and sweeping, like noise from the back of a cave, but then pure and unbidden, like sounds to a surprised eavesdropper.

Children. Laughter. Like recess at grade school.

I opened my eyes and flashed my light around the silver crates. I found them waiting, huddled with me, almost expectant.

Children, I thought, just children.

I ran past Hernandez and Pembry to the comfort pallet. I can't tell you what they saw in my face, but if it was anything like what I saw in the little mirror above the latrine sink, I would have been at once terrified and redeemed.

I looked from the mirror to the interphone. Any problem with the cargo should be reported immediately—procedure demanded it—but what could I tell the AC? I had an urge to drop it all, just eject the coffins and call it a day. If I told them there was a fire in the hold, we would drop below ten thousand feet so I could blow the bolts and send the whole load to the bottom of the Gulf of Mexico, no questions asked.

I stopped then, straightened up, tried to think. *Children*, I thought. *Not monsters, not demons, just the sounds of children playing. Nothing that will get you. Nothing that can get you.* I tossed off the shiver that ran through my body and decided to get some help.

At the bunk, I found Hadley still asleep. A dog-eared copy of a paperback showing two women locked in a passionate embrace lay like a tent on his chest. I shook his arm and he sat up. Neither of us said anything for a moment. He rubbed his face with one hand and yawned.

Then he looked right at me and I watched his face arch into worry. His next action was to grab his portable oxygen. He recovered his game face in an instant. "What is it, Davis?"

I groped for something. "The cargo," I said. "There's a…possible shift in the cargo. I need a hand, sir."

His worry snapped into annoyance. "Have you told the AC?"

"No sir," I said. "I—I don't want to trouble him yet. It may be nothing."

His face screwed into something unpleasant and I thought I'd have words from him, but he let me lead the way aft. Just his presence was enough to revive my doubt, my professionalism. My walk sharpened, my eyes widened, my stomach returned to its place in my gut.

I found Pembry sitting next to Hernandez now, both together in a feigned indifference. Hadley gave them a disinterested look and followed me down the aisle between the coffins.

"What about the main lights?" he asked.

"They don't help," I said. "Here." I handed him the flashlight and asked him, "Do you hear it?"

"Hear what?"

"Just listen."

Again, only engines and the Jetstream. "I don't…"

"Shhh! Listen."

His mouth opened and stayed there for a minute, then shut. The engines quieted and the sounds came, dripping over us like water vapor, the fog of sound around us. I didn't realize how cold I was until I noticed my hands shaking.

"What in the hell is that?" Hadley asked. "It sounds like—"

"Don't," I interrupted. "That can't be it." I nodded at the metal boxes. "You know what's in these coffins, don't you?"

He didn't say anything. The sound seemed to filter around us for a moment, at once close, then far away. He tried to follow the sound with his light. "Can you tell where it's coming from?"

"No. I'm just glad you hear it too, sir."

The engineer scratched his head, his face drawn, like he swallowed something foul and couldn't lose the aftertaste. "I'll be damned," he drawled.

All at once, as before, the sound stopped, and the roar of the jets filled our ears.

"I'll hit the lights." I moved away hesitantly. "I'm not going to call the AC."

His silence was conspiratorial. As I rejoined him, I found him examining a particular row of coffins through the netting.

"You need to conduct a search," he said dully.

I didn't respond. I'd done midair cargo searches before, but never like this, not even on bodies of servicemen. If everything Pembry said was true, I couldn't think of anything worse than opening one of these caskets.

We both started at the next sound. Imagine a wet tennis ball. Now imagine the sound a wet tennis ball makes when it hits the court—a sort of dull THWAK—like a bird striking the fuselage. It sounded again, and this time I could hear it inside the hold. Then, after a buffet of turbulence, the thump sounded again. It came clearly from a coffin at Hadley's feet.

Not a serious problem, his face tried to say. We just imagined it. *A noise from one coffin can't bring a plane down*, his face said. *There are no such things as ghosts.*

"Sir?"

"We need to see," he said.

Blood pooled in my stomach again. *See*, he had said. *I didn't want to see.*

"Get on the horn and tell the AC to avoid the chop," he said. I knew at that moment he was going to help me. He didn't want to, but he was going to do it anyway.

"What are you doing?" Pembry asked. She stood by as I removed the cargo netting from the row of caskets while the engineer undid the individual straps around that one certain row. Hernandez slept head bowed, the downers having finally taken effect.

"We have to examine the cargo," I stated matter-of-factly. "The flight may have caused the load to become unbalanced."

She grabbed my arm as I went by. "Was that all it was? A shifting load?"

There was a touch of desperation in her question. *Tell me I imagined it*, the look on her face said. *Tell me and I'll believe you, and I'll go get some sleep.*

"We think so," I nodded.

Her shoulders dropped and her face peeled into a smile too broad to be real. "Thank God. I thought I was going crazy."

I patted her shoulder. "Strap in and get some rest," I told her. She did.

Finally, I was doing something. As Loadmaster, I could put an end to this nonsense. So I did the work. I unstrapped the straps, climbed the other caskets, shoved the top one out of place, carried it, secured it, removed the next one, carried it, secured it, and again. The joy of easy repetition.

It wasn't until we got to the bottom one, the noisy one, that Hadley stopped. He stood there watching me as I pulled it out of place enough to examine it. His stance was level, but even so it spoke of revulsion, something that, among swaggering Air Force veterans and over beers, he could conceal. Not now, not to me.

I did a cursory examination of the deck where it had sat, of the caskets next to it, and saw no damage or obvious flaws.

A noise sounded—a moist "thunk." From inside. We flinched in unison. The engineer's cool loathing was impossible to conceal. I suppressed a tremble.

"We have to open it," I said.

The engineer didn't disagree, but like me, his body was slow to move. He squatted down and, with one hand firmly planted on the casket lid, unlatched the clasps on his end. I undid mine, finding my finger slick on the cold metal, and shaking a little as I pulled them away and braced my hand on the lid. Our eyes met in one moment that held the last of our resolve. Together we opened the casket.

✈ FLIGHT OR FRIGHT

✈

FIRST, the smell: a mash of rotten fruit, antiseptic, and formaldehyde, wrapped in plastic with dung and sulfur. It stung our nostrils as it filled the hold. The overhead lights illuminated two shiny black body bags, slick with condensation and waste. I knew these would be the bodies of children, but it awed me, hurt me. One bag lay unevenly concealing the other, and I understood at once that there was more than one child in it. My eyes skimmed the juice-soaked plastic, picking out the contour of an arm, the trace of a profile. A shape coiled near the bottom seam, away from the rest. It was the size of a baby.

Then the plane shivered like a frightened pony and the top bag slid away to reveal a young girl, eight or nine at the most, half in and half out of the bag. Wedged like a mad contortionist into the corner, her swollen belly, showing stab wounds from bayonets, had bloated again, and her twisted limbs were now as thick as tree limbs. The pigment-bearing skin had peeled away everywhere but her face, which was as pure and as innocent as any cherub in heaven.

Her face was really what drove it home, what really hurt me. Her sweet face.

My hand fixed itself to the casket edge in painful whiteness, but I dared not remove it. Something caught in my throat and I forced it back down.

A lone fly, fat and glistening, crawled from inside the bag and flew lazily towards Hadley. He slowly rose to his feet and braced himself, as if against a body blow. He watched it rise and flit a clumsy path through the air. Then he broke the moment by stepping back, his hands flailing and hitting it—I heard the slap of his hand—and letting a nauseous sound escape his lips.

When I stood up, my temples throbbed and my legs weakened. I held onto a nearby casket, my throat filled with something rancid.

"Close it," he said like a man with his mouth full. "Close it."

My arms went rubbery. After bracing myself, I lifted one leg and kicked the lid. It rang out like an artillery shell. Pressure pounded into my ears like during a rapid descent.

Hadley put his hands on his haunches and lowered his head, taking deep breaths through his mouth. "Jesus," he croaked.

I saw movement. Pembry stood next to the line of coffins, her face pulled up in sour disgust. "What—is—that—smell?"

"It's okay." I found I could work one arm and tried what I hoped looked like an off-handed gesture. "Found the problem. Had to open it up though. Go sit down."

Pembry brought her hands up around herself and went back to her seat.

I found that with a few more deep breaths, the smell dissipated enough to act. "We have to secure it," I told Hadley.

He looked up from the floor and I saw his eyes as narrow slits. His hands were in fists and his broad torso stood fierce and straight. At the corner of his eyes, wetness glinted. He said nothing.

It became cargo again as I fastened the latches. We strained to fit it back into place. In a matter of minutes, the other caskets were stowed, the exterior straps were in place, the cargo netting draped and secure.

Hadley waited for me to finish up, then walked forwards with me. "I'm going to tell the AC you solved the problem," he said, "and to get us back to speed."

I nodded.

"One more thing," he said. "If you see that fly, kill it."

"Didn't you..."

"No."

I didn't know what else to say, so I said, "Yes, sir."

Pembry sat in her seat, nose wriggled up, feigning sleep. Hernandez sat upright, eyelids half open. He gestured for me to come closer, bend down.

"Did you let them out to play?" he asked.

I stood over him and said nothing. In my heart, I felt that same pang I did as a child, when summer was over.

When we landed in Dover, a funeral detail in full dress offloaded every coffin, affording full funeral rites to each person. I'm told as more bodies flew in, the formality was scrapped and only a solitary Air Force chaplain met the planes. By week's end I was back in Panama with a stomach full of turkey and cheap rum. Then it was off to the Marshall Islands, delivering supplies to the guided missile base there. In the Military Air Command, there is no shortage of cargo.

THE HORROR OF THE HEIGHTS

ARTHUR CONAN DOYLE

In addition to his tales of Sherlock Holmes, Doyle wrote well over a hundred other stories, dozens of them tales of the supernatural. Some of these lack the propulsive, "gotta see what happens next" quality of the Holmes stories, featuring, as most do, upstanding young Englishmen who confront some supernatural horror and triumph through grit and wile, but a few are genuinely scary. "Lot No. 249" is one such; here is another. Like his contemporary, Bram Stoker, Doyle was fascinated by new inventions (he bought a motor car in 1911, without ever having driven one), and that included the aeroplane. When you read "The Horror of the Heights," remember that it was published in 1913, only ten years after the Wright Brothers' *Flyer* lifted off from Kitty Hawk for 59 seconds, with Orville at the rudimentary controls and Wilbur standing by. When Doyle's story was published in *The Strand*, the operating ceiling of most planes would have been from 12,000 to perhaps 18,000 feet. Doyle imagined what might be even higher up there, far beyond the clouds, and in doing so created his most terrifying tale.

he idea that the extraordinary narrative which has been called the Joyce-Armstrong Fragment is an elaborate practical joke evolved by some person, cursed by a perverted and sinister sense of humour, has now been abandoned by all who have examined the matter. The most macabre and imaginative of plotters would hesitate before linking his morbid fancies with the unquestioned and tragic facts which reinforce the statement. Though the assertions contained in it are amazing and even monstrous, it is none the less forcing itself upon the general intelligence that they are true, and that we must readjust our ideas to the new situation. This world of ours appears to be separated by a slight and precarious margin of safety from a most singular and unexpected danger. I will endeavour in this narrative, which reproduces the original document in its necessarily somewhat fragmentary form, to lay before the reader the whole of the facts up to date, prefacing my statement by saying that, if there be any who doubt the narrative of Joyce-Armstrong, there can be no question at all as to the facts concerning Lieutenant Myrtle, R. N., and Mr. Hay Connor, who undoubtedly met their end in the manner described.

The Joyce-Armstrong Fragment was found in the field which is called Lower Haycock, lying one mile to the westward of the village of Withyham, upon the Kent and Sussex border. It was on the 15th September last that an agricultural labourer, James Flynn, in the employment of Mathew Dodd, farmer, of the Chauntry Farm, Withyham, perceived a briar pipe lying near the footpath which skirts the hedge in Lower Haycock. A few paces farther on he picked up a pair of broken binocular glasses. Finally, among some nettles in the ditch, he caught sight of a flat, canvas-backed book, which proved to be a note-book with detachable leaves, some of which had come loose and were fluttering along the base of the hedge. These he collected, but some, including the first, were never recovered, and leave a deplorable hiatus in this all-important statement. The note-book was taken by the labourer to his master, who in turn showed it to Dr. J. H. Atherton, of Hartfield. This gentleman at once recognized the

THE HORROR
OF THE HEIGHTS

ARTHUR CONAN DOYLE

need for an expert examination, and the manuscript was forwarded to the Aero Club in London, where it now lies.

The first two pages of the manuscript are missing. There is also one torn away at the end of the narrative, though none of these affect the general coherence of the story. It is conjectured that the missing opening is concerned with the record of Mr. Joyce-Armstrong's qualifications as an aeronaut, which can be gathered from other sources and are admitted to be unsurpassed among the air-pilots of England. For many years he has been looked upon as among the most daring and the most intellectual of flying men, a combination which has enabled him to both invent and test several new devices, including the common gyroscopic attachment which is known by his name. The main body of the manuscript is written neatly in ink, but the last few lines are in pencil and are so ragged as to be hardly legible—exactly, in fact, as they might be expected to appear if they were scribbled off hurriedly from the seat of a moving aeroplane. There are, it may be added, several stains, both on the last page and on the outside cover which have been pronounced by the Home Office experts to be blood—probably human and certainly mammalian. The fact that something closely resembling the organism of malaria was discovered in this blood, and that Joyce-Armstrong is known to have suffered from intermittent fever, is a remarkable example of the new weapons which modern science has placed in the hands of our detectives.

And now a word as to the personality of the author of this epoch-making statement. Joyce-Armstrong, according to the few friends who really knew something of the man, was a poet and a dreamer, as well as a mechanic and an inventor. He was a man of considerable wealth, much of which he had spent in the pursuit of his aeronautical hobby. He had four private aeroplanes in his hangars near Devizes, and is said to have made no fewer than one hundred and seventy ascents in the course of last year. He was a retiring man with dark moods, in which he would avoid the society of his fellows. Captain Dangerfield, who knew him better than anyone, says that there were times when his eccentricity threatened to develop into something more serious. His habit of carrying a shot-gun with him in his aeroplane was one manifestation of it.

Another was the morbid effect which the fall of Lieutenant Myrtle had upon his mind. Myrtle, who was attempting the height record, fell from an altitude of something over thirty thousand feet. Horrible to narrate, his head was entirely obliterated, though his body and limbs preserved their configuration. At every gathering of airmen, Joyce-Armstrong, according to Dangerfield, would ask, with an enigmatic smile: "And where, pray, is Myrtle's head?"

On another occasion after dinner, at the mess of the Flying School on Salisbury Plain, he started a debate as to what will be the most permanent danger which airmen will have to encounter. Having listened to successive opinions as to air-pockets, faulty construction, and over-banking, he ended by shrugging his shoulders and refusing to put forward his own views, though he gave the impression that they differed from any advanced by his companions.

It is worth remarking that after his own complete disappearance it was found that his private affairs were arranged with a precision which may show that he had a strong premonition of disaster. With these essential explanations I will now give the narrative exactly as it stands, beginning at page three of the blood-soaked note-book:

"Nevertheless, when I dined at Rheims with Coselli and Gustav Raymond I found that neither of them was aware of any particular danger in the higher layers of the atmosphere. I did not actually say what was in my thoughts, but I got so near to it that if they had any corresponding idea they could not have failed to express it. But then they are two empty, vainglorious fellows with no thought beyond seeing their silly names in the newspaper. It is interesting to note that neither of them had ever been much beyond the twenty-thousand-foot level. Of course, men have been higher than this both in balloons and in the ascent of mountains. It must be well above that point that the aeroplane enters the danger zone—always presuming that my premonitions are correct.

"Aeroplaning has been with us now for more than twenty years, and one might well ask: Why should this peril be only revealing itself in our day? The answer is obvious. In the old days of weak engines, when a hundred horse-power Gnome or Green was considered ample for every need, the flights were very restricted. Now that three hundred horse-power is the rule rather than the exception, visits to the upper layers have become easier and more common. Some of us can remember how, in our youth, Garros made a world-wide reputation by attaining nineteen thousand feet, and it was considered a remarkable achievement to fly over the Alps. Our standard now has been immeasurably raised, and there are twenty high flights for one in former years. Many of them have been undertaken with impunity. The thirty-thousand-foot level has been reached time after time with no discomfort beyond cold and asthma. What does this prove? A visitor might descend upon this planet a thousand times and never see a tiger. Yet tigers exist, and if he chanced to come down into a jungle he might be devoured. There are jungles of the upper air, and there are worse things than tigers which inhabit them. I believe in time they will map these jungles accurately out. Even at the present moment I could name two of them. One of them lies over the Pau-Biarritz district of France. Another is just over my head as I write here in my house in Wiltshire. I rather think there is a third in the Homburg-Wiesbaden district.

"It was the disappearance of the airmen that first set me thinking. Of course, everyone said that they had fallen into the sea, but that did not satisfy me at all. First, there was Verrier in France; his machine was found near Bayonne, but they never got his body. There was the case of Baxter also, who vanished, though his engine and some of the iron fixings were found in a wood in Leicestershire. In that case, Dr. Middleton, of Amesbury, who was watching the flight with a telescope, declares that just before the clouds obscured the view he saw the machine, which was at an enormous height, suddenly rise perpendicularly upwards in a succession of jerks in a manner that he would have thought to be impossible. That was the last seen of Baxter. There was a correspondence in the papers, but it never led to anything. There were several other similar cases, and then there was the death of Hay Connor. What a cackle there was about an unsolved mystery of the air, and what columns in the halfpenny papers, and yet how little was ever done to get to the bottom of the business! He came down in a tremendous vol-plane from an unknown height. He never got off his machine and died in his pilot's seat. Died of what? 'Heart disease,' said the doctors. Rubbish! Hay Connor's heart was as sound as mine is. What did Venables say? Venables was the only man who was at his side when he died. He said that he was shivering and looked like a man who had been badly scared. 'Died of fright,' said Venables, but could not imagine what he was frightened about. Only said one word to Venables, which sounded like 'Monstrous.' They could make nothing of that at the inquest. But I could make something of it. Monsters! That was the last word of poor Harry Hay Connor. And he DID die of fright, just as Venables thought.

"And then there was Myrtle's head. Do you really believe—does anybody really believe—that a man's head could be driven clean into his body by the force of a fall? Well, perhaps it may be possible, but

THE HORROR OF THE HEIGHTS

ARTHUR CONAN DOYLE

I, for one, have never believed that it was so with Myrtle. And the grease upon his clothes—'all slimy with grease,' said somebody at the inquest. Queer that nobody got thinking after that! I did—but, then, I had been thinking for a good long time. I've made three ascents—how Dangerfield used to chaff me about my shot-gun—but I've never been high enough. Now, with this new, light Paul Veroner machine and its one hundred and seventy-five Robur, I should easily touch the thirty thousand tomorrow. I'll have a shot at the record. Maybe I shall have a shot at something else as well. Of course, it's dangerous. If a fellow wants to avoid danger he had best keep out of flying altogether and subside finally into flannel slippers and a dressing-gown. But I'll visit the air-jungle tomorrow—and if there's anything there I shall know it. If I return, I'll find myself a bit of a celebrity. If I don't this note-book may explain what I am trying to do, and how I lost my life in doing it. But no drivel about accidents or mysteries, if YOU please.

"I chose my Paul Veroner monoplane for the job. There's nothing like a monoplane when real work is to be done. Beaumont found that out in very early days. For one thing it doesn't mind damp, and the weather looks as if we should be in the clouds all the time. It's a bonny little model and answers my hand like a tender-mouthed horse. The engine is a ten-cylinder rotary Robur working up to one hundred and seventy-five. It has all the modern improvements—enclosed fuselage, high-curved landing skids, brakes, gyroscopic steadiers, and three speeds, worked by an alteration of the angle of the planes upon the Venetian-blind principle. I took a shot-gun with me and a dozen cartridges filled with buck-shot. You should have seen the face of Perkins, my old mechanic, when I directed him to put them in. I was dressed like an Arctic explorer, with two jerseys under my overalls, thick socks inside my padded boots, a storm-cap with flaps, and my talc goggles. It was stifling outside the hangars, but I was going for the summit of the Himalayas, and had to dress for the part. Perkins knew there was something on and implored me to take him with me. Perhaps I should if I were using the biplane, but a monoplane is a one-man show—if you want to get the last foot of life out of it. Of course, I took an oxygen bag; the man who goes for the altitude record without one will either be frozen or smothered—or both.

"I had a good look at the planes, the rudder-bar, and the elevating lever before I got in. Everything was in order so far as I could see. Then I switched on my engine and found that she was running sweetly. When they let her go she rose almost at once upon the lowest speed. I circled my home field once or twice just to warm her up, and then with a wave to Perkins and the others, I flattened out my planes and put her on her highest. She skimmed like a swallow down wind for eight or ten miles until I turned her nose up a little and she began to climb in a great spiral for the cloud-bank above me. It's all-important to rise slowly and adapt yourself to the pressure as you go.

"It was a close, warm day for an English September, and there was the hush and heaviness of impending rain. Now and then there came sudden puffs of wind from the south-west—one of them so gusty and unexpected that it caught me napping and turned me half-round for an instant. I remember the time when gusts and whirls and air-pockets used to be things of danger—before we learned to put an overmastering power into our engines. Just as I reached the cloud-banks, with the altimeter marking three thousand, down came the rain. My word, how it poured! It drummed upon my wings and lashed against my face, blurring my glasses so that I could hardly see. I got down on to a low speed, for it was painful to travel against it. As I got higher it became hail, and I had to turn tail to it. One of my cylinders was out of action—a dirty plug, I should imagine, but still I was rising steadily with plenty of power. After a bit the trouble passed, whatever it was, and I heard the full, deep-throated purr—the ten singing as one. That's where the beauty of our modern silencers comes in. We can at last control our engines by ear. How they squeal and squeak and sob when they are in trouble! All those cries for help were wasted in the old days, when every sound was swallowed up by the monstrous racket of the machine. If only the early aviators could come back to see the beauty and perfection of the mechanism which have been bought at the cost of their lives!

"About nine-thirty I was nearing the clouds. Down below me, all blurred and shadowed with rain, lay the vast expanse of Salisbury Plain. Half a dozen flying machines were doing hackwork at the thousand-foot level, looking like little black swallows against the green background. I dare say they were wondering what I was doing up in cloud-land. Suddenly a grey curtain drew across beneath me and the wet folds of vapours were swirling round my face. It was clammily cold and miserable. But I was above the hail-storm, and that was something gained. The cloud was as dark and thick as a London fog. In my anxiety to get clear, I cocked her nose up until the automatic alarm-bell rang, and I actually began to slide back-wards. My sopped and dripping wings had made me heavier than I thought, but presently I was in lighter cloud, and soon had cleared the first layer. There was a second—opal-coloured and fleecy—at a great height above my head, a white, unbroken ceiling above, and a dark, unbroken floor below, with the monoplane labouring upwards upon a vast spiral between them. It is deadly lonely in these cloud-spaces. Once a great flight of some small water-birds went past me, flying very fast to the westwards. The quick whir of their wings and their musical cry were cheery to my ear. I fancy that they were teal, but I am a wretched zoologist. Now that we humans have become birds we must really learn to know our brethren by sight.

"The wind down beneath me whirled and swayed the broad cloud-plain. Once a great eddy formed in it, a whirlpool of vapour, and through it, as down a funnel, I caught sight of the distant world. A large white biplane was passing at a vast depth beneath me. I fancy it was the morning mail service betwixt Bristol and London. Then the drift swirled inwards again and the great solitude was unbroken.

"Just after ten I touched the lower edge of the upper cloud-stratum. It consisted of fine diaphanous vapour drifting swiftly from the westwards. The wind had been steadily rising all this time and it was now blowing a sharp breeze—twenty-eight an hour by my gauge. Already it was very cold, though my altimeter only marked nine thousand. The engines were working beautifully, and we went droning steadily upwards. The cloud-bank was thicker than I had expected, but at last it thinned out into a golden mist before me, and then in an instant I had shot out from it, and there was an unclouded sky and a brilliant sun above my head—all blue and gold above, all shining silver below, one vast, glimmering plain as far as my eyes could reach. It was a quarter past ten o'clock, and the barograph needle pointed to twelve thousand eight hundred. Up I went and up, my ears concentrated upon the deep purring of my motor, my eyes busy always with the watch, the revolution indicator, the petrol lever, and the oil pump. No wonder aviators are said to be a fearless race. With so many things to think of there is no time to trouble about oneself. About this time I noted how unreliable is the compass when above a certain height from earth. At fifteen thousand feet mine was pointing east and a point south. The sun and the wind gave me my true bearings.

"I had hoped to reach an eternal stillness in these high altitudes, but with every thousand feet of ascent the gale grew stronger. My machine groaned and trembled in every joint and rivet as she faced

THE HORROR OF THE HEIGHTS

ARTHUR CONAN DOYLE

it, and swept away like a sheet of paper when I banked her on the turn, skimming down wind at a greater pace, perhaps, than ever mortal man has moved. Yet I had always to turn again and tack up in the wind's eye, for it was not merely a height record that I was after. By all my calculations it was above little Wiltshire that my air-jungle lay, and all my labour might be lost if I struck the outer layers at some farther point.

"When I reached the nineteen-thousand-foot level, which was about midday, the wind was so severe that I looked with some anxiety to the stays of my wings, expecting momentarily to see them snap or slacken. I even cast loose the parachute behind me, and fastened its hook into the ring of my leathern belt, so as to be ready for the worst. Now was the time when a bit of scamped work by the mechanic is paid for by the life of the aeronaut. But she held together bravely. Every cord and strut was humming and vibrating like so many harp-strings, but it was glorious to see how, for all the beating and the buffeting, she was still the conqueror of Nature and the mistress of the sky. There is surely something divine in man himself that he should rise so superior to the limitations which Creation seemed to impose—rise, too, by such unselfish, heroic devotion as this air-conquest has shown. Talk of human degeneration! When has such a story as this been written in the annals of our race?

"These were the thoughts in my head as I climbed that monstrous, inclined plane with the wind sometimes beating in my face and sometimes whistling behind my ears, while the cloud-land beneath me fell away to such a distance that the folds and hummocks of silver had all smoothed out into one flat, shining plain. But suddenly I had a horrible and unprecedented experience. I have known before what it is to be in what our neighbours have called a tourbillon, but never on such a scale as this. That huge, sweeping river of wind of which I have spoken had, as it appears, whirlpools within it which were as monstrous as itself. Without a moment's warning I was dragged suddenly into the heart of one. I spun round for a minute or two with such velocity that I almost lost my senses, and then fell suddenly, left wing foremost, down the vacuum funnel in the centre. I dropped like a stone, and lost nearly a thousand feet. It was only my belt that kept me in my seat, and the shock and breathlessness left me hanging half-insensible over the side of the fuselage. But I am always capable of a supreme effort—it is my one great merit as an aviator. I was conscious that the descent was slower. The whirlpool was a cone rather than a funnel, and I had come to the apex. With a terrific wrench, throwing my weight all to one side, I levelled my planes and brought her head away from the wind. In an instant I had shot out of the eddies and was skimming down the sky. Then, shaken but victorious, I turned her nose up and began once more my steady grind on the upward spiral. I took a large sweep to avoid the danger-spot of the whirlpool, and soon I was safely above it. Just after one o'clock I was twenty-one thousand feet above the sea-level. To my great joy I had topped the gale, and with every hundred feet of ascent the air grew stiller. On the other hand, it was very cold, and I was conscious of that peculiar nausea which goes with rarefaction of the air. For the first time I unscrewed the mouth of my oxygen bag and took an occasional whiff of the glorious gas. I could feel it running like a cordial through my veins, and I was exhilarated almost to the point of drunkenness. I shouted and sang as I soared upwards into the cold, still outer world.

"It is very clear to me that the insensibility which came upon Glaisher, and in a lesser degree upon Coxwell, when, in 1862, they ascended in a balloon to the height of thirty thousand feet, was due to the extreme speed with which a perpendicular ascent is made.

THE HORROR OF THE HEIGHTS

ARTHUR CONAN DOYLE

Doing it at an easy gradient and accustoming oneself to the lessened barometric pressure by slow degrees, there are no such dreadful symptoms. At the same great height I found that even without my oxygen inhaler I could breathe without undue distress. It was bitterly cold, however, and my thermometer was at zero, Fahrenheit. At one-thirty I was nearly seven miles above the surface of the earth, and still ascending steadily. I found, however, that the rarefied air was giving markedly less support to my planes, and that my angle of ascent had to be considerably lowered in consequence. It was already clear that even with my light weight and strong engine-power there was a point in front of me where I should be held. To make matters worse, one of my sparking-plugs was in trouble again and there was intermittent misfiring in the engine. My heart was heavy with the fear of failure.

"It was about that time that I had a most extraordinary experience. Something whizzed past me in a trail of smoke and exploded with a loud, hissing sound, sending forth a cloud of steam. For the instant I could not imagine what had happened. Then I remembered that the earth is for ever being bombarded by meteor stones, and would be hardly inhabitable were they not in nearly every case turned to vapour in the outer layers of the atmosphere. Here is a new danger for the high-altitude man, for two others passed me when I was nearing the forty-thousand-foot mark. I cannot doubt that at the edge of the earth's envelope the risk would be a very real one.

"My barograph needle marked forty-one thousand three hundred when I became aware that I could go no farther. Physically, the strain was not as yet greater than I could bear but my machine had reached its limit. The attenuated air gave no firm support to the wings, and the least tilt developed into side-slip, while she seemed sluggish on her controls. Possibly, had the engine been at its best, another thousand feet might have been within our capacity, but it was still misfiring, and two out of the ten cylinders appeared to be out of action. If I had not already reached the zone for which I was searching then I should never see it upon this journey. But was it not possible that I had attained it? Soaring in circles like a monstrous hawk upon the forty-thousand-foot level I let the monoplane guide herself, and with my Mannheim glass I made a careful observation of my surroundings. The heavens were perfectly clear; there was no indication of those dangers which I had imagined.

"I have said that I was soaring in circles. It struck me suddenly that I would do well to take a wider sweep and open up a new airtract. If the hunter entered an earth-jungle he would drive through it if he wished to find his game. My reasoning had led me to believe that the air-jungle which I had imagined lay somewhere over Wiltshire. This should be to the south and west of me. I took my bearings from the sun, for the compass was hopeless and no trace of earth was to be seen—nothing but the distant, silver cloud-plain. However, I got my direction as best I might and kept her head straight to the mark. I reckoned that my petrol supply would not last for more than another hour or so, but I could afford to use it to the last drop, since a single magnificent vol-plane could at any time take me to the earth.

"Suddenly I was aware of something new. The air in front of me had lost its crystal clearness. It was full of long, ragged wisps of something which I can only compare to very fine cigarette smoke. It hung about in wreaths and coils, turning and twisting slowly in the sunlight. As the monoplane shot through it, I was aware of a faint taste of oil upon my lips, and there was a greasy scum upon the woodwork of the machine. Some infinitely fine organic matter appeared to be suspended in the atmosphere. There was no life there. It was inchoate and diffuse, extending for many square acres and then fringing off into the void. No, it was not life. But might it not be the remains of life? Above all, might it not be the food of life, of monstrous life, even as the humble grease of the ocean is the food for the mighty whale? The thought was in my mind when my eyes looked upwards and I saw the most wonderful vision that ever man has seen. Can I hope to convey it to you even as I saw it myself last Thursday?

"Conceive a jelly-fish such as sails in our summer seas, bell-shaped and of enormous size—far larger, I should judge, than the dome of St. Paul's. It was of a light pink colour veined with a delicate green, but the whole huge fabric so tenuous that it was but a fairy outline against the dark blue sky. It pulsated with a delicate and regular rhythm. From it there depended two long, drooping, green tentacles, which swayed slowly backwards and forwards. This gorgeous vision passed gently with noiseless dignity over my head, as light and fragile as a soap-bubble, and drifted upon its stately way.

"I had half-turned my monoplane, that I might look after this beautiful creature, when, in a moment, I found myself amidst a perfect fleet of them, of all sizes, but none so large as the first. Some were quite small, but the majority about as big as an average balloon, and with much the same curvature at the top. There was in them a delicacy of texture and colouring which reminded me of the finest Venetian glass. Pale shades of pink and green were the prevailing tints, but all had a lovely iridescence where the sun shimmered through their dainty forms. Some hundreds of them drifted past me, a wonderful fairy squadron of strange argosies of the sky—creatures whose forms and substance were so attuned to these pure heights that one could not conceive anything so delicate within actual sight or sound of earth.

"But soon my attention was drawn to a new phenomenon—the serpents of the outer air. These were long, thin, fantastic coils of vapour-like material, which turned and twisted with great speed, flying round and round at such a pace that the eyes could hardly follow them. Some of these ghost-like creatures were twenty or thirty feet long, but it was difficult to tell their girth, for their outline was so hazy that it seemed to fade away into the air around them. These air-snakes were of a very light grey or smoke colour, with some darker lines within, which gave the impression of a definite organism. One of them whisked past my very face, and I was conscious of a cold, clammy contact, but their composition was so unsubstantial that I could not connect them with any thought of physical danger, any more than the beautiful bell-like creatures which had preceded them. There was no more solidity in their frames than in the floating spume from a broken wave.

"But a more terrible experience was in store for me. Floating downwards from a great height there came a purplish patch of vapour, small as I saw it first, but rapidly enlarging as it approached me, until it appeared to be hundreds of square feet in size. Though fashioned of some transparent, jelly-like substance, it was none the less of much more definite outline and solid consistence than anything which I had seen before. There were more traces, too, of a physical organization, especially two vast, shadowy, circular plates upon either side, which may have been eyes, and a perfectly solid white projection between them which was as curved and cruel as the beak of a vulture.

"The whole aspect of this monster was formidable and threatening, and it kept changing its colour from a very light mauve to a dark, angry purple so thick that it cast a shadow as it drifted between my monoplane and the sun. On the upper curve of its huge body there were three great projections which I can only describe as enormous bubbles, and I was convinced as I looked at them that they were charged with some extremely light gas which served to buoy up

THE HORROR
OF THE HEIGHTS

the misshapen and semi-solid mass in the rarefied air. The creature moved swiftly along, keeping pace easily with the monoplane, and for twenty miles or more it formed my horrible escort, hovering over me like a bird of prey which is waiting to pounce. Its method of progression—done so swiftly that it was not easy to follow—was to throw out a long, glutinous streamer in front of it, which in turn seemed to draw forward the rest of the writhing body. So elastic and gelatinous was it that never for two successive minutes was it the same shape, and yet each change made it more threatening and loathsome than the last.

"I knew that it meant mischief. Every purple flush of its hideous body told me so. The vague, goggling eyes which were turned always upon me were cold and merciless in their viscid hatred. I dipped the nose of my monoplane downwards to escape it. As I did so, as quick as a flash there shot out a long tentacle from this mass of floating blubber, and it fell as light and sinuous as a whip-lash across the front of my machine. There was a loud hiss as it lay for a moment across the hot engine, and it whisked itself into the air again, while the huge, flat body drew itself together as if in sudden pain. I dipped to a vol-pique, but again a tentacle fell over the monoplane and was shorn off by the propeller as easily as it might have cut through a smoke wreath. A long, gliding, sticky, serpent-like coil came from behind and caught me round the waist, dragging me out of the fuselage. I tore at it, my fingers sinking into the smooth, glue-like surface, and for an instant I disengaged myself, but only to be caught round the boot by another coil, which gave me a jerk that tilted me almost on to my back.

"As I fell over I blazed off both barrels of my gun, though, indeed, it was like attacking an elephant with a pea-shooter to imagine that any human weapon could cripple that mighty bulk. And yet I aimed better than I knew, for, with a loud report, one of the great blisters upon the creature's back exploded with the puncture of the buckshot. It was very clear that my conjecture was right, and that these vast, clear bladders were distended with some lifting gas, for in an instant the huge, cloud-like body turned sideways, writhing desperately to find its balance, while the white beak snapped and gaped in horrible fury. But already I had shot away on the steepest glide that I dared to attempt, my engine still full on, the flying propeller and the force of gravity shooting me downwards like an aerolite. Far behind me I saw a dull, purplish smudge growing swiftly smaller and merging into the blue sky behind it. I was safe out of the deadly jungle of the outer air.

"Once out of danger I throttled my engine, for nothing tears a machine to pieces quicker than running on full power from a height. It was a glorious, spiral vol-plane from nearly eight miles of altitude—first, to the level of the silver cloud-bank, then to that of the storm-cloud beneath it, and finally, in beating rain, to the surface of the earth. I saw the Bristol Channel beneath me as I broke from the clouds, but, having still some petrol in my tank, I got twenty miles inland before I found myself stranded in a field half a mile from the village of Ashcombe. There I got three tins of petrol from a passing motor-car, and at ten minutes past six that evening I alighted gently in my own home meadow at Devizes, after such a journey as no mortal upon earth has ever yet taken and lived to tell the tale. I have seen the beauty and I have seen the horror of the heights—and greater beauty or greater horror than that is not within the ken of man.

"And now it is my plan to go once again before I give my results to the world. My reason for this is that I must surely have something to show by way of proof before I lay such a tale before my fellow-men. It is true that others will soon follow and will confirm what I have said, and yet I should wish to carry conviction from the first. Those lovely iridescent bubbles of the air should not be hard to capture. They drift slowly upon their way, and the swift monoplane could intercept their leisurely course. It is likely enough that they would dissolve in the heavier layers of the atmosphere, and that some small heap of amorphous jelly might be all that I should bring to earth with me. And yet something there would surely be by which I could substantiate my story. Yes, I will go, even if I run a risk by doing so. These purple horrors would not seem to be numerous. It is probable that I shall not see one. If I do I shall dive at once. At the worst there is always the shot-gun and my knowledge of…"

Here a page of the manuscript is unfortunately missing. On the next page is written, in large, straggling writing:

"Forty-three thousand feet. I shall never see earth again. They are beneath me, three of them. God help me; it is a dreadful death to die!"

Such in its entirety is the Joyce-Armstrong Statement. Of the man nothing has since been seen. Pieces of his shattered monoplane have been picked up in the preserves of Mr. Budd-Lushington upon the borders of Kent and Sussex, within a few miles of the spot where the note-book was discovered. If the unfortunate aviator's theory is correct that this air-jungle, as he called it, existed only over the south-west of England, then it would seem that he had fled from it at the full speed of his monoplane, but had been overtaken and devoured by these horrible creatures at some spot in the outer atmosphere above the place where the grim relics were found. The picture of that monoplane skimming down the sky, with the nameless terrors flying as swiftly beneath it and cutting it off always from the earth while they gradually closed in upon their victim, is one upon which a man who valued his sanity would prefer not to dwell. There are many, as I am aware, who still jeer at the facts which I have here set down, but even they must admit that Joyce-Armstrong has disappeared, and I would commend to them his own words: "This note-book may explain what I am trying to do, and how I lost my life in doing it. But no drivel about accidents or mysteries, if YOU please."

NIGHTMARE AT 20,000 FEET

RICHARD MATHESON

Is this the greatest fear-of-flying story ever written? Could be. Not to sound like Rod Serling, but consider if you will the thought of one Arthur Jeffrey Wilson, as the DC-7 in which he is a passenger takes off: "Here he was…twenty thousand feet above the earth, trapped in a howling shell of death." Originally published in 1961, when you could smoke on passenger flights and even tote a pistol in your carry-on bag, "Nightmare" walks a knife-edge between two possibilities: either Mr. Wilson is having an anxiety-driven nervous breakdown, or there really is an ugly twisted *thing* on the wing outside his window, trying to bring the plane down. Either way, you're in for a very unpleasant flight. Better fasten your safety belt.

eat belt, please," said the stewardess cheerfully as she passed him.

Almost as she spoke, the sign above the archway which led to the forward compartment lit up— FASTEN SEAT BELT—with, below, its attendant caution—NO SMOKING. Drawing in a deep lungful, Wilson exhaled it in bursts, then pressed the cigarette into the armrest tray with irritable stabbing motions.

Outside, one of the engines coughed monstrously, spewing out a cloud of fume which fragmented into the night air. The fuselage began to shudder and Wilson, glancing through the window, saw the exhaust of flame jetting whitely from the engine's nacelle. The second engine coughed, then roared, its propeller instantly a blur of revolution. With a tense submissiveness, Wilson fastened the belt across his lap.

Now all the engines were running and Wilson's head throbbed in unison with the fuselage. He sat rigidly, staring at the seat ahead as the DC-7 taxied across the apron, heating the night with the thundering blast of its exhausts.

At the edge of the runway, it halted. Wilson looked out through the window at the leviathan glitter of the terminal. By late morning, he thought, showered and cleanly dressed, he would be sitting in the office of one more contact discussing one more specious deal the net result of which would not add one jot of meaning to the history of mankind. It was all so damned—

Wilson gasped as the engines began their warm-up race preparatory to takeoff. The sound, already loud, became deafening—waves of sound that crashed against Wilson's ears like club blows. He opened his mouth as if to let it drain. His eyes took on the glaze of a suffering man, his hands drew in like tensing claws.

He started, legs retracting, as he felt a touch on his arm. Jerking aside his head, he saw the stewardess who had met him at the door. She was smiling down at him.

"Are you all right?" he barely made out her words.

Wilson pressed his lips together and agitated his hand at her as if pushing her away. Her smile flared into excess brightness, then fell as she turned and moved away.

The plane began to move. At first lethargically, like some behemoth struggling to overthrow the pull of its own weight. Then with more speed, forcing off the drag of friction. Wilson, turning to the window, saw the dark runway rushing by faster and faster. On the wing edge, there was a mechanical whining as the flaps descended. Then, imperceptibly, the giant wheels lost contact with the ground, the earth began to fall away. Trees flashed underneath, buildings, the darting quicksilver of car lights. The DC-7 banked slowly to the right, pulling itself upward toward the frosty glitter of the stars.

Finally, it levelled off and the engines seemed to stop until Wilson's adjusting ear caught the murmur of their cruising speed. A moment of relief slackened his muscles, imparting a sense of well-being. Then it was gone. Wilson sat immobile, staring at the NO SMOKING sign until it winked out, then, quickly, lit a cigarette. Reaching into the seat-back pocket in front of him, he slid free his newspaper.

As usual, the world was in a state similar to his. Friction in diplomatic circles, earthquakes and gunfire, murder, rape, tornadoes and collisions, business conflicts, gangsterism. God's in his heaven, all's right with the world, thought Arthur Jeffrey Wilson.

Fifteen minutes later, he tossed the paper aside. His stomach felt awful. He glanced up at the signs beside the two lavatories. Both, illuminated, read OCCUPIED. He pressed out his third cigarette since takeoff and, turning off the overhead light, stared out through the window.

Along the cabin's length, people were already flicking out their lights and reclining their chairs for sleep. Wilson glanced at his watch. Eleven-twenty. He blew out tired breath. As he'd anticipated, the pills he'd taken before boarding hadn't done a bit of good.

He stood abruptly as the woman came out of the lavatory and, snatching up his bag, he started down the aisle.

His system, as expected, gave no cooperation. Wilson stood with a tired moan and adjusted his clothing. Having washed his hands and face, he removed the toilet kit from the bag and squeezed a filament of paste across his toothbrush.

As he brushed, one hand braced for support against the cold bulkhead, he looked out through the port. Feet away was the pale blue of the inboard propeller. Wilson visualized what would happen if it were to tear loose and, like a tri-bladed cleaver, come slicing in at him.

There was a sudden depression in his stomach. Wilson swallowed instinctively and got some paste-stained saliva down his throat. Gagging, he turned and spat into the sink, then, hastily, washed out his mouth and took a drink. Dear God, if only he could have gone by train; had his own compartment, taken a casual stroll to the club car; settled down in an easy chair with a drink and a magazine. But there was no such time or fortune in this world.

He was about to put the toilet kit away when his gaze caught on the oilskin envelope in the bag. He hesitated, then, setting the small briefcase on the sink, drew out the envelope and undid it on his lap.

He sat staring at the oil-glossed symmetry of the pistol. He'd carried it around with him for almost a year now. Originally, when he'd thought about it, it was in terms of money carried, protection from holdup, safety from teenage gangs in the cities he had to attend. Yet, far beneath, he'd always known there was no valid reason except one. A reason he thought more of every day. How simple it would be—here, now—

Wilson shut his eyes and swallowed quickly. He could still taste the toothpaste in his mouth, a faint nettling of peppermint on the buds. He sat heavily in the throbbing chill of the lavatory, the oily gun resting in his hands. Until, quite suddenly, he began to shiver without control. God, let me go! his mind cried out abruptly.

"Let me go, *let me go*." He barely recognized the whimpering in his ears.

NIGHTMARE
AT 20,000 FEET

RICHARD MATHESON

Abruptly, Wilson sat erect. Lips pressed together, he rewrapped the pistol and thrust it into his bag, putting the briefcase on top of it, zipping the bag shut. Standing, he opened the door and stepped outside, hurrying to his seat and sitting down, sliding the overnight bag precisely into place. He indented the armrest button and pushed himself back. He was a business man and there was business to be conducted on the morrow. It was as simple as that. The body needed sleep, he would give it sleep.

Twenty minutes later, Wilson reached down slowly and depressed the button, sitting up with the chair, his face a mask of vanquished acceptance. Why fight it? he thought. It was obvious he was going to stay awake. So that was that.

He had finished half of the crossword puzzle before he let the paper drop to his lap. His eyes were too tired. Sitting up, he rotated his shoulders, stretching the muscles of his back. Now what? he thought. He didn't want to read, he couldn't sleep. And there were still—he checked his watch—seven to eight hours left before Los Angeles was reached. How was he to spend them? He looked along the cabin and saw that, except for a single passenger in the forward compartment, everyone was asleep.

A sudden, overwhelming fury filled him and he wanted to scream, to throw something, to hit somebody. Teeth jammed together so rabidly it hurt his jaws, Wilson shoved aside the curtains with a spastic hand and stared out murderously through the window.

Outside, he saw the wing lights blinking off and on, the lurid flashes of exhaust from the engine cowlings. Here he was, he thought; twenty-thousand feet above the earth, trapped in a howling shell of death, moving through polar night toward—

Wilson twitched as lightning bleached the sky, washing its false daylight across the wing. He swallowed. Was there going to be a storm? The thought of rain and heavy winds, of the plane a chip in the sea of sky was not a pleasant one. Wilson was a bad flyer. Excess motion always made him ill. Maybe he should have taken another few Dramamines to be on the safe side. And, naturally, his seat was next to the emergency door. He thought about it opening accidentally; about himself sucked from the plane, falling, screaming.

Wilson blinked and shook his head. There was a faint tingling at the back of his neck as he pressed close to the window and stared out. He sat there motionless, squinting. He could have sworn—

Suddenly, his stomach muscles jerked in violently and he felt his eyes strain forward. There was something crawling on the wing.

Wilson felt a sudden, nauseous tremor in his stomach. Dear God, had some dog or cat crawled onto the plane before takeoff and, in some way managed to hold on? It was a sickening thought. The poor animal would be deranged with terror. Yet, how, on the smooth, wind-blasted surface, could it possibly discover gripping places? Surely that was impossible. Perhaps, after all, it was only a bird or—

The lightning flared and Wilson saw that it was a man.

He couldn't move. Stupefied, he watched the black form crawling down the wing. *Impossible.* Somewhere, cased in layers of shock, a voice declared itself but Wilson did not hear. He was conscious of nothing but the titanic, almost muscle-tearing leap of his heart—and of the man outside.

Suddenly, like ice-filled water thrown across him, there was a reaction; his mind sprang for the shelter of explanation. A mechanic had, through some incredible oversight, been taken up with the ship and had managed to cling to it even though the wind had torn his clothes away, even though the air was thin and close to freezing.

Wilson gave himself no time for refutation. Jarring to his feet, he shouted: "Stewardess! Stewardess!" his voice a hollow, ringing sound in the cabin. He pushed the button for her with a jabbing finger.

"*Stewardess!*"

She came running down the aisle, her face tightened with alarm. When she saw the look on his face, she stiffened in her tracks.

"There's a man out there! A man!" cried Wilson.

"*What?*" Skin constricted on her cheeks, around her eyes.

"Look, *look!*" Hand shaking, Wilson dropped back into his seat and pointed out the window. "He's crawling on the—"

The words ended with a choking rattle in his throat. There was nothing on the wing.

Wilson sat there trembling. For a while, before he turned back, he looked at the reflection of the stewardess on the window. There was a blank expression on her face.

At last, he turned and looked up at her. He saw her red lips part as though she meant to speak but she said nothing, only placing the lips together again and swallowing. An attempted smile distended briefly at her features.

"'I'm sorry," Wilson said. "It must have been a—"

He stopped as though the sentence were completed. Across the aisle a teenage girl was gaping at him with sleepy curiosity.

The stewardess cleared her throat. "Can I get you anything?" she asked.

"A glass of water," Wilson said.

The stewardess turned and moved back up the aisle.

Wilson sucked in a long breath of air and turned away from the young girl's scrutiny. He felt the same. That was the thing that shocked him most. Where were the visions, the cries, the pummelling of fists on temples, the tearing out of hair?

Abruptly he closed his eyes. There had been a man, he thought. There had, actually, been a man. That's why he felt the same. And yet, there couldn't have been. He knew that clearly.

Wilson sat with his eyes closed, wondering what Jacqueline would be doing now if she were in the seat beside him. Would she be silent, shocked beyond speaking? Or would she, in the more accepted manner, be fluttering around him, smiling, chattering, pretending that she hadn't seen? What would his sons think? Wilson felt a dry sob threatening in his chest. Oh, God—

"Here's your water, sir."

Twitching sharply, Wilson opened his eyes.

"Would you like a blanket?" inquired the stewardess.

"No." He shook his head. "Thank you," he added, wondering why he was being so polite.

"If you need anything, just ring," she said.

Wilson nodded.

Behind him, as he sat with the untouched cup of water in his hand, he heard the muted voices of the stewardess and one of the passengers. Wilson tightened with resentment. Abruptly, he reached down and, careful not to spill the water, pulled out the overnight bag. Unzipping it, he removed the box of sleeping capsules and washed two of them down. Crumpling the empty cup, he pushed it into the seat-pocket in front of him, then, not looking, slid the curtains shut. There—it was ended. One hallucination didn't make insanity.

Wilson turned onto his right side and tried to set himself against the fitful motion of the ship. He had to forget about this, that was the most important thing. He mustn't dwell on it. Unexpectedly, he found a wry smile forming on his lips. Well, by God, no one could accuse him of mundane hallucinations anyway. When he went at it, he did a royal job. A naked man crawling down a DC-7's wing at twenty-thousand feet—there was a chimera worthy of the noblest lunatic.

The humor faded quickly. Wilson felt chilled. It had been so clear, so vivid. How could the eyes see such a thing when it did not exist? How could what was in his mind make the physical act of seeing work to its purpose so completely? He hadn't been groggy, in a daze—nor had it been a shapeless, gauzy vision. It had been sharply three-dimensional, fully a part of the things he saw which he *knew* were real. That was the frightening part of it. It had not been dreamlike in the least. He had looked at the wing and—

Impulsively, Wilson drew aside the curtain.

He did not know, immediately, if he would survive. It seemed as if all the contents of his chest and stomach were bloating horribly, the excess pushing up into his throat and head, choking away breath, pressing out his eyes. Imprisoned in this swollen mass, his heart pulsed strickenly, threatening to burst its case as Wilson sat, paralyzed.

Only inches away, separated from him by the thickness of a piece of glass, the man was staring at him.

It was a hideously malignant face, a face not human. Its skin was grimy, of a wide-pored coarseness; its nose a squat, discolored lump; its lips misshapen, cracked, forced apart by teeth of a grotesque size and crookedness; its eyes recessed and small—unblinking. All framed by shaggy, tangled hair which sprouted, too, in furry tufts from the man's ears and nose, birdlike, down across his cheeks.

Wilson sat riven to his chair, incapable of response. Time stopped and lost its meaning. Function and analysis ceased. All were frozen in an ice of shock. Only the beat of heart went on—alone, a frantic leaping in the darkness. Wilson could not so much as blink. Dull-eyed, breathless, he returned the creature's vacant stare.

Abruptly then, he closed his eyes and his mind, rid of the sight, broke free. It isn't there, he thought. He pressed his teeth together, breath quavering in his nostrils. It isn't there, *it simply is not there.*

Clutching at the armrests with pale-knuckled fingers, Wilson braced himself. There is no man out there, he told himself. It was impossible that there should be a man out there crouching on the wing looking at him.

He opened his eyes—

—to shrink against the seat back with a gagging inhalation. Not only was the man still there but he was grinning. Wilson turned his fingers in and dug the nails into his palms until pain flared. He kept it there until there was no doubt in his mind that he was fully conscious.

Then, slowly, arm quivering and numb, Wilson reached up for the button which would summon the stewardess. He would not make the same mistake again—cry out, leap to his feet, alarm the creature into flight. He kept reaching upward, a tremor of aghast excitement in his muscles now because the man was watching him, the small eyes shifting with the movement of his arm.

He pressed the button carefully once, twice. Now come, he thought. Come with your objective eyes and see what I see—but *hurry.*

In the rear of the cabin, he heard a curtain being drawn aside and, suddenly, his body stiffened. The man had turned his caliban head to look in that direction. Paralyzed, Wilson stared at him. Hurry, he thought. For God's sake, hurry!

It was over in a second. The man's eyes shifted back to Wilson, across his lips a smile of monstrous cunning. Then with a leap, he was gone.

"Yes, sir?"

NIGHTMARE AT 20,000 FEET

RICHARD MATHESON

For a moment, Wilson suffered the fullest anguish of madness. His gaze kept jumping from the spot where the man had stood to the stewardess's questioning face, then back again. Back to the stewardess, to the wing, to the stewardess, his breath caught, his eyes stark with dismay.

"What *is* it?" asked the stewardess.

It was the look on her face that did it. Wilson closed a vise on his emotions. She couldn't possibly believe him. He realized it in an instant.

"I'm—I'm sorry," he faltered. He swallowed so dryly that it made a clicking noise in his throat. "It's nothing. I—apologize."

The stewardess obviously didn't know what to say. She kept leaning against the erratic yawing of the ship, one hand holding on to the back of the seat beside Wilson's, the other stirring limply along the seam of her skirt. Her lips were parted slightly as if she meant to speak but could not find the words.

"Well," she said finally and cleared her throat, "if you—need anything."

"Yes, yes. Thank you. Are we—going into a storm?"

The stewardess smiled hastily. "Just a small one," she said. "Nothing to worry about."

Wilson nodded with little twitching movements. Then, as the stewardess turned away, breathed in suddenly, his nostrils flaring. He felt certain that she already thought him mad but didn't know what to do about it because, in her course of training, there had been no instruction on the handling of passengers who thought they saw small men crouching on the wing.

Thought?

Wilson turned his head abruptly and looked outside. He stared at the dark rise of the wing, the spouting flare of the exhausts, the blinking lights. He'd *seen* the man—to that he'd swear. How could he be completely aware of everything around him—be, in all ways, sane and still imagine such a thing? Was it logical that the mind, in giving way, should, instead of distorting all reality, insert, within the still intact arrangement of details, one extraneous sight?

No, not logical at all.

Suddenly, Wilson thought about war, about the newspaper stories which recounted the alleged existence of creatures in the sky who plagued the Allied pilots in their duties. They called them gremlins, he remembered. Were there, actually, such beings? Did they, truly, exist up here, never falling, riding on the wind, apparently of bulk and weight, yet impervious to gravity?

He was thinking that when the man appeared again.

One second the wing was empty. The next, with an arcing descent, the man came jumping down to it. There seemed no impact. He landed almost fragilely, short, hairy arms outstretched as if for balance. Wilson tensed. Yes, there was knowledge in his look. The man—was he to think of it as a man?—somehow understood that he had tricked Wilson into calling the stewardess in vain. Wilson felt himself tremble with alarm. How could he prove the man's existence to others? He looked around desperately. That girl across the aisle. If he spoke to her softly, woke her up, would she be able to—

No, the man would jump away before she could see. Probably to the top of the fuselage where no one could see him, not even the pilots in their cockpit. Wilson felt a sudden burst of self-condemnation that he hadn't gotten that camera Walter had asked for. Dear Lord, he thought, to be able to take a picture of the man.

He leaned in close to the window. What was the man doing?

Abruptly, darkness seemed to leap away as the wing was chalked with lightning and Wilson saw. Like an inquisitive child, the man was squatted on the hitching wing edge, stretching out his right hand toward one of the whirling propellers.

As Wilson watched, fascinatedly appalled, the man's hand drew closer and closer to the blurring gyre until, suddenly, it jerked away and the man's lips twitched back in a soundless cry. He's lost a finger! Wilson thought, sickened. But, immediately, the man reached forward again, gnarled finger extended, the picture of some monstrous infant trying to capture the spin of a fan blade.

If it had not been so hideously out of place it would have been amusing for, objectively seen, the man, at that moment, was a comic sight—a fairy tale troll somehow come to life, wind whipping at the hair across his head and body, all of his attention centered on the turn of the propeller. How could this be madness? Wilson suddenly thought. What self-revelation could this farcical little horror possibly bestow on him?

Again and again, as Wilson watched, the man reached forward. Again and again jerked back his fingers, sometimes, actually, putting them in his mouth as if to cool them. And, always, apparently checking, he kept glancing back across at his shoulder looking at Wilson. *He knows*, thought Wilson. Knows that this is a game between us. If I am able to get someone else to see him, then he loses. If I am the only witness, then he wins. The sense of faint amusement was gone now. Wilson clenched his teeth. Why in hell didn't the pilots see!

Now the man, no longer interested in the propeller, was settling himself across the engine cowling like a man astride a bucking horse. Wilson stared at him. Abruptly a shudder plaited down his back. The little man was picking at the plates that sheathed the engine, trying to get his nails beneath them.

Impulsively, Wilson reached up and pushed the button for the stewardess. In the rear of the cabin, he heard her coming and, for a second, thought he'd fooled the man, who seemed absorbed with his efforts. At the last moment, however, just before the stewardess arrived, the man glanced over at Wilson. Then, like a marionette jerked upward from its stage by wires, he was flying up into the air.

"Yes?" She looked at him apprehensively.

"Will you—sit down, please?" he asked.

She hesitated. "Well, I—"

"Please."

She sat down gingerly on the seat beside his.

"What is it, Mr. Wilson?" she asked.

He braced himself.

"That man is still outside," he said.

The stewardess stared at him.

"The reason I'm telling you this," Wilson hurried on, "is that he's starting to tamper with one of the engines."

She turned her eyes instinctively toward the window.

"No, no, don't look," he told her. "He isn't there now." He cleared his throat viscidly. "He—jumps away whenever you come here."

A sudden nausea gripped him as he realized what she must be thinking. As he realized what he, himself, would think if someone told him such a story, a wave of dizziness seemed to pass across him and he thought—I *am* going mad!

"The point is this," he said, fighting off the thought. "If I'm not imagining this thing, the ship is in danger."

"Yes," she said.

"I know," he said. "You think I've lost my mind."

"Of course not," she said.

"All I ask is this," he said, struggling against the rise of anger. "Tell the pilots what I've said. Ask them to keep an eye on the wings. If they see nothing—all right. But if they do—"

The stewardess sat there quietly, looking at him. Wilson's hands curled into fists that trembled in his lap.

"*Well?*" he asked.

She pushed to her feet. "I'll tell them," she said.

Turning away, she moved along the aisle with a movement that was, to Wilson, poorly contrived—too fast to be normal yet, clearly, held back as if to reassure him that she wasn't fleeing. He felt his stomach churning as he looked out at the wing again.

Abruptly, the man appeared again, landing on the wing like some grotesque ballet dancer. Wilson watched him as he set to work again, straddling the engine casing with his thick, bare legs and picking at the plates.

Well, what was he so concerned about? thought Wilson. That miserable creature couldn't pry up rivets with his fingernails. Actually, it didn't matter if the pilots saw him or not—at least as far as the safety of the plane was concerned. As for his own, personal reasons—

It was at that moment that the man pried up one edge of a plate.

Wilson gasped. "Here, quickly!" he shouted, noticing, up ahead, the stewardess and the pilot coming through the cockpit doorway.

The pilot's eyes jerked up to look at Wilson, then abruptly, he was pushing past the stewardess and lurching up the aisle.

"*Hurry!*" Wilson cried. He glanced out the window in time to see the man go leaping upward. That didn't matter now. There would be evidence.

"What's going on?" the pilot asked, stopping breathlessly beside his seat.

"He's torn up one of the engine plates!" said Wilson in a shaking voice.

"He's what?"

"The man outside!" said Wilson. "I tell you he's—!"

"Mister Wilson, keep your voice down!" ordered the pilot. Wilson's jaw went slack.

"I don't know what's going on here," said the pilot, "but—"

"Will you look?!" shouted Wilson.

"Mister Wilson, I'm warning you."

"For God's sake!" Wilson swallowed quickly, trying to repress the blinding rage he felt. Abruptly, he pushed back against his seat and pointed at the window with a palsied hand. "Will you, for God's sake, *look?*" he asked.

Drawing in an agitated breath, the pilot bent over. In a moment, his gaze shifted coldly to Wilson's. "Well?" he asked.

Wilson jerked his head around. The plates were in their normal position.

"Oh, now wait," he said before the dread could come. "I saw him pry that plate up."

"Mister Wilson, if you don't—"

"*I said I saw him pry it up,*" said Wilson.

The pilot stood there looking at him in the same withdrawn, almost aghast way as the stewardess had. Wilson shuddered violently.

"Listen, I *saw* him!" he cried. The sudden break in his voice appalled him.

In a second, the pilot was down beside him. "Mister Wilson, please," he said. "All right, you saw him. But remember there are other people aboard. We mustn't alarm them."

Wilson was too shaken to understand at first.

"You—mean you've *seen* him then?" he asked.

"Of course," the pilot said, "but we don't want to frighten the passengers. You can understand that."

"Of course, of course, I don't want to—"

NIGHTMARE AT 20,000 FEET

RICHARD MATHESON

Wilson felt a spastic coiling in his groin and lower stomach. Suddenly, he pressed his lips together and looked at the pilot with malevolent eyes.

"I understand," he said.

"The thing we have to remember—" began the pilot.

"We can stop now," Wilson said.

"Sir?"

Wilson shuddered. "Get out of here," he said.

"Mister Wilson, what—?"

"*Will you stop?*" Face whitening, Wilson turned from the pilot and stared out at the wing, eyes like stone.

He glared back suddenly.

"Rest assured I'd not say another word!" he snapped.

"Mr. Wilson, try to understand our—"

Wilson twisted away and stared out venomously at the engine. From a corner of his vision, he saw two passengers standing in the aisle looking at him. *Idiots!* his mind exploded. He felt his hands begin to tremble and, for a few seconds, was afraid that he was going to vomit. It's the motion, he told himself. The plane was bucking in the air now like a storm-tossed boat.

He realized that the pilot was still talking to him and, refocusing his eyes, he looked at the man's reflection in the window. Beside him, mutely somber, stood the stewardess. Blind idiots, both of them, thought Wilson. He did not indicate his notice of their departure. Reflected on the window, he saw them heading toward the rear of the cabin. They'll be discussing me now, he thought. Setting up plans in case I grow violent.

He wished now that the man would reappear, pull off the cowling plate and ruin the engine. It gave him a sense of vengeful pleasure to know that only he stood between catastrophe and the more than

73

thirty people aboard. If he chose, he could allow that catastrophe to take place. Wilson smiled without humor. There would be a royal suicide, he thought.

The little man dropped down again and Wilson saw that what he'd thought was correct—the man had pressed the plate back into place before jumping away. For, now, he was prying it up again and it was raising easily, peeling back like skin excised by some grotesque surgeon. The motion of the wing was very broken but the man seemed to have no difficulty staying balanced.

Once more Wilson felt panic. What was he to do? No one believed him. If he tried to convince them any more they'd probably restrain him by force. If he asked the stewardess to sit by him it would be, at best, only a momentary reprieve. The second she departed or, remaining, fell asleep, the man would return. Even if she stayed awake beside him, what was to keep the man from tampering with the engines on the other wing? Wilson shuddered, a coldness of dread misting along his bones.

Dear God, there was nothing to be done.

He twitched as, across the window through which he watched the little man, the pilot's reflection passed. The insanity of the moment almost broke him—the man and the pilot within feet of each other, both seen by him yet not aware of one another. No, that was wrong. The little man had glanced across his shoulder as the pilot passed. As if he knew there was no need to leap off any more, that Wilson's capacity for interfering was at an end. Wilson suddenly trembled with mind-searing rage. I'll kill you! he thought! You filthy little animal, I'll *kill* you!

Outside, the engine faltered.

It lasted only for a second, but, in that second, it seemed to Wilson as if his heart had, also, stopped. He pressed against the window, staring. The man had bent the cowling plate far back and now was on his knees, poking a curious hand into the engine.

"Don't," Wilson heard the whimper of his own voice begging. "Don't..."

Again, the engine failed. Wilson looked around in horror. Was everyone deaf? He raised his hand to press the button for the stewardess, then jerked it back. No, they'd lock him up, restrain him somehow. And he was the only one who knew what was happening, the only one who could help.

"God..." Wilson bit his lower lip until the pain made him whimper. He twisted around again and jolted. The stewardess was hurrying down the rocking aisle. She'd heard it! He watched her fixedly and saw her glance at him as she passed his seat.

She stopped three seats down the aisle. Someone else had heard! Wilson watched the stewardess as she leaned over, talking to the unseen passenger. Outside, the engine coughed again. Wilson jerked his head around and looked out with horror-pinched eyes.

"*Damn you!*" he whined.

He turned again and saw the stewardess coming back up the aisle. She didn't look alarmed. Wilson stared at her with unbelieving eyes. It wasn't possible. He twisted around to follow her swaying movement and saw her turn in at the kitchen.

"*No.*" Wilson was shaking so badly now he couldn't stop. No one had heard.

No one knew.

Suddenly, Wilson bent over and slid his overnight bag out from under the seat. Unzipping it, he jerked out his briefcase and threw it on the carpeting. Then, reaching in again, he grabbed the oilskin envelope and straightened up. From the corners of his eyes, he saw the stewardess coming back and pushed the bag beneath the seat with his shoes, shoving the oilskin envelope beside himself. He sat there rigidly, breath quavering in his chest, as she went by.

Then he pulled the envelope into his lap and untied it. His movements were so feverish that he almost dropped the pistol. He caught it by the barrel, then clutched at the stock with white-knuck-led fingers and pushed off the safety catch. He glanced outside and felt himself grow cold.

The man was looking at him.

Wilson pressed his shaking lips together. It was impossible that the man knew what he intended. He swallowed and tried to catch his breath. He shifted his gaze to where the stewardess was handing some pills to the passenger ahead, then looked back at the wing. The man was turning to the engine once again, reaching in. Wilson's grip tightened on the pistol. He began to raise it.

Suddenly, he lowered it. The window was too thick. The bullet might be deflected and kill one of the passengers. He shuddered and stared out at the little man. Again the engine failed and Wilson saw an eruption of sparks cast light across the man's animal features. He braced himself. There was only one answer.

He looked down at the handle of the emergency door. There was a transparent cover over it. Wilson pulled it free and dropped it. He looked outside. The man was still there, crouched and probing at the engine with his hand. Wilson sucked in trembling breath. He put his left hand on the door handle and tested. It wouldn't move downward. Upward there was play.

Abruptly, Wilson let go and put the pistol in his lap. No time for argument, he told himself. With shaking hands, he buckled the belt across his thighs. When the door was opened, there would be a tremendous rushing out of air. For the safety of the ship, he must not go with it.

NIGHTMARE AT 20,000 FEET

RICHARD MATHESON

Now. Wilson picked the pistol up again, his heartbeat staggering. He'd have to be sudden, accurate. If he missed, the man might jump onto the other wing—worse, onto the tail assembly where, inviolate, he could rupture wires, mangle flaps, destroy the balance of the ship. No, this was the only way. He'd fire low and try to hit the man in the chest or stomach. Wilson filled his lungs with air. Now, he thought. *Now.*

The stewardess came up the aisle as Wilson started pulling at the handle. For a moment, frozen in her steps, she couldn't speak. A look of stupefied horror distended her features and she raised one hand as if imploring him. Then, suddenly, her voice was shrilling above the noise of the engines.

"*Mr. Wilson, no!*"

"Get back!" cried Wilson and he wrenched the handle up.

The door seemed to disappear. One second it was by him, in his grip. The next, with a hissing roar, it was gone.

In the same instant, Wilson felt himself enveloped by a monstrous suction which tried to tear him from his seat. His head and shoulders left the cabin and, suddenly, he was breathing tenuous, freezing air. For a moment, eardrums almost bursting from the thunder of the engines, eyes blinded by the arctic winds, he forgot the man. It seemed he heard a prick of screaming in the maelstrom that surrounded him, a distant shout.

Then Wilson saw the man.

He was walking across the wing, gnarled form leaning forward, talon-twisted hands outstretched in eagerness. Wilson flung his arm up, fired. The explosion was like a popping in the roaring violence of the air. The man staggered, lashed out and Wilson felt a streak of pain across his head. He fired again at immediate range and saw the man go flailing backward—then, suddenly, disappear with no more solidity than a paper doll swept in a gale. Wilson felt a bursting numbness in his brain. He felt the pistol torn from failing fingers.

Then all was lost in winter darkness.

HE stirred and mumbled. There was a warmness trickling in his veins, his limbs felt wooden. In the darkness, he could hear a shuffling sound, a delicate swirl of voices. He was lying, face up, on something—moving, joggling. A cold wind sprinkled on his face, he felt the surface tilt beneath him.

He sighed. The plane was landed and he was being carried off on a stretcher. His head wound, likely, plus an injection to quiet him.

"Nuttiest way of tryin' to commit suicide *I* ever heard of," said a voice somewhere.

Wilson felt the pleasure of amusement. Whoever spoke was wrong, of course. As would be established soon enough when the engine was examined and they checked his wound more closely. Then they'd realize that he'd saved them all.

Wilson slept without dreams.

THE FLYING MACHINE

AMBROSE BIERCE

Although Bierce lived into the age of flight (he died in 1914), one doubts if he ever actually flew. The vignette that follows is less about airplanes than it is about the gullibility of people willing to invest in them, and it certainly helps to explain his nickname, which was "Bitter" Bierce. My own favorite Bierce *bon mot*: "War is God's way of teaching Americans geography."

n Ingenious Man who had built a flying-machine invited a great concourse of people to see it go up. At the appointed moment, everything being ready, he boarded the car and turned on the power. The machine immediately broke through the massive substructure upon which it was builded, and sank out of sight into the earth, the aeronaut springing out barely in time to save himself.

"Well," said he, "I have done enough to demonstrate the correctness of my details. The defects," he added, with a look at the ruined brick-work, "are merely basic and fundamental."

Upon this assurance the people came forward with subscriptions to build a second machine.

LUCIFER!

E.C. TUBB

Here's the thing about air travel: once the plane takes off, you're in it for the duration. Tubb combines that simple, irrefutable fact with an extremely original—and sinister—time travel concept. To say more would spoil this nasty, chilling, one-of-a-kind story. Edwin Charles Tubb was one of Great Britain's most prolific science fiction writers. In a career spanning almost sixty years, he wrote at least 150 novels and over a dozen short story collections. He edited *Authentic Science Fiction* in the 1956-57 and, under a variety of pseudonyms, wrote most of the stories himself (including the book review column). "Lucifer!" is one of his best. It received a Special Award for Best Short Story at the first Eurocon in 1972.

I t was a device of great social convenience and everyone used it. Everyone, in this case, meaning the Special People all of whom were rich, charming and socially successful. Those who had dropped in to study an amusing primitive culture and those who, for personal reasons, preferred to remain on a world where they could be very large fish in a very small sea.

The Special People, dilettantes of the Intergalactic Set, protected and cosseted by their science, playing their games with the local natives and careful always to preserve their anonymity. But accidents can happen even to the superhuman. Stupid things which, because of their low order of probability, were statistically impossible.

Like a steel cable snapping when the safe it was supporting hung twenty feet above the ground. The safe fell, smashing the sidewalk but doing no other damage. The cable, suddenly released from strain, snapped like a whip, the end jerking in a random motion impossible to predict. The odds against it hitting any one particular place were astronomical. The odds against one of the Special People being in just that spot at that exact time were so high as to negate normal probability. But it happened. The frayed end of the cable hit a skull, shredding bone, brain and tissue in an ungodly mess. A surgically implanted mechanism sent out a distress call. The man's friends received the signal. Frank Weston got the body.

Frank Weston, anachronism. In a modern age no man should have to drag a twisted foot through 28 years of his life. Especially when he has the face of a Renaissance angel. But if he looked like an angel he was a fallen one. The dead couldn't be hurt but their relatives could. Tell a suicide's father that his dead girl was pregnant. A doting mother that the apple of her eye was loathsomely diseased. They didn't bother to check, why should they? And, even if they did, so what? Anyone could make a mistake and he was a morgue attendant not a doctor.

Dispassionately he examined the new delivery. The cable had done a good job of ruining the face—visual identification was impossible. Blood had ruined the suit but enough remained to show the wearer had bought pricey material. The wallet contained few bills but a lot of credit cards. There was some loose change, a cigarette case, a cigarette lighter, keys, wrist-watch, tiepin...They made little rustling noises as Frank fed them into an envelope. He paused when he saw the ring.

Sometimes, in his job, an unscrupulous man could make a little on the side. Frank had no scruples only defensive caution. The ring could have been lost before the stiff arrived in his care. The hand was caked with blood and maybe no one had noticed it. Even if they had it would be his word against theirs. If he could get it off, wash the hand free of blood, stash it away and act innocent, the ring would be his. And he would get it off if he had to smash the hand to do it. Accidents sometimes made strange injuries.

An hour later they arrived to claim the body. Quiet men, two of them, neatly dressed and calmly determined. The dead man was their business associate. They gave his name and address, the description of the suit he was wearing, other information. There was no question of crime and no reason to hold the body.

One of them looked sharply at Frank. "Is this all he had on him?"

"That's right," said Frank. "You've got it all. Sign here and he's yours."

"One moment." The two men looked at each other then the one who had spoken turned to Frank. "Our friend wore a ring. It was something like this." He extended his hand. "The ring had a stone and a wide band. Could we have it please?"

Frank was stubborn. "I haven't got it. I haven't even seen it. He wasn't wearing it when he came in here."

Again the silent conference. "The ring has no intrinsic value but it does have sentimental worth. I would be prepared to pay one hundred dollars for it and no questions will be asked."

"Why tell me?" said Frank coldly. Inside he felt the growing warmth that stemmed from sadistical pleasure. How he didn't know but he was hurting this man. "You gonna sign or what?" He turned the knife. "You think I stole something you call the cops. Either way get out of here."

✈ FLIGHT OR FRIGHT

IN the dog hours he examined what he had stolen. Sitting hunched in his usual corner of the canteen, masked by a newspaper, to the others in the place just another part of the furniture. Slowly he turned the ring. The band was thick and wide, raised in one part, a prominence which could be flattened by the pressure of a finger. The stone was flat, dull, probably a poorly ground specimen of the semi-precious group. The metal could have been plated alloy. If it was, a hundred dollars could buy any of a dozen like it.

But—would a man dressed as the stiff had been dressed wear such a ring?

The corpse had reeked of money. The cigarette case and lighter had been of jewelled platinum—too hot to think of stealing. The credit cards would have taken him around the world and first class all the way. Would a man like that wear a lousy hundred-dollar ring?

Blankly he stared across the canteen. Facing his table three men sat over their coffee. One of them straightened, rose, stretched and headed towards the door.

Scowling Frank dropped his eyes to the ring. Had he thrown away a hundred dollars for the sake of some junk? His fingernail touched the protuberance. It sank a little and, impatiently, he pressed it flush.

Nothing happened.

Nothing aside from the fact that the man who had risen from the facing table and who had walked towards the door was suddenly sitting at the table again. As Frank watched he rose, stretched and walked towards the door. Frank pressed the stud. Nothing happened.

Literally nothing.

He frowned and tried again. Abruptly the man was back at his table. He rose, stretched, headed towards the door. Frank pressed the stud and held it down, counting. Fifty-seven seconds and suddenly the man was back at his table again. He rose, stretched, headed towards the door. This time, Frank let him go.

He knew now what it was he had.

He leaned back filled with the wonder of it. Of the Special People he knew nothing but his own race had bred scientists and, even though a sadist, Frank was no fool. A man would want to keep something like this to himself. He would need to have it close to hand at all times. It would need to be in a form where he could use it quickly. So what better than a ring? Compact. Ornamental. Probably everlasting.

A one-way time machine.

LUCK, the fortuitous combination of favourable circumstances, but who needs luck when they know what is going to happen fifty-seven seconds in advance? Call it a minute. Not long?

Try holding your breath that long. Try resting your hand on a red-hot stove for even half that time. In a minute you can walk a hundred yards, run a quarter of a mile, fall three. You can conceive, die, get married. Fifty-seven seconds is enough for a lot of things.

For a card to turn, a ball to settle, a pair of dice tumble to rest. Frank was a sure-fire winner and in more ways than one.

He stretched, enjoyed the shower, the impact of hot water driven at high pressure. He turned a control and gasped as the water turned to ice and made goose pimples rise on his skin. A cold bath in winter is hardship when you have no choice, a pleasant titivation when you have. He jerked the control back to hot, waited, then cut the spray and stepped from the shower drying himself on a fluffy towel.

"Frank, darling, are you going to be much longer?"

A female voice with the peculiar intonation of the inbred upper classes; a member of the aristocracy by marriage and birth. The Lady Jane Smyth-Connors was rich, curious, bored and impatient.

"A moment, honey," he called and dropped the towel. Smiling he looked down at himself. Money had taken care of the twisted foot. Money had taken care of a lot of other things, his clothes, his accent, the education of his tastes. He was still a fallen angel but there was bright new gilt on his broken wings.

"Frank, darling!"

"Coming!" His jaws tightened until the muscles ached. The high-toned, high-stepping bitch! She'd fallen for his face and reputation and was going to pay for her curiosity. But that could wait. First the spider had to get the fly well and truly in his web.

A silk robe to cover his nakedness. Brushes to tidy his hair. A spray gave insurance against halitosis. The stallion was almost ready to perform.

The bathroom had a window. He drew the curtains and looked at the night. Way down low a scatter of lights carpeted the misty ground. London was a nice city, England a nice place. Very nice, especially to gamblers—they paid no tax on winnings. And here, more than anywhere, high prizes were to be won. Not just for cash, that was for plebians, but make the right connections and every day would be Christmas.

London. A city the Special People held in high regard.

"Frank!"

Impatience. Irritation. Arrogance. The woman waited to be served.

She was tall with a peculiar angularity, an overgrown schoolgirl who should be wearing tweeds and carrying a hockey stick. But the appearance was deceptive. Generations of inbreeding had done more than fashion the distribution of flesh and bone. It had developed a ripe decadence and created a mass of seething frustrations. She was clinically insane but in her class people were never thought insane only "eccentric," never stupid only "thoughtless," never spiteful or cruel only "amusing."

He reached out, took her in his arms, pressed the ball of each thumb against her eyes. She strained back from the sudden pain. He pressed harder and she screamed from agony and the stomach-wrenching fear of blindness. In his mind a mental clock counted seconds. Fifty-one…fifty-two…

His fingers clamped down on the ring.

"Frank!"

He reached out and took her in his arms, heart still pounding from the pleasure of having inflicted pain. He kissed her with practiced skill, nibbling her gently with his teeth. He ran his hands over her body, thin material rustling as it fell from her shoulders. He bit a little harder and felt her tense.

"Don't do that!" she said abruptly. "I hate anyone doing that!"

One bad mark. Frank counted seconds as he reached for the light switch. With darkness she squirmed, pushed herself free of his arms.

"I hate the dark! Must you be like all the others?"

Two bad marks. Twenty-seconds to go. Time for one more quick exploration. His hands groped, made contact, moved with educated determination. She sighed with pleasure.

He activated the ring.

"Frank!"

He reached out and took her in his arms, this time making no attempt to either nibble or bite. Her clothing rustled to the floor and the skin gleamed like pearl in the light. He looked at her, boldly admiring, and his hands moved in the way which gave her pleasure.

She closed her eyes, fingernails digging into his back. "Talk to me," she demanded. "Talk to me!"

He began counting seconds.

⇒⇒

LATER, as she lay in satiated sleep, he rested, smoking, thinking, oddly amused. He had been the perfect lover. He had said and done the exact things she wanted in the exact order she wanted them and, more important than anything else, had said and done them without her prompting him at any time. He had been a reflection of herself. An echo of her needs—and why not? He had worked hard to map the blueprint of her desires. Exploring, investigating, erasing all false starts and mistakes. What else could he have been but perfect?

He turned, looking down at the woman, seeing her not as flesh and blood but as the rung of a ladder leading to acceptance. Frank Weston had come a long way. He intended to keep climbing.

She sighed, opened her eyes, looked at the classical beauty of his face. "Darling!"

He said what she wanted him to say.

She sighed again, same sound different meaning. "I'll see you tonight?"

"No."

"Frank!" Jealousy reared her upright. "Why not? You said—"

"I know what I said and I meant every word of it," he interrupted. "But I have to fly to New York. Business," he added. "After all I do have to make a living."

She caught the bait. "You don't have to worry about that. I'll speak to Daddy and—"

He closed her lips with his own. "I still have to go," he insisted.

Beneath the covers his hands did what she wanted them to do. "And when I return—"

"I'll get a divorce," she said. "We'll be married."

Christmas, he thought, as dawn paled the sky.

COME, *fly with me!* said the song, me being a gleaming new Comet, two stewardesses all legs and eyes and silken hair with a "you may look at me because I'm beautiful but you must never, ever touch" attitude, a flight crew and seventy-three other passengers only eighteen of which were travelling first class. Room for everyone and Frank was glad of it.

He felt tired. The night had been hectic and the morning no better. It was good to sit and relax neatly strapped in a form-fitting chair as the jets gulped air and spewed it behind in a man-made hurricane which sent the plane down the runway and up into the sky. London fell away to one side, the clouds dropped like tufts of dirty cotton and then there was only the sun, a watchful eye in an immense iris of blue.

Go West, young man, he thought smugly. Why? For no reason other than he liked to travel and a little absence could make a heart grow fonder. And there was a kick in flying. He liked to look down and think of all the emptiness between him and the ground. Feel his stomach tighten with acrophobia, the delicious sensation of fear experienced in perfect safety. Height had no meaning in a plane. All you had to do was to look straight ahead and you could be in a Pullman.

He unstrapped, stretched his legs, glanced through a window as the captain's voice came over the speakers telling him that they were flying at a height of 34,000 feet at a speed of 536 miles per hour.

Through the window he could see very little. The sky, the clouds below, the tip of a quivering sheet of metal which was a wing. Old stuff. The blonde stewardess was far from that. She swayed down the aisle, caught his eyes, responded with instant attention. Was he quite comfortable? Would he like a pillow? A newspaper? A magazine? Something to drink?

"Brandy," he said. "With ice and soda."

He sat on the inner seat close to the wall of the cabin so that she had to step from the aisle in order to lower the flap and set out his drink. He lifted his left hand and touched her knee, slid the hand up the inside of her thigh, felt her stiffen, saw the expression on her face. It was a compound of incredulity, outrage, interest and speculation. It didn't last long. His right hand reached out and dug fingers into her throat. Congested blood purpled her cheeks, eyes popped, the discarded tray made a mess as her hands fluttered in helpless anguish.

Within his mind the automatic clock counted off the seconds. Fifty-two...fifty-three...fifty-four...

He pressed the stud on his ring.

The flap made a little thudding sound as it came to rest, the brandy a liquid gurgling as it gushed from the miniature bottle over the ice. She smiled, poising the punctured can of soda. "All of it, sir?"

He nodded, watching as she poured, remembering the soft warmth of her thigh, the touch of her flesh. Did she know that he had almost killed her? Could she possibly guess?

No, he decided as she moved away. How could she? To her nothing had happened. She had served him a drink and that was all. That *was* all but—?

Brooding he stared at the ring. You activated it and went back fifty-seven seconds in time. All you had done during that period was erased. You could kill, rob, commit mayhem and none of it mattered because none of it had happened. But it *had* happened. It could be remembered. Could you remember what had never taken place?

That girl, for example. He had felt her thigh, the warm place between her legs, the yielding softness of her throat. He could have poked out her eyes, doubled her screaming, mutilated her face. He had done that and more to others, pandering to his sadism, his love of inflicting pain. And he had killed. But what was killing when you could undo the inconvenience of your crime? When you could watch the body smile and walk away?

The plane rocked a little. The voice from the speaker was calm, unhurried. "Will all passengers please fasten their safety belts. We are heading into an area of minor disturbance. You may see a little lightning but there is absolutely nothing to worry about. We are, of course, flying well above the area of storm."

Frank ignored the instruction, still engrossed with the ring. The unpolished stone looked like a dead eye, suddenly malevolent, somehow threatening. Irritably he finished his drink. The ring was nothing but a machine.

The blonde passed down the aisle, tutted when she saw his unfastened belt, made to tighten it. He waved her away, fumbled with the straps, let the belt fall open. He didn't need it and didn't like it. Frowning he settled back, thinking.

Time. Was it a single line or one with many branches? Could it be that each time he activated the ring an alternate universe was created? That somewhere was a world in which he had attacked the stewardess and had to pay for the crime? But he had only attacked her because he'd known he could erase the incident. Without the ring he wouldn't have touched her. With the ring he could do as he liked because he could always go back and escape the consequences. Therefore the alternate universe theory couldn't apply. What did?

He didn't know and it didn't matter. He had the ring and that was enough. The ring they had offered a lousy hundred dollars for.

SOMETHING hit the roof of the cabin. There was a ripping sound, a blast of air, an irresistible force which tore him from his seat and flung him into space. Air gushed from his lungs as he began to fall. He gulped, trying to breathe, to understand. Arctic cold numbed his flesh. He twisted, saw through streaming eyes the plane with one wing torn loose, the metal tearing free as he watched, the plane accompanying his fall to the sea five miles below.

An accident, he though wildly. A fireball, a meteor, metal fatigue even. A crack in the cabin wall and internal pressure would do the rest. And now he was falling. Falling!

His fingers squeezed in frenzied reaction.

"Please, Mr. Weston." The blonde stewardess came forward as he reared from his seat. "You must remain seated and with your safety belt fastened. Unless—?" Diplomatically she looked towards the toilets at the rear of the cabin.

"Listen!" He grabbed her by both arms. "Tell the pilot to change course. Tell him now. Hurry!"

A fireball or a meteor could be dodged that way. They could find safety if the course was changed fast enough. But it had to be fast! Fast!

"Quick." He ran towards the flight deck, the girl at his heels. Damn the stupid bitch! Couldn't she understand? "This is an emergency!" he shouted. "The pilot must change course immediately!"

Something hit the roof of the cabin. The compartment popped open, metal coiling like the peeled skin of a banana. The blonde vanished. The shriek of tearing metal was lost in the explosive gusting of escaping air. Desperately Frank clung to a seat, felt his hands being torn from the fabric, his body sucked towards the opening. Once again he was ejected into space to begin the long stomach-twisting five mile fall.

"No!" he screamed, frantic with terror. "Dear God, no!"

He activated.

"Mr. Weston, I really must insist. If you do not want to go to the toilet you must allow me to fasten your safety belt."

He was standing by his seat and the blonde was showing signs of getting annoyed. Annoyed!

"This is important," he said, fighting to remain calm. "In less than a minute this plane is going to fall apart. Do you understand? We are all going to die unless the pilot changes course immediately."

Why did she have to stand there looking so dumb? He had told her all this before!

"You stupid cow! Get out of my way!" He pushed her to one side and lunged again towards the flight deck. He tripped, fell, came raging to his feet. "Change course!" he yelled. "For God's sake listen and—"

Something hit the roof. Again the roar, the blast, the irresistible force. Something struck his head and he was well below the clouds before he managed to regain full control. He activated and found himself still in space, gulping at rarified air and shivering with savage cold. To one side the shattered plane hung as though suspended, a mass of disintegrating debris as it fell. Tiny fragments hung around it; one of them perhaps the blonde.

The clouds passed. Below the sea spread in a shimmer of light and water. His stomach constricted with overwhelming terror as he stared at the waves, his lurking acrophobia aroused and tearing at every cell. Hitting the sea would be like smashing into a floor of solid concrete and he would be conscious to the very end. Spasmodically he activated and, immediately, was high in the air again with almost a minute of grace in which to fall.

Fifty-seven seconds of undiluted hell.

Repeated.

Repeated.

Repeated over and over because the alternative was to smash into the waiting sea.

THE FIFTH CATEGORY

TOM BISSELL

Tom Bissell is one of America's best and most interesting (they are not always the same) writers. In addition to nonfiction, such as the book-length *Extra Lives: Why Video Games Matter*, he has written scripts for video games such as *Gears of War* and co-wrote the critically acclaimed *The Disaster Artist: My Life Inside The Room, the Greatest Bad Movie Ever Made*, which became an award-winning film starring and directed by James Franco. Bissell, who has covered the gulf wars as a journalist, has also found time to write some extraordinary short stories. This tale of the author of several controversial legal memos awakening on a deserted airliner on a flight from Estonia is one of his best.

ohn woke statically electric from some unremembered dream. He recalibrated with Gatling blinks, his brain malnourished. Falling asleep on a plane was like paying someone to assault you in the middle of the night. Oddly, though, he did not remember falling asleep. For that matter, he did not remember wanting to fall asleep.

His last memory: drinking a Diet Coke, chatting with his neighbor, Janika, a tall Estonian woman with a mischievous-wood-sprite face, who said she was on her way to the United States for her first visit. John certainly did not remember pulling the blanket up to his chin or inserting behind his head the wondrously soft pillow he felt there. And he would have remembered. A bedtime habit of his, dating from childhood, was putting a memory lock on his sleeping position—the spoon, the scissor, the dead man, the fetus, the sprawl—just before the final fade. Only twice in his life had he found himself in the same position upon waking. John thought of sleep as a form of time travel. Things happened, mental labors occurred, body parts moved, and you would never know.

Janika was gone, and the darkened plane was now over the mid-Atlantic, he guessed. She had probably left for a stretch. Europeans and their in-flight calisthenics, their applause on landing. The cabin's every lozenge-shaped window shade had been pulled down. The only illumination was provided by the glowing orange ellipses of the cabin's running lights. John lifted his window shade. What he saw could not be. His flight landed in New York at 4:00 p.m. It was not a night flight. And yet, outside: night. Janika's seat, John now realized, was not the only vacant one. The remaining forty-odd business-class seats were also empty. He lunged for his seatbelt.

The cozily paired thrones of business class were spread spaciously throughout the cabin, and no overhead luggage compartments hindered his movement around them. Many were draped with twisty blankets. Others had headphones still plugged into their armrest jacks. Half a dozen pillows littered the floor. Carry-ons remained stuffed under a number of seats. One aisle over, someone had left the seat tray extended, and on it sat a perfume-sized bottle of red wine and a plastic glass. Hovering above every seat was the same sense of sudden abandonment.

Something had happened, he thought, that gathered everyone's attention back in coach. A drunken Finn punching out a flight attendant. A heart attack. He drew a crisp mental X, for now, through any other possibilities. John whipped aside the thin blue curtain that allowed those in coach merely to imagine their deprivation. His hand sought the steadying reality of the gray, white-speckled partition from which the curtain hung.

Before him spanned thirty darkened rows of unfilled seats. Out of shock he took a single step forward. He reached for his iPhone, sensing its absence before his hand even touched his pocket. Despite the darkness, he saw a few crude shapes on the first row of seats: paperbacks, newspapers, a briefcase. It grew darker the deeper into the rows he walked, as though he were entering a synthetic jungle.

How fundamentally wrong it felt to run down the narrow aisle of a commercial aircraft. When he reached the tight dark aft quarters he felt trapped in a bewilderingly unfamiliar closet. His hands fumbled for the Braille of the visible world. The attendants' jump seats were up. Adjacent to one of them was a mounted flashlight, which he pulled from its cradle. He slashed a blade of light across the kitchen, its long silver drawers looking like they belonged in a submarine, and over an unloaded dinner cart pushed into the kitchen's deepest recess. He turned, the light passing an overhead container marked FIRST AID, then brought the beam to bear on one of the plane's exit doors—an immense thing, less like a door than an igloo's facade. Out of its tiny porthole John saw layers of wing-sliced cloud swirl in the starless night. He turned to the attendants' control panel, complicated by numerous knobs and buttons. Even though it was a Finnair flight, everything was in English. At the bottom of the panel was a red EVAC button. He worked his way up past several CALL buttons (all dark), a small green screen glowing with utterly unfathomable information, a public announcement button, and finally the lighting panel, which held not buttons but knobs, all of which he began turning.

In the harsh new light he opened the door to the lavatory, half expecting to find a magically immense room in which the several hundred people who boarded this flight were waiting with pointy party hats and confetti. But it was empty, shockingly white, and smelled of shit and spearmint. Transparent blisters of standing water adorned the sink's metal basin.

He charged back up coach, through business class, and found himself at the cockpit door, which had a thick, reinforced look. "Hardened," was the technical term, he believed. How to proceed was unclear. Any display of forcefulness so close to the pilots seemed to John both unwise and potentially unlawful. So he knocked. When no one answered he attempted to open it. Locked. He knocked again. He noticed a small, knee-level cabinet. Inside were four yellow life jackets and some kind of heavy steel air compressor. He looked at the fore's exit door, another glacial immensity he was not sure he could figure out how to open if he tried. But why would he want to? That he was already considering this a possible exit did not, he realized, bode particularly well.

He was sweating now. His body, as though having at last accepted, analyzed, and rejected the information his mind had sent forth, began some pointless counterattack. From his stomach, the staging area, his body spit his most recent meal into his intestinal coils. He stood there, clenched, listening to his heart pump, his lungs fill and empty. The curtain hanging between voluntary and involuntary function had been torn from its runners. His nervous system seemed a single concentration lapse from going off-line.

He pounded on the cockpit door, shouting that something had happened, that he needed help. When, finally, he stopped, his forehead came to rest against the door's hardened outer shell. His breath was as sour and microbial as a Petri dish. He felt weak, white-bellied, and exposed. He then heard something on the door's other side and jumped back. Slowly, he closed back in, fitting his ear within the cup his hand formed against the cold metal. On the other side of the door, in the cockpit of a plane with no passengers, someone was weeping.

He had been advised not to travel outside the United States by his lawyer, his sympathetic university colleagues (he had more than most would have guessed—John was nothing if not the soul of faculty-meeting affability), and those few from Justice to whom he still spoke. But when an invitation to speak at a conference ("International Law and the Future of American-European Relations") in Tallinn, Estonia, was first extended six months ago, John did what he always did: he talked to his wife.

One of the things he appreciated most about leaving government service was that he could, once again, talk to his wife about work. Anyone who lived within his mind to the degree that John did asked for nothing more perfect than a companion able to step inside that mind when invited and leave before asking was necessary. For the last two years she had been his confidante, sentinel, nurse, and ballast. It was, nevertheless, one of his marriage's longer, more difficult nights when a number of his so-called torture memos were leaked, and then, without any warning to him, declassified and disavowed. His wife was not the only person with whom he had proved able to clarify his intentions in writing the memos. Any journalist who took the time to see John invariably came away admitting that the purported werewolf seemed a decent enough sort.

After telling his wife about the conference invitation, he admitted, "My first thought was to say no. But I think I may want to go."

Two years ago, a complaint accusing John of war crimes had been filed in a German court; the gears of this particular justice had since scarcely turned. Another suit was filed six months ago, in a California court, by a convicted American terrorist and his mother, who claimed John's memos had led to his maltreatment while in U.S. custody. John did not dispute—though of course could not admit—that the wretch had been poorly treated in custody, but drawing the line back to him evidenced a kind of naive legal creationism. While John's travel was by no means formally restricted, the thought of leaving American airspace filled him with unfamiliar apprehension. This shocked him. It also emboldened him.

"Don't route your flight through Germany," his wife said. "Or France. Or Spain. I'd avoid Italy, too, for that matter."

She thought he was joking about wanting to go, he realized, and he waited a moment before telling her what he liked about Estonia, a young country with memories of actual oppression. He had always been interested in the nations of the former Soviet bloc and post-communist countries in general. (His parents' flight from Korean Communism was, after all, the only reason he was an American.) He did not think he had any cause to fear Estonia, which was an official American ally in the war. Was his wife aware that there were only a million Estonians in the world? Maybe it was a Korean thing, but he felt strange kinship with small, frequently invaded, routinely pushed-around nations. He admired, he said somewhat grandly, their parochial ambitions. He was now shamelessly appealing to his wife's own complicated feelings concerning her Vietnamese heritage.

She asked how he could be certain it was not simply a trap to publicly humiliate him. To that he already had something of an answer. The event's organizers had promised, unprompted, that no topics would be discussed beyond John's willingness to discuss them. They were aware of the lawsuits and promised him full escape-pod capability during any line of questioning. ("Escape pod." His words, not theirs. Like any nerd who grew up in the 1970s, John was always good for a *Star Wars* reference.) The U.S. embassy, moreover, was "aware of" John's invitation. ("Aware of." Their words, not his. A middling embassy like Estonia's was no doubt heavily staffed with Administration flunkies and professional vacationists. Given that John was the only former member of the Administration who insisted on talking about the decisions he had made while part of it, he was as popular among them as a leper bell.)

"But you'll talk about it all anyway," she said, "won't you?" John often reduced his lawyer to similar frustration. He was not afraid to defend himself, provided his interlocutor was not obviously carrying a torch and kindling. After John had granted an interview to *Esquire* his lawyer did not speak to him for a week. Then his lawyer read the not entirely unflattering profile that resulted. "You're a smooth one, Counsel," he told John.

John smiled at his wife. Of course he would talk about it all. He knew what he could and could not say. He was a lawyer.

When he told the event's organizers he would be able to come, they expressed as much surprise as excitement. He would be the only American, they said, and as such an invaluable part of the discussion. It was agreed he would speak alone, at the close of the conference, for an hour, and then answer questions, some of which, they warned, might be hostile. It all sounded fine, John emailed back. He had faced more bloodthirsty rooms than he imagined Estonia could muster. Before agreeing, he checked in with the embassy in Tallinn. They acknowledged the conference and wished him a successful trip. The last he would hear from them, he suspected.

Six months later, he spent two hours laid over in Helsinki's airport. When two Finnish security guards stopped near John's exit to chat, he was not sure why he felt so nervous. It was not as if Interpol had issued a warrant for his arrest. But what man could truly relax knowing that courts on two continents entertained the possibility he had committed crimes against humanity? He supposed he was brave for being here. No, actually. This thought disgusted him. He was a teacher and a lawyer, in that order. He did not recall the last time he raised his voice. He did not recall once, in his four decades, having intentionally hurt anyone. The Finnish guards walked away.

He boarded the flight to Tallinn with reenergized anonymity. By the time he saw his spired, red-roofed, seaside destination appear outside the starboard window, he knew he had made the right choice. It was noon by the time he reached his hotel in Tallinn's Old Town. Check-in was surreally pleasant. The conference's organizers had sent flowers. He called them to ask for directions to that night's conference hall, which, as it happened, was less than three blocks away, in another hotel, the Viru. No, no thank you, he could make his way there on his own. His talk was scheduled for 8:00 p.m. This meant he had an afternoon to spend in Tallinn. He did so by sleeping off the circadian catastrophe of shooting across ten time zones.

By 5:00, he was awake, showered, dressed in a cement-colored suit with a blue shirt (no tie), and wandering Tallinn's Old Town in search of dinner. The organizers had offered to send someone, but no. He wanted to announce his conference presence with the same powerful abruptness he used to enter his classrooms. If any of the conference's participants were indeed seeking to confront him, the fewer pressure points with which they had time to acquaint themselves the better.

The charms of Tallinn's Old Town were myriad and entirely preposterous. No actual human beings could live here. It looked like a soundstage for some elvish epic. The streets—the most furiously cobbled he had ever seen—appeared to shed their names at every intersection. Most took him past pubs, restaurants, shops selling amber, and nothing else. It was easy to distinguish the tourists

THE FIFTH CATEGORY TOM BISSELL

from the locals: everyone not working was a tourist. Outside a medieval restaurant off the town square, young Estonians dressed like the maidens and squires of the Hanseatic League watched as their co-workers reenacted a swordfight. On one block-long side street, a blast of methane wind took hold of him: the sewage coursing through three-hundred-year-old plumbing was one bit of Tallinn's past in no need of recreation. The similarity of the Old Town's many ornate black church spires confused him. Every time he settled on one as his compass back toward the Viru, he realized it was the wrong tower. For two hours, he was always at least slightly lost.

From its height and brutalist design, he correctly surmised that the Viru had once been the Intourist Hotel during the Soviet era. In its lobby he found a Wall of Fame listing some of the hotel's notable guests: Olympians, musicians, actors, Arab princes, and the President himself. A note written to the hotel manager on White House letterhead was framed: "Thanks also for the good-looking sweater and hat." After inquiries at the front desk, an elevator ride to the conference floor, and an olfactory napalming courtesy of a perfumed woman riding up with him, John walked down a lushly carpeted hallway toward the registration desk. The young man sitting there pointed further down the hall, toward a small group of people politely waiting outside the conference room proper for the current speaker to finish. John was on in half an hour. He joined the waiting listeners outside the conference room, a golden and chandeliered cavern.

The speaker was German. From the translation projected onto a screen behind the woman (in French, Estonian, and English—he, too, had been asked to send the text of his talk beforehand to the organizers, after extracting from them a promise that native English speakers would translate it) John knew he was in for a slightly rougher night than he had been anticipating. He had heard all the tropes of the German woman's talk before. She finished to applause and answered questions, after which a ten-minute break was announced. As people rose from their seats, another woman near the back of the room turned, spotted John, and, with a smile of recognition, walked toward him. John met her halfway, maneuvering through the human cross-stream of intermission.

This was Ilvi, one of the organizers, his contact and a professor of law at the University of Tartu. A very young professor of law, which warmed the still-youthful-looking John to her instantly. They shook, after which Ilvi began knotting her hands as though shaping a small clay ball. Pleasantries, then: flights, sleep, Tallinn. She asked, "Are you ready?" John laughed and said he thought so. She laughed, too, her enamel giving off a slight yellow tinge. Ilvi had chapped lips and a mushroom of curly brown hair. Her long and angular face was almost cubist, its unusual prettiness cohering only after you spent some time looking at her.

For some incomprehensible reason, Ilvi guided John to the German speaker who had just finished condemning his country. She was speaking to four people at once, all of whom stood around her. She appeared accustomed to being the center of attention; they appeared accustomed to providing it. These conferences were all the same. Attendees may as well be given scripts and assigned parts. At Ilvi's announcement of John's name, they all turned to consider him. He smiled, his hand thrust out. Only one person, an older man wearing a heavy wool sport coat, deigned to shake, though he did so with the dutiful air of a prisoner meeting his warden. John's smile was now a dying man's attempt at serenity. No one said anything after that.

For far longer than John appreciated, Ilvi—whether mortified or oblivious he had no good way of surmising—stood beside him, then escorted him to a few other small bundles of conference-goers. He was received with only a few more calories of warmth. Finally, she led him to the dais. He plunked down upon the lone chair and withdrew his talk from a breast pocket. Ilvi stood at the maple podium, schoolmarmishly looking at her watch.

He was by now inured to the pariah treatment, which was not to say it did not wound him. Sometimes students (never his; his classes were always over-enrolled) wore black armbands and stood in silence on the steps outside the law school, waiting for John to pass en route to his office. A couple of times they had worn Gitmo-orange jumpsuits. He always wished them good morning. Once, and only once, he had stopped to talk to them. Their complaints were so numerous and multidisciplinary it had been like arguing with Beatnik poetry. He came away from all such experiences less befuddled than disappointed. John did not want them or anyone else to agree with him. He respected considered disagreement. All he wanted was someone other than himself to admit that it was complicated.

Early in the war, two detainees were captured. One was an American citizen, the other an Australian. What laws applied to them? As John learned, you had to go very far back in the history of American jurisprudence—the Indian Wars, piracy law—to find legally appropriate analogies. Some members of the Justice Department wanted the captured American Mirandized, but every court on this planet accepted that more amorphous laws governed battlefield conduct. Treating these men as criminals meant the loss of what they knew. The American and Australian detainees did not, John argued, enjoy the protections granted to prisoners of war under Common Article III of the Geneva Conventions. Enjoying no rank, no clearly defined army, and no obvious chain of command—prerequisites upon which war-prisoner protections under Common Article

III were dependent—these men could not be considered prisoners of war in any legal sense.

When the third-highest ranking member of al-Qaeda was captured in Pakistan, John was asked to provide the CIA with legal guidance. This took much of the summer of 2002, and John could not recall having worked harder or more thoroughly on a memo. He had to determine whether interrogation techniques used by the CIA outside the United States violated American obligations under the 1984 Torture Convention. So he looked at what these obligations entailed. The first thing he learned was that torture was "any act by which severe pain or suffering, whether physical or mental, is intentionally inflicted on a person." "Severe," then, was part of the legal definition. The United States had attached to its instrument of ratification a further definition of torture as an act "specifically intended to inflict severe physical or mental pain." What was "severe pain"? What did "specifically intended" actually mean? John checked the relevant medical literature. Could a doctor define "severe pain"? A doctor could not. Did the law itself? The law did not. The fact was, you could look far and wide in legal documents for a working definition of "severe pain" and never find it. So John, with no relish, provided one: in order to constitute torture, the "severe pain" must rise "to a level that would ordinarily be associated with a sufficiently serious physical condition such as death, organ failure, or serious impairment of body functions." As for "prolonged mental harm," another bit of unexplained language from the Torture Convention, it appeared nowhere in U.S. law, medical literature, or international human rights reports. Again, John had to provide his own definition. For purely mental pain or suffering to amount to torture, thus satisfying the legal requirement of "prolonged mental harm," the end result, he judged, must be akin to post-traumatic stress disorder or chronic depression of significant duration, which is to say, months or years. John had intended these guidelines to apply only to the CIA and only with regard to what were known as "high-value intelligence targets," never to common prisoners and especially not in Iraq, where Common Article III of the Geneva Convention absolutely applied. Due to the interrogation limits the FBI agents at Guantánamo were insisting upon—they wanted everything gathered from the prisoners to hold up in court, forgetting (or choosing to forget) that none of these men would be tried by anything but military tribunals—prisoners could not be offered so much as a Twinkie without it being deemed coercive. Until John's memo. Shortly after its guidance went into wide and, to John, unanticipated effect, the FBI's head counsel wrote his own memo that claimed the interrogations his agents were seeing at Guantánamo were illegal. The day John's memos were declassified, Gonzales disavowed them at a press conference, claiming they "did not reflect the policies of the Administration." For this John would not forgive him.

The audience clapped, at least, after Ilvi's introduction, an idle plagiarism of the curriculum vitae John had sent her. He made his way to the podium, leaned toward the mic, glanced at the screen behind him, leaned toward the mic, and glanced again at the screen behind him. Leaning toward the mic a final time, and making sure his already soft voice was as mild as a child's aspirin, he said he was not sure which speech should begin first. A few scattered chuckles, then actual laughter. John turned to the screen one last time to see that his talk's first block of translated text had obligingly appeared. Okay, he thought. Good.

He flattened out the first page of his talk, which he had given several times, and looked out on the facial pointillism of his audience. Three hundred people? Their expressions were more curious than hostile, he thought. Something then popped into his mind as suddenly as the words had appeared on the screen behind him: This was too far to have come. He was a tenured professor of law at a major American university. He wondered, once again, why he was so determined to defend himself. Was the solace of knowing he could that important?

At the beginning of September 2001, John was 34 years old and reviewing a treaty whose most legally substantive issue involved polar bears.

Before returning to his seat John tried a couple of things. He hit the cockpit door with the steel air compressor approximately four dozen times. He then returned aft, held down the PA button of the attendant's control panel, and screamed. Becoming hysterical solved nothing. Calmer now, and sitting, he tried to formulate a reasonable explanation for what was happening. He did not think he had been drugged. He had eaten nothing that day and drunk only a can of Diet Coke shortly after boarding. The attendant had given the can to John and he himself had opened it.

He replayed various short-term-memory fragments. The morning flight from Tallinn. Forty-five minutes in Helsinki. The bovine ordeal of boarding. He recalled as many fellow passengers as he could. Chatty Janika, the Estonian on her way to the United States. The neckless, bullfrogish man John had sat beside at the gate. The amply eyebrowed young woman in the Oxford sweatshirt who smiled at John as she passed his seat on her way to coach. (No Asian man forgets a white girl who smiles at him, unibrow or no.) A young man he recalled only because he was black. A studious, string-haired girl in a loose white blouse. A kid in his early twenties in a YOU SUCK tee shirt. The female flight attendants in their powder-blue pantsuits. John had been conscious of his Asianness on this Finnair flight, in this northern clime, and recalled, now, anticipating his relief at returning to California, his university town, its sidewalks of multiracial buffet, its music stores and eateries, the varieties of its cannabis enfleurage.

But there was the matter of his iPhone. Someone had clearly taken it. He had looked for it under his and every other seat in business class. What would he do? What could he do? The air compressor had done real damage to the door, denting its hardened shell and knocking off the handle. The handle was now in John's pocket, in case he needed to fix it later, though he had no idea how he might do that. He found some tools in an aft storage cabinet, which were now on the seat beside him. The door itself had not budged.

In sudden need of the transporting thereness of an outside item, he pulled a magazine from the mesh basket on the side of his seat, its heavily laminated cover as cold and slippery as glass. Finnair's in-flight shopping magazine. Even under his present circumstances, the appeal of shopping while aboard a plane remained mysterious. He nonetheless slapped at the crisp, thick pages. Fifty-euro pearl necklaces. Twenty-euro sticks of Dolce & Gabbana deodorant. Thirty-euro Glam Bronze Sunset & Glam Shine foundation by L'Oréal. Pages of European chocolates and confections. He came to the last pages, electronics, and stopped at a 245-euro solar-powered BlackBerry Curve 8310 Smartphone. Almost certainly, dozens of passengers aboard this plane had been carrying phones, any number of which might still be in their carry-ons. While getting reception was unlikely, he might find a device that allowed the sending of a stored email or text once the plane reached a lower altitude.

As he rose, the plane shook as though withstanding atmospheric reentry. He sat and buckled his seatbelt. His fear, having almost come under the control of his hope, felt newly feral. He breathed. He was not sure what time it was, or how long he had been on this plane, but his window shade, like every other window in business class, was now open, and once again he stared into the freezing darkness of the troposphere. He thought of his wife, his students, their concern for him, and, yet again, rose.

John felt strangely better once he had all the business class carry-ons gathered around his seat. Remaining close to his appointed seat seemed important, though he could not explain why. He worked his way through the bags, most of which were small. People who paid business class fares did not hesitate to check their luggage. They had no cab line to beat; they landed to find Jordanian men holding small white signs bearing their last names. Unzipping luggage, John slipped his hand into one opening after another and felt and squeezed and searched. He did not want to unnecessarily disturb anyone's items. Anything that felt at all promising he pulled out through its zippered caul. By the end of his search he sat among shaving kits, digital cameras, iPods, duty-free bottles of vodka with Cyrillic lettering, several Montblanc pens, and a smooth pink plastic torpedo he had realized only incrementally was a sex toy. Also accounted for were half a dozen computer cases, every one of them empty.

He moved on to coach, but before he had managed to empty a single overhead container, his stomach sent another dose of fiery waste toward its point of egress. He staggered to the bathroom, unbuckling his pants, and sprayed before he could get himself atop the metal-basined toilet's plastic ring. The smell had no equivalent he could name. It was, somehow, an orange smell. His intestinal spigot opened again; waste escaped him in avid bursts. He was sick now, and dizzy, his brain an invalid whom no one had thought to visit in months. When he was finished he washed his hands.

THE FIFTH CATEGORY   TOM BISSELL

Decorousness no longer concerned him. He walked down the first aisle opening overheads and savagely throwing their contents to the floor. Soon enough it was knee-deep with baggage. Would he really go through all of it? No. His anger was too overriding now, and he had to allow himself to regenerate the care and attentiveness searching the bags would require. He moved to the second aisle, pushing overhead release buttons as he traversed it. After a satisfying pop the doors slowly lifted open. So much of this plane was kept in place by plastic hinges. He was within a metal tube, sailing just beneath the fringe of outer space, while huge engines fifty feet from him spewed invisible 1,000-degree fire. Was this any less remarkable than the reality that he was now trapped inside?

He found Janika in the aisle's third-to-last overhead—though given that the overheads were triply connected, she occupied all of them, however unhappily she fit. Her bruised, cross-eyed face and masking-taped mouth sent John to the floor as resoundingly as a blow. When he finally looked back up at her he saw that one of her arms had slipped from its containment. Her hand vibrated lightly in turbulence he could no longer feel. He carefully removed her from the overhead. When the last of her body pulled free she seemed to gain one hundred spontaneous pounds. John fell back, Janika on top of him, onto a bed of carry-ons and their jutting contents.

Janika's crossed eyes, so close to John's own but unable to meet them, seemed troubled by some final, unwanted knowledge. Dried red crumbles of blood filled her nostrils. Her cheeks were spider-webbed with broken capillaries, the veins of her forehead and temples subcutaneously livid. John pushed her away and made long loud primate sounds. He tried pulling the masking tape from Janika's mouth, but the sound of dead skin tugging against musculature was so nightmarishly sloppy he stopped and ran screaming back toward business class.

He decided to once again beat the cockpit door with the air compressor. This time, however, he would not stop. He entered business class to find that the screen upon which the pre-flight PSA had been broadcast was lowering. The lights went soundlessly out. Panic spun him around. Two steps into his flight he stumbled and fell. Unable to see and crawling back toward coach on an uneven reef of luggage, his thoughts turned Neanderthal. Back, back to shelter. But there was no shelter. What he had been feeling until now was not fear. Fear was liquid; it traveled the bloodstream; it sought the reservoir of the brain. Real fear, he now knew, took its power not from what could happen but what you realize will happen. Above him was a sound of small, whirring industry. He recognized it for what it was: throughout coach smaller screens were lowering into place. John looked at the closest one. It was on but blank. The screen glowed like vinyl: darker, somehow, than actual darkness.

Then, an image of crisp digital-video quality, though its bottom edge vaguely flickered with waveform. John was too far away to make sense of it. He stood. What he saw when close enough was a small plywood room filmed from the impersonal high-corner angle unique to surveillance. In this room were two figures. In a chair, behind a small table: a woman. Circling her: a man in boots, loose black pants, black tank top, black ski mask. The audio was tinny, faraway, obviously unmic'd. In the blizzardy imperfection of poorly lit digital video, John did not immediately recognize Janika. She appeared to be tied to her chair and was crying in a steady and quietly hopeless way. The man looked at the camera, walked toward it, and finally reached up and grabbed it. The camera was not fixed in some surveillance perch at all; it was a hand-held. The image went whirlwind but quickly stabilized, save for a few hand-held jiggles.

THE FIFTH CATEGORY

TOM BISSELL

A second man, identically dressed, entered the room through a hitherto unnoticed door. Looking directly into the camera, he pulled the door shut with a strange gentleness. The first, camera-wielding man must have gone into zoom as the second approached: his ski-masked face less filled the screen than violently annexed it. John stared at this man staring back at him. This too was time travel. Now that she was blocked from sight, Janika's soft, wet sobs were sharper, more keening. Or perhaps she was simply reacting to the second man's entrance.

The man himself said nothing. His eyes were animate in no remarkable way. When, at last, he turned away, he busied himself at the table. The man was writing something, John realized, and once he had finished he again faced the camera. He held out a piece of thin white cardboard filled with letters of nearly perfect contiguousness. John did not expect the sign to say what it did. He nonetheless felt grateful, for now he understood what was happening, and why. The man placed the sign on the table before fixing his attention upon Janika, who now screamed. As for the sign, John could still see it: CATEGORY 1.

AFTER his speech, Ilvi asked John if he would like to join her and some others, including the speaker who preceded him, for drinks in the Old Town. Was this woman truly that stupid? John extricated himself from the offer with an obsequious bow, a claim of exhaustion, and multiple thank-yous. He was beginning to feel both ghostly and loathed here, less a man than an unpleasant idea. As he made his way toward the exit, people scattered from his path as though he were lobbing lit firecrackers. How much longer, he wondered, would this be his life?

A few of the questions he had taken were indeed hostile, the most pointed posed by an older woman in the front row with a face as tight-skinned as a kayak. She had huffily asked what John would do in the event of a formal accusation of war crimes by the International Criminal Court. John told her he did not anticipate that happening and then lied: "I'm not that worried about it, to be perfectly honest."

John had another day scheduled in Tallinn. At the first thought of this, he stepped into a men's room off the hallway outside of the conference room and stabbed at his iPhone until he was online. The conference had paid for John's flight but, at his request, left the return ticket open. Within a couple of minutes his ticket was changed. Magic. Less magical was the fact that he was now $1,500 poorer. It was hard to regard this as anything but a bargain.

John exited the men's room to find a gleamingly clean-shaven man waiting for him. His outfit was a Halloween version of a tech-industry executive: navy blue sport coat, no tie, jeans, cross-trainers. He was obviously American. His face filled with an expression of unilateral recognition John had still not grown used to, probably because it was an expression that always failed to acknowledge itself as unilateral. He knew who John was; therefore John would be happy to meet him. Everyone was the star of his own story.

He said John's name and extended his hand. A business card emblazoned with the embassy seal materialized. RUSSELL GALLAGHER, CULTURAL LIAISON OFFICER. In John's limited experience, words such as "cultural" and "officer" tended to serve as camouflage for intelligence work.

John tried to give the card back but Gallagher insisted John keep it. John put it in his pocket and asked, "Are you my envoy?"

Gallagher had a boyish, I'm-being-tickled laugh, though age was beginning its work around his eyes and had begun pushing back his hairline. "I'm not, unfortunately. You're not too popular at the embassy. You probably know this already but they tried to get you uninvited to this thing."

John was aware that, among the remaining loyalist vestiges of the Administration, he could expect no grata shown his persona. But that an embassy would attempt to block his appearance at an international conference seemed astonishing. Did these people not have anything better to do? "As a matter of fact," he told Gallagher, "I did not know that."

This indiscretion was cause for yet more Gallagher laughter. He was trying too hard, John thought.

"It turns out your friend, Professor Armastus, doesn't like to be pushed around. She also has friends. The harder the embassy lobbied the more determined they were to get you here. Great speech, by the way."

"Tonight is the first time I met her. But thank you."

"Look," Gallagher said, aware that whatever he wanted to talk about was now thunking along the berm, "I'm here, under my own volition, to tell you that a lot of us are grateful to you and what you did."

"Thank you again."

He looked at John, his face sweetly bold. "My father was a Vietnam vet, seventy-one to seventy-two. One of the things he was involved with was the Phoenix Program. He always said the reason it got such a bad name was because it was created by geniuses and carried out by idiots. But even then it was the most effective thing we ever threw against the Viet Cong. The Communists admitted as much after the war. My dad was in Saigon, and he told me that by 1972 the average life expectancy of a Communist cell leader in the city was about four months. And nothing you argued for was worse than what my dad was proud to have done with Phoenix. Just wanted you to know there are a lot of us who admire you."

While drafting his memos John had actually looked into the Phoenix Program. He learned the CIA had made internal promises that Phoenix would be "operated under the normal laws of war." He also learned that several American officers involved with Phoenix asked to be relieved of their duties because they thought what they were doing was immoral. John stood there looking at Gallagher. His posting in the target-poor environment of Estonia spoke for itself. His father hunted down Communists. The hottest action the son could scare up for himself was defying his embassy in order to tell John to keep his chin up. The conservatism of which Gallagher was doubtless a disciple was not a proper philosophy. It was a bad mood. Neither of them said anything for several seconds.

"You want a drink?" Gallagher asked. "You look like you could use one."

John did not want a drink. He could, however, use one. They walked out of the Viru together and into the enduring 10:00 p.m. sunlight of a Tallinn summer evening. John asked Gallagher how long he had been posted here. "I was in Greece before this. Ten years in. Before that, the Marines. Made captain in 1998. Got out too early for any of the fun stuff."

They walked toward the center of the Old Town. In the weakening light the buildings seemed as bright as animation cells. People were drinking in the cafés along the sidewalk, drinking while they walked, drinking while they waited for ATM slots to stick out their tongues of currency. John noted the packs of young Russian men with hard eyes and unsteady gaits, the singing arm-entwined Scotsmen, the wobbling smokers standing outside every pub. He also noticed the tiny old begging women dressed in tatterdemalion, seasonally inappropriate clothing, every one looking as though she had suffered some unbreakable gypsy curse. John asked Gallagher, "With what sort of culture do you typically liaise around here?"

Gallagher looked at him. "You might be surprised. But it's a fun place to live, even if Estonians are sort of inscrutable. A buddy of mine plays bass, and he told me that wherever he's lived in the world he's always been able to show up at open mics. Everyone needs a bass player. When he got to Tallinn he'd show up at an open mic and there'd be five Estonian guys standing there with their basses, looking for a lead guitarist. This is a nation of bass players."

John's eyes snagged on two high-heeled Freyas in dermally tight jeans walking toward him. These two carried themselves with the steel-spined air of women secretly covetous of constant low-grade harassment, which they were getting. In their wake they left all manner of shouted Russian entreaties.

Gallagher noticed the women, too. "And, of course, there's that. In Tallinn even the ugly girls are kind of pretty. This is offset by the fact that even the intelligent ones are kind of stupid."

Gallagher went on as they walked. Talk of women became talk of Finland, which became talk of the Soviet Special Forces, which became a condensed narrative history of the 1990s. Segues were nonexistent. Soon the soliloquy returned to his father. John was no longer listening. Instead he considered Gallagher. His hair was thin, limp, the color of rye, and Gallagher was often petting it forward—a naughty schoolboy tic reactivated in middle age to conceal his retreating hairline. Discussing his father left Gallagher wallowing in unspecified grievances, though he still insisted on laughing every third or fourth sentence. "And that's what my dad always said," Gallagher closed.

John, having failed to catch the gist of Gallagher's finale (there may not have been one), nodded.

Gallagher did, too. Then: "He died only last year, you know."

"I'm sorry for your loss."

"When your memos were leaked we even talked about it. I asked him for his opinion. He predicted that the terrorists were going to use our own courts against us. He said, 'Shit, I personally violated Article III of the Geneva Conventions. Several times!'"

Gentle crinkles of preoccupation formed across John's brow. This was a mistake.

"Here we go." Gallagher was pointing to a belowground bar just off of Pikk, an absurdly pretty street John had wandered up and down earlier that day. Christmas lights were strung up in its basement windows; there was no sign. John did not drink, at least not in any way that conceptually honored what people meant by "drinking." A glass of wine every few nights, always with a meal; an occasional imported beer on hot Sunday afternoons; a good single malt after an expensive dinner. When Gallagher mentioned a drink John had imagined the two of them sharing a tumbler of cognac in a wine bar. It was one of those social laws you broke only at great risk: never go anywhere with anyone you don't know well.

John followed Gallagher down concrete bomb-shelter stairs. Already uncomfortable, he became more so when Gallagher pushed open the door—a hail fellow, well met—and instantly repaired to the bar, where he had words with the gorgeous apparition toiling behind it. John decided to play a little game with himself to see how long he could last there. He found a table and waited for Gallagher to join him, but when he looked back, Gallagher was holding the bartender's hand. He turned it over and traced with his index finger some elaborate fortune-teller augury on her palm. Smiling, the

bartender pulled her hand free and worked the tap while Gallagher looked smugly around. She air-kissed him while handing over two pints. Gallagher raised the glasses to her. The moment his back was to her she stopped smiling.

As for the bar's other patrons: there did not appear to be any. John had chosen as his landing site the most centrally located of the room's four tables. Sparsely arranged along one wall's tragically upholstered booth were half a dozen cross-armed young women staring at the ceiling, their purses in their laps. At the other end of the room another woman danced on a stage no larger than the table at which John now sat. Thankfully, she was not stripping, and did not appear interested in stripping, but rather moved in a languidly bored way to music so timidly broadcast John could barely hear it. The walls and carpet were inferno red—the only recognizable motif. That this was exactly what John imagined hell looked like did not abate the impression. Gallagher planted himself in the chair across from John and pushed a beer toward him. "It doesn't usually get hopping around here till one or two."

John motioned around. "What is this?"

In mid-sip, Gallagher's eyebrows lifted. When he lowered the glass his tongue agilely shaved off his froth mustache. "A place for discerning gentlemen. Don't worry. It's nothing you don't want it to be."

With that the dancing woman came and sat next to John. She was violently pretty and wearing a black dress that could have fit inside a coin purse. Her dancing had left her sweaty and luminous, an ecosystem in miniature.

John looked plaintively at his host. "Gallagher, please."

Gallagher laughed again. "One drink, Counsel. It's a nice place to relax if you let yourself." To the dancing woman he said, "Sweetheart, davei. Come sit next to me." She did. The next woman who came over Gallagher tried to wave off; she sat next to John anyway.

John shook her hand. Her legs were ruinously thin, her stretch pants tight around her thighs but barely holding shape against her calves. Her neck was a veiny stalk. She sniffled in an affected way and pulled two silver clips from her black hair. They were purely for show: not one displaced strand fell into her face. She scrutinized the clips as though she had panned them from a riverbed. She was waiting for John to speak. She replaced the clips and studied her foot as she tapped it against the red carpeting, which looked as though it had been the recipient of many gastric sorrows. Her toenails were the color of aluminum foil. John still said nothing to her. Gallagher, meanwhile, was getting along well with the dancing girl. Honestly. It appeared they were having a fairly serious conversation. The woman next to John lit a cigarette and took one of those long, crackling drags that actually made cigarettes seem appealing. Smoke leaked from the corners of her mouth. After another minute of this, she left, and John was alone with his beer.

What they did not ask after his speech was whether he had suffered any reservations at the time he had written his memos. John did have occasional reservations. They all did. John worried first that interrogators might not feel restrained by the same moral qualms that he, John, would. He also worried about what was called "force drift," where force applied unsuccessfully had no choice but to become force applied again, but more intently. After all, enhanced interrogation was excusable only if the person being interrogated was assumed to know something. This was why he never imagined it being applied to anyone but al-Qaeda members.

John understood his arguments were controversial and sometimes even repellent, but they were legal rather than moral judgments.

THE FIFTH CATEGORY TOM BISSELL

John did not craft policy or devise what form "enhanced interrogation" actually took. He simply measured legality against relevant statutes. His memos had been concerned with eighteen methods, and they came in three categories. The first category was limited to two techniques: yelling and deception. The second category comprised twelve: stress positions, isolation, forced standing for up to four hours, phobia exploitation, false documents, removal from standard interrogation sites, twenty-four-hour-long interrogations, food variation, removal of clothing, forced grooming, deprivation of light, and loud music. The third category, intended for use only against the hardest cases, broke down into four techniques: mild physical contact, scenarios that threatened the death of the detainee or his family, extreme element exposure, and simulated drowning. There was also a fourth category, which, thankfully, he had never been asked to rule on. The fourth category was also the loneliest. Its one technique: extraordinary rendition.

John had told himself, while contemplating leaving Justice, that it would be better outside. Walks across an autumn quad, adoring students waiting outside his office, all the intramural atmosphere Washington could never provide except in venal approximation. Justice was a museum, and its cold marble hallways led to a kind of intellectual progeria: even the young there quickly became old. Addington was the saddest to see John go. Do you really, Addington asked, want to teach spoiled rich kids who give murdering proletarian mobs a good name?

Within months after John's departure, many of his judgments were withdrawn and then suspended. John later learned that Addington protested this by saying the President had been relying on John's views. In that case, the answer came back, the President may have been breaking the law. Five months later, Abu Ghraib.

Seven months later, John's memos were declassified. Gonzales, at the press conference, claimed to want to show the media that due diligence and proper legal vetting had occurred at every step in the enhanced interrogation process. That was what he actually believed was at issue.

John would never forget the rattlesnake energy coiled in those War Council meetings. They were all as confident as Maoists. Feith, Haynes, Addington, Gonzales, Flanigan—men one step away from the President. The lawyer's lawyers. The nation had suffered a heart attack and they were holding the paddles of defibrillation, working together to improvise legal strategies for something no law as yet existed to contain. They met in Gonzales's office in the White House, sometimes at Defense. Simple, uncatered, unrecorded meetings in which the most luxurious staples were a few Diet Cokes. John often looked at himself and Gonzales during these meetings. John was a first-generation American, Gonzales the son of immigrants so impoverished they did not even have a telephone. And yet here he was, drafting policy during the most serious national-security crisis in half a century, serving as personal counsel to the world's most powerful man. This was the America John had been willing to do anything legal to protect.

Then you had Feith and Addington, androids who regarded other human beings as little more than collections of interesting mental malfunctions. The dimples within Feith's rumpled Muppet face were venom repositories. He circulated memos without buckslips so no one could be sure to whom they were routed or cc'd them to people who never actually received them. He made speeches on the sanctity of Geneva only to heighten the incongruity of its sacred shroud being filthied by terrorists. His was such manifestly confusing lawyering that those who heard Feith talk about Geneva came away believing Article III would apply to everyone the United States captured. By the end of one of Feith's monologues he had one of the Joint Chiefs mistakenly believing that all eighteen enhanced interrogation techniques were sanctioned by the Army's Field Manual. Not one of them actually was. The idea to launch a new intelligence agency called Total Information Awareness, the logo of which was a crazy Masonic eye overlooking the world? Only Feith.

As for Addington: the eyes of a Russian icon, the bearing of Lincoln, the disposition of a hand grenade. After the attacks, Addington began carrying a copy of the Constitution in his pocket so worn and flimsy it looked like it served as a hankie or coaster or both. Whenever anyone disagreed with him, he pulled it out and started reading from it. It was Addington's special genius to frame every legal and moral argument in warlike terms, whereas any argument about actual warfare came draped in diaphanous euphemism. Maybe that was why, out of all of them, only Addington escaped. Only he had managed to keep his name off every relevant document.

They had attempted to legislate within an atmosphere in which the ticking time bomb was the operational assumption rather than the outlying statistical Pluto it was. Now John could see that, but that was only one way of thinking about it. Another was this: intelligence was the ability to discern the applicability of incoming outside information. The better part of knowledge was knowing what you were allowed to forget.

Three people had been subjected to waterboarding. Three people. And for that he had to answer questions about war crimes. John had heard that his successor allowed himself to be waterboarded before supplying a decision about whether it was over the line. The answer: it was. But for all that, for all the debate and decapitated careers, the CIA was still allowed to use simulated drowning (John actually preferred this more honest term), just as John had originally argued. His core arguments were still in place. Of course, no one in Justice wanted to sign off on CIA use of the technique, but the President found his man. He always did. But that was bitterness. John was not bitter. He would have liked to see Feith or Gonzales or Ashcroft, or any of them, alone in a European city, answering questions on policies they had endorsed and were now ashamed of.

John looked into his pint glass, now an empty crystal well. Somehow he had drunk his beer. He could brood here, he knew, all night, and let the dark wave carry him.

"I'm ready to leave," he told Gallagher, who was still having his edifying conversation with the dancer.

He looked at John. "I hope you've made time to see the Museum of Occupation tomorrow."

"I can't, actually. I'm leaving in the morning." John looked at his watch. It was already past midnight.

Gallagher sat back. "A shame. Tallinn's a nice place to spend a day in."

"Thank you for the drink," John said, standing. "Feel free to stay. I can find my way back."

Gallagher remained seated but extended his hand. "I hope someday we might meet again. Have a good flight tomorrow."

At the door, John turned for one last glimpse of Gallagher. He was already on his cell, bent over in his chair, the dancer getting up to leave. Gallagher noticed John lingering in the doorway and shot him a not-very-sharp salute. Hard to believe that guy was a Marine. John wondered, though only for a moment, to whom Gallagher might be speaking.

Janika's interrogation film had been over for twenty minutes or two hours. It was impossible to keep track of time in the darkness.

THE FIFTH CATEGORY   TOM BISSELL

Light gave time's passage handholds and markers. Time passed in the dark was like driving through cornfields—an endless similarity, full of the unseen.

What the exercise was intended to provoke in him he did not know. He was no more or less sympathetic to those he had helped doom to torture than he was before it began. They misunderstood him. They did not comprehend what he had actually argued for. Those in command of this plane and, now, his life, had nothing to gain from him, other than invigorating their sadism. He, in return, had nothing he could give them, other than the gift of his torment. Torture, he had written, was a matter of intent. He now knew that torture was many more things than that. The exchange of dark knowledge, a revelation of hidden capacities, the annihilation of connection.

Suddenly John was staring at the plane's ceiling, its vaguely surgical nozzles gushing air. The lights were back on. He wrenched around in his adopted coach seat and was not quite prepared to see Janika's broken body, still tangled in luggage. When he stood, gusts of sickness-spiced air pushed through the cloth chimneys of his clothing.

After Janika's tormentor had moved through Category I and the more visually operatic techniques of Categories II and III, several other men entered the room. What happened next was as dreadful as anything John had seen. He refused to watch most of it and opened his eyes only after the sounds of her struggle had ceased. While the men were verifying the extinguishment of Janika's vital signs, the film stopped.

John returned to his designated seat. Upon it sat his iPhone, white as a wafer. A dumb flood of thought branched off toward what few remaining lowlands it could. One of them was Gallagher, the only person who knew that John had changed his flight. Gallagher's card was still in his breast pocket. He took it out and looked at it, his thumb playing over the raised embassy seal. He wondered how Gallagher knew he would not throw the card away. He wondered how it could be that Janika was wearing the same clothes in the interrogation video as she had been on this plane. He wondered how long he had actually been unconscious and whether this was the plane he had boarded. He wondered where on this plane those who were doing this to him were hiding. He wondered, too, how his iPhone was receiving any service, but there it was: two bars of reception. An answer came to one of his questions: Gallagher had not anticipated John keeping his card. John was four digits into Gallagher's number when the recognition application tripped. It had been added to his phone.

Gallagher answered after the third ring. "Tallinn is a nice place to spend a day. You should have listened to me."

What could John say? They had what they wanted.

"Nothing to ask? I don't blame you. You have bigger problems, Counsel. Right now you should probably turn around."

He did. A man in a black ski mask, and a YOU SUCK tee shirt, hit John in the face with an instrument of formidably metal bluntness. When his knees met the carpet he saw the item clearly: the same air compressor he had used to beat the cockpit door. John's head turned mutant with pain. He did not remember the second blow but it must have come, because he woke, once again suddenly, in a plywood room, tied to a chair. One of his eyes no longer worked. Some of his teeth were gone and his tongue felt as swollen and bloody as a leech. He looked down at his shirt: a butcher's apron. The plane's engine was still in his ears. Turbulence shook the room. He could hear weeping somewhere close by. Sitting across from John was Gallagher, whose hands were folded atop yet another sign. He did not show it to John, but John could read it. Gallagher told John he

could promise questions but not answers. He also told him this was new territory for all involved. Not even he was sure where this would go. "Are you ready?" Gallagher asked him. "I need to know if you're ready." John nodded, feeling somehow covetous of his mouthful of blood. The door behind him opened. Footsteps. Hands like toothless lupine muzzles took hold of him. Category VI had begun.

TWO MINUTES FORTY-FIVE SECONDS

DAN SIMMONS

Dan Simmons has written award-winning science fiction novels (*Hyperion*), award-winning fantasy/horror novels (*Carrion Comfort*), and stories which contain elements of both. Here is one of his very best stories, remarkable for its clarity and its brevity. Simmons suggests that two minutes and forty-five seconds can be the length of a pop song...a rollercoaster ride...or just enough time to contemplate one's onrushing death.

oger Colvin closed his eyes and the steel bar clamped down across his lap and they began the steep climb. He could hear the rattle of the heavy chain and the creak of steel wheels on steel rails as they clanked up the first hill of the rollercoaster. Someone behind him laughed nervously. Terrified of heights, heart pounding painfully against his ribs, Colvin peeked out from between spread fingers.

The metal rails and white wooden frame rose steeply ahead of him. Colvin was in the first car. He lowered both hands and tightly gripped the metal restraining bar, feeling the dried sweat of past palms there. Someone giggled in the car behind him. He turned his head only far enough to peer over the side of the rails.

They were very high and still rising. The midway and parking lots grew smaller, individuals growing too tiny to be seen and the crowds becoming mere carpets of color, fading into a larger mosaic of geometries of streets and lights as the entire city became visible, then the entire county. They clanked higher. The sky darkened to a deeper blue. Colvin could see the curve of the earth in the haze-blued distance. He realized that they were far out over the edge of a lake now as he caught the glimmer of light on wavetops miles below through the wooden ties. Colvin closed his eyes as they briefly passed through the cold breath of a cloud, then snapped them open again as the pitch of chain rumble changed, as the steep gradient lessened, as they reached the top.

And went over.

There was nothing beyond. The two rails curved out and down and ended in air.

Colvin gripped the restraining bar as the car pitched forward and over. He opened his mouth to scream. The fall began.

"Hey, the worst part's over." Colvin opened his eyes to see Bill Montgomery handing him a drink. The sound of the Gulfstream's jet engines was a dull rumble under the gentle hissing of air from the overhead ventilator nozzle. Colvin took the drink, turned down the flow of air, and glanced out the window. Logan International was already out of sight behind them and Colvin could make out Nantasket Beach below, a score of small white triangles of sail in the expanse of bay and ocean beyond. They were still climbing.

"Damn, we're glad you decided to come with us this time, Roger," Montgomery said to Colvin. "It's good having the whole team together again. Like the old days." Montgomery smiled. The three other men in the cabin raised their glasses.

Colvin played with the calculator in his lap and sipped his vodka. He took a breath and closed his eyes.

Afraid of heights. *Always* afraid. Six years old and in the barn, tumbling from the loft, the fall seemingly endless, time stretching out, the sharp tines of the pitchfork rising toward him. Landing, wind knocked out of him, cheek and right eye against the straw, three inches from the steel points of the pitchfork.

"The company's ready to see better days," said Larry Miller. "Two and a half years of bad press is enough. Be good to see the launch tomorrow. Get things started again."

"Here, here," said Tom Weiscott. It was not yet noon but Tom had already had too much to drink.

Colvin opened his eyes and smiled. Counting himself, there were four corporate vice presidents in the plane. Weiscott was still a Project Manager. Colvin put his cheek to the window and watched Cape Cod Bay pass below. He guessed their altitude to be eleven or twelve thousand feet and climbing.

Colvin imagined a building nine miles high. From the carpeted hall of the top floor he would step into the elevator. The floor of the elevator would be made of glass. The elevator shaft drops away 4,600 floors beneath him, each floor marked with halogen lights, the parallel lights drawing closer in the nine miles of black air beneath him until they merged in a blur below.

He looks up in time to see the cable snap, separate. He falls, clutching futilely at the inside walls of the elevator, walls which have grown as slippery as the clear glass floor. Lights rush by, but already the concrete floor of the shaft is visible miles below—a tiny blue concrete square, growing as the elevator car plummets. He knows that he has almost three minutes to watch that blue square come closer, rise up to smash him. Colvin screams and the spittle floats in the air in front of him, falling at the same velocity, hanging there. The lights rush past. The blue square grows.

Colvin took a drink, placed the glass in the circle set in the wide arm of his chair, and tapped away at his calculator.

⚑ FLIGHT OR FRIGHT

Falling objects in a gravity field follow precise mathematical rules, as precise as the force vectors and burn rates in the shaped charges and solid fuels Colvin had designed for twenty years, but just as oxygen affects combustion rates, so air controls the speed of a falling body. Terminal velocity depends upon atmospheric pressure, mass distribution, and surface area as much as upon gravity.

Colvin lowered his eyelids as if to doze and saw what he saw every night when he pretended to sleep; the billowing white cloud, expanding outward like a time-lapse film of a slanting, tilting stratocumulus blossoming against a dark blue sky, the reddish brown interior of nitrogen tetroxide flame, and—just visible below the two emerging, mindless contrails of the SRBs—the tumbling, fuzzy square of the forward fuselage, flight deck included. Even the most amplified images had not shown him the closer details—the intact pressure vessel that was the crew compartment, scorched on the right side where the runaway SRB had played its flame upon it, tumbling, falling free, trailing wires and cables and shreds of fuselage behind it like an umbilical and afterbirth. The earlier images had not shown these details, but Colvin had seen them, touched them, after the fracturing impact with the merciless blue sea. There were layers of tiny barnacles growing on the ruptured skin. Colvin imagined the darkness and cold waiting at the end of that fall; small fish feeding.

"Roger," said Steve Cahill, "where'd you get your fear of flying?"

Colvin shrugged, finished his vodka. "I don't know." In Viet Nam—not "Nam" or "in-country"—a place Colvin still wanted to think of as a place rather than a condition, he had flown. Already an expert on shaped charges and propellants, Colvin was being flown out to Bong Son Valley near the coast to see why a shipment of standard C-4 plastic explosive was not detonating for an ARVN unit

TWO MINUTES FORTY-FIVE SECONDS

DAN SIMMONS

when the Jesus nut came off their Huey and the helicopter fell, rotorless, 280 feet into the jungle, tore through almost a hundred feet of thick vegetation, and came to a stop, upside down, in vines ten feet above the ground. The pilot had been neatly impaled by a limb that smashed up through the floor of the Huey. The co-pilot's skull had smashed through the windshield. The gunner was thrown out, breaking his neck and back, and died the next day. Colvin walked away with a sprained ankle.

Colvin looked down as they crossed Nantucket. He estimated their altitude at eighteen thousand feet and climbing steadily. Their cruising altitude, he knew, was to be thirty-two thousand feet. Much lower than forty-six thousand, especially lacking the vertical thrust vector, but so much depended upon surface area.

When Colvin was a boy in the 1950s, he saw a photograph in the "old" *National Enquirer* of a woman who had jumped off the Empire State Building and landed on the roof of a car. Her legs were crossed almost casually at the ankles; there was a hole in the toe of one of her nylon stockings. The roof of the car was flattened, folded inward, almost like a large goosedown mattress, molding itself to the weight of a sleeping person. The woman's head looked as if it were sunk deep in a soft pillow.

Colvin tapped at his calculator. A woman stepping off the Empire State Building would fall for almost fourteen seconds before hitting the street. Someone falling in a metal box from 46,000 feet would fall for two minutes and forty-five seconds before hitting the water.

What did she think about? What did *they* think about?

Most popular songs and rock videos are about three minutes long, thought Colvin. *It is a good length of time; not so long one gets bored, long enough to tell a complete story.*

"We're damned glad you're with us," Bill Montgomery said again.

"Goddammit," Bill Montgomery had whispered to Colvin outside the company teleconference room twenty-seven months earlier, "are you with us or against us on this?"

A teleconference was much like a séance. The group sat in semi-darkened rooms hundreds or thousands of miles apart and communed with voices which came from nowhere.

"Well, that's the weather situation here," came the voice from KSC. "What's it to be?"

"We've seen your telefaxed stuff," said the voice from Marshall, "but still don't understand why we should consider scrubbing based on an anomaly that small. You assured us that this stuff was so failsafe that you could kick it around the block if you wanted to."

Phil McGuire, the chief engineer on Colvin's project team, squirmed in his seat and spoke too loudly. The four-wire teleconference phones had speakers near each chair and could pick up the softest tones. "You *don't* understand, do you?" McGuire almost shouted. "It's the *combination* of these cold temperatures and the likelihood of electrical activity in that cloud layer that causes the problems. In the past five flights there've been three transient events in the leads that run from SRB linear shaped charges to the Range Safety command antennas..."

"Transient events," said the voice from KSC, "but within flight certification parameters?"

"Well...yes," said McGuire. He sounded close to tears. "But it's within parameters because we keep signing papers and rewriting the goddamn parameters. We just don't *know* why the C-12B shaped range safety charges on the SRBs and ET record a transient current flow when no enable functions have been transmitted. Roger thinks maybe the LSC enable leads or the C-12 compound itself can accidentally allow the static discharge to simulate a command signal... Oh, hell, *tell* them, Roger."

"Mr. Colvin?" came the voice from Marshall.

Colvin cleared his throat. "That's what we've been watching for some time. Preliminary data suggests that temperatures below 28 degrees Fahrenheit allow the zinc oxide residue in the C-12B stacks to conduct a false signal...if there's enough static discharge... theoretically..."

"But no solid database on this yet?" said the voice from Marshall.

"No," said Colvin.

"And you did sign the Critically One waiver certifying flight readiness on the last three flights?"

"Yes," said Colvin.

"Well," said the voice from KSC, "we've heard from the engineers at Beaunet-HCS, what do you say we have recommendations from management there?"

Bill Montgomery had called a five-minute break and the management team met in the hall. "Goddammit, Roger, are you with us or against us on this one?"

Colvin had looked away.

"I'm serious," snapped Montgomery. "The LCS division has brought this company 215 million dollars *in profit* this year, and your work has been an important part of that success, Roger. Now you seem ready to flush that away on some goddamn transient telemetry readings that don't mean *anything* when compared to the work we've done as a team. There's a vice-presidency opening in a few months, Roger. Don't screw your chances by losing your head like that hysteric McGuire."

"Ready?" said the voice from KSC when five minutes had passed.

"Go," said Vice-President Bill Montgomery.

"Go," said Vice-President Larry Miller.

"Go," said Vice-President Steve Cahill.

"Go," said Project Manager Tom Weiscott.

"Go," said Project Manager Roger Colvin.

"Fine," said KSC. "I'll pass along the recommendation. Sorry you gentlemen won't be here to watch the liftoff tomorrow."

Colvin turned his head as Bill Montgomery called from his side of the cabin, "Hey, I think I see Long Island."

"Bill," said Colvin, "how much did the company make this year on the C-12B redesign?"

Montgomery took a drink and stretched his legs in the roomy interior of the Gulfstream. "About four hundred million, I think, Rog. Why?"

"And did the Agency ever seriously consider going to someone else after...after?"

"Shit," said Tom Weiscott, "where else could they go? We got them by the short hairs. They thought about it for a few months and then came crawling back. You're the best designer of shaped range safety devices and solid hypergolics in the country, Rog."

Colvin nodded, worked with his calculator a minute and closed his eyes.

The steel bar clamped down across his lap and the car he rode in clanked higher and higher. The air grew thin and cold, the screech of wheel on rail dwindling into a thin scream as the rollercoaster lumbered above the six mile mark.

In case of loss of cabin pressure, oxygen masks will descend from the ceiling. Please fasten them securely over your mouth and nose and breath normally.

Colvin peeked ahead, up the terrible incline of the rollercoaster, sensing the summit of the climb and the emptiness beyond.

The tiny air tank-and-mask combinations were called PEAPs— Personal Egress Air Packs. PEAPs from four of the five crew-members were recovered from the ocean bottom. All had been activated. Two minutes and forty-five seconds of each five-minute air supply had been used up.

Colvin watched the summit of the rollercoaster's first hill arrive.

There was a raw metallic noise and a lurch as the rollercoaster went over the top and off the rails. People in the cars behind Colvin screamed and kept on screaming. Colvin lurched forward and grabbed the restraining bar as the rollercoaster plummeted into nine miles of nothingness. He opened his eyes. A single glimpse out the Gulfstream window told him that the thin lines of shaped charges he had placed there had removed all of the port wing cleanly, surgically. The tumble rate suggested that enough of a stub of the starboard wing was left to provide the surface area needed to keep the terminal velocity a little lower than maximum. Two minutes and forty-five seconds, plus or minus four seconds.

Colvin reached for his calculator but it had flown free in the cabin, colliding with hurtling bottles, glasses, cushions, and bodies that had not been securely strapped in. The screaming was very loud.

Two minutes and forty-five seconds. Time to think of many things. And perhaps, just perhaps, after two and a half years of no sleep without dreams, perhaps it would be time enough for a short nap with no dreams at all. Colvin closed his eyes.

DIABLITOS

CODY GOODFELLOW

What's worse than being stopped at customs in a South American country while trying to smuggle out contraband? How about being sealed in a 727 at 30,000 feet with a hellishly lively stolen artifact in your carry-on bag? In this story, Ryan Rayburn III is faced with both. Cody Goodfellow is something of a mystery. Did he really study literature at UCLA? Does he live in Burbank? Did he once earn a living as an "undistinguished composer of scores for pornographic videos?" Maybe some of the above, maybe all, maybe none. Two things are for sure: he knows how to chill your blood, and you'll thank God Ryan Rayburn isn't your seatmate.

nvisible and invincible, Ryan Rayburn III betrayed no trace of worry as he breezed through security and passport control of Nicoya's Guanacaste Airport, a cool American tourist right up until they culled him out of the boarding line, took him behind a screen and ordered him to open his bag.

Smiling guilelessly, he presented his boarding pass, declaration form and passport to the hangdog customs agent. *No big deal, you're just doing your job.* None of the other passengers looked his way as they filed by. It had to be random, but he was a white man traveling alone. He probably wasn't going to blow up the plane, but odds were excellent he was holding contraband, maybe even a mule for *las drogas...*

This wasn't some banana republic where tourists got disappeared. Costa Rica was almost civilization—hell, even better, since they didn't even have an army, and a "safety patrol" in lieu of state police. But *la mordida* was still king. Ryan looked around for a supervisor or a camera, smiled nonchalantly and fished five twenties out of his money belt. The customs agent strapped on a pair of baby blue rubber gloves before commencing an autopsy of Ryan's duffel bag.

Guanacaste was slightly fancier than most modern Latin American airports, but still had the ambience of a cheap 70s sci-fi film set in a futuristic prison. Signs everywhere tried to shame flyers with images of hooded and handcuffed prisoners with tormented thought bubbles: *Why Did I Try To Smuggle?*

Stiff upper lip. Don't smile or try to chat him up. Don't do their job for them. The idiots they caught always broadcast their guilt in creepy, toxic waves that would kill a canary. He was doing nothing wrong. The security checkpoint didn't even know what they were looking at, and even if this guy did, it was hardly worth delaying the flight. He wasn't smuggling drugs, or weapons. He was just another tourist, bringing back tourist stuff.

The customs agent laid out clothing, camera equipment and toiletries with the odd delicacy of a servant setting out a picnic. He excavated the whole bag, then reached in and peeled back the inner lining and unzipped the false bottom.

"It's just a souvenir, sir." Ryan gulped like he was breathing through a wet towel. "Is there a problem? I bought it at a souvenir shop—"

The customs agent did not acknowledge him. He just stared into Ryan's bag with his hands planted on the scuffed stainless steel table. Then he coughed into his hand.

Ryan looked around, fanning the cash in his hand, pushing it at the agent. A steady stream of passengers filed through the metal detector towards the departure gate. "My flight leaves in ten minutes, friend."

Still coughing, the customs agent dropped Ryan's travel documents and waved him away like a mosquito cloud. Strings of mucus sprayed out around his fist.

Ryan hurriedly stuffed his bag and pocketed his cash, turned to go up a broken escalator and down a long, mostly unlit terminal to his gate before he noticed that his papers were sticky with saliva, dappled with blood.

Jesus, some security… Tries to shake you down and gives you TB. It wasn't funny, but he had to laugh, or he'd scream. They'd had him— caught him red-handed. The look in the agent's eyes when he opened the false bottom, just before he got sick… It had gone a sickly pale olive, and his eyes just about rolled down his cheeks to fall in with the thing in his dirty laundry pouch. The sad bastard had known what he was looking at. He'd *known*, but he'd said nothing, neither did he touch the money.

If there was anything in the world that could make Ryan cross himself and utter a prayer, it would be the thing in his bag, but not because he believed in magic. Smuggling a kilo of uncut Colombian shouting powder might net thirty grand before it got stepped on. For the two pounds of handcarved hardwood in his bag, Ryan might take twice that amount, but if he got caught down here, extradition and federal time in the states would be the best he could pray for.

Ryan Rayburn III never set out to create the life he lived. He casually baited the lines and let it come to him. He blew his trust fund on a BA in art history, then trashed all remaining parental goodwill by bumming around South America instead of getting a job. After three years of misadventures and hard-won discoveries in the darkest corners of the earth, he finally learned the one lesson that his parents had tried to teach him, back in Palo Alto. Being poor sucked.

Back in California, Ryan resolved to convert his impractical degree into a career. He trawled the gallery scene and started picking up contacts for private art collectors and stumbled into the hothouse sub-culture of pre-Columbian artifact freaks. He did shopping trips from Mexico to Tierra Del Fuego, cutting out layers of middle-men until he had a dozen dot-com millionaires in his client list. Half the antiquities in South American museums were fake, and archae-ologists worked in secret to keep looters at bay. The UN and US Customs had cracked several rings that operated around Palo Alto and Stanford, but Ryan didn't move in show-off circles. His clients didn't flash their grave robbery trophies at charity galas, and he didn't trade in the crap you'd see in *National Geographic*.

The Xorocua lived in the high alpine valleys of the Cordillera de Talamanca, less than two hundred miles from the capitol, and yet a day's hike from the nearest navigable road. They were initially believed to be a virgin Stone Age tribe until 1950, when they were documented by a Smithsonian photographer.

His photographs of the Xorocua harvest ritual told a tragic story of prior contact buried in the bizarre ceremony. A man in a crude bull costume rampaged around the huts of the village all night until just before dawn, when a procession of masked guardian spirits arrived to defeat the bull by spitting blood upon it until it weakened and died. The guardians in their carven masks drank corn liquor mixed with various poisons to summon into their bellies the *diablitos*, who repaid in kind the torments and genocide that decimated their tribe and drove the survivors into the most remote cloud-forests of Talamanca.

The Xorocua were primitive by any standard, having struggled too long and hard with basic survival to devise any elaborate cultural treasures. Their greeting to strangers was a formalized plea for food. But the harvest festival masks in those photographs were a revelation.

Each mask was "mouth-painted"—airbrushed using paint spat through a reed—in livid, smoldering colors and elaborate motifs more like runes than abstract motifs. Despite their hostile rejection of the outside world, the Xorocua masks inspired a collectors' frenzy in the 70s. By 1982, the last Xorocua had died from influenza. But the neighboring tribes still feared their masks.

With no analog anywhere in the region, they were stranger and more elaborate and fearsome than any Maya or Aztec deities, almost Polynesian in their fusion of human, insect, floral and animal features, and imbued with a feral malevolence that made the most severe Gothic gargoyles look like Care Bears.

From what he could find in print, he gathered they were a nasty variant on the Latin American fairies, known as *duendes*. The word came from the Spanish *duenos*—or owners—because they were the true owners of any habitat they shared with humans. But the neighboring tribes' Spanish name for them, and for the Xorocua themselves—was more fitting for spirits never quite seen, but keenly feared—*diablitos*, or "little devils."

Ryan had scored some incredible Moche burial charms on a sweep through Colombia and Peru and successfully posted them to his drop contact in California. He flew to Panama City, drove a jeep into the Cordillera de Talamanca just to hike Cerro La Muerte and chill out. He didn't expect to find any remnant of the Xorocua in the rudimentary museums and tourist traps in the nameless mountain villages, and he didn't. Fakes and pastiche trash chiseled out of balsa wood and haphazardly airbrushed with acrylics by *mestizo* hillbillies who knew less about the Xorocua than Ryan's dumbest clients.

Ryan Rayburn III never got anywhere by forcing success. That way lay madness and ulcers; just ask Ryan II and Ryan I. He simply let good things gravitate to him, as they always had. An old blind woman outside a hut with a cooler full of blood-warm Fanta had made a strange gesture and coughed into her hand when he asked her granddaughter about the Xorocua. Coughed into her arthritic claw and opened it up and a red butterfly took flight from her hand.

The girl played mute, but while he was drinking his third Fanta, Ryan poked around the compound. All the men were off hunting or logging, and nobody saw him except a naked boy whose testicles had yet to descend. The huts were huddled in an octagon around a well beside a waist-high soapstone idol, weathered and worn until its chiseled features were only vague dimples in the stone.

Ryan nearly shouted and threw his soda in the air. It was a Xorocua village, or the revival of one, which was highly unlikely. Many tribes in the region buried their dead under their homes, then moved far away. The site of a tribal extinction would be like a stone age Chernobyl.

The old blind woman appeared, then, and sold him the mask for two hundred dollars. That was what he would tell anyone who asked. He'd told himself the story enough times by now, that he almost believed it. What really happened was hardly the worst thing he'd ever done, and there was simply no point in reliving it.

The mask was authentic. It looked like it weighed a hundred pounds, but was carved of some unidentified purple-black jungle softwood that weighed less than water. The paints were indigenous pigments; the deep indigo derived from *azul mata*, the pale, liquid gold extracted from onion skin, the fiery orange from *achiote* fruit, the lurid violet extracted from the glands of an endangered mollusk called *munice*. The unexpected splash of deeper, duller red on the inside of the mask looked less like an accident than a savage signature, and would probably only increase its value.

He had a standing buyer on the line—two, actually, and fiercely jealous competitors. When his plane touched down at LAX, he could unload the mask for fifty thousand, maybe double that, if he held it long enough for discreetly seeded rumors to spark a bidding war.

The exhausted purser at the gate held the door open for him without checking his papers. Stepping out onto the tarmac was like walking into a whirlwind of animal breath. The jungle closed in on all sides of the runway like walls of emerald fire. The Pura Vida Air 727 idled as the last straggling passengers hustled up the rolling stairway and into the hatch.

The flight was just over half full. About fifty passengers, two-thirds American. Most of them had already turned out their lights and were trying to go to sleep, huddled under thin nylon blankets against recycled paper pillows.

He groaned as he found his seat. 11A, by the window, just aft of the wing, beside a longhaired Caucasian beardo and a buxom Asian lady snuggling and tinkering with the faulty fans set into the ceiling. Perking up alarmingly as they got up to let him squeeze into the window seat, the man introduced himself as Dan, his wife Lori. "Need something to read?" he asked, holding out a paperback. "I wrote it myself."

"Quit bothering people, honey," his wife murmured. Ryan shook his head and spread out in the empty seats across the aisle.

The stewardess began the preflight emergency pantomime, gesturing to masks and escape hatches in time with the crackling recording in Spanish, when the last passenger stumbled down the narrow aisle and nearly sat on his bag.

Ryan grabbed his bag out of the shadow of the large descending ass just in time. He started to say, "Watch where you're going, idiot," when he saw the white cane gripped in the fat old woman's hand.

Ryan's whole body went rigid. He pushed back against the window, and if he'd been seated next to an escape hatch, he might've grabbed the latch and popped it and leapt out onto the wing.

He threw up a defensive arm and tried to squeeze out of the seat. The blind woman stumbled against the steward who had helped her to the seat, then rebounded off the arm of 11C and threw out an arm to catch herself before she fell into his arms.

At second glance, his seatmate was just a girl, maybe thirteen, with a long horsy face and terrible acne scars. Her eyes bulged out of her head like unscrewed lightbulbs. Her pupils rolled up to stare through the ceiling, half obscured by heavy, sleepy lids. Her white cane snapped out to jab his ankles.

He took a second to catch his breath, longer to collect his thoughts. With so many empty seats, why on earth would they put her next to him? A young American man traveling alone sitting next to a blind foreign girl was asking for trouble. "Aren't there a lot of other seats on the plane?"

The steward returned to the tail of the aisle to help lipsync the tail end of the safety instructions.

Perhaps deaf as well as blind—or perhaps she didn't speak Spanish—the girl lowered herself into 11D and sat with her knees tightly together and a handwoven native bag trapped in her arms.

The plane bumbled backwards and then taxied onto the runway with a woozy, rolling speed that made Ryan wonder who was flying the plane. Maybe the blind girl could go to the cockpit and help.

The turbines were winding up when Ryan noticed the girl hadn't buckled her seatbelt. "Señorita, your belt should be fastened…"

She rocked slightly but didn't respond. A tiny crucifix and a string of glow-in-the-dark plastic rosary beads clutched in her hands, frequently rising up to kiss her thick, chapped lips.

The stewardess was buckled in at the front. Apparently, it was his responsibility. *For duty and humanity*, he thought, as he reached over to fasten the belt. "Let me help you…"

The girl's hands trapped his in a sweaty, trembling vise. She cried out as if he'd woken her from a sound sleep to find herself groped, empty eyes staring as if she could see his face floating in her perpetual darkness.

Wrenching his hands free, he tried to calm her down without touching her again, but it was no use. She didn't seem to hear or understand him, and she was already in a panic over the flight and being pawed by some strange man in the middle of it. Feeling vaguely ashamed, he looked around for help, but no one seemed to notice. The escalating howl of the engines drowned out her screaming, and then the drunken lurch of acceleration flattened them into their seats.

When the landing gear folded up and the plane leveled off, she went back to her silent prayer. Ryan turned his face to the wall and wadded his sweatshirt into a pillow. Outside, the blinking red light on the wing danced and bled as streaks of rain raced across the glass. The little coastal city was engulfed in tufts of fog like giant kites snarled in the trees. Only a few lost lights that might have been ships at sea testified that the city he'd just escaped was still down there.

Ryan was a seasoned traveler. He could sleep anywhere, under any circumstances. He clenched his legs tight around the duffel bag on the floor and tried to empty his mind. It took a while, though, because every time he felt himself sliding into slumber, the blind girl coughed loudly into her fist.

His mind kept circling back around to the mask. The customs agent had started coughing up blood at the sight of it, but let him go. Was that just some kind of crazy coincidence? The Xorocua were wiped out by disease, so it figured their folklore would invent some kind of magical spirits for protection or revenge, but fat fucking lot of good it did them... They were long gone, their weird, sad little religion just an anthro text footnote that fascinated millionaires who needed bloodthirsty pagan gods for poker partners. Were the masks some kind of vector for spreading a virus? That would explain something, if he had gotten sick, but aside from the usual tropical rashes and maladies, he felt fine. He didn't believe in curses, unless you counted poverty.

They had leveled off at 30,000 feet when Ryan decided he wasn't going to sleep, and decided to work on getting drunk. He rubbed his eyes with the heels of his hands for a while. Maybe he should try to apologize to the blind girl, or better yet, move to another seat. He turned to size her up and found himself eye to eye with the Xorocua mask.

She was wearing it. The whites of her empty eyes glinted through the slits cut into the beetling, jaguar-mottled brow. Every plane of the angular face was painted a different animal texture, as if to tie all the life of the jungle into its vengeful visage. But now, on the blind girl's face, it came to life.

The stylized, branching horns jutting from the jawline and temples glowed cobalt blue, like gas-jet flames. The interlaced fangs in the snarling mouth slid apart like the tumblers of a lock and a torrent of black, rancid blood jetted out over the curled lips to splash down the front of his shirt.

He jumped up and smashed his head into the luggage compartment, fell back into his seat. The blood all over him was cold and sticky and alive with twitching, scuttling things that disappeared under his clothing before he could tear them off. His screams went unheard by the other passengers. The blind girl's bony arms barred his escape. She pressed closer, still coughing up gouts of infested blood and he was drenched and drowning in it when he threw out his hands to pry the mask off her face.

The mask came off with a sound like rusty nails worming out of rotten wood. It took her face off with it and she crushed him into the wall, her cold, slimy cheekbone hard against his chest.

He might've screamed when he woke up. His face was stuck to the cold window. Every other part of his body was crawling with sweat. He was groggy as if he'd popped a couple Ambien on top of a few shots of tequila.

Slowly, deliberately, he turned and looked at the blind girl. She sat bolt-upright in her seat, her head thrown back against the unyielding headrest, her steady breath like plumbing gurgling past a ferocious blockage.

Her traytable was unfolded, and a half-empty Styrofoam cup rested on it beside a foil bag with some kind of pickled fruit spilling out of it, and her plastic rosary beads, glowing like plutonium in the blue murk. Beverage service had come and gone while he slept.

Her dress was homespun cotton, richly embroidered with garish butterflies and birds. As he studied her, fighting the urge to pinch himself, she was wracked with a string of wet, red choking coughs. Fuck this noise, he thought, and grabbed his bag. Gingerly clearing the junk from her traytable, he folded it against the back of 10C and undid his seatbelt.

The cabin was hotter than the fucking Yucatan. His inner ears throbbed as they always did when he flew, but they felt like he was deep underwater, and not skipping over the upper atmosphere. The only light came from the spotty fiber-optic strips along the aisle, and a couple spotlights over passengers nodding over laptops or reading Kindles with iPod plugs in their ears.

Moving one limb at a time with total concentration, he levered himself out of his seat and threw a leg over the girl's knees to plant his foot in the aisle. It was a good plan, and he was careful as hell, but his foot slipped on something and he skidded into the splits with a stifled yelp.

The girl's knees jabbed his ass. He braced himself for the shrieking and batting fists, but they never came. The girl coughed so hard he felt the wet force of her expelled breath through his shirt. Fighting panic, he lurched over her into the aisle, dragging his duffel bag and swinging it over the slumbering head of the passenger in 10C, a fat mother with a mustache and a double armload of squirming kids in her lap.

He must've been out for a couple hours. The plane bounced off roiling pockets of turbulence somewhere over the lightless Mexican interior. The aisle was clear, except for a couple of cups rolling in loopy circles with the rise and fall of the plane. The stewardess was nowhere in sight.

Ryan hurried down the aisle, trying not to bump into passengers' dangling arms and legs. The last row of seats before the restroom was empty, and he made for them like a seasick drunk.

The plane dipped alarmingly just as he reached the seats and fell into them. His heart raced, muscles jittered with spurts of misspent adrenaline. His bag felt weightless as he dropped it into the window seat. Holy shit, but he'd got himself worked up. He needed a drink. Maybe the stewardess would let him buy a bottle of hard stuff. Hell, maybe she'd share it with him. He deserved something good, after everything he'd been through.

He cradled the duffel bag against his hip. It was weightless because it was empty.

Shock galvanized him. Ripping the zipper open, he plunged his hand into the bag and found himself looking at his grabbing hand again, when it popped out the ragged hole in the bottom of the bag. Only a couple pairs of rolled-up tube socks and some boxer shorts were still in the bag, and they were wet, clinging to the walls of the bag in a slimy black paste. The hole was not just a rip in the double-walled nylon. It was a gaping circular fucking hole, like the material had been dissolved... or chewed up.

"Fuck!" he seethed through gritted teeth, looking up the aisle at the scattered yard sale of his possessions trailing all the way back to his old seat. He staggered down the aisle, scooping up slimy piles of clothing. Finally, his hand caught something with heft to it that he snatched up with a grateful whimper, but it turned out to be his shaving kit.

He felt eyes tracking him and the unmistakable sense of someone laughing at his predicament, but every face was turned away, tucked into its neighbor's shoulder or tilted back, mouth agape.

The whine of the engines seemed to subside, the plane to rock laterally and the cups in the aisle tumbled towards the nose. Were they descending already?

Finally, he reached his old seat. Dan and Lori were fast asleep. The carpet was spongy with pooled fluid all around the blind girl in 11D. She must have thrown up, he thought with distaste, or wet herself. His mask was not anywhere in the aisle, so it must have fallen out under his seat when he made his escape. From there, it could have rolled away with the turbulence, could be anywhere in the goddamned plane. There was nothing else to do, but go looking.

He started to kneel beside the blind girl. The plane tilted nose-down and sent him sprawling to the floor. He threw his hand out to save his head and caught an armrest in the eye. He fell to the deck and laughed at his clumsiness when something stabbed him.

A bolt of pure agony was driven by his falling weight into his right leg, just under his right kneecap, until it popped through the tender flesh between the thongs of tendon and muscle at the back of his knee.

It hurt worse than anything he'd ever experienced, until he tried to straighten his leg, and whatever had intruded into the delicate mechanism of his knee snapped inside him, and then pain became his whole, wide world.

Howling, he crumpled on the deck, hugging his impaled knee to his chest. He screamed over and over, but it didn't dawn on him right away how strange it was that, for all his screaming, nobody on the plane had reacted at all.

Reaching out for the couple in 11B and C, he yanked the blanket off them so Dan's novel fell into the aisle. They knocked heads and the husband slumped onto his traytable. A rivulet of deep red flowed out from his left nostril, out of which protruded the hilt of a coffee stirrer. His wife belched and something crawled out of her open mouth, a red shadow slathered in bright arterial blood.

A moan escaped his slack, flapping lips. He rocked back on his leg and was jolted by a fresh stroke of agony. His right leg had a knife in it. Pulling back the leg of his jeans, he saw a white plastic hilt protruding from the wound in the depression just under his kneecap.

A wave of nausea threatened to carry him away when he looked at it, but pure disbelief kept him staring. He'd been stabbed with a plastic knife. The point of it poked out the other side, whittled or chewed until it was sharp as a scalpel.

He turned and pawed at the blind girl, hoping to make her scream like a fire alarm, but she only flopped over her armrest to knock her long, hollow skull against Ryan's forehead. Her mouth hung open, lips flecked with glossy red stains that matched the mire he was sitting in. Her skin was cold as marble, her limbs loose and inert as a doll's, but she shook against him, wracked by a postmortem coughing fit.

They came out of her mouth. With the wracking cough, they scrambled out over her lips and down into the sunken meadow of her lap to leer at him over the armrest.

They looked like beetles or stick insects, with their fluted thoraxes and tapered, exoskeletal limbs. Their bodies borrowed promiscuously from the insect, reptile and amphibian clades, but their hideous faces were (or were hidden behind) miniature Xorocua harvest masks.

The tallest of them was not quite eight inches high, but looking down on him from their perch, they owned him.

Ryan dragged himself backwards, down the aisle towards the cockpit. Everywhere he looked, he saw them creeping over corpses, peering down at him from behind headrests. He passed the mother with her children—bloated and black with asphyxiation—and a business man slouched over his laptop—ballpoint pens shoved into the ruins of his eyes—and the stewardess—the broken neck of an Imperial beer bottle sticking out of a new mouth in her neck. He dragged himself backwards until the solid armored bulk of the cockpit door stopped him.

Everyone in the plane was dead, but cockpits were like bank vaults these days. He thrashed against the door, screaming for them to open it before he was killed, something killed everyone on the plane, but it wasn't him, he was innocent and he didn't deserve to die—

"Ladies and gentleman, we thank you for flying Pura Vida Air, and ask that you wait until the plane has come to a complete stop before activating personal electronics or attempting to retrieve luggage..."

It was a calm, almost sleepy voice, soothing… and pre-recorded. They weren't scheduled to be over Los Angeles for another hour.

The door stayed sealed. The crew on the other side might be dead, too, or they might be totally oblivious to what was going on. He turned to look for a phone.

The darkness leapt out of the seats to fill the aisle and came streaming towards him like army ants. He pounded on the door, shrieking beyond words, but they did not come to kill him.

They wanted him to have the mask. They brought it to him and laid it on the deck.

They wanted him to wear it.

The plane shuddered as its landing gear was lowered into the screaming wind. The cabin was still a lightless cavern, but the ugly amber sodium glow of Tijuana poured in the windows like the overflow of a public urinal.

Huddled against the door, it slowly dawned on him that he didn't have to die. Numbly, he picked up the mask, seeing it too late with new eyes. It was not a trinket or a treasure, or even a mask.

It was a door.

The blood he'd spilled had opened it. To let them leave this place, the door only had to open again. It was simple, when there was no other choice but to accept.

Ryan put the mask to his face. The hard, rough inner surface caressed him with splinters that grew and intertwined under his skin.

They climbed each other to reach his lips. The narrow, fanged mouth only allowed one at a time, and they were beyond counting. They scuttled up his shivering body and into the gate of teeth, but he could feel them piling up inside his belly, restless, hungry for trouble, and he could feel a whole new world, cold, black and infinite, inside.

Before the last one had disappeared into his mouth, the 727 touched down with a rough jerk and skidded on the tarmac as if the runway were a plain of loose boulders.

When the plane finally pirouetted to a stop and the cabin lights turned on, not a single passenger stirred to turn on cell phones or try to pull their luggage out of the overheads. Ryan hauled himself to his feet and knocked once more on the cockpit door, but whatever was on the other side was quite content to stay behind.

He pulled the latch on the cabin door and turned the wheel. Two baggage handlers pressed quizzical faces to the porthole and tapped on the glass. Ryan smiled at them, forgetting he was wearing a mask, and threw open the door.

He tried to explain, but they didn't see him at all. They fell to their knees, choking on red phlegm. He pushed past them and skipped down the stairs to kneel and kiss the tarmac with a forked black tongue.

It was so good, after all his wandering, to be at home...

AIR RAID

JOHN VARLEY

John Varley was born in Texas and went to Michigan State University on a National Merit scholarship—supposedly because of the schools he could afford, MSU was the farthest from Texas. There are science fiction writers who have brilliant ideas, and science fiction writers who are fine prose stylists. Varley is one of the fortunate few who are both. "Air Raid" was published in 1977 (under the pen name Herb Boehm, an amalgam of his middle name and his mother's maiden name, because he had another story appearing in the same issue of *Asimov's*), was nominated for both a Hugo and a Nebula Award, was expanded into the novel *Millennium* in 1983, and became a movie in 1989. Once you start this one, you won't be able to put it down. So welcome aboard Sun-Belt Airlines Flight 128, departing Miami and bound for New York. The passengers, however, may be heading for a far different destination.

was jerked awake by the silent alarm vibrating my skull. It won't shut down until you sit up, so I did. All around me in the darkened bunkroom the Snatch Team members were sleeping singly and in pairs. I yawned, scratched my ribs, and patted Gene's hairy flank. He turned over. So much for a romantic send-off.

Rubbing sleep from my eyes, I reached to the floor for my leg, strapped it on and plugged it in. Then I was running down the rows of bunks toward Ops.

The situation board glowed in the gloom. Sun-Belt Airlines Flight 128, Miami to New York, September 15, 1979. We'd been looking for that one for three years. I should have been happy, but who can afford it when you wake up?

Liza Boston muttered past me on the way to Prep. I muttered back, and followed. The lights came on around the mirrors, and I groped my way to one of them. Behind us, three more people staggered in. I sat down, plugged in, and at last I could lean back and close my eyes.

They didn't stay closed for long. Rush! I sat up straight as the sludge I use for blood was replaced with supercharged go-juice. I looked around me and got a series of idiot grins. There was Liza, and Pinky and Dave. Against the far wall Cristabel was already turning slowly in front of the airbrush, getting a caucasian paint job. It looked like a good team.

I opened the drawer and started preliminary work on my face. It's a bigger job every time. Transfusion or no, I looked like death. The right ear was completely gone now. I could no longer close my lips; the gums were permanently bared. A week earlier, a finger had fallen off in my sleep. And what's it to you, bugger?

While I worked, one of the screens around the mirror glowed. A smiling young woman, blonde, high brow, round face. Close enough. The crawl line read *Mary Katrina Sondergard, born Trenton, New Jersey, age in 1979: 25.* Baby, this is your lucky day.

The computer melted the skin away from her face to show me the bone structure, rotated it, gave me cross-sections. I studied the similarities with my own skull, noted the differences. Not bad, and better than some I'd been given.

I assembled a set of dentures that included the slight gap in the upper incisors. Putty filled out my cheeks. Contact lenses fell from the dispenser and I popped them in. Nose plugs widened my nostrils. No need for ears; they'd be covered by the wig. I pulled a blank plastiflesh mask over my face and had to pause while it melted in. It took only a minute to mold it to perfection. I smiled at myself. How nice to have lips.

The delivery slot clunked and dropped a blonde wig and a pink outfit into my lap. The wig was hot from the styler. I put it on, then the pantyhose.

"Mandy? Did you get the profile on Sondergard?" I didn't look up; I recognized the voice.

"Roger."

"We've located her near the airport. We can slip you in before take-off, so you'll be the joker."

I groaned, and looked up at the face on the screen. Elfreda Baltimore-Louisville, Director of Operational Teams: lifeless face and tiny slits for eyes. What can you do when all the muscles are dead?

"Okay." You take what you get.

She switched off, and I spent the next two minutes trying to get dressed while keeping my eyes on the screens. I memorized names and faces of crew members plus the few facts known about them. Then I hurried out and caught up with the others. Elapsed time from the first alarm: twelve minutes and seven seconds. We'd better get moving.

"Goddam Sun-Belt," Cristabel groused, hitching at her bra.

"At least they got rid of the high heels," Dave pointed out. A year earlier we would have been teetering down the aisles on three-inch platforms. We all wore short pink shifts with blue and white stripes, diagonally across the front, and carried matching shoulder bags. I fussed trying to get the ridiculous pillbox cap pinned on.

We jogged into the dark Operations Control Room and lined up at the gate. Things were out of our hands now. Until the gate was ready, we could only wait.

I was first, a few feet away from the portal. I turned away from it; it gives me vertigo. I focused instead on the gnomes sitting at their consoles, bathed in yellow lights from their screens. None of them looked back at me. They don't like us much. I don't like them, either. Withered, emaciated, all of them. Our fat legs and butts and breasts are a reproach to them, a reminder that Snatchers eat five times their ration to stay presentable for the masquerade. Meantime we continue to rot. One day I'll be sitting at a console. One day I'll be *built in to* a console, with all my guts on the outside and nothing left of my body but stink. The hell with them.

I buried my gun under a clutter of tissues and lipsticks in my purse. Elfreda was looking at me.

"Where is she?" I asked.

"Motel room. She was alone from 10 PM to noon on flight day."

Departure time was 1:15. She cut it close and would be in a hurry. Good.

"Can you catch her in the bathroom? Best of all, in the tub?"

"We're working on it." She sketched a smile with a fingertip drawn over lifeless lips. She knew how I liked to operate, but she was telling me I'd take what I got. It never hurts to ask. People are at their most defenseless stretched out and up to their necks in water.

"Go!" Elfreda shouted. I stepped through, and things started to go wrong.

I was faced the wrong way, stepping *out* of the bathroom door and facing the bedroom. I turned and spotted Mary Katrina Sondergard through the haze of the gate. There was no way I could reach her without stepping back through. I couldn't even shoot without hitting someone on the other side.

Sondergard was at the mirror, the worst possible place. Few people recognize themselves quickly, but she'd been looking right at herself. She saw me and her eyes widened. I stepped to the side, out of her sight.

"What the hell is...hey? Who the hell..." I noted the voice, which can be the trickiest thing to get right.

I figured she'd be more curious than afraid. My guess was right. She came out of the bathroom, passing through the gate as if it wasn't there, which it wasn't, since it only has one side. She had a towel wrapped around her.

"Jesus Christ! What are you doing in my—" Words fail you at a time like that. She knew she ought to say something, but what? *Excuse me, haven't I seen you in the mirror?*

I put on my best stew smile and held out my hand.

"Pardon the intrusion. I can explain everything. You see, I'm—" I hit her on the side of the head and she staggered and went down hard. Her towel fell to the floor. "—working my way through college." She started to get up, so I caught her under the chin with my artificial knee. She stayed down.

"Standard fuggin' *oil!*" I hissed, rubbing my injured knuckles. But there was no time. I knelt beside her, checked her pulse. She'd be okay, but I think I loosened some front teeth. I paused a moment. Lord, to look like that with no makeup, no prosthetics! She nearly broke my heart.

I grabbed her under the knees and wrestled her to the gate. She was a sack of limp noodles. Somebody reached through, grabbed her feet, and pulled. *So long, love! How would you like to go on a long voyage?*

I sat on her rented bed to get my breath. There were car keys and cigarettes in her purse, genuine tobacco, worth its weight in blood. I lit six of them, figuring I had five minutes of my very own. The room filled with sweet smoke. They don't make 'em like that anymore.

✈ FLIGHT OR FRIGHT

The Hertz sedan was in the motel parking lot. I got in and headed for the airport. I breathed deeply of the air, rich in hydrocarbons. I could see for hundreds of yards into the distance. The perspective nearly made me dizzy, but I live for those moments. There's no way to explain what it's like in the pre-meck world. The sun was a fierce yellow ball through the haze.

The other stews were boarding. Some of them knew Sondergard so I didn't say much, pleading a hangover. That went over well, with a lot of knowing laughs and sly remarks. Evidently it wasn't out of character. We boarded the 707 and got ready for the goats to arrive.

It looked good. The four commandos on the other side were identical twins for the women I was working with. There was nothing to do but be a stewardess until departure time. I hoped there would be no more glitches. Inverting a gate for a joker run into a motel room was one thing, but in a 707 at twenty thousand feet...

The plane was nearly full when the woman that Pinky would impersonate sealed the forward door. We taxied to the end of the runway, then we were airborne. I started taking orders for drinks in first.

The goats were the usual lot, for 1979. Fat and sassy, all of them, and as unaware of living in a paradise as a fish is of the sea. *What would you think, ladies and gents, of a trip to the future? No? I can't say I'm surprised. What if I told you this plane is going to—*

My arm beeped as we reached cruising altitude. I consulted the indicator under my Lady Bulova and glanced at one of the restroom doors. I felt a vibration pass through the plane. *Damn it, not so soon.*

The gate was in there. I came out quickly, and motioned for Diana Gleason—Dave's pigeon—to come to the front.

"Take a look at this," I said with a disgusted look. She started to enter the restroom, stopped when she saw the green glow. I planted a boot on her fanny and shoved. Perfect. Dave would have a chance to hear her voice before popping in. Though she'd be doing little but screaming when she got a look around...

Dave came through the gate, adjusting his silly little hat. Diana must have struggled.

"Be disgusted," I whispered.

"What a mess," he said as he came out of the restroom. It was a fair imitation of Diana's tone, though he'd missed the accent. It wouldn't matter much longer.

"What is it?" It was one of the stews from tourist. We stepped aside so she could get a look, and Dave shoved her through. Pinky popped out very quickly.

"We're minus on minutes," Pinky said. "We lost five on the other side."

"Five?" Dave-Diana squeaked. I felt the same way. We had a hundred and three passengers to process.

"Yeah. They lost control after you pushed my pigeon through. It took that long to re-align."

You get used to that. Time runs at different rates on each side of the gate, though it's always sequential, past to future. Once we'd started the Snatch with me entering Sondergard's room, there was no way to go back any earlier on either side. Here, in 1979, we had a rigid ninety-four minutes to get everything done. On the other side, the gate could never be maintained longer than three hours.

"When you left, how long was it since the alarm went in?"

"Twenty-eight minutes."

It didn't sound good. It would take at least two hours just customizing the wimps. Assuming there was no more slippage on 79-time, we might just make it. But there's *always* slippage. I shuddered, thinking about riding it in.

"No time for any more games, then," I said. "Pink, you go back to tourist and call both of the other girls up here. Tell 'em to come one at a time, and tell 'em we've got a problem. You know the bit."

"Biting back the tears. Got you." She hurried aft. In no time the first one showed up. Her friendly Sun-Belt Airlines smile was stamped on her face, but her stomach would be churning. *Oh God, this is it!*

I took her by the elbow and pulled her behind the curtains in front. She was breathing hard.

"Welcome to the twilight zone," I said, and put the gun to her head. She slumped, and I caught her. Pinky and Dave helped me shove her through the gate.

"Fug! The rotting thing's flickering."

Pinky was right. A very ominous sign. But the green glow stabilized as we watched, with who-knows-how-much slippage on the other side. Cristabel ducked through.

"We're plus thirty-three," she said. There was no sense talking about what we were all thinking: things were going badly.

"Back to tourist," I said. "Be brave, smile at everyone, but make it just a little bit too good, got it?"

"Check," Cristabel said.

We processed the other quickly, with no incident. Then there was no time to talk about anything. In eighty-nine minutes Flight 128 was going to be spread all over a mountain whether we were finished or not.

Dave went into the cockpit to keep the flight crew out of our hair. Me and Pinky were supposed to take care of first class, then back up Cristabel and Liza in tourist. We used the standard "coffee, tea, or milk" gambit, relying on our speed and their inertia.

I leaned over the first two seats on the left.

"Are you enjoying your flight?" Pop, pop. Two squeezes on the trigger, close to the heads and out of sight of the rest of the goats.

"Hi, folks. I'm Mandy. Fly me." Pop, pop.

Halfway to the galley, a few people were watching us curiously. But people don't make a fuss until they have a lot more to go on. One goat in the back row stood up, and I let him have it. By now there were only eight left awake. I abandoned the smile and squeezed off four quick shots. Pinky took care of the rest. We hurried through the curtains, just in time.

There was an uproar building in the back of tourist, with about sixty percent of the goats already processed. Cristabel glanced at me, and I nodded.

"Okay, folks," she bawled. "I want you to be quiet. Calm down and listen up. *You*, fathead, *pipe down* before I cram my foot up your ass sideways."

The shock of hearing her talk like that was enough to buy us a little time, anyway. We had formed a skirmish line across the width of the plane, guns out, steadied on seat backs, aimed at the milling, befuddled group of thirty goats.

The guns are enough to awe all but the most foolhardy. In essence, a standard-issue stunner is just a plastic rod with two grids about six inches apart. There's not enough metal in it to set off a hijack alarm. And to people from the Stone Age to about 2190 it doesn't look any more like a weapon than a ballpoint pen. So Equipment Section jazzes them up in a plastic shell to real Buck Rogers blasters, with a dozen knobs and lights that flash and a barrel like the snout of a hog. Hardly anyone ever walks into one.

"We are in great danger, and time is short. You must all do exactly as I tell you, and you will be safe."

You can't give them time to think, you have to rely on your status as the Voice of Authority. The situation is just *not* going to make sense to them, no matter how you explain it.

"Just a minute, I think you owe us—"

An airborne lawyer. I made a snap decision, thumbed the fireworks switch on my gun, and shot him.

The gun made a sound like a flying saucer with hemorrhoids, spit sparks and little jets of flame, and extended a green laser finger to his forehead. He dropped.

All pure kark, of course. But it sure is impressive.

And it's damn risky, too. I had to choose between a panic if the fathead got them to thinking, and a possible panic from the flash of the gun. But when a 20th gets to talking about his "rights" and what he is "owed," things can get out of hand. It's infectious.

It worked. There was a lot of shouting, people ducking behind seats, but no rush. We could have handled it, but we needed some of them conscious if we were ever going to finish the Snatch.

"Get up. Get *up*, you *slugs!*" Cristabel yelled. "He's stunned, nothing worse. But I'll *kill* the next one who gets out of line. Now *get to your feet* and do what I tell you. *Children first! Hurry*, as fast as you can, to the front of the plane. Do what the stewardess tells you. Come on, kids, *move!*"

I ran back into first class just ahead of the kids, turned at the open restroom door, and got on my knees.

They were petrified. There were five of them—crying, some of them, which always chokes me up—looking left and right at dead people in the first class seats, stumbling, near panic.

"Come on, kids," I called to them, giving my special smile. "Your parents will be along in just a minute. Everything's going to be all right, I promise you. Come on."

I got three of them through. The fourth balked. She was determined not to go through that door. She spread her legs and arms and
I couldn't push her through. I will not hit a child, never. She raked
her nails over my face. My wig came off, and she gaped at my bare
head. I shoved her through.

Number five was sitting in the aisle, bawling. He was maybe seven.
I ran back and picked him up, hugged him and kissed him, and tossed
him through. God, I needed a rest, but I was needed in tourist.

"You, you, you, and you. Okay, you too. Help him, will you?"
Pinky had a practiced eye for the ones that wouldn't be any use to
anyone, even themselves. We herded them toward the front of the
plane, then deployed ourselves along the left side where we could
cover the workers. It didn't take long to prod them into action. We
had them dragging the limp bodies forward as fast as they could go.
Me and Cristabel were in tourist, with the others up front.

Adrenaline was being catabolized in my body now; the rush of
action left me and I started to feel very tired. There's an unavoid-
able feeling of sympathy for the poor dumb goats that starts to get
me about this stage of the game. Sure, they were better off, sure
they were going to die if we didn't get them off the plane. But
when they saw the other side they were going to have a hard time
believing it.

The first ones were returning for a second load, stunned at what
they'd just seen: dozens of people being put into a cubicle that was
crowded when it was empty. One college student looked like he'd
been hit in the stomach. He stopped by me and his eyes pleaded.

"Look, I want to *help* you people, just…what's going *on*? Is this
some new kind of rescue? I mean, are we going to crash—"

I switched my gun to prod and brushed it across his cheek. He
gasped, and fell back.

"Shut your fuggin' mouth and get moving, or I'll kill you." It would be hours before his jaw was in shape to ask any more stupid questions.

We cleared tourist and moved up. A couple of the work gang were pretty damn pooped by then. Muscles like horses, all of them, but they can hardly run up a flight of stairs. We let some of them go through, including a couple that were at least fifty years old. Je-zuz. Fifty! We got down to a core of four men and two women who seemed strong, and worked them until they nearly dropped. But we processed everyone in twenty-five minutes.

The portapak came through as we were stripping off our clothes. Cristabel knocked on the door to the cockpit and Dave came out, already naked. A bad sign.

"I had to cork 'em," he said. "Bleeding Captain just *had* to make his Grand March through the plane. I tried *everything.*"

Sometimes you have to do it. The plane was on autopilot, as it normally would be at this time. But if any of us did anything detrimental to the craft, changed the fixed course of events in any way, that would be it. All that work for nothing, and Flight 128 inaccessible to us for all Time. I don't know sludge about time theory, but I know the practical angles. We can do things in the past only at times and in places where it won't make any difference. We have to cover our tracks. There's flexibility; once a Snatcher left her gun behind and it went in with the plane. Nobody found it, or if they did, they didn't have the smoggiest idea of what it was, so we were okay.

Flight 128 was mechanical failure. That's the best kind; it means we don't have to keep the pilot unaware of the situation in the cabin right down to ground level. We can cork him and fly the plane, since there's nothing he could have done to save the flight anyway. A pilot-error smash is almost impossible to Snatch. We mostly work mid-air, bombs, and structural failures. If there's even one survivor, we can't touch it. It would not fit the fabric of space-time, which is immutable (though it can stretch a little), and we'd all just fade away and appear back in the ready-room.

My head was hurting. I wanted that portapak very badly.

"Who has the most hours on a 707?" Pinky did, so I sent her to the cabin, along with Dave, who could do the pilot's voice for air traffic control. You have to have a believable record in the flight recorder, too. They trailed two long tubes from the portapak, and the rest of us hooked in up close. We stood there, each of us smoking a fistful of cigarettes, wanting to finish them but hoping there wouldn't be time. The gate had vanished as soon as we tossed our clothes and the flight crew through.

But we didn't worry long. There's other *nice* things about Snatching, but nothing to compare with the rush of plugging into a portapak. The wake-up transfusion is nothing but fresh blood, rich in oxygen and sugars. What we were getting now was an insane brew of concentrated adrenaline, super-saturated hemoglobin, methedrine, white lightning, TNT, and Kickapoo joyjuice. It was like a firecracker in your heart; a boot in the box that rattled your sox.

"I'm growing hair on my chest," Cristabel said solemnly. Everyone giggled.

"Would someone hand me my eyeballs?"

"The blue ones, or the red ones?"

"I think my ass just fell off."

We'd heard them all before, but we howled anyway. We were strong, *strong*, and for one golden moment we had no worries. Everything was hilarious. I could have torn sheet metal with my eyelashes.

But you get hyper on that mix. When the gage didn't show, and didn't show, and *didn't sweetjeez show* we all started milling. This bird wasn't going to fly all that much longer.

Then it did show, and we turned on. The first of the wimps came through, dressed in the clothes taken from a passenger it had been picked to resemble.

"Two thirty-five elapsed upside time," Cristabel announced.

"Je-zuz."

It is a deadening routine. You grab the harness around the wimp's shoulders and drag it along the aisle, after consulting the seat number painted on its forehead. The paint would last three minutes. You seat it, strap it in, break open the harness and carry it back to toss through the gate as you grab the next one. You have to take it for granted they've done the work right on the other side: fillings in the teeth, fingerprints, the right match in height and weight and hair color. Most of those things don't matter much, especially on Flight 128, which was a crash-and-burn. There would be bits and pieces, and burned to a crisp at that. But you can't take chances. Those rescue workers are pretty thorough on the parts they do find; the dental work and fingerprints especially are important.

I hate wimps. I really hate 'em. Every time I grab the harness of one of them, if it's a child, I wonder if it's Alice. *Are you my kid, you vegetable, you slug, you slimy worm?* I joined the Snatchers right after the brain bugs ate the life out of my baby's head. I couldn't stand to think she was the last generation, that the last humans there would ever be would live with nothing in their heads, medically dead by standards that prevailed even in 1979, with computers working their muscles to keep them in tone. You grow up, reach puberty still fertile—one in a thousand—rush to get pregnant in your first heat. Then you find out your mom or pop passed on a chronic disease bound right into the genes, and none of your kids will be immune. I *knew* about the para-leprosy; I grew up with my toes rotting away. But this was too much. What do you do?

Only one in ten of the wimps had a customized face. It takes time and a lot of skill to build a new face that will stand up to a doctor's autopsy. The rest came pre-mutilated. We've got millions of them; it's not hard to find a good match in the body. Most of them would stay breathing, too dumb to stop, until they went in with the plane.

The plane jerked hard. I glanced at my watch. Five minutes to impact. We should have time. I was on my last wimp. I could hear Dave frantically calling the ground. A bomb came through the gate, and I tossed it into the cockpit. Pinky turned on the pressure sensor on the bomb and came running out, followed by Dave. Liza was already through. I grabbed the limp dolls in stewardess costume and tossed them to the floor. The engine fell off and a piece of it came through the cabin. We started to depressurize. The bomb blew away part of the cockpit (the ground crash crew would read it—we hoped—that part of the engine came through and killed the crew: no more words from the pilot on the flight recorder) and we turned, slowly, left and down. I was lifted toward the hole in the side of the plane, but I managed to hold onto a seat. Cristabel wasn't so lucky. She was blown backwards.

We started to rise slightly, losing speed. Suddenly it was uphill from where Cristabel was lying in the aisle. Blood oozed from her temple. I glanced back; everyone was gone, and three pink-suited wimps were piled on the floor. The plane began to stall, to nose down, and my feet left the floor.

"Come on, Bel!" I screamed. The gate was only three feet away from me, but I began pulling myself along to where she floated. The plane bumped, and she hit the floor. Incredibly, it seemed to wake her up. She started to swim toward me, and I grabbed her hand as the floor came up to slam us again. We crawled as the plane went through its final death agony, and we came to the door. The gate was gone.

There wasn't anything to say. We were going in. It's hard enough to keep the gate in place on a plane that's moving in a straight line. When a bird gets to corkscrewing and coming apart, the math is fearsome. So I've been told.

I embraced Cristabel and held her bloodied head. She was groggy, but managed to smile and shrug. You take what you get. I hurried into the restroom and got both of us down on the floor. Back to the forward bulkhead, Cristabel between my legs, back to front. Just like in training. We pressed our feet against the other wall. I hugged her tightly and cried on her shoulder.

And it was there. A green glow to my left. I threw myself toward it, dragging Cristabel, keeping low as two wimps were thrown head-first through the gate above our heads. Hands grabbed and pulled us through. I clawed my way a good five yards along the floor. You can leave a leg on the other side and I didn't have one to spare.

I sat up as they were carrying Cristabel to Medical. I patted her arm as she went by on the stretcher, but she was passed out. I wouldn't have minded passing out myself.

For a while, you can't believe it all really happened. Sometimes it turns out it *didn't* happen. You come back and find out all the goats in the holding pen have softly and suddenly vanished away because the continuum won't tolerate the changes and paradoxes you've put into it. The people you've worked so hard to rescue are spread like tomato surprise all over some goddam hillside in Carolina and all you've got left is a bunch of ruined wimps and an exhausted Snatch Team. But not this time. I could see the goats milling around in the holding pen, naked and more bewildered than ever. And just starting to be *really* afraid.

Elfreda touched me as I passed her. She nodded, which meant well-done in her limited repertoire of gestures. I shrugged, wondering if I cared, but the surplus adrenaline was still in my veins and I found myself grinning at her. I nodded back.

Gene was standing by the holding pen. I went to him, hugged him. I felt the juices start to flow. *Damn it, let's squander a little ration and have us a good time.*

Someone was beating on the sterile glass wall of the pen. She shouted, mouthing angry words at us. *Why? What have you done to us?* It was Mary Sondergard. She implored her bald, one-legged twin to make her understand. She thought she had problems. God, was she pretty. I hated her guts.

Gene pulled me away from the wall. My hands hurt, and I'd broken off all my fake nails without scratching the glass. She was sitting on the floor now, sobbing. I heard the voice of the briefing officer on the outside speaker.

"...Centauri 3 is hospitable, with an Earth-like climate. By that, I mean your Earth, not what it has become. You'll see more of that later. The trip will take five years, shiptime. Upon landfall, you will be entitled to one horse, a plow, three axes, two hundred kilos of seed grain..."

I leaned against Gene's shoulder. At their lowest ebb, this very moment, they were so much better than us. I had maybe ten years, half of that as a basketcase. They are our best, our very brightest hope. Everything is up to them.

"...that no one will be forced to go. We wish to point out again, not for the last time, that you would all be dead without our intervention. There are things you should know, however. You cannot breathe our air. If you remain on Earth, you can never leave this building. We are not like you. We are the result of a genetic winnowing, a mutation process. We are the survivors, but our enemies have evolved along with us. They are winning. You, however, are immune to the diseases that afflict us..."

I winced, and turned away.

"...the other hand, if you emigrate you will be given a chance at a new life. It won't be easy, but as Americans you should be proud of your pioneer heritage. Your ancestors survived, and so will you. It can be a rewarding experience, and I urge you..."

Sure. Gene and I looked at each other and laughed. *Listen to this, folks. Five percent of you will suffer nervous breakdowns in the next few days, and never leave. About the same number will commit suicide, here and on the way. When you get there, sixty to seventy percent will die in the first three years. You will die in childbirth, be eaten by animals, bury two out of three of your babies, starve slowly when the rains don't come. If you live, it will be to break your back behind a plow, sunup to dusk. New Earth is Heaven, folks!*

God, how I wish I could go with them.

You Are Released

Joe Hill

Joe Hill began his career with a short story called "Better Than Home," almost twenty years ago, and published his first novel—the bestselling *Heart-Shaped Box*—in 2007. He's written three more highly regarded novels, a book of novellas (*Strange Weather*), dozens of short stories (many published in *20th Century Ghosts*), and the award-winning graphic novel series, *Locke & Key*. He is the son of your humble editor, who could not be more proud of the relationship. Here, written especially for this collection, is one of his scariest stories. May we all pray it never comes true.

GREGG HOLDER IN BUSINESS

older is on his third Scotch and playing it cool about the famous woman sitting next to him when all the TVs in the cabin go black and a message in white block text appears on the screens. AN ANNOUCEMENT IS IN PROGRESS.

Static hisses from the public address system. The pilot has a young voice, the voice of an uncertain teenager addressing a crowd at a funeral.

"Folks, this is Captain Waters. I've had a message from our team on the ground, and after thinking it over, it seems proper to share it with you. There's been an incident at Andersen Air Force Base in Guam and—"

The PA cuts out. There is a long, suspenseful silence.

"—I am told," Waters continues abruptly, "that U.S. Strategic Command is no longer in contact with our forces there or with the regional governor's office. There are reports from off-shore that—that there was a flash. Some kind of flash."

Holder unconsciously presses himself back into his seat, as if in response to a jolt of turbulence. What the hell does that mean, *there was a flash*? Flash of what? So many things can flash in this world. A girl can flash a bit of leg. A high roller can flash his money. Lightning flashes. Your whole life can flash before your eyes. Can Guam flash? An entire island?

"Just say if they were nuked, please," murmurs the famous woman on his left in that well-bred, moneyed, honeyed voice of hers.

Captain Waters continues, "I'm sorry I don't know more and that what I do know is so…" His voice trails off again.

"Appalling?" the famous woman suggests. "Disheartening? Dismaying? Shattering?"

"Worrisome," Waters finishes.

"Fine," the famous woman says, with a certain dissatisfaction.

"That's all I know right now," Waters says. "We'll share more information with you as it comes in. At this time we're cruising at thirty-seven thousand feet and we're about halfway through your flight. We should arrive in Boston a little ahead of schedule."

There's a scraping sound and a sharp click and the monitors start playing films again. About half the people in business class are watching the same superhero movie, Captain America throwing his shield like a steel-edged Frisbee, cutting down grotesques that look like they just crawled out from under the bed.

A black girl of about nine or ten sits across the aisle from Holder. She looks at her mother and says, in a voice that carries, "Where is

Guam, precisely?" Her use of the word "precisely" tickles Holder, it's so teacherly and unchildlike.

The girl's mother says, "I don't know, sweetie. I think it's near Hawaii." She isn't looking at her daughter. She's glancing this way and that with a bewildered expression, as if reading an invisible text for instructions. *How to discuss a nuclear exchange with your child.*

"It's closer to Taiwan," Holder says, leaning across the aisle to address the child.

"Just south of Korea," adds the famous woman.

"I wonder how many people live there," Holder says.

The celebrity arches an eyebrow. "You mean as of this moment? Based on the report we just heard, I should think very few."

ARNOLD FIDELMAN IN COACH

THE violinist Fidelman has an idea the very pretty, very sick-looking teenage girl sitting next to him is Korean. Every time she slips her headphones off—to speak to a flight attendant, or to listen to the recent announcement—he's heard what sounds like K-Pop coming from her Samsung. Fidelman himself was in love with a Korean for several years, a man ten years his junior, who loved comic books and played a brilliant if brittle viol, and who killed himself by stepping in front of a Red Line train. His name was So as in "so it goes," or "so there we are" or "little Miss So-and-So" or "so what do I do now?" So's breath was always sweet, like almond milk, and his eyes were always shy, and it embarrassed him to be happy. Fidelman always thought So was happy, right up to the day he leapt like a ballet dancer into the path of a 52-ton engine.

Fidelman wants to offer the girl comfort and at the same time doesn't want to intrude on her anxiety. He mentally wrestles with what to say, if anything, and finally nudges her gently. When she pops out her earbuds, he says, "Do you need something to drink? I've got half a can of Coke that I haven't touched. It isn't germy, I've been drinking from the glass."

She shows him a small, frightened smile. "Thank you. My insides are all knotted up."

She takes the can and has a swallow.

"If your stomach is upset, the fizz will help," he says. "I've always said that on my deathbed, the last thing I want to taste before I leave this world is a cold Coca-Cola." Fidelman has said this exact thing to others, many times before, but as soon as it's out of his mouth, he wishes he could have it back. Under the circumstances, it strikes him as a rather infelicitous sentiment.

"I've got family there," she says.

"In Guam?"

"In Korea," she says and shows him the nervous smile again. The pilot never said anything about Korea in his announcement, but anyone who's watched CNN in the last three weeks knows that's what this is about.

"Which Korea?" says the big man on the other side of the aisle. "The good one or the bad one?"

The big man wears an offensively red turtleneck that brings out the color in his honeydew melon of a face. He's so large, he overspills his seat. The woman sitting next to him—a small, black-haired lady with the high-strung intensity of an overbred greyhound—has been crowded close to the window. There's an enamel American flag pin in the lapel of his suit coat. Fidelman already knows they could never be friends.

The girl gives the big man a startled glance and smooths her dress over her thighs. "South Korea," she says, declining to play his game of good versus bad. "My brother just got married in Jeju. I'm on my way back to school."

"Where's school?" Fidelman asks.

"M.I.T."

"I'm surprised you could get in," says the big man. "They've got to draft a certain number of unqualified inner city kids to meet their quota. That means a lot less space for people like you."

"People like what?" Fidelman asks, enunciating slowly and deliberately. *People. Like. What?* Nearly fifty years of being gay has taught Fidelman that it is a mistake to let certain statements pass unchallenged.

The big man is unashamed. "People who are qualified. People who earned it. People who can do the arithmetic. There's a lot more to math than counting out change when someone buys a dime bag. A lot of the model immigrant communities have suffered because of quotas. The Orientals especially."

Fidelman laughs—sharp, strained, disbelieving laughter. But the M.I.T. girl closes her eyes and is still and Fidelman opens his mouth to tell the big son-of-a-bitch off and then shuts it again. It would be unkind to the girl to make a scene.

"It's Guam, not Seoul," Fidelman tells her. "And we don't know what happened there. It might be anything. It might be an explosion at a power station. A normal accident and not a... catastrophe of some sort." The first word that occurred to him was *holocaust*.

"Dirty bomb," says the big man. "Bet you a hundred dollars. He's upset because we just missed him in Russia."

He is the Supreme Leader of the DPRK. There are rumors someone took a shot at him while he was on a state visit to the Russian side of Lake Khasan, a body of water on the border between the two nations. There are unconfirmed reports that he was hit in the shoulder, hit in the knee, not hit at all; that a diplomat beside him was hit and killed; that one of the Supreme Leader's impersonators was killed. According to the Internet the assassin was either a radical anti-Putin anarchist, or a C.I.A. agent masquerading as a member of the Associated Press, or a K-Pop star named Extra Value Meal. The U.S. State Department and the North Korean media, in a rare case of agreement, insist there were no shots fired during the Supreme Leader's visit to Russia, no assassination attempt at all. Like many following the story, Fidelman takes this to mean the Supreme Leader came very close to dying indeed.

It is also true that eight days ago, a U.S. submarine patrolling the Sea of Japan shot down a North Korean test missile in North Korean airspace. A DPRK spokesman called it an act of war and promised to retaliate in kind. Well, no. He had promised to fill the mouths of every American with ashes. The Supreme Leader himself didn't say anything. He hasn't been seen since the assassination attempt that didn't happen.

"They wouldn't be that stupid," Fidelman says to the big man, talking across the Korean girl. "Think about what would happen."

The small, wiry, dark-haired woman stares at the big man sitting beside her with a slavish pride, and Fidelman suddenly realizes why she tolerates his paunch intruding on her personal space. They're together. She loves him. Perhaps adores him.

The big man replies, placidly, "Hundred dollars."

LEONARD WATERS IN THE COCKPIT

NORTH Dakota is somewhere beneath them but all Waters can see is a hilly expanse of cloud stretching to the horizon. Waters has never visited North Dakota and when he tries to visualize it, imagines rusting antique farm equipment, Billy Bob Thornton, and furtive acts of buggery in grain silos. On the radio, the controller in Minneapolis

instructs a 737 to ascend to flight level three-six-zero and increase speed to Mach Seven Eight.

"Ever been to Guam?" asks his first officer, with a false fragile cheer.

Waters has never flown with a female co-pilot before and can hardly bear to look at her, she is so heart-breakingly beautiful. Face like that, she ought to be on magazine covers. Up until the moment he met her in the conference room at LAX, two hours before they flew, he didn't know anything about her except her name was Bronson. He had been picturing someone like the guy in the original *Death Wish*.

"Been to Hong Kong," Waters says, wishing she wasn't so terribly lovely.

Waters is in his mid-forties and looks about nineteen, a slim man with red hair cut to a close bristle and a map of freckles on his face. He is only just married and soon to be a father: a photo of his gourd-ripe wife in a sundress has been clipped to the dash. He doesn't want to be attracted to anyone else. He feels ashamed of even spotting a handsome woman. At the same time, he doesn't want to be cold, formal, distant. He's proud of his airline for employing more female pilots, wants to approve, to support. All gorgeous women are an affliction upon his soul. "Sydney. Taiwan. Not Guam, though."

"Me and friends used to freedive off Fai Fai beach. Once I got close enough to a blacktip shark to pet it. Freediving naked is the only thing better than flying."

The word *naked* goes through him like a jolt from a joy buzzer. That's his first reaction. His second reaction is that of course she knows Guam, she's ex-navy, which is where she learned to fly. When he glances at her sidelong, he's shocked to find tears in her eyelashes.

Kate Bronson catches his gaze and gives him a crooked embarrassed grin that shows the slight gap between her two front teeth. He tries to imagine her with a shaved head and dog tags. It isn't hard. For all her cover girl looks, there is something slightly feral underneath, something wiry and reckless about her.

"I don't know why I'm crying. I haven't been there in ten years. It's not like I have any friends there."

Waters considers several possible reassuring statements, and discards each in turn. There is no kindness in telling her it might not be as bad as she thinks, when, in fact, it is likely to be far worse.

There's a rap at the door. Bronson hops up, wipes her cheeks with the back of her hand, glances through the peephole, turns the bolts.

It's Vorstenbosch, the senior flight attendant, a plump, effete man with wavy blond hair, a fussy manner, and small eyes behind his thick gold-framed glasses. He's calm, professional, and pedantic when sober, and a potty-mouthed swishy delight when drunk.

"Did someone nuke Guam?" he asks, without preamble.

"I don't have anything from the ground except we've lost contact," Waters says.

"What's that mean, specifically?" Vorstenbosch asks. "I've got a planeload of very frightened people and nothing to tell them."

Bronson thumps her head, ducking behind the controls to sit back down. Waters pretends not to see. He pretends not to notice her hands are shaking.

"It means—" Waters begins, but there's an alert tone, and then the controller is on with a message for everyone in ZMP airspace. The voice from Minnesota is sandy, smooth, untroubled. He might be talking about nothing more important than a region of high pressure. They're taught to sound that way.

"This is Minneapolis Center with high priority instructions for all aircraft on this frequency, be advised we have received instructions from U.S. Strategic Command to clear this airspace for operations from Ellsworth. We will begin directing all flights to the closest appropriate airport. Repeat, we are grounding all commercial and recreational aircraft in the ZMP. Please remain alert and ready to respond promptly to our instructions." There is a momentary hiss and then, with what sounds like real regret, Minneapolis adds, "Sorry about this, ladies and gents. Uncle Sam needs the sky this afternoon for an unscheduled world war."

"Ellsworth Airport?" Vorstenbosch says. "What do they have at Ellsworth Airport?"

"The 28th Bomb Wing," Bronson says, rubbing her head.

VERONICA D'ARCY IN BUSINESS

THE plane banks steeply and Veronica D'Arcy looks straight down at the rumpled duvet of cloud beneath. Shafts of blinding sunshine stab through the windows on the other side of the cabin. The good-looking drunk beside her—he has a loose lock of dark hair on his brow that makes her think of Cary Grant, of Clark Kent—unconsciously squeezes his armrests. She wonders if he's a white-knuckle flier, or just a boozer. He had his first Scotch as soon as they reached cruising altitude, three hours ago, just after ten A.M.

The screens go black and another ANNOUNCEMENT IS IN PROGRESS. Veronica shuts her eyes to listen, focusing the way she might at a table read as another actor reads lines for the first time.

CAPTAIN WATERS (V.O.)

Hello, passengers, Captain Waters again. I'm afraid we've had an unexpected request from air traffic control to reroute to Fargo and put down at Hector International Airport. We've been asked to clear this airspace, effective immediately—

(uneasy beat)

—for military maneuvers. Obviously the situation in Guam has created, um, complications for everyone in the sky today. There's no reason for alarm, but we are going to have to put down. We expect to be on the ground in Fargo in forty minutes. I'll have more information for you as it comes in.

(beat)

My apologies, folks. This isn't the afternoon any of us was hoping for.

If it were a movie, the captain wouldn't sound like a teenage boy going through the worst of adolescence. They would've cast someone gruff and authoritative. Hugh Jackman maybe. Or a Brit, if they wanted to suggest erudition, a hint of Oxford-acquired wisdom. Derek Jacobi perhaps.

Veronica has acted alongside Derek off and on for almost thirty years. He held her backstage the night her mother died and talked her through it in a gentle, reassuring murmur. An hour later they were both dressed as Romans in front of four hundred and eighty people and God he was good that night, and she was good too, and that was the evening she learned she could act her way through anything, and she can act her way through this, too. Inside, she is already growing calmer, letting go of all cares, all concern. It has been years since she felt anything she didn't decide to feel first.

"I thought you were drinking too early," she says to the man beside her. "It turns out I started drinking too late." She lifts the little plastic cup of wine she was served with her lunch, and says "chin-chin" before draining it.

He turns a lovely, easy smile upon her. "I've never been to Fargo although I did watch the TV show." He narrows his eyes. "Were you

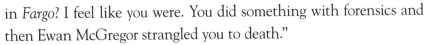

in *Fargo?* I feel like you were. You did something with forensics and then Ewan McGregor strangled you to death."

"No, darling. You're thinking of *Contract: Murder* and it was James McAvoy with a garrote."

"So it was. I knew I saw you die once. Do you die a lot?"

"Oh all the time. I did a picture with Richard Harris, it took him all day to bludgeon me to death with a candlestick. Five set-ups, forty takes. Poor man was exhausted by the end of it."

Her seatmate's eyes bulge and she knows he's seen the picture and remembers her role. She was twenty-two at the time and naked in every scene, no exaggeration. Veronica's daughter once asked, "Mom, when exactly did you discover clothing?" Veronica had replied, "Right after you were born, darling."

Veronica's daughter is beautiful enough to be in movies herself but she makes hats instead. When Veronica thinks of her, her chest aches with pleasure. She never deserved to have such a sane, happy, grounded daughter. When Veronica considers herself—when she reckons with her own selfishness and narcissism, her indifference to mothering, her preoccupation with her career—it seems impossible that she should have such a good person in her life.

"I'm Gregg," says her neighbor. "Gregg Holder."

"Veronica D'Arcy."

"What brought you to L.A.? A part? Or do you live there?"

"I had to be there for the apocalypse. I play a wise old woman of the wasteland. I assume it will be a wasteland. All I saw was a green screen. I hope the real apocalypse will hold off long enough for the film to come out. Do you think it will?"

Gregg looks out at the landscape of cloud. "Sure. It's North Korea, not China. What can they hit us with? No apocalypse for us. For them maybe."

"How many people live in North Korea?" This from the girl on the other side of the aisle, the one with the comically huge glasses. She has been listening to them intently and is leaning toward them now in a very adult way.

Her mother gives Gregg and Veronica a tight smile, and pats her daughter's arm. "Don't disturb the other passengers, dear."

"She's not disturbing me," Gregg says. "I don't know, kid. But a lot of them live on farms, scattered across the countryside. There's only the one big city I think. Whatever happens, I'm sure most of them will be okay."

The girl sits back and considers this, then twists in her seat to whisper to her mother. Her mother squeezes her eyes shut and shakes her head. Veronica wonders if she even knows she is still patting her daughter's arm.

"I have a girl about her age," Gregg says.

"I have a girl about *your* age," Veronica tells him. "She's my favorite thing in the world."

"Yep. Me too. My daughter, I mean, not yours. I'm sure yours is great as well."

"Are you headed home to her?"

"Yes. My wife called to ask if I would cut a business trip short. My wife is in love with a man she met on Facebook and she wants me to come take care of the kid so she can drive up to Toronto to meet him."

"Oh my God. You're not serious. Did you have any warning?"

"I thought she was spending too much time online, but to be fair, she thought I was spending too much time being drunk. I guess I'm an alcoholic. I guess I might have to do something about that now. I think I'll start by finishing this." And he swallows the last of his Scotch.

YOU ARE RELEASED

Veronica has been divorced—twice—and has always been keenly aware that she herself was the primary agent of domestic ruin. When she thinks about how badly she behaved, how badly she used Robert and François, she feels ashamed and angry at herself, and so she is naturally glad to offer sympathy and solidarity to the wronged man beside her. Any opportunity to atone, no matter how small.

"I'm so sorry. What a terrible bomb to have dropped on you."

"What did you say?" asks the girl across the aisle, leaning toward them again. The deep brown eyes behind those glasses never seem to blink. "Are we going to drop a nuclear bomb on them?"

She sounds more curious than afraid, but at this, her mother exhales a sharp, panicked breath.

Gregg leans toward the child again, smiling in a way that is both kindly and wry, and Veronica suddenly wishes she were twenty years younger. She might've been good for a fellow like him. "I don't know what the military options are, so I couldn't say for sure. But—"

Before he can finish the cabin fills with a nerve-shredding sonic howl.

An airplane slashes past, then two more flying in tandem. One is so near off the port wing that Veronica catches a glimpse of the man in the cockpit, helmeted, face cupped in some kind of breathing apparatus. These aircraft bear scant resemblance to the 777 carrying them east…these are immense iron falcons, the gray hue of bullet-tips, of lead. The force of their passing causes the whole airliner to shudder. Passengers scream, grab each other. The punishing sound of the bombers crossing their path can be felt intestinally, in the bowels. Then they're gone, having raked long contrails across the bright blue.

A shocked, shaken silence follows.

Veronica D'Arcy looks at Gregg Holder and sees he has smashed his plastic cup, made a fist and broken it into flinders. He notices what he's done at the same time and laughs and puts the wreckage on the armrest.

Then he turns back to the little girl and finishes his sentence as if there had been no interruption. "But I'd say all signs point to 'yes.'"

JENNY SLATE IN COACH

"B-1S," her love says to her, in a relaxed, almost pleased tone of voice. "Lancers. They used to carry a fully nuclear payload, but black Jesus did away with them. There's still enough firepower onboard to cook every dog in Pyongyang. Which is funny, because usually if you want cooked dog in North Korea, you have to make reservations."

"They should've risen up," Jenny says. "Why didn't they rise up when they had a chance? Did they *want* work camps? Did they want to starve?"

"That's the difference between the Western mindset and the Oriental world view," Bobby says. "There, individualism is viewed as aberrant." In a murmur, he adds, "There's a certain ant-colony quality to their thinking."

"Excuse me," says the Jew in the middle aisle, sitting next to the Oriental girl. He couldn't be any more Jewish if he had the beard and his hair in ringlets and the prayer shawl over his shoulders. "Could you lower your voice, please? My seatmate is upset."

Bobby *had* lowered his voice, but even when he's trying to be quiet, he has a tendency to boom. This wouldn't be the first time it's got them in trouble.

Bobby says, "She shouldn't be. Come tomorrow morning, South Korea will finally be able to stop worrying about the psychopaths on the other side of the DMZ. Families will be reunited. Well. Some families. Cookie Cutter bombs don't discriminate between military and civilian populations."

Bobby speaks with the casual certainty of a man who has spent twenty years producing news segments for a broadcasting company that owns something like seventy local TV stations and specializes in distributing content free of mainstream media bias. He's been to Iraq, to Afghanistan. He went to Liberia during the Ebola outbreak to do a piece investigating an ISIS plot to weaponize the virus. Nothing scares Bobby. Nothing rattles him.

Jenny was an unwed pregnant mother who had been cast out by her parents, and sleeping in the supply room of a gas station between shifts, on the day Bobby bought her an Extra Value Meal and told her he didn't care who the father was. He said he would love the baby as much as if it were his own. Jenny had already scheduled the abortion. Bobby told her, calmly, quietly, that if she came with him, he would give her and the child a good, happy life, but if she drove to the clinic, she would murder a child, and lose her own soul. She had gone with him and it had been just as he said, all of it. He had loved her well, had adored her from the first; he was her miracle. She did not need the loaves and fishes to believe. Bobby was enough. Jenny fantasized, sometimes, that a liberal—a Code Pinker, maybe, or one of the Bernie people—would try to assassinate him, and she would manage to step between Bobby and the gun to take the bullet herself. She had always wanted to die for him. To kiss him with the taste of her own blood in her mouth.

"I wish we had phones," the pretty Oriental girl says suddenly. "Some of these planes have phones. I wish there was a way to call—someone. How long before the bombers get there?"

"Even if we could make calls from this aircraft," Bobby says, "it would be hard to get a call through. One of the first things the U.S.

will do is wipe out communications in the region, and they might not limit themselves to just the DPRK. They won't want to risk agents in the South—a sleeper government—coordinating a counterstrike. Plus, everyone with family in the Korean peninsula will be calling right now. It would be like trying to call Manhattan on 9/11, only this time it's *their* turn."

"Their turn?" says the Jew. "*Their* turn? I must've missed the report that said North Korea was responsible for bringing down the World Trade Towers. I thought that was al-Qaeda."

"North Korea sold them weapons and intel for years," Bobby lets him know. "It's all connected. North Korea has been the number one exporter of Destroy America Fever for decades."

Jenny butts her shoulder against Bobby and says, "Or they used to be. I think they've been replaced by the Black Lives Matter people." She is actually repeating something Bobby said to friends only a few nights before. She thought it was a witty line and she knows he likes hearing his own best material repeated back to him.

"Wow. Wow!" says the Jew. "That's the most racist thing I've ever heard in real life. If millions of people are about to die, it's because millions of people like *you* put unqualified, hate-filled morons in charge of our government."

The girl closes her eyes and sits back in her chair.

"My wife is *what* kind of people?" Bobby asks, lifting one eyebrow.

"Bobby," Jenny cautions him. "I'm fine. I'm not bothered."

"I didn't ask if you were bothered. I asked this gentleman what kind of people he thinks he's talking about."

The Jew has hectic red blotches in his cheek. "People who are cruel, smug—and ignorant."

He turns away, trembling.

Bobby kisses his wife's temple and then unbuckles his seatbelt.

YOU ARE RELEASED

MARK VORSTENBOSCH IN THE COCKPIT

VORSTENBOSCH is ten minutes calming people down in coach and another five wiping beer off Arnold Fidelman's head and helping him change his sweater. He tells Fidelman and Robert Slate that if he sees either of them out of their seats again before they land, they will both be arrested in the airport. The man Slate accepts this placidly, tightening his seat belt and placing his hands in his lap, staring serenely forward. Fidelman looks like he wants to protest. Fidelman is shaking helplessly and his color is bad and he calms down only when Vorstenbosch tucks a blanket in around his legs. As he's leaning toward Fidelman's seat, Vorstenbosch whispers that when the plane lands, they'll make a report together, and that Slate will be written up for verbal and physical assault. Fidelman gives him a glance of surprise and appreciation, one gay to another, looking out for each other in a world full of Robert Slates.

The senior flight attendant himself feels nauseated and steps into the head long enough to steady himself. The cabin smells of vomit and fear, fore and aft. Children weep inconsolably. Vorstenbosch has seen two women praying.

He touches his hair, washes his hands, draws one deep breath after another. Vorstenbosch's role model has always been the Anthony Hopkins character from *The Remains of the Day*, a film he has never seen as a tragedy, but rather as an encomium to a life of disciplined service. Vorstenbosch sometimes wishes he was British. He recognized Veronica D'Arcy in business right away, but his professionalism requires him to resist acknowledging her celebrity in any overt way.

When he has composed himself, he exits the head, and begins making his way to the cockpit to tell Captain Waters they will require airport security upon landing. He pauses in business to tend to a woman who is hyperventilating. When Vorstenbosch takes her hand, he is reminded of the last time he held his grandmother's hand; at the time she was in her coffin, and her fingers were just as cold and lifeless. Vorstenbosch feels a quavering indignation when he thinks about the bombers—those idiotic hot dogs—blasting by so close to the plane. The lack of simple human consideration sickens him. He practices deep breathing with the woman, assures her they'll be on the ground soon.

The cockpit is filled with sunshine and calm. He isn't surprised. Everything about the work is designed to make even a crisis—and this *is* a crisis, albeit one they never practiced in the flight simulators—a matter of routine, of checklists and proper procedure.

The first officer is a scamp of a girl who brought a brown-bag lunch onto the plane with her. When her left sleeve was hiked up, Vorstenbosch glimpsed part of a tattoo, a white lion, just above the wrist. He looks at her and sees in her past a trailer park, a brother hooked on opioids, divorced parents, a first job in Walmart, a desperate escape to the military. He likes her immensely—how can he not? His own childhood was much the same, only instead of escaping to the army, he went to New York to be queer. When she let him into the cockpit last time she was trying to hide tears, a fact that twists Vorstenbosch's heart. Nothing distresses him quite like the distress of others.

"What's happening?" Vorstenbosch asks.

"On the ground in ten," says Bronson.

"Maybe," Waters says. "They've got half a dozen planes stacked up ahead of us."

"Any word from the other side of the world?" Vorstenbosch wants to know.

For a moment neither replies. Then, in a stilted, distracted voice, Waters says, "The U.S. Geological Survey reports a seismic event in Guam that registered about six-point-three on the Richter Scale."

"That would correspond to two hundred and fifty kilotons," Bronson says.

"It was a warhead," Vorstenbosch says. It's not quite a question.

"Something happened in Pyongyang, too," Bronson says. "An hour before Guam, state television switched over to color bars. There's intelligence about a whole bunch of high-ranking officials being killed within minutes of one another. So we're either talking a palace coup or we tried to bring down the leadership with some surgical assassinations and they didn't take it too well."

"What can we do for you, Vorstenbosch?" says Waters.

"There was a fight in coach. One man poured beer on another—"

"Oh for fuck's sake," Waters says.

"—they've been warned, but we might want Fargo Pee Dee on hand when we put down. I believe the victim is going to want to file charges."

"I'll radio Fargo, but no promises. I get the feeling the airport is going to be a madhouse. Security might have their hands full."

"There's also a woman in business having a panic attack. She's trying not to scare her daughter, but she's having trouble breathing. I have her huffing into an air sickness bag. But I'd like emergency services to meet her with an oxygen tank when we get down."

"Done. Anything else?"

"There are a dozen other mini crises unfolding, but the team has it in hand. There is one *other* thing, I suppose. Would either of you like a glass of beer or wine in violation of all regulations?"

They glance back at him. Bronson grins.

"I want to have your baby, Vorstenbosch," she says. "We would make a lovely child."

Waters says, "Ditto."

"That's a yes?"

Waters and Bronson look at each other.

"Better not," Bronson decides and Waters nods.

Then the captain adds, "But I'll have the coldest Dos Equis you can find as soon as we're parked."

"You know what my favorite thing about flying is?" Bronson asks. "It's always a sunny day up this high. It seems impossible anything so awful could be happening on such a sunny day."

They are all admiring the cloudscape when the white and fluffy floor beneath them is lanced through a hundred times. A hundred pillars of white smoke thrust themselves into the sky, rising from all around. It's like a magic trick, as if the clouds had hidden quills that have suddenly erupted up and out. A moment later the thunderclap hits them and with it turbulence, and the plane is *kicked*, knocked up and to one side. A dozen red lights stammer on the dash. Alarms shriek. Vorstenbosch sees it all in an instant as he is lifted off his feet. For a moment, Vorstenbosch floats, suspended like a parachute, a man made of silk, filled with air. His head clubs the wall. He drops so hard and fast, it's as if a trapdoor has opened in the floor of the cockpit and plunged him into the bright fathoms of the sky beneath.

JANICE MUMFORD IN BUSINESS

"MOM!" Janice shouts. "Mom, lookat! What's that?"

What's happening in the sky is less alarming than what's happening in the cabin. Someone is screaming: a bright silver thread of sound that stitches itself right through Janice's head. Adults groan in a way that makes Janice think of ghosts.

The 777 tilts to the left, and then rocks suddenly hard to the right. The plane sails through a labyrinth of gargantuan pillars, the cloisters of some impossibly huge cathedral. Janice had to spell CLOISTERS (an easy one) in the Englewood Regional.

YOU ARE RELEASED   JOE HILL

Her mother, Millie, doesn't reply. She's breathing steadily into a white paper bag. Millie has never flown before, has never been out of California. Neither has Janice, but unlike her mother, she was looking forward to both. Janice has always wanted to go up in a big airplane; she'd also like to dive in a submarine someday, although she'd settle for a ride in a glass-bottomed kayak.

The orchestra of despair and horror sinks away to a soft diminuendo (Janice spelled DIMINUENDO in the first round of the State Finals and came thi-i-i-is close to blowing it and absorbing a humiliating early defeat). Janice leans toward the nice-looking man who has been drinking iced tea the whole trip.

"Were those rockets?" Janice asks.

The woman from the movies replies, speaking in her adorable British accent. Janice has only ever heard British accents in films and she loves them.

"ICBMs," says the movie star. "They're on their way to the other side of the world."

Janice notices the movie star is holding hands with the much younger man who drank all the iced tea. Her features are set in an expression of almost icy calm. The man beside her, on the other hand, looks like he wants to throw up. He's squeezing the older woman's hand so hard his knuckles are white.

"Are you two related?" Janice asks. She can't think why else they might be holding hands.

"No," says the nice-looking man.

"Then why are you holding hands?"

"Because we're scared," says the movie star, although she doesn't look scared. "And it makes us feel better."

"Oh," Janice says, and then quickly takes her mother's free hand. Her mother looks at her gratefully over the bag that keeps inflating and deflating like a paper lung. Janice glances back at the nice-looking man. "Would you like to hold my hand?"

"Yes please," the man says, and they take each other's hand across the aisle.

"What's I-C-B-M stand for?"

"InterContinental Ballistic Missile," the man says.

"That's one of my words! I had to spell 'intercontinental' in the regional."

"For real? I don't think I can spell 'intercontinental' off the top of my head."

"Oh it's easy," Janice says, and proves it by spelling it for him.

"I'll take your word for it. You're the expert."

"I'm going to Boston for a spelling bee. It's International Semi-Finals, and if I do well *there*, I get to go to Washington, D.C., and be on television. I didn't think I'd ever go to either of those places. But then I didn't think I'd ever go to Fargo, either. Are we still landing at Fargo?"

"I don't know what else we'd do," says the nice-looking man.

"How many ICBMs was that?" Janice asks, craning her neck to look at the towers of smoke.

"All of them," says the movie star.

Janice says, "I wonder if we're going to miss the spelling bee."

This time it is her mother who responds. Her voice is hoarse, as if she has a sore throat, or has been crying. "I'm afraid we might, sweetie."

"Oh," Janice says. "Oh no." She feels a little like she did when they had Secret Santa last year, and she was the only one who didn't get a gift, because her Secret Santa was Martin Cohassey, and Martin was out with mononucleosis.

"You would've won," her mother says and shuts her eyes. "And not just the semi-finals, either."

"They aren't till tomorrow night," Janice says. "Maybe we could get another plane in the morning."

"I'm not sure anyone will be flying tomorrow morning," says the nice-looking man, apologetically.

"Because of something happening in North Korea?"

"No," her friend across the aisle says. "Not because of something that's going to happen there."

Millie opens her eyes and says, "*Sh.* You'll scare her."

But Janice isn't scared, she just doesn't understand. The man across the aisle swings her hand back and forth, back and forth.

"What's the hardest word you ever spelled?" he asks.

"Anthropocene," Janice says promptly. "That's the word I lost on *last* year, at semis. I thought it had an 'I' in it. It means 'in the era of human beings.' As in 'the Anthropocene era looks very short when compared to other geological periods.'"

The man stares at her for a moment, and then barks with laughter. "You said it, kid."

The movie star stares out her window at the enormous white columns. "No one has ever seen a sky like this. These towers of cloud. The bright sprawling day caged in its bars of smoke. They look like they're holding up heaven. What a lovely afternoon. You might soon get to see me perform another death, Mr. Holder. I'm not sure I can promise to play the part with my usual flair." She shuts her eyes. "I miss my daughter. I don't think I'm going to get to—" She opens her eyes and looks at Janice and falls quiet.

"I've been thinking the same thing about mine," says Mr. Holder. Then he turns his head and peers past Janice at her mother. "Do you know how lucky you are?" He glances from Millie to Janice and back, and when Janice looks, her mother is nodding, a small gesture of acknowledgment.

"Why are you lucky, Mom?" Janice asks her.

Millie squeezes her and kisses her temple. "Because we're together today, silly bean."

"Oh," Janice says. It's hard to see the luck in that. They're together *every* day.

At some point Janice realizes the nice-looking man has let go of her hand and when she next looks over, he is holding the movie star in his arms, and she is holding him, and they are kissing each other, quite tenderly, and Janice is shocked, just *shocked*, because the movie star is a lot older than her seatmate. They're kissing just like lovers at the end of the film, right before the credits roll and everyone has to go home. It's so outrageous, Janice just has to laugh.

A RA LEE IN COACH

FOR a moment at her brother's wedding in Jeju, A Ra thought she saw her father, who has been dead for seven years. The ceremony and reception were held in a vast and lovely private garden, bisected by a deep, cool, man-made river. Children threw handfuls of pellets into the current and watched the water boil with rainbow carp, a hundred heaving, brilliant fish in all the colors of treasure: rose-gold and platinum and new-minted copper. A Ra's gaze drifted from the kids to the ornamental stone bridge crossing the brook and there was her father in one of his cheap suits, leaning on the wall, grinning at her, his big homely face seamed with deep lines. The sight of him startled her so badly she had to look away, was briefly breathless with shock. When she looked back, he was gone. By the time she was in her seat for the ceremony, she had concluded that she had only seen Jum, her father's younger brother, who cut his hair the same way. It would be easy, on such an emotional day, to momentarily

confuse one for another… especially given her decision not to wear her glasses to the wedding.

On the ground, the student of evolutionary linguistics at M.I.T. places her faith in what can be proved, recorded, known, and studied. But now she is aloft and feeling more open-minded. The 777—all three hundred-odd tons of it—hurtles through the sky, lifted by immense, unseen forces. Nothing carries everything on its back. So it is with the dead and the living, the past and the present. *Now* is a wing and history is beneath it, holding it up. A Ra's father loved fun—he ran a novelty factory for forty years, fun was his actual business. Here in the sky, she is willing to believe he would not have let death get between him and such a happy evening.

"I'm so fucking scared right now," Arnold Fidelman says.

She nods. She is too.

"And so fucking angry. *So* fucking angry."

She stops nodding. She isn't and chooses not to be. In this moment more than any other she chooses not to be.

Fidelman says, "That motherfucker, Mister Make-America-So-Fucking-Great over there. I wish we could bring back the stocks, just for one day, so people could hurl dirt and cabbages at him. Do you think this would be happening if Obama was in office? Any of this—*this*—lunacy? *Listen.* When we get down—*if* we get down. Will you stay with me on the jetway? To report what happened? You're an impartial voice in all this. The police will listen to you. They'll arrest that fat creep for pouring his beer on me, and he can enjoy the end of the world from a dank little cell, crammed in with shitty raving drunks."

She has shut her eyes, trying to place herself back in the wedding garden. She wants to stand by the man-made river and turn her head and see her father on the bridge again. She doesn't want to be afraid of him this time. She wants to make eye contact and smile back.

But she isn't going to get to stay in her wedding garden of the mind. Fidelman's voice has been rising along with his hysteria. The big man across the aisle, Bobby, catches the last of what he has to say.

"While you're making your statement to the police," Bobby says, "I hope you won't leave out the part where you called my wife smug and ignorant."

"Bobby," says the big man's wife, the little woman with the adoring eyes. "Don't."

A Ra lets out a long slow breath and says, "No one is going to report anything to police in Fargo."

"You're wrong about that," Fidelman says, his voice shaking. His legs are shaking too.

"No," A Ra says, "I'm not. I'm sure of it."

"Why are you so sure?" asks Bobby's wife. She has bright bird-like eyes and quick bird-like gestures.

"Because we aren't landing in Fargo. The plane stopped circling the airport a few minutes after the missiles launched. Didn't you notice? We left our holding pattern some time ago. Now we're headed north."

"How do you know that?" asks the little woman.

"The sun is on the left side of the plane. Hence, we go north."

Bobby and his wife look out the window. The wife makes a low hum of interest and appreciation.

"What's north of Fargo?" the wife asks. "And why would we go there?"

Bobby slowly lifts a hand to his mouth, a gesture which might indicate he's giving the matter his consideration, but which A Ra sees as Freudian. He already knows why they aren't landing in Fargo and has no intention of saying.

A Ra only needs to close her eyes to see in her mind exactly where the warheads must be now, well outside of the earth's atmosphere, already past the crest of their deadly parabola and dropping back into gravity's well. There is perhaps less than ten minutes before they strike the other side of the planet. A Ra saw at least thirty missiles launch, which is twenty more than are needed to destroy a nation smaller than New England. And the thirty they have all witnessed rising into the sky are certainly only a fraction of the arsenal that has been unleashed. Such an onslaught can only be met with a proportional response, and no doubt America's ICBMs have crossed paths with hundreds of rockets sailing the other way. Something has gone horribly wrong, as was inevitable when the fuse was lit on this string of geopolitical firecrackers.

But A Ra does not close her eyes to picture strike and counter-strike. She prefers instead to return to Jeju. Carp riot in the river. The fragrant evening smells of lusty blossoms and fresh-cut grass. Her father puts his elbows on the stone wall of the bridge and grins mischievously.

"This guy—" says Fidelman. "This guy and his goddamn wife. Calls Asians 'Orientals.' Talks about how your people are ants. Bullies people by throwing beer at them. This guy and his goddamn wife put reckless, stupid people just like themselves in charge of this country and now here we are. The missiles are flying." His voice cracks with strain and A Ra senses how close he is to crying.

She opens her eyes once more. "This guy and his goddamn wife are on the plane with us. We're *all* on this plane." She looks over at Bobby and his wife, who are listening to her. "However we got here, we're *all* on this plane now. In the air. In trouble. Running as hard as we can." She smiles. It feels like her father's smile. "Next time you feel like throwing a beer, give it to me instead. I could use something to drink."

Bobby stares at her for an instant with thoughtful, fascinated eyes—then laughs.

Bobby's wife looks up at him and says, "*Why* are we running north? Do you really think Fargo could be hit? Do you really think we could be hit *here?* Over the middle of the United States?" Her husband doesn't reply, so she looks back at A Ra.

A Ra weighs in her heart whether the truth would be a mercy or yet another assault. Her silence, however, is answer enough.

The woman's mouth tightens. She looks at her husband and says, "If we're going to die, I want you to know I'm glad I'll be next to you when it happens. You were good to me, Robert Jeremy Slate."

He turns to his wife and kisses her and draws back and says, "Are you kidding me? I can't believe a fat man like me wound up married to a knock-out like you. It'd be easier to draw a million dollar lottery ticket."

Fidelman stares at them and then turns away. "Oh for fuck's sake. Don't start being human on me now." He crumples up a beery paper towel and throws it at Bob Slate.

It bounces off Bobby's temple. The big man turns his head and looks at Fidelman... and laughs. Warmly.

A Ra closes her eyes, puts her head against the back of her seat.

Her father watches her approach the bridge, through the silky spring night.

As she steps up onto the stone arch, he reaches out to take her hand, and lead her on to an orchard, where people are dancing.

KATE BRONSON IN THE COCKPIT

BY the time Kate finishes field dressing Vorstenbosch's head injury, the flight attendant is groaning, stretched out on the cockpit floor. She tucks his glasses into his shirt pocket. The left lens was cracked in the fall.

"I have never *ever* lost my footing," Vorstenbosch says, "in twenty years of doing this. I am the Fred-Effing-Astaire of the skies. *No.* The

Grace-Effing-Kelly. I can do the work of all other flight attendants, but backward and in heels."

Kate says, "I've never seen a Fred Astaire film. I was always more of a Sly Stallone girl."

"Serf," Vorstenbosch says.

"Right to the bone," Kate agrees, and squeezes his hand. "Don't try and get up. Not yet."

Kate springs lightly to her feet and slips into the seat beside Waters. When the missiles launched, the imaging system lit up with bogeys, a hundred red pinpricks and more, but there's nothing now except the other planes in the immediate vicinity. Most of the other aircraft are behind them, still circling Fargo. Captain Waters turned them to a new heading while Kate tended to Vorstenbosch.

"What's going on?" she asks.

His face alarms her. He's so waxy he's almost colorless.

"It's all happening," he says. "The president has been moved to a secure location. The cable news says Russia launched."

"Why?" she asks, as if it matters.

He shrugs helplessly, but then replies, "Russia, or China, or both put defenders in the air to turn back our bombers before they could get to Korea. A sub in the South Pacific responded by striking a Russian aircraft carrier. And then. And then."

"So," Kate says.

"No Fargo."

"Where?" Kate can't seem to load more than a single word at a time. There is an airless, tight sensation behind her breastbone.

"There must be somewhere north we can land, away from—from what's coming down behind us. There must be somewhere that isn't a threat to anyone. Nunavut maybe? They landed a seven-seventy-seven at Iqaluit last year. Short little runway at the end of the world but it's technically possible and we might have enough fuel to make it."

"Silly me," Kate says. "I didn't think to pack a winter coat."

He says, "You must be new to long-haul flying. You never know where they're going to send you, so you always make sure to have a swimsuit and mittens in your bag."

She *is* new to long-haul flying—she attained her 777 rating just six months ago—but she doesn't think Waters's tip is worth taking to heart. Kate doesn't think she'll ever fly another commercial aircraft. Neither will Waters. There won't be anywhere to fly *to*.

Kate isn't going to see her mother, who lives in Pennsyltucky, ever again, but that's no loss. Her mother will bake, along with the stepfather who tried to put a hand down the front of Kate's Wranglers when she was fourteen. When Kate told her mom what he had tried to do, her mother said it was her own fault for dressing like a slut.

Kate will also never see her twelve-year-old half-brother again, and that *does* make her sad. Liam is sweet, peaceful, and autistic. Kate got him a drone for Christmas and his favorite thing in the world is to send it aloft to take aerial photographs. She understands the appeal. It has always been her favorite part of getting airborne, too, that moment when the houses shrink to the size of models on a train set. Trucks the size of ladybugs gleam and flash as they slide, friction-less, along the highways. Altitude reduces lakes to the size of flashing silver hand mirrors. From a mile up, a whole town is small enough to fit in the cup of your palm. Her half-brother Liam says he wants to be little, like the people in the pictures he takes with his drone. He says if he was as small as them, Kate could put him in her pocket, and take him with her.

They soar over the northernmost edge of North Dakota, gliding in the way she once sliced through the bathwater-warm water off Fai

Fai Beach, through the glassy bright green of the Pacific. How good that felt, to sail as if weightless above the oceanworld beneath. To be free of gravity is, she thinks, to feel what it must be like to be pure spirit, to escape the flesh itself.

Minneapolis calls out to them. "Delta two-three-six, you are off course. You are about to vacate our airspace, what's your heading?"

"Minneapolis," Waters says, "our heading is zero-six-zero, permission to redirect to Yankee Foxtrot Bravo, Iqaluit Airport."

"Delta two-three-six, why can't you land at Fargo?"

Waters bends over the controls for a long time. A drop of sweat plinks on the dash. His gaze shifts briefly and Kate sees him looking at the photograph of his wife. "Minneapolis, Fargo is a first-strike location. We'll have a better chance north. There are two hundred and forty seven souls onboard."

The radio crackles. Minneapolis considers.

There is a snap of intense brightness, almost blinding, as if a flashbulb the size of the sun has gone off somewhere in the sky, behind the plane. Kate turns her head away from the windows and shuts her eyes. There is a deep muffled whump, felt more than heard, a kind of existential shudder in the frame of the aircraft. When Kate looks up again, there are green blotchy afterimages drifting in front of her eyeballs. It's like diving Fai Fai again; she is surrounded by neon fronds and squirming fluorescent jellyfish.

Kate leans forward and cranes her neck. Something is glowing under the cloud cover, possibly as much as a hundred miles away behind them. The cloud itself is beginning to deform and expand, bulging upward.

As she settles back into her seat, there is another deep, jarring, muffled crunch, another burst of light. The inside of the cockpit momentarily becomes a negative image of itself. This time she feels a flash of heat against the right side of her face, as if someone switched a sunlamp on and off.

Minneapolis says, "Copy, Delta two-three-six. Contact Winnipeg Center one-two-seven-point-three." The air traffic controller speaks with an almost casual indifference.

Vorstenbosch sits up. "I'm seeing flashes."

"Us too," Kate says.

"Oh my God," Waters says. His voice cracks. "I should've tried to call my wife. Why didn't I try to call my wife? She's five months pregnant and she's all alone."

"You can't," Kate says. "You couldn't."

"Why didn't I call and *tell* her?" Waters says, as if he hasn't heard.

"She knows," Kate tells him. "She already knows." Whether they are talking about love or the apocalypse, Kate couldn't say.

Another flash. Another deep, resonant, meaningful thump.

"Call now Winnipeg FIR," says Minneapolis. "Call now Nav Canada. Delta two-three-six, you are released."

"Copy, Minneapolis," Kate says, because Waters has his face in his hands and is making tiny anguished sounds and can't speak. "Thank you. Take care of yourselves, boys. This is Delta two-three-six. We're gone."

Joe Hill
Exeter, New Hampshire
December 3rd, 2017

Author's note: my thanks to retired airline pilot Bruce Black for talking me through proper procedure in the cockpit. Any technical errors are mine and mine alone.

WARBIRDS

DAVID J. SCHOW

David Schow is perhaps best known for his work in the splat-terpunk subgenre (he is said to have invented the word), but he has also written straight fiction, crime stories, and screen-plays which include *The Crow* and the best of the *Texas Chainsaw Massacre* reboots (*The Texas Chainsaw Massacre: The Beginning*, for those of you keeping score). "Warbirds" is a stunning and amazingly detailed re-creation of the bombing runs over Germany in World War II. It's also a powerful portrait of the forces that are unleashed when men go to war. "I think we woke something up back then, with all that conflict," old Jorgenson says. "All that hate. All those lives..." Which may (or may not) explain what the crew of the *Shady Lady* saw while the bullets were flying and the air was exploding all around them.

arbirds was real," said the old man sitting across the table from me. "I seen 'em. More real than gremlins, say; less real than the weight of a pistol in your hand."

I had traveled several hundred miles to listen to this man reminisce about my late father, and he was spinning me a tale of flying monsters, his spidery white eyebrows gauging how much hogwash I might buy. We'd never met before, and all the trust assumed implicit between us was mere courtesy, standing at ease until something more fundamental could replace it.

I should have paid more attention to that part about the pistol.

"Good man, your dad," said Jorgensen, top turret gunner. That would be the Martin turret on the B-24D. Blame my homework. I knew each crew member by their position; I'd based a lot of my anticipation on a photo I found from 1943—one of the few times the entire core team held together long enough for a snapshot. I appended last names to each man, my roster denying them their full names or nicknames, and back then *everybody* had a nickname, usually a diminution of their given name: Bobby, Willy, Frankie, no different from kids in a neighborhood mob. And kids these guys were. As I sat there drinking coffee served by Jorgensen's sister Katie, that defocused black and white photo was sixty-five years old and most of the fresh faces were barely out of their teens. At least two of the crew had lied about their age in order to join up. Jorgensen, today, was not pushing eighty; he was pulling it. One more burden. He suffered arthritis that had closed his hands to cramped claws. He wouldn't admit that he was a bit deaf, even though his hearing aid was plain to see (one of the older, bigger ones, a behind-the-ear rig with a so-called "flesh-colored" braided wire that snaked to a box stationed in his shirt pocket). His eyes were blue, paled by a patina of yellowed sclera. Polished spectacles. He was bowed but unbent by time and expected me to believe what he told me, because, after all, he was my elder, and what do kids really know, anyway?

Brett Jorgensen, like most men in bomber crews during World War II, had come out of training and landed in Europe as a sergeant. He joked that before the Normandy invasion, German prison camps were overcrowded with thousands of shot-down sergeants. He leaked items like this to suss me out; was I for real and did I know what I was talking about, or was I just another ground-pounder who had seen fit to drop the last Great War from history and memory?

"Sergeants and lieutenants," I said, dumping powdered chemicals into my lukewarm coffee. Jorgensen drank his straight, black. Naturally. If you repeat what a person tells you, usually they illuminate.

He pushed back from our table, then moved forward. He had a tough time finding biz to do with his hands, since they had degenerated to basic grasping tools. I felt a sympathetic twinge, not for the first time.

"Your dad was a sergeant, too, outta Chicago. He tried to train on AT-6s but wasn't a very good pilot. He pulled back'a the bus—twin Fifties." He snorted out a chuckle and searched for a napkin. "This one time, he got his butt cooked by a piece of flak that came through the fuselage and tore through his flight suit and wound up sizzling against his ass."

"Yeah, he told me about that one. Bernberg airport, part of Berlin's outer ring of protective bases, mission number three, March of '44."

"You *have* been paying attention," Jorgensen said. "Well, then, maybe you won't find this story so weird. You've seen war movies. Ever seen combat?"

"No, sir." I was in high school when the draft lottery was instigated. I drew a fairly high number on first cull.

"Well, it ain't like that, and aerial combat is a whole different gorilla. Mostly what it is is a lot of noise and panic, and somehow, if you live through it, you try to figure out later why you're not dead. In the moment, it's all adrenaline and the kind of fear that makes you shit yourself. Planes coming apart around you, bomb loads dropping, ten big Fifties all snackering away, enemy fighters throwing twenty-millimeter cannon shells at your snoot, and around you, *all* around you, you see other planes going down— guys you knew, trailing smoke, blowing up in midair, and you want to look for chutes but there's no time. You ever listen to that heavy metal music?"

He painted such a vivid thumbnail that I was momentarily lost in it, groundless. "What? Oh, yeah, some. You know."

"I never liked it," said Jorgensen. Pause for me to construct a mental image of Jorgensen sitting down all cozy with a Black Sabbath greatest hits disc. A taste of Mudhoney thrash. Perhaps a jot of some Norwegian speed-metal band's idea of meltdown.

"Know why? It sounds like combat, that's why."

⚑

THE B-24 Liberator called the *Turk*, according to its nose paint, chomped into the ground and belched flaming parts all over the runway shoulder while what was left of her crew scattered. Two crewmen still in thermal suits were flattened by the explosion. One did not get up to slap himself out. Fire crews hustled from one half-extinguished conflagration to this new one as other crippled heavies tried to dodge the debris and land. Liberators—nineteen tons each, empty—were packed and stacked on approach and literally dropping out of the sky. A tower spotter was busy counting returning planes and racking up a death toll.

The weather, typical for England, was an oppressive haze of fog and overcast. Blazing planes seared painfully bright peepholes in the mist, hot spots that corkscrewed black contrails of smoke toward the sky.

Wheatrow, a just-arrived belly gunner from Oklahoma City, as blond and corn-fed as his name, rushed up to Harry Mars, a lieutenant who was the *Shady Lady's* co-pilot. Mars stood with his hands thrust into his back pockets, an attitude he affected when he had no idea of what to fix first.

"Jesus H. Christ!" said Wheatrow. "What hit her?"

"Came in with her nose wheel cocked and didn't watch the crash film, I guess," said Mars. "Welcome to Shipdham, laddie buck."

Shipdham was a parish in Norfolk, a jut of the Isles northeast of London, now home to the 44th Bomb Group and one of the Allies' coastal rally points for European missions. This British postcard of pubs and cottages had been despoiled by Nissen huts and landing strips, engirded by anti-aircraft batteries, then overrun by brash American flyers demanding to know what was really going on. Usually loudly and with a pointed absence of tact—cultural shock, writ large.

Watching a gut-shot B-24 slide home was almost operatic in its extravagant horror. Liberators were big-bellied birds that ceased to look ungainly only in flight. On water ditches they tended to "squash," making survival ten times less likely than if you splashed a Flying Fort. The *Turk's* skipper took the lousy hand he had been dealt and played it by the manual, feathering his two working engines, stomping flaps and keeping his snout off the tarmac as long as possible. His locked-down starboard wheel had snapped on impact, guttering him into the mud and shearing off the right wing between the huge Pratt-Whitney engines. Then something had caught fire. No bomb load, little ammo, and littler fuel, but something aboard had touched off and blew the beast apart at the waist like a firecracker in a beer bottle.

Practically everything aboard these planes was flammable, anyway, and the fire would not be extinguished by the United Kingdom's omnipresent cold, gray mud and moisture-laden air.

Everybody got more bad news from Madsen in the mess hall, which doubled as the briefing shack. Wheatrow checked the mission board for *Shady Lady*. Their space was still blank. Madsen was a stiff piece of Sam Browne-belted British business, with a swagger stick he employed as a pointer and map-whacking tool, addressing a full complement of fidgeting officers and noncoms in the too-small corrugated hut.

"...a total of one hundred nine-point-two tons of five-hundred and 1000-pound bombs, fused at a one-tenth of a second nose and one-quarter-second tail, were successfully dropped from eighteen thousand to twenty thousand feet. Apart from the Messerschmitt plant at Regensburg—"

Madsen's swagger stick whacked the map and a general cheer went up at this.

"Yes, yes." Madsen waited it out. "Two other targets in the vicinity were hit, successfully severing air, water, and electrical lines. A screw factory and a rubber plant. Of course, some machine parts were left salvageable, but not without major testing and repair."

Nearly nine hundred lit cigarettes formed an inversion layer of smoke in the dome of the hut. Wheatrow recognized a few faces fresh from his training in Casper, Wyoming, guys he'd shipped over with, guys with unmemorable names. But now he was socked in with his new crew, the fresh meat on their plate. He sat next to Sgt. Jorgensen, who was rocking in his folding chair.

"All this Limey ever talks about," said Jorgensen. "Screwing and rubbers."

Alvin Tewks, a cowboy from California, leaned in from Jorgensen's far side to jerk a thumb toward the *Shady Lady's* navigator. "Ol' Lieutenant Max, he *married* a Limey almost as soon as he hit the beach. Ba-boom!"

Tewks immediately cringed under the scrutiny of Lt. Keith Stackpole, bombardier and nose gunner. He was, after all, talking about an officer. "Shit," he said. "Sorry, sir."

Stackpole, one of the grownups among them at age 22, held out a flat hand. *Keep that blather stowed.* Just as they were raiding the Axis, a similarly militant contingent of British ladies were raiding homesick Yanks, in a potent atmosphere of material privation and imminent death. Max Gentry, their green-eyed navigator, had claimed different. He had fallen in love. Of course. He had also bought himself a double truckload of ribbing and bullshit, which Stackpole admired him for bearing with a calm deference that suggested he was acclimating to the whole indigenous stiff-upper-lip posture. As long as Gentry did not start wearing a flight scarf or speaking with a nasal accent, Stackpole would be A-OK with the *Lady's* map-man.

Stackpole passed a cigarette to Sgt. Jones, the radioman, who broke it in half and passed it on to Sgt. Smith, his best buddy, engineer and right waist gunner. Smith and Jones. Sometimes you had to laugh to keep from crying.

"To hell with all the scores," Jones groused. "How *many?*"

"Forty, fifty, something like that," said Smith. Both men lit up off the same match.

Wheatrow's expression curdled. "Out of how many?"

"Two hundred, something like that." Jimmy Beck had appeared behind them, since there were no more seats. The tail gunner wore military-issue glasses and transferred his smoke from one hand to the other to permit Lt. Mars and their pilot, Lt. Coggins, to squeeze in. Every fact and statistic, no matter how clear, was *something like that.*

Wheatrow lost his breath. "*Two hundred...?!*"

"Out of a total of one hundred seventy-seven B-24s," Madsen boomed from the paltry little stage upfront, "at least one hundred twenty-seven and possibly as many as one hundred thirty-three reached and bombed the target. Forty-two aircraft were shot down or crashed en route—"

"N-root?" said Tewks, still with a newcomer's fascination at the British penchant for not speaking English.

"—of which fifteen, we estimate, were lost over the target."

"We're not on the mission board, again," Coggins said to Stackpole.

"In addition," said Madsen, "eight planes landed in neutral Turkey and were interned. One hundred and four returned to base, and twenty-three to other friendly bases, for a total loss of fifty. The casualty tallies at present are four hundred forty men killed or missing in action. We are informed the Axis holds twenty of the missing crews."

Wheatrow felt his stomach drop away. One mission, nearly four hundred fifty guys lost. The crews of forty-five lost planes. *Something like that.*

"Goddamned Krauts," Jorgensen muttered.

Madsen delivered the cold comfort part of the briefing: "A total of fifty-one enemy fighters were downed."

"Great," said Tewks. "Almost one fighter for every bomber fulla guys."

Some of the men applauded anyway.

Lt. Mars was already past it, ribbing Beck. "Hey Jimmy—know what the life expectancy is for a tail gunner in combat?"

It was an ancient joke for these youngsters. At least three of them chimed, "Nine seconds!"

"Thanks, fellows," said Beck, exhaling smoke. "I feel a whole lot better. Warm inside."

Coggins silently scoped reaction among his crew. Good. Big death numbers would make them all hate the Fuehrer a little more tomorrow, and maybe that hate could help him bring them all back alive, not barbecued in bomber wreckage like those poor sonsabitches aboard the *Turk*, whose skipper was currently logging bunk time in the hospital with his left arm deep-fried medium rare and his leg busted in four places.

This was war. This was important. In 1941, six months before Pearl Harbor, the US Army Air Corps had been renamed US Army Air Forces under General Hap Arnold, and this hut-full of belligerent Americans had a lot to stand up for. Tons to prove. Now, their pride was pricked every day. The warriors of the clouds were *almost* as legitimate and autonomous as the Navy or the tank jockeys. After the States entered the fray, the War Department reorganized the Army Ground Forces and Army Air Forces into co-equal commands, but the shuffle would not result in something called the United States Air Force until after the war. Many of the veteran fliers still wore their Air Corps insignia with understandable self-esteem even though they were all now part of the AAF.

The pride did not count for much when you were rousted out of your rack at one o'clock in the morning. Half the guys in the hut were aware of the intruder even before he clicked on his flashlight. That would be Carlisle, the C.O., so that would be Carlisle's beam bouncing off Coggins' bald cueball skull in the chilly darkness.

"Coggins," Carlisle whispered. "J.J. Wakey-wakey."

"I'm awake," Coggins husked, rolling over.

Carlisle seated himself on the edge of the cot. "Listen, I hate to do this to you, but—"

"What time is it?" Everybody except Tewks was awake now.

"One-fifteen. Look... the mission. Can you make it?"

"Sure," said Coggins, as if he were sure of everything.

"We're leading the Eighth this morning, and we need the whole group to muster maximum effort."

"What's he saying?" said Wheatrow, rubbing his face to consciousness.

"Shh," said Beck. "It's a surprise."

"It's a big deal," said Carlisle, louder now, for the general benefit. "Heavy flak, then fighters. An oil refinery. I know your crew isn't quite combat-ready, but we can't co-pilot you out with a more experienced guy because—"

"My crew *is* combat-ready, sir," Coggins returned, and nobody contradicted him.

There it was, then. The thing Coggins would later describe as a "massacre."

Coggins had gotten "*Shady Lady*" painted on his ship during his North African leg. This green crew was sleeping inside a hut that several days before had been occupied by a completely different crew, now MIA. Tomorrow, who knew? Technically, they had flown four of their 25-mission stint, but had always been recalled or otherwise aborted. They had yet to make it all the way across the Channel. Their much-vaunted first mission had decayed into a complete embarrassment when they lost a supercharger at 12,000 feet and had to turn back and dump their bombs in the North Atlantic. Their right waist gunner, a Texan named MacCardle, had been seconded out to an active combat crew on their twelfth run, *Hometown Gal*, leaving a slot that had just been filled by Wheatrow.

A belly gunner from a ship called the *Double Diamond* had related the mission to Coggins: "I saw the *Ratpacker* take an 88 shell right in the cockpit. It heeled over with a full load of bombs and cut *Hometown Gal* right in half. I didn't see any chutes." Was MacCardle alive or dead? Nobody knew, and past a certain minimal concern, it was a bad idea to care too much.

So here they were: scalding hot coffee, joints cracking in the accursed British damp, struggling into their gear, sleep dirt blurring their vision, becoming roly-poly flyboys. Electrical suits, flak vests, backpack chutes for the pilots, chest chutes for the rest, Mae Wests, helmets, goggles, oxygen masks. They all smelled like wet sheepskin and leather.

"Goddamned fog," said Tewks on the truck to the field. "Too thin to eat and too thick to drink."

Visibility was zilch. "We're going to have to follow a Jeep just to find the runway," said Stackpole. "Where are we in the formation?"

"Coffin corner," said Coggins, trying to make it sound normal.

"Oh, outstanding," grumbled Beck, the Guy in Back.

"What?" said Wheatrow, damp blond hair plastered to his head inside his flight cap.

Lt. Mars recited the verdict: "Outside edge of the box, rear element."

"So the flak can kill us easier," noted Beck.

Jorgensen boffed Wheatrow on one thickly-padded arm. "Newcomer position. For virgins."

"We're supposed to tag along until there's an abort," said Coggins. "So we can fill in." At least they had graduated from the aborts. Coggins had pulled the wire from the brim of his garrison cap with pliers, to permit the proper "mission crush" when he donned his headphones.

Stackpole was whistling "The Way You Look Tonight."

And *Shady Lady* abruptly loomed up before them, filling their world. Dull green, bitch mother, sky lover, their womb, their fate.

The 44th Bomb Group was known as the Flying Eight-Balls, the first Liberator unit in the AAF, though not the first to Europe, which distinction went to the Ninth Air Force's Pyramiders. The Eight-Balls flew their first sortie in support of Flying Forts in November of '42, and as the other groups converted to night missions, the Eight-Balls were left in the unenviable position of being the sole Liberator group assigned to daylight bombing raids. There was a lot of talk about one

Lib, *Boomerang* by name, part of the 93rd Bomb Group's October 9th raid on Lille. She came back wearing thousands of holes, destined for scrap, but her pilot and crew chief fought for her, patched up her bullet punctures with aluminum, and she became the first B-24 in the Eighth to complete her fifty missions. Her men defended her honor, and she repaid them with their lives. Not to put too fine a point on it, snickers aside, the Lille mission was also the breaking point for command, which was compelled to incontrovertibly report that the B-24 was a better bombardment craft, hands down, than the much sexier "glamour girl" B-17—the Libs were faster, longer-range, capable of ferrying heavier bomb loads with superior armament. In essence, the history of the Eight-Balls was the saga of the Liberator in wartime; aerial conflict had birthed her, and she would be practically obsolete by VJ Day. Many of the 24s at Shipdham had arrived with the newer armor, self-sealing tanks, turbo-superchargers, and the retractable Sperry ball turret.

Which is where Wheatrow was headed this morning.

"Big pot-bellied bitch," said Mars, echoing the words of a skipper named Keith Schuyler.

"I like big women," said Tewks. "More to grab on to."

"She moves fast for a big'un," said Coggins. He might have been talking about his wife back in the States, or his aircraft, thought Jorgensen. Like the difference mattered. Maybe his old lady's wingspan was longer than her fuselage.

The flight crew had completed hoisting 500-pounders into the *Lady's* bomb bay, and the ten Fifties aboard were glutted with eleven thousand rounds of ammo in disintegrating link belts. Coggins' men began levering themselves into the underside of the plane. There they'd spend the next twelve hours in almost unbearable cramp, pissing through relief tubes, sucking artificial air, fighting not to die. God help you if you were struck with the trots in mid-mission.

Mars clambered into the co-pilot bucket to Coggins' right, noting that the skipper, as usual, had locked his seat full-forward. You'd think shorter men would be ideal for bombers, but the jokers back in San Diego or Fort Worth always liked to rack the pedals just out of reach for an average human being.

"Could be a milk run," Mars said, snugging in.

"Could be a nightmare, if fighters pick our group to plaster," said Coggins, not looking at him. He mashed down his (now-wireless) cap to accommodate his headphones.

They ran through the preflight check with the flight engineer. Mars stowed the control latch overhead (so it would not slap him in the face later) and popped out the hatch to check movement on the ailerons, elevators and rudder. They were starting up from a battery cart, so he killed the ignition switches. The engineer pulled the props through by hand, six turns or "blades" each, starting with #3, inboard to outboard. The process was dull, administrative, and by rote, but even a misstep at this stage could cause an explosion, from a closed intercooler or an overlooked supercharger switch. The flight engineer placed the wheel chocks and stood by with a portable extinguisher for the actual engine startup, #3 first, to drive the hydraulics. At 1000 rpm, the dials read properly:

45-50 pounds for the oil pressure, 4-1/2 inches for the vacuum pumps, about 975 pounds pressure in the accumulators, for braking power. Coggins throttled to one-third power while Mars amplified the fuel mix to auto-lean. After taxiing out, Mars would rev all four powerhouses to "exercise" the props.

Coggins went on the air: "Checking interphone."

"Christ, I can't even see past the nose of the plane," Mars returned as the crew began to check in from their positions. As usual, the fog would lift only when they broke above it.

Stackpole's voice: "Bombardier, roger." He was down by their feet, near Jones, at the radio station, who said, "Radioman, check."

Behind Smith always came Jones: "Roger, left waist."

"Rodger-dodger, you old codger." That was Tewks, across from Smith at the right waist gun.

"Top turret, Jorgensen here." If Mars or Coggins turned around, they'd see Jorgensen's boots on the turret footbar.

"Wheatrow. Ball turret is okay." The poor lad had to be dogged in and lowered away, without a chute. No room for a chute. To use one, he'd have to clamber out—with help—and strap one on, theoretically while the aircraft was plummeting earthward in a fireball. Easy peasy.

Lt. Gentry jack-in-the-boxed out from his station to give a thumbs up. Per procedure, he had to be heard, so he was.

"Heads up, Jimmy," said Coggins.

"The tail is ready, Skipper," said Beck from what Jorgensen had called the "back of the bus."

In that moment, Coggins seemed to compress from the weight he imagined on his yoke. Mars' eyebrows went up. Coggins finally cracked a half-smile and said, "This goddamned seat's too short."

Despite their bulky gear, armament, and sleepless disposition, when the *Lady* lofted skyward, it felt like riding in a limousine. They finally got to see some daylight and blue sky. Every little taste of reward was deeply important.

At 3000 feet, they all lit up cigarettes, because at 10,000 feet, they'd have to go on ship oxygen. Then sheer ball-sweat would have to carry them until they turned around, empty, and showed the Continent their tail.

"**WE** got swamped by Focke-Wulfs," said Jorgensen. "One-nineties everywhere. After flak always comes fighters. And the next thing I know, Mars is screaming into his intercom that *Vargas Doll* was on fire, just off our left wing. I couldn't *not* see it from my turret. Flak hit an oxygen bottle near ole Jonesy's head and blew his radio apart. Wheatrow's electrical suit shorted out and burned him. Everybody's yelling, the guns are all blazing, Focke-Wulfs zipping past close enough to spit on. Tewks snapped his gun tether and accidentally shot up our right stabilizer trying to nail one of the sonsabitches, and we started to shake like a drunk old whore. And that's when I saw it, first time."

"The Warbird," I said. Katie had dutifully refreshed our coffee. Jorgensen's older sister was also in her eighties. The last Mrs. Jorgensen had died a decade ago.

"At first, I thought it was one of them Stukas," said Jorgensen. "When they dived, they made this weird whine. Then I saw its wings flap and I thought, *This ain't no airplane.* It was nearly as *big* as a fighter. Wings like a bat, snout like one of them needle-bills. Eyes like onyx and pewter." He cleared his throat. "About now you're thinking to yourself, gee, this old coot has lost his marbles, right?" His feathery brows arched, to indict me.

"Actually, no sir. I could never get my father to talk about the war, but some of the *Shady Lady's* other crew had a few tales to tell, over the years it took me to find them. I've heard weirder."

He seemed to arrive at some momentous inner decision. "Well, okay, then, as long as Katie's in the kitchen or watching soaps or whatever it is she does with her free time." No protest came from the back of the house, so Jorgensen was satisfied we were in confidence, here.

"I thought the same thing you just probably thought," he went on. "That it was a hallucination. I don't think so. I just saw this big, impossible thing coming straight for me, claws out. Next thing I know, all my plexi is gone and I'm laid out on the deck with my head tore open. Still got the scar." He smoothed his hair back to favor a white line that zigged from his left eyebrow up into his scalp. It resembled a knife wound. "Damned near lost my eye. By the time we were back to base, I was in shock from loss of blood. I barely remember the haul back home. They told me later that the belly turret was gone when we landed, and so was Wheatrow, the new guy."

"The whole turret was just gone from the plane?"

"Yeah—pretty tough to do with just cannon fire or machine guns. And all of us would have felt a direct flak hit. Jerry was using 128-millimeter guns for flak, so if Wheatrow had been blown out of the ball by a burst, we would have known about it because half the plane would have been on fire. We had seven thousand pounds of incendiaries and our wings were full of high-test gasoline."

"You think that—"

He overrode me. "I don't think. I suspect. Some things I know. Now, I suspect what happened to poor ole Wheatrow, but I'll tell you what I think: I think that a war that big doesn't just go away because you shake hands and sign some paper."

"Or nuke a couple of cities into Japanese-flavored vapor." I didn't mean it to sound that flip, but Jorgensen stayed on track, either ignoring it or being polite.

"Think of it: the whole world at war. Years of war. Every birthday, every Christmas, the war is still there. Then we suddenly get all civilized and agree to pretend there ain't no war. Sometimes I think... sometimes..." He petered out. Why bother? He barely knew me, and I was just the callow spawn of one of his old crewmates, Jimmy Beck, who'd died five years ago and never sent a holiday card, ever.

"It ain't about heroics or glory," he said, starting up a different avenue of attack. "Where you're up there in the air, shooting all around, guys bleeding and guys hollering, explosions, it's about keeping your skin on. Sheer survival. If you believe in God, you pray constantly to yourself, silently: *God, please don't let me die on this mission.* If you believe in good luck charms, you tote 'em. Stackpole had a little Kilroy sock doll his wife made for him, and you better believe we all treated Kilroy like one of our crew, made sure he was accounted for on every mission. Gentry had a St. Christopher's medal. Wheatrow came with his rabbit's foot, even though that wasn't very lucky for him or the rabbit. And your Daddy had this ritual. Before he checked his guns, he'd pull the first slug out of the chain belt and write the date on it and put it in his pocket next to his heart."

A fifty-caliber round was nearly six inches long and weighed more than a roll of quarters. My father had flown at least eight successful missions over enemy territory. I wondered what had become of the bullet collection.

"Everybody does stuff like that," I said, although my father's quirk was news to me. "You don't need combat to believe in little rituals, patterns. Who does it harm?"

"You're missing the point." He waved his hand dismissively.

I seemed to be part of a larger picture, one that was right behind me, part of a vista that Jorgensen could perceive, but I could not. He was seeing it right now.

"That feeling, that battle feeling, it's come back," he said. "Every day. Just little bits at first. More every time. Not flashbacks, not jitters. I'm not senile, goddammit. It's as real as the part in your hair. Now I'm gonna tell you what I believe, and I'll call you a liar if you tell anyone else, but I'm saying this out of respect for your dad."

He was passing something on to me, a weight more massive than I expected, and it was everything I could manage to not interrupt him with all my wise modernity.

"I think we woke something up back then, with all that conflict. All that hate. All those lives, feeding the war. Something that big doesn't just stop, there one day and gone the next. I think maybe it got gorged and fat, and it went to sleep for a while. We had other wars, here and there, but they weren't the same. This war had a child. It birthed up something bad. Something that awoke from its nap and realized, why, it was hungry again, and it hadn't yanked *all* of us out of the air, where it feeds."

"The Warbird. But why you? Why now, after all this time?"

"You want logic from me? I don't have it. All I have is the thought that maybe some of us were supposed to die back then and didn't. And it knows who were are, and it's got a little checklist, like a menu. And we're easy pickings, because it waited, and now we aren't full of sperm and vinegar anymore. We can't run away, and we can't shoot back. The Warbird is on the wing again, eating leftovers, and none of this matters, because who in hell is going to believe a crusty old fart like me?"

"Mr. Jorgensen, my father died of a heart attack. A thrombosis. He technically died four times before he died for real and stayed that way. He had a quadruple bypass. An angioplasty. He had two pacemakers in his chest when he finally went down. Nobody was more stubborn than him when it came to dying. And he did not die in fear or pain. He accepted it. He didn't act like he was..." I hated that I had to grope for an appropriate word, "...haunted."

"Yeah," Jorgensen said. There was a hint of *gotcha* in his eyes, past the tears he was manfully damming back. Men of his generation were not supposed to cry, ever. "But you just said he never talked to you about the war, did he?"

224

"Yet you talked to me about the Warbird." He was not funnin' me in the way of a wacky grampaw. He was dead serious, and the admission had cost him in emotional viscera, reeled out and inelegantly splayed for inspection. Whether I was trustworthy or not, I had fallen into that bizarre gap that permits people to confide to strangers intimacies they would never reveal to their closest loved ones. I had gotten an explanation. It seemed unfair to retroactively impose preconditions now.

"I did, didn't I?" he said, coming back into himself. "That was stupid of me. I'm sorry, young man. I'm sorry for your dad, and I'm sorry for dumping this on you. You seem like a stand-up fella. I'd'a been proud to serve with you. But please don't let this foolishness hector you none. I'm past it. I'm at the end of my rope and I'm hearing things every once in a while, and the joke is, I don't even hear so good. Senescence can be liberating. Bet you didn't think I knew a word like senescence, now didja? I looked it up."

Sometime later that evening, Brett Jorgensen put the muzzle of a vintage Luger beneath his chin and blew the back of his head apart with a nine-millimeter hollow point.

I had left him alone to do that. Made my excuses, said my goodbyes, and sincerely promised to keep in touch. I had, I realized, abandoned him.

From what I could piece together later, he'd had the pistol for over half a century.

Brett Jorgensen, the man I had just spoken with, had been the son of immigrant parents from Oslo, Norway. His middle name was Eric. After the war, he had graduated with a degree in political science from the University of Missouri, courtesy of the GI Bill. Two marriages, three children. His obituary would be cursory. He had done time at a brokerage firm and retired with a decent nut. His down-home manner of speech was mostly a put-on. Nobody much cared that he had once risked his life daily to drop fire on the Axis war machine. Since 1939, he had smoked two packs of Luckies a day and never caught a smidge of cancer.

Apparently, he had made several attempts at a suicide note and burned them all in a punchbowl-sized ashtray as self-pitying drivel. Near the ashtray and butted smokes was a pewter frame with a photograph of Teresa, his first wife, his big wartime love, his girl back home. He had buried her in 1981 after pathologists dug out a tumor the size of a deflated volleyball from her insides. Against popular odds, he had fallen in love again and ultimately buried his second wife, Millicent, in the same cemetery in New Jersey.

The Luger had not come from enemy spoils. Jorgensen had fought Germany in the abstract but never glimpsed a Nazi, except maybe for one time when he swore he could make out a face, grimacing behind goggles and a leather flight helmet, firing salvos of twenty-mil cannonfire right at his noggin, ten thousand feet up, lost in foreign clouds. That had been mission number six, railyards at Bremen. Or perhaps that cruise had been Hamburg, a munitions factory. Or another kind of factory, something like that.

He never thought he would live to grow old. Yet it was all they ever talked about, stranded in Shipdham, flying missions: Marry that girl back home. Raise that family. Carve out that piece of the red, white and blue pie. Survive to accomplish it all.

He hadn't trusted a politician since Kennedy. He remembered the outrage of the world focusing on that single assassination, and recalled where he was and what he was doing when he heard the news. Today, all people knew was that Kennedy had been some kind of randy, dirty joke. Sordid exposés; muck-raking. John F. Kennedy had been a war hero, dammit all to hell. If the revisionism was true, then what had Jorgensen been fighting to preserve, way back when? He had seen that cartoon, the one captioned *We Have Met the Enemy and He is Us*, and thought, *I wish I could tell when that meeting took place, because I missed it.* His country's flag was still the same, but he had seen too many men and women, hypocrites all, standing before that flag and lying. Even his political science degree seemed a cruel trick, permitting him to perceive too much, and he stopped entertaining notions about fighting for a country in which he no longer seemed to have any rightful place.

He had loaded the pistol at half-past three a.m., alone in his den, fifteen feet away from where we had shared coffee. He knew the sounds of fighter planes in the air, ours and theirs. What he was hearing then was not a police helicopter or semis crawling up the interstate. To make sure, he pulled out his hearing aid and all that remained was a screeching noise that came from no kind of aircraft, not even a Stuka bomber.

This is guesswork, I know, but now I can see it, clear as expensive stemware: An old man rips out his hearing aid and the world falls silent. The mantel clock stops ticking, the outside world goes away, the creaks and settling lumber of his home cease their punctuation of the night, and he is left alone with the sound of the Warbird. He finishes his bourbon, snubs his Lucky, and pulls the trigger with closed and tearless eyes, hoping his sister will understand and forgive him. There is a loud noise, and the war comes pouring out of his head.

Just another old fart, self-destructing.

Except that now I can hear the sounds, too. Sounds that cannot be mistaken for anything else. Now I see strange black shapes in the night sky. Hungry, still unsatiated, coming back for more.

THE FLYING MACHINE

RAY BRADBURY

After an early start writing effective (and sometimes gruesome) short stories of horror, such as "Small Assassin" and "The Emissary," Ray Bradbury grew to be one of the giants of 20th century fantasy fiction. He wrote one classic novel, *Something Wicked This Way Comes*, and his stories set in Greentown, Illinois, rival those of Sherwood Anderson about Winesburg, Ohio. In this tale, however, Bradbury takes us to ancient China, and clearly delineates the dark side of flight in a mere 1500 words. "Here is a man who has made a certain machine," the Emperor says, "and yet asks us what he has created. He does not know himself." Ambrose Bierce's flying machine story is ironic; Bradbury's is allegorical, asking a deceptively simple question: Do we understand the implications of the things we create? Underlying this is another: Once created, can anything be *un*-created?

n the year A.D. 400, the Emperor Yuan held his throne by the Great Wall of China, and the land was green with rain, readying itself toward the harvest, at peace, the people in his dominion neither too happy nor too sad.

Early on the morning of the first day of the first week of the second month of the new year, the Emperor Yuan was sipping tea and fanning himself against a warm breeze when a servant ran across the scarlet and blue garden tiles, calling, "Oh, Emperor, Emperor, a miracle!"

"Yes," said the Emperor, "the air is sweet this morning."

"No, no, a miracle!" said the servant, bowing quickly.

"And this tea is good in my mouth, surely that is a miracle."

"No, no, Your Excellency."

"Let me guess then—the sun has risen and a new day is upon us. Or the sea is blue. That now is the finest of all miracles."

"Excellency, a man is flying!"

"What?" The Emperor stopped his fan.

"I saw him in the air, a man flying with wings. I heard a Voice call out of the sky, and when I looked up, there he was, a dragon in the heavens with a man in its mouth, a dragon of paper and bamboo, colored like the sun and the grass."

"It is early," said the Emperor, "and you have just wakened from a dream."

"It is early, but I have seen what I have seen! Come, and you will see it too."

"Sit down with me here," said the Emperor. "Drink some tea. It must be a strange thing, if it is true, to see a man fly. You must have time to think of it, even as I must have time to prepare myself for the sight."

They drank tea.

"Please," said the servant at last, "or he will be gone."

The Emperor rose thoughtfully. "Now you may show me what you have seen."

They walked into a garden, across a meadow of grass, over a small bridge, through a grove of trees, and up a tiny hill.

"There!" said the servant.

The Emperor looked into the sky.

And in the sky, laughing so high that you could hardly hear him laugh, was a man; and the man was clothed in bright papers and

THE FLYING MACHINE   RAY BRADBURY ◄

reeds to make wings and a beautiful yellow tail, and he was soaring all about like the largest bird in a universe of birds, like a new dragon in a land of ancient dragons.

The man called down to them from high in the cool winds of morning. "I fly, I fly!"

The servant waved to him. "Yes, yes!"

The Emperor Yuan did not move. Instead he looked at the Great Wall of China now taking shape out of the farthest mist in the green hills, that splendid snake of stones which writhed with majesty across the entire land. That wonderful wall which had protected them for a timeless time from enemy hordes and preserved peace for years without number. He saw the town, nestled to itself by a river and a road and a hill, beginning to waken.

"Tell me," he said to his servant, "has anyone else seen this flying man?"

"I am the only one, Excellency," said the servant, smiling at the sky, waving.

The Emperor watched the heavens another minute and then said, "Call him down to me."

"Ho, come down, come down! The Emperor wishes to see you!" called the servant, hands cupped to his shouting mouth.

The Emperor glanced in all directions while the flying man soared down the morning wind. He saw a farmer, early in his fields, watching the sky, and he noted where the farmer stood.

The flying man alit with a rustle of paper and a creak of bamboo reeds. He came proudly to the Emperor, clumsy in his rig, at last bowing before the old man.

"What have you done?" demanded the Emperor.

"I have flown in the sky, Your Excellency," replied the man.

"What have you done?" said the Emperor again.

"I have just told you!" cried the flier.

"You have told me nothing at all." The Emperor reached out a thin hand to touch the pretty paper and the birdlike keel of the apparatus. It smelled cool, of the wind.

"Is it not beautiful, Excellency?"

"Yes, too beautiful."

"It is the only one in the world!" smiled the man. "And I am the inventor."

"The only one in the world?"

"I swear it!"

"Who else knows of this?"

"No one. Not even my wife, who would think me mad with the sun. She thought I was making a kite. I rose in the night and walked to the cliffs far away. And when the morning breezes blew and the sun rose, I gathered my courage, Excellency, and leaped from the cliff. I flew! But my wife does not know of it."

"Well for her, then," said the Emperor. "Come along."

They walked back to the great house. The sun was full in the sky now, and the smell of the grass was refreshing. The Emperor, the servant, and the flier paused within the huge garden.

The Emperor clapped his hands. "Ho, guards!"

The guards came running.

"Hold this man." The guards seized the flier. "Call the executioner," said the Emperor.

"What's this!" cried the flier, bewildered. "What have I done?" He began to weep, so that the beautiful paper apparatus rustled.

"Here is the man who has made a certain machine," said the Emperor, "and yet asks us what he has created. He does not know himself. It is only necessary that he create, without knowing why he has done so, or what this thing will do."

THE FLYING MACHINE   RAY BRADBURY

The executioner came running with a sharp silver ax. He stood with his naked, large-muscled arms ready, his face covered with a serene white mask.

"One moment," said the Emperor. He turned to a nearby table upon which sat a machine that he himself had created. The Emperor took a tiny golden key from his own neck. He fitted his key to the tiny, delicate machine and wound it up. Then he set the machine going.

The machine was a garden of metal and jewels. Set in motion, the birds sangs in tiny metal trees, wolves walked through miniature forests, and tiny people ran in and out of sun and shadow, fanning themselves with miniature fans, listening to tiny emerald birds, and standing by impossibly small but tinkling fountains.

"Is it not beautiful?" said the Emperor. "If you asked me what I have done here, I could answer you well. I have made birds sing, I have made forests murmur, I have set people to walking in this woodland, enjoying the leaves and shadows and songs. That is what I have done."

"But, oh, Emperor!" pleaded the flier, on his knees, the tears pouring down his face. "I have done a similar thing! I have found beauty. I have flown on the morning wind. I have looked down on all the sleeping houses and gardens. I have smelled the sea and even seen it, beyond the hills, from my high place. And I have soared like a bird; oh, I cannot say how beautiful it is up there, in the sky, with the wind about me, the wind blowing me here like a feather, there like a fan, the way the sky smells in the morning! And how free one feels! That is beautiful, Emperor, that is beautiful too!"

"Yes," said the Emperor sadly, "I know it must be true. For I felt my heart move with you in the air and I wondered: What is it like? How does it feel? How do the distant pools look from so high? And how my houses and servants? Like ants? And how the distant towns not yet awake?"

"Then spare me!"

"But there are times," said the Emperor, more sadly still, "when one must lose a little beauty if one is to keep what little beauty one already has. I do not fear you, yourself, but I fear another man."

"What man?"

"Some other man who, seeing you, will build a thing of bright papers and bamboo like this. But the other man will have an evil face and an evil heart, and the beauty will be gone. It is this man I fear."

"Why? Why?"

"Who is to say that someday just such a man, in just such an apparatus of paper and reed, might not fly in the sky and drop huge stones upon the Great Wall of China?" said the Emperor.

No one moved or said a word.

"Off with his head," said the Emperor.

The executioner whirled his silver ax.

"Burn the kite and the inventor's body and bury their ashes together," said the Emperor.

The servants retreated to obey.

The Emperor turned to his hand-servant, who had seen the man flying. "Hold your tongue. It was all a dream, a most sorrowful and beautiful dream. And that farmer in the distant field who also saw, tell him it would pay him to consider it only a vision. If ever the word passes around, you and the farmer die within the hour."

"You are merciful, Emperor."

"No, not merciful," said the old man. Beyond the garden wall he saw the guards burning the beautiful machine of paper and reeds that smelled of the morning wind. He saw the dark smoke climb into

234

the sky. "No, only very much bewildered and afraid." He saw the guards digging a tiny pit wherein to bury the ashes. "What is the life of one man against those of a million others? I must take solace from that thought."

He took the key from its chain about his neck and once more wound up the beautiful miniature garden. He stood looking out across the land at the Great Wall, the peaceful town, the green fields, the rivers and streams. He sighed. The tiny garden whirred its hidden and delicate machinery and set itself in motion; tiny people walked in forests, tiny faces loped through sun-speckled glades in beautiful shining pelts, and among the tiny trees flew little bits of high song and bright blue and yellow color, flying, flying, flying in that small sky.

"Oh," said the Emperor, closing his eyes, "look at the birds, look at the birds!"

ZOMBIES ON A PLANE

BEV VINCENT

Your co-pilot, Bev Vincent, has published over four score short stories and a few books of non-fiction, but this is his only story thus far that involves airplanes. The title was inspired by a certain movie starring Samuel L. Jackson, but you won't find a single thirteen-lettered epithet in the following tale. Yippee ki-yay!

The guy wearing the Phish t-shirt told Myles he can fly anything, and if he's lying they're all dead. It's that simple. The guy—Barry, who looks like he's under thirty—says he trained to be a pilot "over there," where it all started, but he's skimpy with the details and it sounds like an idle boast, the kind of line someone trots out in a bar late at night to impress women. If women were still hanging out in bars, that is.

"A lot of people said the war was a bad idea. I supported it at first," Barry says with a shrug. "Never figured it would turn out like this." An understatement if Myles ever heard one.

Myles met up with this small group of survivors—nineteen in total, counting himself—in the auditorium of an inner city school, a place with strong doors and sturdy locks that provided temporary sanctuary. Once Barry announced he could get them airborne, Myles presented his sketchy plan. Just like that, he became their leader.

"We'll go someplace remote," he tells those gathered around him, apparently attracted by the aura of confidence he cultivated during thirty years in sales and middle management. "A place where we'll be safe until all this is over." No one asks what they'll do if "this" is *never* over.

Heading for the airport seems like their best option. The city's overrun, much of it on fire, and people are being killed in the streets. Those that aren't consumed by their attackers get up again a few seconds later to join the ravenous army of the undead. Myles wishes his plan didn't rely on the unproven skills of a guy who looks like he's never worked a day in his life.

But if the others want to treat him like their leader, he's going to lead, goddammit. Under his direction, they raid the cafeteria for food and the work shed for tools and weapons. Barry also claims he can start the bus parked near the loading dock if they can't find the keys. Myles doesn't ask if he learned this trick "over there," too, but Barry proves up to the task. Maybe there's hope after all.

The fuel gauge on the aging school bus registers something less than a quarter of a tank. The last working gas station in the county ran dry six days ago, and the promised supply tankers never showed up. Probably never would. They have enough gas to reach the airport—barely—but if Barry can't figure out how to get one of the planes going, they're screwed. Seventeen people follow him and Barry onto the bus like rats after the pied piper.

The bus is a piece of crap, but it runs, so long as they take it easy. Every time Barry pushes it past fifty kilometers an hour, the engine light comes on, so he eases back on the accelerator. They can't afford to break down. They haven't seen many of those abominations outside Halifax, but no place is safe. Those devils can pop up anywhere at any time, and Myles' group has only knives and axes for weapons. Like gasoline, bullets are a precious and rare commodity.

ZOMBIES ON A PLANE BEV VINCENT

Fifty kilometers per hour is fast enough, though. If there's a plane with enough jet fuel to get them wherever they decide to go, it can wait for them to lumber along the highway. When he was in field sales, before being forced into a desk job, Myles hated the long trek out to Stanfield International, but today he's happy to put distance between himself and the city.

There's no other traffic as far as the eye can see in either direction. They pass stalled vehicles on the side of the road, but when they slow to check if any occupants need help, the bus wheezes, hiccups, and threatens to stall. Barry eases it back up to fifty, the only speed at which it seems content. Myles thinks he sees a head pop up behind the steering wheel of one car after they pass, but he can't be sure, and it could just as easily be one of *them* instead of a real person.

He pushes the fleeting glimpse from his mind. It might have been a trick of the light, after all, and even if it wasn't, they can't save everyone—he's not even sure they can save themselves. Never give up, though, that's his mantra. His most rewarding sales were the ones where the other person intended to buy from a competitor and Myles won him over with persistence and passion.

He wonders what will happen after the zombies kill nearly everyone. Will they wander the planet in a futile quest for food until they fall to pieces and writhe on the ground like a child's toy with failing batteries? Seven billion zombies searching for the few remaining survivors of the human race?

Then there's the fact that even if his group escapes, they won't live forever. They'll all die eventually, and when they do, the virus—or whatever it is—will bring each of them back as one of those creatures. All they can do is forestall the inevitable and hope that somewhere people are working on a solution. *Mankind has survived for thousands of years. This scourge won't eradicate us,* Myles thinks.

Someone will find a way to cure this plague. They always do. This belief is what drives him. Otherwise he might as well set himself on fire and be done with it.

When they reach the airport, Myles tells everyone to hold on tight and orders Barry to crash the bus through the fence that separates the parking lot from the runways. The bus lurches and pulls to one side as the fence wraps itself like chain mail around the bumper and the windshield, but they make it through and onto the tarmac.

There are several Airbuses and Boeings parked at the terminal, but Barry opts for a commuter jet, big enough to hold them all but small enough that they'll be able to land it wherever they want, even on a remote airstrip designed for private aircraft. It's an Embraer ERJ-145 with a range of at least 4000 kilometers, according to Barry. Maybe a little more, since they'll be flying light. Enough to get them far from here.

But that's the catch—where should they go? Barry releases the jet's door, which drops to reveal a set of stairs. He ducks inside and emerges a few minutes later with a set of navigational maps. Myles spreads them out on a bus seat while Barry and a former taxi driver named Gilbert hotwire a fuel truck and pull it up next to the Embraer's wing.

Alfie, who in another life was a financial analyst, leans over the seat back. "How about Alaska?"

"We can't get that far. We could make Labrador or northern Ontario."

"Too cold," Terri, the former yoga instructor, says, hugging herself. Myles isn't surprised. She's complained about everything since she joined their group.

"Snow slows them down," a barber named Phil says.

ZOMBIES ON A PLANE   BEV VINCENT ▰

Even if that's true, they have to go someplace where they can survive, perhaps even grow crops. Also a place where they can stay in touch with the rest of the world, so they'll know when the situation improves. Myles doesn't share his thought process with the others, though. He doesn't want them to realize he's as uncertain as they are.

"Look," Emily yells. She's the youngest of their group, a teenager who has barely said a word since they left the city, concentrating instead on trying to reach someone—anyone—on her iPhone, clicking the keys with her thumbs.

Myles looks in the direction of her outstretched arm. Several zombies emerge from the airport terminal, shambling across the tarmac toward them, guided by some primal instinct.

Barry and Gilbert are stowing the hose on the fuel truck, so they must be finished. Myles grabs the wad of maps and dashes out onto the airstrip. "We have to go," he yells. "Now."

The two men look up and see the zombies headed their way. Gilbert gets behind the wheel of the truck and drives it clear of the wing.

"On board, everybody," Myles yells, and the others push past him without any further encouragement, backpacks full of food and supplies slung over their shoulders, weapons clutched in their hands. The zombies may be slow, but they're relentless, and they've already covered almost half the distance between the terminal and the bus. Another few minutes and they'll be on them, ripping and tearing and shredding humanity's last, best hope for survival.

Myles is the last one to board the jet, huffing and panting and trying to ignore the pain shooting down his left arm. Two men—Myles thinks their names are Matt and Chet—pull the door closed while Barry heads into the cockpit. Gilbert volunteers to be the copilot, even though he's never flown a plane before. This is it, the moment of truth. If Barry can't get this thing started and off the ground, they're through, trapped like sardines in a tin can.

Myles leans back in his seat and tries to catch his breath. When he closes his eyes and concentrates, the pain in his chest subsides. He has only three pills left in the little plastic case in his front pocket, and the odds of finding a refill range between slim and none, so he isn't about to waste one now. *This will pass. This will pass.* Another mantra.

He looks out the window. The zombies have reached the bus and are sniffing around the open door. A moment later they lurch toward the jet again. *They know we're in here,* Myles thinks. He pulls back from the small oval, not wanting to fall under their penetrating gaze.

The other passengers are pressed up against the windows, watching the slow but steady procession. The cabin door is closed, so they're safe for now. But what if the creatures take a bite out of their tires before they start taxiing? Or if they're smart enough to find a way in—through the luggage compartment, perhaps?

The thought no sooner enters his mind than he hears a thump coming from the underside of the aircraft. It reminds him of the sound of handlers opening or closing the cargo bay doors.

"We have to get going," he yells, hoping their putative pilot can hear him. He prays that Barry isn't sitting in the cockpit staring at the dizzying array of readouts, dials and switches wondering which one is the ignition key.

Another thump, this one strong enough to cause the fuselage to sway.

"I can't see them any more," Alfie says. "They're under the plane."

"How many?" Terri asks, her voice barely more than a whisper.

"Eight, maybe ten," Alfie says. "More on the way."

Myles looks out the porthole window again. A second group of zombies is crossing the tarmac, at least forty or fifty strong.

ZOMBIES ON A PLANE

BEV VINCENT

"What's taking him so long?" Myles mutters. He inhales deeply, assesses the tightness in his chest and decides that moving won't kill him. Besides, if they don't get in the air soon, a heart attack will be the least of his worries.

He lunges from his seat and heads toward the cockpit. Through the door he sees Barry flipping switches as Gilbert reads instructions from a sheet of paper on a clipboard.

"Can you fly this thing or not?" Myles demands, dreading the answer.

"Of course," Barry says. Gilbert looks up from the checklist and shrugs.

More thumps come from beneath Myles' feet. "Now would be good. Reinforcements are on the way—and not for us."

Barry nods, waves Gilbert off, and throws a few switches. "To hell with the checklist," he says. "I've got this." The small jet trembles as one engine roars to life and then the other. Myles can feel the power building, the potential energy that will get them off the ground and headed...where? In the panic and confusion, he still hasn't picked a destination. The others are expecting him to decide for them.

"Just get us out of here," he tells Barry.

Barry pushes a lever and the jet begins to roll forward. "Hope one of those things doesn't get sucked into the engine," he mutters.

The thumping beneath the plane is non-stop now. There's nothing they can do about it, so Myles refuses to worry. If one of them manages to get into the luggage compartment, they'll deal with that once they're in the air. They still have their axes and knives. Most of them are part of this group because they know how to fend those creatures off.

As the jet picks up speed, the thumping peters out, then stops. Myles tries to look behind the plane, but the view out the small window is limited. All he can see is the second group of zombies standing on the tarmac, staring at them like a group of well-wishers saying "bon voyage."

He takes a deep breath. "Everyone strapped in?" he asks. "We're about to take off." He hopes that's true, that they aren't about to hurtle off the end of the runway into the trees beyond. If that happens, the best-case scenario would be for the plane to burst into flames and consume them. That would put an end to their misery, at least.

The others take their seats and fasten their belts. Myles wonders if they should be worrying about weight distribution, but Barry didn't mention anything about that and so far he seems to know what he's doing. He picks up the navigational charts. He has to make a decision soon.

The jet jerks to the left and pauses. They've reached the head of the runway. The engines roar and the jet lunges forward, accelerating rapidly. Trees whip past the side windows. Myles leans back, waiting for the nose to rotate upward and, a few seconds later, it does just that. Gravity presses him into his seat as the small jet leaps into the air, buffeted by the invisible pressure of air beneath their wings. All the problems of the world fall away below them. If they could remain airborne forever, they'd be fine.

The jet levels off a few minutes later. Out of habit, Myles' eyes are on the seatbelt sign, but Barry probably isn't worried about the niceties of commercial air travel. He undoes his seatbelt and returns his attention to the charts. He might as well close his eyes and point at a random spot. He doesn't have any information to aid his decision. Are there places where the plague hasn't yet spread? An island, perhaps, like Iceland, which is comfortably within range? Maybe Barry can pick up something on the radio.

ZOMBIES ON A PLANE

BEV VINCENT

He has only one chance to get this right. The need to choose a destination before they burn up too much fuel paralyzes him. *Why do they expect me to make all the decisions? All I want to do is go to sleep,* he thinks. *I'm so tired.*

Weight pushes against his chest again, the same sensation he felt during takeoff. But he shouldn't be feeling the pressure of acceleration now—they're at cruising altitude, high enough to minimize the friction of the air around them and maximize their range. He tries to inhale, but his chest is constricted. Suddenly he can't catch his breath—the heaviness is so great that his lungs refuse to expand.

The others are staring out the windows, like zombies. There's nothing to see, just the clouds and the occasional glimpse of the earth below. *They're probably wondering what lies ahead,* he thinks. *What we'll find when we touch down.*

Myles no longer cares. He knows what lies ahead, and there's nothing he can do about it. Shooting pain immobilizes him. He can't reach the plastic case in his pants pocket, or make a sound to attract anyone's attention. His breath comes in short bursts. The pressure in his chest builds, like a wall of water at a dam ready to burst.

He hopes the others will be prepared when he comes after them. He wonders whether zombies feel pain. *It can't be worse than this. Can it?*

THEY SHALL NOT GROW OLD

ROALD DAHL

Although best known for his books for children—*Charlie and the Chocolate Factory* and *James and the Giant Peach*, among others—Dahl was also a talented short story writer. His most famous tale may be "Lamb to the Slaughter," in which a woman cooks the frozen leg of lamb she murdered her husband with, and then feeds it to the police. Dahl was an ace fighter pilot in World War II, surviving one crash and downing many enemy aircraft, including at least two Junkers 88s. He flew a Hawker Hurricane exactly like the one Fin flies in this story, which was originally published in *Ladies' Home Journal* near the end of the war.

The two of us sat outside the hangar on wooden boxes.

It was noon. The sun was high and the heat of the sun was like a close fire. It was hotter than hell out there by the hangar. We could feel the hot air touching the inside of our lungs when we breathed and we found it better if we almost closed our lips and breathed in quickly; it was cooler that way. The sun was upon our shoulders and upon our backs, and all the time the sweat seeped out from our skin, trickled down our necks, over our chests and down our stomachs. It collected just where our belts were tight

247

around the tops of our trousers and it filtered under the tightness of our belts where the wet was very uncomfortable and made prickly heat on the skin.

Our two Hurricanes were standing a few yards away, each with that patient, smug look which fighter planes have when the engine is not turning, and beyond them the thin black strip of the runway sloped down towards the beaches and towards the sea. The black surface of the runway and the white grassy sand on the sides of the runway shimmered and shimmered in the sun. The heat haze hung like a vapour over the aerodrome.

The Stag looked at his watch.

"He ought to be back," he said.

The two of us were on readiness, sitting there for orders to take off. The Stag moved his feet on the hot ground.

"He ought to be back," he said.

It was two and a half hours since Fin had gone and he certainly should have come back by now. I looked up into the sky and listened. There was the noise of airmen talking beside the petrol wagon and there was the faint pounding of the sea upon the beaches; but there was no sign of an aeroplane. We sat a little while longer without speaking.

"It looks as though he's had it," I said.

"Yep," said the Stag. "It looks like it."

The Stag got up and put his hands into the pockets of his khaki shorts. I got up too. We stood looking northwards into the clear sky, and we shifted our feet on the ground because of the softness of the tar and because of the heat.

"What was the name of that girl?" said the Stag without turning his head.

"Nikki," I answered.

THEY SHALL NOT GROW OLD

The Stag sat down again on his wooden box, still with his hands in his pockets and he looked down at the ground between his feet. The Stag was the oldest pilot in the squadron; he was twenty-seven. He had a mass of coarse ginger hair which he never brushed. His face was pale, even after all this time in the sun, and covered with freckles. His mouth was wide and tight closed. He was not tall but his shoulders under his khaki shirt were broad and thick like those of a wrestler. He was a quiet person.

"He'll probably be all right," he said, looking up. "And anyway, I'd like to meet the Vichy Frenchman who can get Fin."

We were in Palestine fighting the Vichy French in Syria. We were at Haifa, and three hours before the Stag, Fin and I had gone on readiness. Fin had flown off in response to an urgent call from the Navy, who had phoned up and said that there were two French destroyers moving out of Beyrouth harbour. Please go at once and see where they are going, said the Navy. Just fly up the coast and have a look and come back quickly and tell us where they are going.

So Fin had flown off in his Hurricane. The time had gone by and he had not returned. We knew that there was no longer much hope. If he hadn't been shot down, he would have run out of petrol some time ago.

I looked down and I saw his blue RAF cap which was lying on the ground where he had thrown it as he ran to his aircraft, and I saw the oil stains on top of the cap and the shabby bent peak. It was difficult now to believe that he had gone. He had been in Egypt, in Libya and in Greece. On the aerodrome and in the mess we had had him with us all of the time. He was gay and tall and full of laughter, this Fin, with black hair and a long straight nose which he used to stroke up and down with the tip of his finger. He had a way of listening to you while you were telling a story, leaning back in his chair with his face to the ceiling but with his eyes looking down on the ground, and it was only last night at supper that he had suddenly said, "You know, I wouldn't mind marrying Nikki. I think she's a good girl."

The Stag was sitting opposite him at the time, eating baked beans.

"You mean just occasionally," he said.

Nikki was in a cabaret in Haifa.

"No," said Fin. "Cabaret girls make fine wives. They are never unfaithful. There is no novelty for them in being unfaithful; that would be like going back to the old job."

The Stag had looked up from his beans. "Don't be such a bloody fool," he said. "You wouldn't really marry Nikki."

"Nikki," said Fin with great seriousness, "comes of a fine family. She is a good girl. She never uses a pillow when she sleeps. Do you know why she never uses a pillow when she sleeps?"

"No."

The others at the table were listening now. Everyone was listening to Fin talking about Nikki.

"Well, when she was very young she was engaged to be married to an officer in the French Navy. She loved him greatly. Then one day when they were sunbathing together on the beach he happened to mention to her that he never used a pillow when he slept. It was just one of those little things which people say to each other for the sake of conversation. But Nikki never forgot it. From that time onwards she began to practise sleeping without a pillow. One day the French officer was run over by a truck and killed; but although to her it was very uncomfortable, she still went on sleeping without a pillow to preserve the memory of her lover."

Fin took a mouthful of beans and chewed them slowly. "It is a sad story," he said. "It shows that she is a good girl. I think I would like to marry her."

That was what Fin had said last night at supper. Now he was gone and I wondered what little thing Nikki would do in his memory.

The sun was hot on my back and I turned instinctively in order to take the heat upon the other side of my body. As I turned, I saw Carmel and the town of Haifa. I saw the steep pale green slope of the mountain as it dropped down towards the sea, and below it I saw the town and the bright colours of the houses shining in the sun. The houses with their whitewashed walls covered the sides of Carmel and the red roofs of the houses were like a rash on the face of the mountain.

Walking slowly towards us from the grey corrugated-iron hangar, came the three men who were the next crew on readiness. They had their yellow Mae Wests slung over their shoulders and they came walking slowly towards us, holding their helmets in their hands as they came.

When they were close, the Stag said, "Fin's had it," and they said, "Yes, we know." They sat down on the wooden boxes which we had been using, and immediately the sun was upon their shoulders and upon their backs and they began to sweat. The Stag and I walked away.

The next day was a Sunday and in the morning we flew up the Lebanon valley to ground-strafe an aerodrome called Rayak. We flew past Hermon who had a hat of snow upon his head, and we came down out of the sun on to Rayak and on to the French bombers on the aerodrome and began our strafing. I remember that as we flew past, skimming low over the ground, the doors of the French bombers opened. I remember seeing a whole lot of women in white dresses running out across the aerodrome; I remember particularly their white dresses.

You see, it was a Sunday and the French pilots had asked their ladies out from Beyrouth to look over the bombers. The Vichy pilots had said, come out on Sunday morning and we will show you our aeroplanes. It was a very Vichy French thing for them to do.

So when we started shooting, they all tumbled out and began to run across the aerodrome in their white Sunday dresses.

I remember hearing Monkey's voice over the radio, saying, "Give them a chance, give them a chance," and the whole squadron wheeled around and circled the aerodrome once while the women ran over the grass in every direction. One of them stumbled and fell twice and one of them was limping and being helped by a man, but we gave them time. I remember watching the small bright flashes of a machine-gun on the ground and thinking that they should at least have stopped their shooting while we were waiting for their white-dressed women to get out of the way.

That was the day after Fin had gone. The next day the Stag and I sat once more at readiness on the wooden boxes outside the hangar. Paddy, a big fair-haired boy, had taken Fin's place and was sitting with us.

It was noon. The sun was high and the heat of the sun was like a close fire. The sweat ran down our necks, down inside our shirts, over our chests and stomachs, and we sat there waiting for the time when we would be relieved. The Stag was sewing the strap on to his helmet with a needle and cotton and telling of how he had seen Nikki the night before in Haifa and of how he had told her about Fin.

Suddenly we heard the noise of an aeroplane. The Stag stopped his talking and we all looked up. The noise was coming from the north, and it grew louder and louder as the aeroplane flew closer, and then the Stag said suddenly, "It's a Hurricane."

The next moment it was circling the aerodrome, lowering its wheels to land.

"Who is it?" said the fair-haired Paddy. "No one's gone out this morning."

Then, as it glided past us on to the runway, we saw the number on the tail of the machine, H4427, and we knew that it was Fin.

We were standing up now, watching the machine as it taxied towards us, and when it came up close and swung round for parking we saw Fin in the cockpit. He waved his hand at us, grinned and got out. We ran up and shouted at him, "Where've you been?" "Where in the hell have you been?" "Did you force-land and get away again?" "Did you find a woman in Beyrouth?" "Fin, where in the hell have you been?"

Others were coming up and crowding around him now, fitters and riggers and the men who drove the fire tender, and they all waited to hear what Fin would say. He stood there pulling off his helmet, pushing back his black hair with his hand, and he was so astonished at our behaviour that at first he merely looked at us and did not speak. Then he laughed and he said, "What in the hell's the matter? What's the matter with all of you?"

"Where have you been?" we shouted. "Where have you been for two days?"

Upon the face of Fin there was a great and enormous astonishment. He looked quickly at his watch.

"Five past twelve," he said. "I left at eleven, one hour and five minutes ago. Don't be a lot of damn fools. I must go and report quickly. The Navy will want to know that those destroyers are still in the harbour at Beyrouth."

He started to walk away; I caught his arm.

"Fin," I said quietly, "you've been away since the day before yesterday. What's the matter with you?"

He looked at me and laughed.

"I've seen you organize much better jokes than this one," he said. "It isn't so funny. It isn't a bit funny." And he walked away.

We stood there, the Stag, Paddy and I, the fitters, the riggers and the men who drove the fire-engine, watching Fin as he walked away. We looked at each other, not knowing what to say or to think, understanding nothing, knowing nothing except that Fin had been serious when he spoke and that what he said he had believed to be true. We knew this because we knew Fin, and we knew it because when one has been together as we had been together, then there is never any doubting of anything that anyone says when he is talking about his flying; there can only be a doubting of one's self. These men were doubting themselves, standing there in the sun doubting themselves, and the Stag was standing by the wing of Fin's machine peeling off with his fingers little flakes of paint which had dried up and cracked in the sun.

Someone said, "Well, I'll be buggered," and the men turned and started to walk quietly back to their jobs. The next three pilots on readiness came walking slowly towards us from the grey corrugated-iron hangar, walking slowly under the heat of the sun, and swinging their helmets in their hands as they came. The Stag, Paddy and I walked over to the pilots' mess to have a drink and lunch.

The mess was a small white wooden building with a veranda. Inside there were two rooms, one a sitting-room with armchairs and magazines and a hole in the wall through which you could buy drinks, and the other a dining-room with one long wooden table. In the sitting-room we found Fin talking to Monkey, our CO. The other pilots were sitting around listening and everybody was drinking beer. We knew that it was really a serious business in spite of the beer and the armchairs; that Monkey was doing what he had to do and doing it in the only way possible. Monkey was a rare man, tall

with a handsome face, an Italian bullet wound in his leg and a casual friendly efficiency. He never laughed out loud, he just choked and grunted deep in his throat.

Fin was saying, "You must go easy, Monkey; you must help me to stop thinking that I've gone mad."

Fin was being serious and sensible, but he was worried as hell.

"I have told you all I know," he said. "That I took off at eleven o'clock, that I climbed up high, that I flew to Beyrouth, saw the two French destroyers and came back, landing at five past twelve. I swear to you that that is all I know."

He looked around at us, at the Stag and me, at Paddy and Johnny and the half-dozen other pilots in the room, and we smiled at him and nodded to show him that we were with him, not against him, and that we believed what he said.

Monkey said, "What in the hell am I going to say to Headquarters at Jerusalem? I reported you missing. Now I've got to report your return. They'll insist on knowing where you've been."

The whole thing was getting to be too much for Fin. He was sitting upright, tapping with the fingers of his left hand on the leather arm of his chair, tapping with quick sharp taps, leaning forward, thinking, thinking, fighting to think, tapping on the arm of the chair and then he began tapping the floor with his foot as well. The Stag could stand it no longer.

"Monkey," he said, "Monkey, let's just leave it all for a bit. Let's leave it and perhaps Fin will remember something later on."

Paddy, who was sitting on the arm of the Stag's chair, said, "Yes, and meanwhile we could tell HQ that Fin had force-landed in a field in Syria, taken two days to repair his aircraft, then flown home."

Everybody was helping Fin. The pilots were all helping him. In the mind of each of us was the certain knowledge that here was something that concerned us greatly. Fin knew it, although that was all he knew, and the others knew it because one could see it upon their faces. There was a tension, a fine high-drawn tension in the room, because here for the first time was something which was neither bullets nor fire nor the coughing of an engine nor burst tyres nor blood in the cockpit nor yesterday nor today, nor even tomorrow. Monkey felt it too, and he said, "Yes, let's have another drink and leave it for a bit. I'll tell HQ that you force-landed in Syria and managed to get off again later."

We had some more beer and went in to lunch. Monkey ordered bottles of Palestine white wine with the meal to celebrate Fin's return.

After that no one mentioned the thing at all; we did not even talk about it when Fin wasn't there. But each one of us continued to think about it secretly, knowing for certain that it was something important and that it was not finished. The tension spread quickly through the squadron and it was with all the pilots.

Meanwhile the days went by and the sun shone upon the aerodrome and upon the aircraft and Fin took his place among us flying in the normal way.

Then one day, I think it was about a week later, we did another ground-strafe of Rayak aerodrome. There were six of us, with Monkey leading and Fin flying on his starboard side. We came in low over Rayak and there was plenty of light flak, and as we went in on the first run, Paddy's machine was hit. As we wheeled for the second run we saw his Hurricane wing gently over and dive straight to the ground at the edge of the aerodrome. There was a great billow of white smoke as it hit, then the flames, and as the flames spread the smoke turned from white to black and Paddy was with it. Immediately there was a crackle over the radio and I heard Fin's voice, very excited, shouting into his microphone, shouting, "I've remembered it. Hello, Monkey,

I've remembered it all," and Monkey's calm, slow reply, "OK Fin, OK; don't forget it."

We did our second run and then Monkey led us quickly away, weaving in and out of the valleys, with the bare grey-brown hills far above us on either side, and all the way home, all through the half-hour's flight, Fin never stopped shouting over the RT. First he would call to Monkey and say, "Hello, Monkey, I've remembered it, all of it; every bit of it." Then he would say, "Hello, Stag, I've remembered it, all of it; I can't forget it now." He called me and he called Johnny and he called Wishful; he called us all separately over and over again, and he was so excited that sometimes he shouted too loudly into his mike and we could not hear what he was saying.

When we landed, we dispersed our aircraft and because Fin for some reason had to park his at the far side of the aerodrome, the rest of us were in the Operations room before him.

The Ops room was beside the hangar. It was a bare place with a large table in the middle of the floor on which there was a map of the area. There was another smaller table with a couple of telephones, a few wooden chairs and benches and at one end the floor was stacked with Mae Wests, parachutes and helmets. We were standing there taking off our flying clothing and throwing it on to the floor at the end of the room when Fin arrived. He came quickly into the doorway and stopped. His black hair was standing up straight and untidy because of the way in which he had pulled off his helmet; his face was shiny with sweat and his khaki shirt was dark and wet. His mouth was open and he was breathing quickly. He looked as though he had been running. He looked like a child who had rushed downstairs into a room full of grown-ups to say that the cat has had kittens in the nursery and who does not know how to begin.

We had all heard him coming because that was what we had been waiting for. Everyone stopped what they were doing and stood still, looking at Fin.

Monkey said, "Hello, Fin," and Fin said, "Monkey, you've got to believe this because it's what happened."

Monkey was standing over by the table with the telephones; the Stag was near him, square, short, ginger-haired Stag, standing up straight, holding a Mae West in his hand looking at Fin. The others were at the far end of the room: When Fin spoke, they began to move up quietly until they were closer to him, until they reached the edge of the big map table which they touched with their hands. There they stood, looking at Fin, waiting for him to begin.

He started at once, talking quickly, then calming down and talking more slowly as he got into his story. He told everything, standing there by the door of the Ops room, with his yellow Mae West still on him and with his helmet and oxygen mask in his hand. The others stayed where they were and listened, and as I listened to him, I forgot that it was Fin speaking and that we were in the Ops room at Haifa; I forgot everything and went with him on his journey, and did not come back until he had finished.

"I was flying at about twenty thousand," he said. "I flew over Tyre and Sidon and over the Damour River and then I flew inland over the Lebanon hills, because I intended to approach Beyrouth from the east. Suddenly I flew into cloud, thick white cloud which was so thick and dense that I could see nothing except the inside of my cockpit. I couldn't understand it, because a moment before everything had been clear and blue and there had been no cloud anywhere.

"I started to lose height to get out of the cloud and I went down and down and still I was in it. I knew that I must not go too low because of the hills, but at six thousand the cloud was still around me. It was so thick that I could see nothing, not even the nose of my machine nor the wings, and the cloud condensed on the windshield and little rivers of water ran down the glass and got blown away by the slipstream. I have never seen cloud like that before. It was thick and white right up to the edges of the cockpit. I felt like a man on a magic carpet, sitting there alone in this little glass-topped cockpit, with no wings, no tail, no engine and no aeroplane.

"I knew that I must get out of this cloud, so I turned and flew west over the sea away from the mountains; then I came down low by my altimeter. I came down to five hundred feet, four hundred, three hundred, two hundred, one hundred, and the cloud was still around me. For a moment I paused. I knew that it was unsafe to go lower. Then, quite suddenly, like a gust of wind, came the feeling that there was nothing below me; no sea nor earth nor anything else and slowly, deliberately, I opened the throttle, pushed the stick hard forward and dived.

"I did not watch the altimeter; I looked straight ahead through the windshield at the whiteness of the cloud and I went on diving. I sat there pressing the stick forward keeping her in the dive, watching the vast clinging whiteness of the cloud and I never once wondered where I was going. I just went.

"I do not know how long I sat there; it may have been minutes and it may have been hours; I know only that as I sat there and kept her diving, I was certain that what was below me was neither mountains nor rivers nor earth nor sea and I was not afraid.

"Then I was blinded. It was like being half asleep in bed when someone turns on the light.

"I came out of the cloud so suddenly and so quickly that I was blinded. There was no space of time between being in it and being out of it. One moment I was in it and the whiteness was thick around me and in that same moment I was out of it and the light was so bright that I was blinded. I screwed up my eyes and held them tight closed for several seconds.

"When I opened them everything was blue, more blue than anything that I had ever seen. It was not a dark blue, nor was it a bright blue; it was a blue blue, a pure shining colour which I had never seen before and which I cannot describe. I looked around. I looked up above me and behind me. I sat up and peered below me through the glass of the cockpit and everywhere it was blue. It was bright and clear, like pleasant sunlight, but there was no sun.

"Then I saw them.

"Far ahead and above I saw a long thin line of aircraft flying across the sky. They were moving forward in a single black line, all at the same speed, all in the same direction, all close up, following one behind the other, and the line stretched across the sky as far as the eye could see. It was the way they moved ahead, the urgent way in which they pressed forward like ships sailing before a great wind, it was from this that I knew everything. I do not know why or how I knew it but I knew as I looked at them that these were the pilots and aircrews who had been killed in battle, who now, in their own aircraft were making their last flight, their last journey.

"As I flew higher and closer I could recognize the machines themselves. I saw in that long procession nearly every type there was. I saw Lancasters and Dorniers, Halifaxes and Hurricanes, Messerschmitts, Spitfires, Sterlings, Savoia 79s, Junkers 88s, Gladiators, Hampdens, Macchi 200s, Blenheims, Focke-Wulfs, Beaufighters, Swordfish and Heinkels. All these and many more I saw, and the moving line reached across the blue sky both to the one side and to the other until it faded from sight.

"I was close to them now and I began to sense that I was being sucked towards them regardless of what I wished to do. There was a wind which took hold of my machine, blew it over and tossed it about like a leaf and I was pulled and sucked as by a giant vortex towards the other aeroplanes. There was nothing I could do for I was in the vortex and in the arms of the wind. This all happened very quickly, but I remember it clearly. I felt the pull on my aircraft becoming stronger. I was whisked forward faster and faster, and then suddenly I was flying in the procession itself, moving forward with the others, at the same speed and on the same course. Ahead of me, close enough for me to see the colour of the paint on its wings, was a Swordfish, an old Fleet Air Arm Swordfish. I could see the heads and helmets of the observer and the pilot as they sat in their cockpits, the one behind the other. Ahead of the Swordfish there was a Dornier, a Flying Pencil, and beyond the Dornier there were others which I could not recognize from where I was.

"We flew on and on. I could not have turned and flown away even if I had wanted to. I do not know why, although it may have been something to do with the vortex and with the wind, but I knew that it was so. Moreover, I was not really flying my aircraft; it flew itself. There was no manoeuvring to reckon with, no speed, no height, no throttle, no stick, no nothing. Once I glanced down at my instruments and saw that they were all dead, just as they are when the machine is sitting on the ground.

"So we flew on. I had no idea how fast we went. There was no sensation of speed and, for all I know, it was a million miles an hour. Now I come to think of it, I never once during that time felt either hot or cold or hungry or thirsty; I felt none of those things. I felt no fear, because I knew nothing of which to be afraid. I felt no worry, because I could remember nothing or think of nothing about which to be worried. I felt no desire to do anything that I was not doing or to have anything that I did not have, because there was nothing that I wished to do and there was nothing that I wished to have. I felt only pleasure at being where I was, at seeing the wonderful light and the beautiful colour around me. Once I caught sight of my face in the cockpit mirror and I saw that I was smiling, smiling with my eyes and with my mouth, and when I looked away I knew that I was still smiling, simply because that was the way I felt. Once, the observer in the Swordfish ahead of me turned and waved his hand. I slid back the roof of my cockpit and waved back. I remember that even when I opened the cockpit, there was no rush of air and no rush of cold or heat, nor was there any pressure of the slipstream on my hand. Then I noticed that they were all waving at each other, like children on a rollercoaster and I turned and waved at the man in the Macchi behind me.

"But there was something happening along the line. Far up in front I could see that the aeroplanes had changed course, were wheeling around to the left and losing height. The whole procession, as it reached a certain point, was banking around and gliding downwards in a wide, sweeping circle. Instinctively I glanced down over the cockpit and there I saw spread out below me a vast green plain. It was green and smooth and beautiful; it reached to the far edges of the horizon where the blue of the sky came down and merged with the green of the plain.

"And there was the light. Over to the left, far away in the distance was a bright white light, shining bright and without any colour. It was as though the sun, but something far bigger than the sun, something without shape or form whose light was bright but not blinding, was lying on the far edge of the green plain. The light spread outwards from a centre of brilliance and it spread far up into the sky and far out over the plain. When I saw it, I could not at first look away from it. I had no desire to go towards it, into it, and almost at once the desire and the longing became so intense that several times I tried to pull my aircraft out of the line and fly straight towards it; but it was not possible and I had to fly with the rest.

"As they banked around and lost height I went with them, and we began to glide down towards the green plain below. Now that I was closer, I could see the great mass of aircraft upon the plain itself. They were everywhere, scattered over the ground like currants upon a green carpet. There were hundreds and hundreds of them, and each minute, each second almost, their numbers grew as those in front of me landed and taxied to a standstill.

"Quickly we lost height. Soon I saw that the ones just in front of me were lowering their wheels and preparing to land. The Dornier next but one to me levelled off and touched down. Then the old Swordfish. The pilot turned a little to the left out of the way of the Dornier and landed beside him. I turned to the left of the Swordfish and levelled off. I looked out of the cockpit at the ground, judging the height, and I saw the green of the ground blurred as it rushed past me and below me.

"I waited for my aircraft to sink and to touch down. It seemed to take a long time. 'Come on,' I said. 'Come on, come on.' I was only about six feet up, but she would not sink. 'Get down,' I shouted, 'please *get down.*' I began to panic. I became frightened. Suddenly I noticed that I was gaining speed. I cut all the switches, but it made no difference. The aircraft was gathering speed, going faster and faster, and I looked around and saw behind me the long procession of aircraft dropping down out of the sky and sweeping in to land. I saw the mass of machines upon the ground, scattered far across the plain and away on one side I saw the light, that shining white light which shone so brightly over the great plain and to which I longed to go. I know that had I been able to land, I would have started to run towards that light the moment I got out of my aircraft.

"And now I was flying away from it. My fear grew. As I flew faster and farther away, the fear took hold of me until soon I was fighting crazy mad, pulling at the stick, wrestling with the aeroplane, trying to turn it around, back towards the light. When I saw that it was impossible, I tried to kill myself. I really wanted to kill myself then. I tried to dive the aircraft into the ground, but it flew on straight. I tried to jump out of the cockpit, but there was a hand upon my shoulder which held me down. I tried to bang my head against the sides of the cockpit, but it made no difference and I sat there fighting with my machine and with everything until suddenly I noticed that I was in cloud. I was in the same thick white cloud as before; and I seemed to be climbing. I looked behind me, but the cloud had closed in all round. There was nothing now but this vast impenetrable whiteness. I began to feel sick and giddy. I did not care any longer what happened one way or the other, I just sat there limply, letting the machine fly on by itself.

"It seemed a long time and I am sure that I sat there for many hours. I must have gone to sleep. As I slept, I dreamed. I dreamed not of the things that I had just seen, but of the things of my ordinary life, of the squadron, of Nikki and of the aerodrome here at Haifa. I dreamed that I was sitting at readiness outside the hangar with two others, that a request came from the Navy for someone to do a quick recce over Beyrouth; and because I was first up, I jumped into my Hurricane and went off. I dreamed that I passed over Tyre and Sidon and over the Damour River, climbing up to twenty thousand as I went. Then I turned inland over the Lebanon hills, swung around and approached Beyrouth from the east. I was above the town, peering over the side of the cockpit, looking for the harbour and trying to find the two French destroyers. Soon I saw them, saw them clearly, tied up close alongside each other by the wharf, and I banked around and dived for home as fast as I could.

THEY SHALL NOT GROW OLD

"The Navy's wrong, I thought to myself as I flew back. The destroyers are still in the harbour. I looked at my watch. An hour and a half. 'I've been quick,' I said. 'They'll be pleased.' I tried to call up on the radio to give the information, but I couldn't get through.

"Then I came back here. When I landed, you all crowded around me and asked me where I had been for two days, but I could remember nothing. I did not remember anything except the flight to Beyrouth until just now, when I saw Paddy being shot down. As his machine hit the ground, I found myself saying, 'You lucky bastard. You lucky, lucky bastard,' and as I said it, I knew why I was saying it and remembered everything. That was when I shouted to you over the radio. That was when I remembered."

Fin had finished. No one had moved or said anything all the time that he had been talking. Now it was only Monkey who spoke. He shuffled his feet on the floor, turned and looked out of the window and said quietly, almost in a whisper, "Well, I'll be damned," and the rest of us went slowly back to the business of taking off our flying clothing and stacking it in the corner of the room on the floor; all except the Stag, square short Stag, who stood there watching Fin as Fin walked slowly across the room to put away his clothing.

After Fin's story, the squadron returned to normal. The tension which had been with us for over a week, disappeared. The aerodrome was a happier place in which to be. But no one ever mentioned Fin's journey. We never once spoke about it together, not even when we got drunk in the evening at the Excelsior in Haifa.

The Syrian campaign was coming to an end. Everyone could see that it must finish soon, although the Vichy people were still fighting fiercely south of Beyrouth. We were still flying. We were flying a great deal over the fleet, which was bombarding the coast, for we had the job of protecting them from the Junkers 88s which came over from Rhodes. It was on the last one of these flights over the fleet that Fin was killed.

We were flying high above the ships when the Ju-88s came over in force and there was a battle. We had only six Hurricanes in the air; there were many of the Junkers and it was a good fight. I do not remember much about what went on at the time. One never does. But I remember that it was a hectic, chasing fight, with the Junkers diving for the ships, with the ships barking at them, throwing up everything into the air so that the sky was full of white flowers which blossomed quickly and grew and blew away with the wind. I remember the German who blew up in mid-air, quickly, with just a white flash, so that where the bomber had been, there was nothing left except tiny little pieces falling slowly downwards. I remember the one that had its rear turret shot away, which flew along with the gunner hanging out of the tail by his straps, struggling to get back into the machine. I remember one, a brave one who stayed up above to fight us while the others went down to dive-bomb. I remember that we shot him up and I remember seeing him turn slowly over on to his back, pale green belly upwards like a dead fish, before finally he spun down.

And I remember Fin.

I was close to him when his aircraft caught fire. I could see the flames coming out of the nose of his machine and dancing over the engine cowling. There was black smoke coming from the exhaust of his Hurricane.

I flew up close and I called to him over the RT. "Hello, Fin," I called, "you'd better jump."

His voice came back, calm and slow. "It's not so easy."

"Jump," I shouted, "jump quickly."

I could see him sitting there under the glass roof of the cockpit. He looked towards me and shook his head.

"It's not so easy," he answered. "I'm a bit shot up. My arms are shot up and I can't undo the straps."

"Get out," I shouted. "For God's sake, get out," but he did not answer. For a moment his aircraft flew on, straight and level, then gently, like a dying eagle, it dipped a wing and dived towards the sea. I watched it as it went; I watched the thin trail of black smoke which it made across the sky, and as I watched, Fin's voice came again over the radio, clear and slow. "I'm a lucky bastard," he was saying. "A lucky, lucky bastard."

MURDER IN THE AIR

PETER TREMAYNE

No book of stories featuring airplanes would be complete without at least one locked room mystery (planes being the ultimate locked rooms), but in this case, you'll find *two* locked rooms. Welcome aboard a Global Airways jumbo jet, where the body of an unlucky traveler is about to be discovered. Luckily for the crew of Flight 162, one of the passengers is criminologist Gerry Fane, and he is very much on the case. Peter Tremayne is the pseudonym of Peter Ellis, who—in addition to being the author of nearly one hundred novels and over a hundred short stories—holds a Master's Degree in Celtic Studies. He was born in Coventry, worked as a reporter, and became a full-time writer in the mid-seventies. This one is a gem.

hief Steward Jeff Ryder noticed the worried expression on the face of Stewardess Sally Beech the moment that she entered the premier class galley of the Global Airways 747, Flight GA 162. He was surprised for a moment, as he had never seen the senior stewardess looking so perturbed before.

"What's up, Sal?" he greeted in an attempt to bring back her usual impish smile. "Is there a wolf among our first-class passengers causing you grief?"

She shook her head without a change of her pensive expression. "I think one of the passengers is locked in the toilet," she began.

Jeff Ryder's smile broadened, and he was about to make some ribald remark.

"No," she interrupted as if she had interpreted his intention. "I am serious. I think that something might have happened. He has been in there for some time, and the person with whom he was traveling asked me to check on him. I knocked on the door, but there was no reply."

Ryder suppressed a sigh. A passenger locked in the toilet was uncommon but not unknown. He had once had to extricate a two-hundred-and-fifty-pound Texan from an aircraft toilet once. It was not an experience that he wanted to remember.

"Who is this unfortunate passenger?"

"He's down on the list as Henry Kinloch Gray."

Ryder gave an audible groan. "If a toilet door is stuck on this aircraft, then it just had to be Kinloch Gray who gets stuck with it. Do you know who he is? He's the chairman of Kinloch Gray and Brodie, the big multinational media company. He has a reputation for eating company directors alive, but as for the likes of you and me, poor minnows in the great sea of life…" He rolled his eyes expressively. "Oh Lord! I'd better see to it."

With Sally trailing in his wake, Ryder made his way to the premier-class toilets. There was no one about, and he saw immediately which door was flagged as "engaged." He went to it and called softly: "Mr. Kinloch Gray? Is everything all right, sir?" He waited and then knocked respectfully on the door.

There was still no response.

Ryder glanced at Sally. "Do we know roughly how long he has been in there?"

"His traveling companion said he went to the toilet about half an hour ago."

Ryder raised an eyebrow and turned back to the door. His voice rose an octave. "Sir. Mr. Kinloch Gray, sir, we are presuming that you are in some trouble in there. I am going to break the lock. If you can, please stand back from the door."

He leaned back, raised a foot, and sent it crashing against the door by the lock. The flimsy cubicle lock dragged out its attaching screws and swung inward a fraction.

"Sir?..." Ryder pressed against the door. He had difficulty pushing it; something was causing an obstruction. With some force, he managed to open it enough to insert his head into the cubicle and then only for a moment. He withdrew it rapidly; his features had paled. He stared at Sally, not speaking for a moment or two. Finally he formed some words. "I think he has been shot," he whispered.

◥◢

THE toilets had been curtained off, and the captain of the aircraft, Moss Evans, one of Global Airways's senior pilots, had been sent for, having been told briefly what the problem was. The silver-haired, sturdily built pilot had hid his concerns as he made his way from the flight deck through the premier-class section, smiling and nodding affably to passengers. His main emotion was one of irritation, for it had been only a few moments since the aircraft had passed its midpoint, the "point of no return," halfway into its flight. Another four hours to go, and he did not like the prospect of diverting to another airport now and delaying the flight for heaven knew how long. He had an important date waiting for him.

Ryder had just finished making an announcement to premier-class passengers with the feeble excuse that there was a mechanical malfunction with the forward premier-class toilets, and directing passengers to the midsection toilets for their safety and comfort. It was typical airline jargon. Now he was waiting with Sally Beech for the captain. Evans knew Ryder well, for Jeff had been flying with him for two years. Ryder's usually good humor was clearly absent. The girl also looked extremely pale and shaken.

Evans glanced sympathetically at her; then he turned to the shattered lock of the cubicle door. "Is that the toilet?"

"It is."

Evans had to throw his weight against the door and managed to get his head inside the tiny cubicle.

The body was sprawled on the toilet seat, fully dressed. The arms dangled at the sides, the legs were splayed out, thus preventing the door from fully opening. The balance of the inert body was precarious. From the mouth to the chest was a bloody mess. Bits of torn flesh hung from the cheeks. Blood had splayed on the side walls of the cubicle. Evans felt the nausea well up in him but suppressed it.

As Ryder had warned him, it looked as though the man had been shot in the mouth. Automatically, Evans peered down, not knowing what he was looking for until he realized that he should be looking for a gun. He was surprised when he did not see one. He peered around again. The hands dangling at the sides of the body held nothing. The floor of the cubicle to which any gun must have fallen showed no sign of it. Evans frowned and withdrew. Something in the back of his mind told him that something was wrong about what he had seen, but he could not identify it.

"This is a new one for the company's air emergency manual," muttered Ryder, trying to introduce some humor into the situation.

"I see that you have moved passengers back from this section," Evans observed.

"Yes. I've moved all first-class passengers from this section, and we are rigging a curtain. I presume the next task is to get the body out of there?"

"Has his colleague been told? The person he was traveling with?"

"He has been told that there has been an accident. No details."

"Very well. I gather our man was head of some big corporation?"

"Kinloch Gray. He was Henry Kinloch Gray."

Evans pursed his lips together in a silent whistle. "So we are talking about an influence backed by megabucks, eh?"

"They don't come any richer."

"Have you checked the passenger list for a doctor? It looks like our man chose a hell of a time and place to commit suicide. But I think we'll need someone to look at him before we move anything. I'll proceed on company guidelines of a medical emergency routine. We'll notify head office."

Ryder nodded an affirmative. "I've already had Sally check if there are any doctors on board. As luck would have it, we have two in the premier class. They are both seated together. C one and C two."

"Right. Get Sally to bring one of them up here. Oh, and where is Mr. Gray's colleague?"

"Seated B three. His name is Frank Tilley, and I understand he is Gray's personal secretary."

"I'm afraid he'll have to stand by to do a formal identification. We'll have to play this strictly by the company rule book," he added again as if seeking reassurance.

Sally Beech approached the two men in seats C one and two. They were both of the same age, mid-forties; one was casually dressed with a mop of fiery red hair, looking very unlike the stereotype idea of a doctor. The other appeared neat and more smartly attired. She halted and bent down.

"Doctor Fane?" It was the first of the two names she had memorized. The smartly dressed man glanced up with a smile of inquiry.

"I'm Gerry Fane. What can I do for you, miss?"

"Doctor, I am afraid that we have a medical emergency with one of the passengers. The captain extends his compliments and would greatly appreciate it if you could come and take a look."

It sounded like a well-repeated formula. In fact, it was a formula out of the company manual. Sally did not know how else to deliver it but in the deadpan way that she had been trained to do.

The man grimaced wryly. "I am afraid my doctorate is a Ph.D. in criminology, miss. Not much help to you. I think that you will need my companion, Hector Ross. He's a medical doctor."

The girl glanced apologetically to the red-haired man in the next seat and was glad to see that he was already rising so that she did not have to repeat the same formula.

"Don't worry, lass. I'll have a look, but I am not carrying my medical bag. I'm actually a pathologist returning from a conference, you understand? Not a GP."

"We have some emergency equipment on board, Doctor, but I don't think that you will need it."

Ross glanced at her with a puzzled frown, but she had turned and was leading the way along the aisle.

HECTOR Ross backed out of the toilet cubicle and faced Captain Evans and Jeff Ryder. He glanced at his watch. "I am pronouncing death at thirteen-fifteen hours, Captain."

Evans stirred uneasily. "And the cause?"

Ross bit his lip. "I'd rather have the body brought out where I can make a full inspection." He hesitated again. "Before I do, I would like my colleague, Doctor Fane, to have a look. Doctor Fane is a criminal psychologist, and I have great respect for his opinion."

Evans stared at the doctor, trying to read some deeper meaning behind his words. "How would a criminal psychologist be able to help in this matter unless—?"

"I'd appreciate it all the same, Captain. If he could just take a look?" Ross's tone rose persuasively.

Moments later, Gerry Fane was backing out of the same toilet door and regarding his traveling companion with some seriousness.

"Curious," he observed. The word was slowly and deliberately uttered.

"Well?" demanded Captain Evans impatiently. "What is that supposed to mean?"

Fane shrugged eloquently in the confined space. "It means that it's not well at all, Captain," he said with just a hint of sarcasm. "I think we should extricate the body so that my colleague here can ascertain the cause of death, and then we can determine how this man came by that death."

Evans sniffed, trying to hide his annoyance. "I have my company's chairman waiting on the radio, Doctor. I would like to be able to tell him something more positive. I think you will understand when I tell you that he happens to know Mr. Gray. Same golf club or something."

Fane was ironic. "*Knew*, I'm afraid. Past tense. Well, you can tell your chairman that it rather looks as though his golfing partner was murdered."

Evans was clearly shocked. "That's impossible. It must have been suicide."

Hector Ross cleared his throat and looked uneasily at his friend. "Should you go that far, old laddie?" he muttered. "After all—"

Fane was unperturbed and interrupted him in a calm decisive tone. "Whatever the precise method of inflicting the fatal wound, I would think that you would agree that it looked pretty instantaneous. The front parts of the head, below the eyes and nose, are almost blown away. Nasty. Looks like a gunshot wound to the mouth."

Evans had recovered the power of speech. Now, as he thought about it, he realized the very point that had been puzzling him. It was his turn to be sarcastic.

"If a gun was fired in there, even one of low caliber with a body to cushion the impact of the bullet, it would have had the force to pierce the side of the aircraft, causing decompression. Do you know what a bullet can do if it pierces an aircraft fuselage at thirty-six thousand feet?"

"I did not say for certain that it was a gun." Fane maintained his gentle smile. "I said that it looked like a gunshot."

"Even if it were a gunshot that killed him, why could it not have been a suicide?" the chief steward interrupted. "He was in a locked toilet, for Chrissake! It was locked on the inside."

Fane eyed him indulgently. "I made a point about the instantaneous nature of the wound. I have never known a corpse to be able to get up and hide a weapon after a successful suicide bid. The man is sprawled in there dead, with a nasty mortal wound that was pretty instantaneous in causing death...and no sign of any weapon. Curious, isn't it?"

Evans stared at him in disbelief. "That's ridiculous..." There was no conviction in his voice. "You can't be serious? The weapon must be hidden behind the door or somewhere."

Fane did not bother to reply.

"But," Evans plunged on desperately, knowing that Fane had articulated the very thing that had been worrying him: the missing weapon. "Are you saying that Gray was killed and then placed in the toilet?"

Fane shook his head firmly. "More complicated than that, I'm afraid. Judging from the blood splayed out from the wound, staining the walls of the cubicle, he was already in the toilet when he was killed and with the door locked from the inside, according to your chief steward there."

Jeff Ryder stirred uncomfortably. "The door was locked from the inside," he confirmed defensively.

"Then how—?" began Evans.

"That is something we must figure out. Captain, I have no wish to usurp any authority, but if I might make a suggestion?..."

Evans did not answer. He was still contemplating the impossibility of what Fane had suggested.

"Captain?..."

"Yes? Sorry, what did you say?"

"If I might make a suggestion? While Hector does a preliminary examination to see if we can discover the cause of death, will you allow me to question Gray's colleague, and then we might discover the why as well as the how?"

Evans lips compressed thoughtfully. "I don't feel that I have the authority. I'll have to speak to the chairman of the company."

"As soon as possible, Captain. We'll wait here," Fane replied calmly. "While we are waiting, Doctor Ross and I will get the body out of the toilet."

HARDLY any time passed before Moss Evans returned. By then Ross and Fane had been able to remove the body of Kinloch Gray from the toilet and lay it in the area between the bulkhead and front row of the premier-class seats.

Evans cleared his throat awkwardly. "Doctor Fane. My chairman has given you full permission to act as you see fit in this matter...until the aircraft lands, that is. Then, of course, you must hand over matters to the local police authority." He shrugged and added, as if some explanation were necessary: "It seems that my chairman has heard of your reputation as a...a criminologist? He is happy to leave the matter in the hands of Doctor Ross and yourself."

Fane inclined his head gravely. "Will you be diverting the aircraft?" he asked.

"My chairman has ordered us to continue to our point of destination, Doctor. As the man is dead, it is pointless to divert in search of any medical assistance."

"Good. Then we have over three hours to sort this out. Can your steward provide me with a corner where I can speak with Gray's colleague? She tells me that he is his personal secretary. I want a word without causing alarm to other passengers."

"See to it, Jeff," Captain Evans ordered the chief steward. He glanced at Fane. "Don't they say that murder is usually committed by someone known to the victim? Doesn't that make this secretary the prime suspect? Or will every passenger have to be checked out to see if they have some connection with Gray?"

Fane smiled broadly. "I often find that you cannot make general rules in these matters."

Evans shrugged. "If it helps, I could put out an address asking all passengers to return to their seats and put on their seat belts. I could say that we are expecting turbulence. It would save any curious souls from trying to enter this area."

"That would be most helpful, Captain," Hector Ross assured him, looking up from his position by the corpse.

Evans hesitated a moment more. "I am going back to the flight deck. Keep me informed of any developments."

Within a few minutes of Evans's leaving, there came the sound of raised voices. Fane looked up to see the stewardess, Sally Beech, trying her best to prevent a young man from moving forward toward them.

The young man was very determined. "I tell you that I work for him." His voice was raised in protest. "I have a right to be here."

"You are in tourist class, sir. You have no right to be here in premier class."

"If something has happened to Mr. Gray, then I demand..."

Fane moved quickly forward. The young man was tall, well spoken, and, Fane observed, his handsome looks were aided by a tan that came from a lamp rather than the sun. He was immaculately dressed. He sported a gold signet ring on his slim tapering fingers. Fane had a habit of noticing hands. He felt much could be told about a person from their hands and how they kept their fingernails. This young man obviously paid a great deal of attention to maintaining well-manicured nails.

"Is this Mr. Gray's secretary?" he asked Sally.

The stewardess shook her head. "No, Doctor. This is a passenger from tourist class. He claims to have worked for Mr. Gray."

"And your name is?" queried Fane swiftly, his sharp eyes on the young man's handsome features.

"Oscar Elgee. I was Mr. Gray's manservant." The young man spoke with a modulated voice that clearly betrayed his prep school background. "Check with Frank Tilley, in premier class. He is Mr. Gray's personal secretary. He will tell you who I am."

Fane smiled encouragingly at Sally Beech. "Would you do that for me, Miss Beech, and also tell Mr. Tilley that I would like to see him here when convenient?" When she hurried away, Fane turned back to the new arrival. "Now, Mr. Elgee, how did you hear that there had been an...an accident?"

"I heard one of the stewardesses mentioning it to another back in the tourist class," Elgee said. "If Mr. Gray has been hurt—"

"Mr. Gray is dead."

Oscar Elgee stared at him for a moment. "A heart attack?"

"Not exactly. Since you are here, you might formally identify your late employer. We need an identification for Doctor Ross's record."

He stood aside and allowed the young man to move forward to where the body had been laid out ready for Ross's examination. Ross moved to allow the young man to examine the face. Elgee halted over the body and gazed down for a moment.

"*Terra es, terram ibis*," he muttered. Then his face broke in anguish. "How could this have happened? Why is there blood on his face? What sort of accident happened here?"

"That's exactly what we are attempting to find out," Ross told him. "I take it that you formally identify this man as Henry Kinloch Gray?"

The young man nodded briefly, turning away. Fane halted him beyond the curtained area.

"How long did you work for him, Mr. Elgee?"

"Two years."

"What exactly was your job with him?"

"I was his manservant. Everything. Chauffeur, butler, cook, valet, handyman. His *factotum*."

"And he took you on his trips abroad?"

"Of course."

"But I see he was a stickler for the social order, eh?" smiled Fane.

The young man flushed. "I don't understand."

"You are traveling tourist class."

"It would not be seemly for a manservant to travel first class."

"Quite so. Yet, judging from your reactions to his death, you felt a deep attachment to your employer?"

The young man's chin raised defiantly, and a color came to his cheeks. "Mr. Gray was an exemplary employer. A tough businessman, true. But he was a fair man. We never had a cross word. He was a good man to work for. A great man."

"I see. And you looked after him? Took care of his domestic needs. If I recall the newspaper stories, Harry Gray was always described as an eligible bachelor."

Fane saw a subtle change of expression on the young man's face. "If he had been married, then he would hardly have needed my services, would he? I did everything for him. Even repairing his stereo system or his refrigerator. No, he was not married."

"Just so." Fane smiled, glancing again at Elgee's hands. "Repairing a stereo system requires a delicate touch. Unusual for a handyman to be able to do that sort of thing."

"My hobby is model making. Working models." There was a boastful note in his voice.

"I see. Tell me, as you would be in the best position to know, did your employer have any enemies?"

The young man actually winced. "A businessman like Harry Gray is surrounded by enemies." He looked up and saw Sally Beech ushering a bespectacled man into the compartment. "Some enemies work with him and pretended to be his confidants," he added with a sharp note. He paused and frowned as the thought seemed to occur to him. "Are you saying that his death was...was suspicious?"

Fane noticed, with approval, that Sally had motioned her new charge to sit down and did not come forward to interrupt him. He turned to the young man.

"That we will have to find out. Now, Mr. Elgee, perhaps you would return to your seat? We will keep you informed of the situation."

The young man turned and went out, hardly bothering to acknowledge the new arrival, who, in turn, seemed to drop his eyes to avoid contact with the personable young man. There was obviously no love lost between the manservant and secretary.

Leaving Hector Ross to continue his examination with the aid of the aircraft's emergency medical kit, Fane went up to where the newcomer had been seated.

Sally Beech, waiting with her charge, gave him a nervous smile. "This is Mr. Francis Tilley. He was traveling with Mr. Gray."

Frank Tilley was a thin and very unattractive man in his mid-thirties. His skin was pale, and his jaw showed a permanent blue shadow, which no amount of shaving would erase. He wore thick, horn-rimmed spectacles that seemed totally unsuited to his features. His hair was thin and receding, and there was a nervous twitch at the corner of his mouth.

Fane motioned the stewardess to stand near the door to prevent any other person entering the premier-class compartment, and he turned to Tilley.

"He's dead, eh?" Tilley's voice was almost a falsetto. He giggled nervously. "Well, I suppose it had to happen sometime, even to the so-called great and the good."

Fane frowned at the tone in the man's voice. "Are you saying that Mr. Gray was ill?" he asked.

Tilley raised a hand and let it fall as if he were about to make a point and changed his mind. Fane automatically registered the shaky hand, the thick trembling fingers, stained with nicotine, and the raggedly cut nails.

"He was prone to asthma, that's all. Purely a stress condition."

"Then, why?..."

Tilley looked slightly embarrassed. "I suppose that I was being flippant."

"You do not seem unduly upset by the death of your colleague?"

Tilley sniffed disparagingly. "Colleague? He was my boss. He never let anyone who worked for him forget that he was the boss, that he was the arbiter of their fate in the company. Whether the man was a doorman or his senior vice-president, Harry Kinloch Gray was a 'hands on' chairman, and his word was law. If he took a dislike to you, then you were out immediately, no matter how long you had worked with the company. He was the archetypical Victorian, self-made businessman. Autocratic, mean, and spiteful. He should have had no place in the modern business world."

Fane sat back and listened to the bitterness in the man's voice. "Was he the sort of man who had several enemies then?"

Tilley actually smiled at the humor. "He was the sort of man who did not have any friends."

"How long have you worked for him?"

"'I've spent ten years in the company. I was his personal secretary for the last five of those years."

"Rather a long time to spend with someone you don't like? You must have been doing something right for him not to take a dislike to you and sack you, if, as you say, that was his usual method of dealing with employees."

Tilley shifted uneasily at Fane's sarcasm. "What has this to do with Mr. Gray's death?" he suddenly countered.

"Just seeking some background."

"What happened?" Tilley went on. "I presume that he had some sort of heart attack?"

"Did he have a heart condition then?"

"Not so far as I know. He was overweight and ate like a pig. With all the stress he carried about with him, it wouldn't surprise me to know that that was the cause."

"Was this journey a particularly stressful one?"

"No more than usual. We were on our way to a meeting of the executives of the American subsidiaries."

"And so far as you noticed, Mr. Gray was behaving in his usual manner?"

Tilley actually giggled. It was an unpleasant noise. "He was his usual belligerent, bullying, and arrogant self. He had half a dozen people to sack and he wanted to do it in a public ritual to give them the maximum embarrassment. It gave him a buzz. And then..." Tilley hesitated and a thoughtful look came into his eyes. "He was going through some documents from his case. One of them seemed to fascinate him, and after a moment or two he started to have one of his attacks—"

"Attacks? I thought you said that he had no health problems?"

"What I actually said was that he was prone to asthma. He did have these stress-related asthma attacks."

"So you did. So he began to have an asthma attack? Did he take anything for it?"

"He carried one of those inhalers around with him. He was vain and thought that none of us knew about it. The great chairman did not like to confess to a physical weakness. So when he had his attacks, he would disappear to treat himself with the inhaler. It was so obvious. Ironic that he had a favorite quotation from Ecclesiastes, 'Vanitas vanitatum, omnis vanitas'!"

"So are you saying that he went to the toilet to take his inhaler?"

"That is what I am saying. After a considerable time had passed, I did get concerned."

"Concerned?" Fane smiled thinly. "From what you are telling me, concern about your boss's well-being was not exactly a priority with you."

Tilley lips thinned in a sneer. "Personal feelings do not enter into it. I was not like Elgee, who puts his all into the job. I was being paid to do a job, and I did it with integrity and with professionalism. I did not have to like Harry Gray. It was no concern of mine what Harry Gray did or did not do outside of the job he paid me to do. It did not concern me who his lover was nor who his mortal enemies were."

"Very well. So he went to the toilet and did not come back?"

"As I said, after a while, I called the stewardess and she went to check on him. That was no more nor less the concern of my position as his secretary."

"Wait there a moment, Mr. Tilley."

Fane moved to where Sally Beech was standing, still pale and slightly nervous, and said quietly: "Do you think you could go to Mr. Gray's seat and find his attaché case? I'd like you to bring it here."

She returned in a short while with a small brown leather case.

Fane took it to show to Frank Tilley. "Do you identify this as Gray's case?"

The man nodded reluctantly. "I don't think you should do that," he protested as Fane snapped open the clasps.

"Why not?"

"Confidential company property."

"I think an investigation into a possible homicide will override that objection."

Frank Tilley was surprised. "Homicide?...But that means...murder. No one said anything about murder."

Fane was too busy shifting through the papers to respond. He pulled out a sheet and showed it to Tilley. "Was this what he was looking at just before he began to have breathing difficulties?"

"I don't know. Perhaps. It was a piece of paper like it—that's all I can say."

The sheet was a tear sheet from a computer printout. It had two short sentences on it:

You will die before this aircraft lands. *Memento, "homo," quia pulvis es et in pulverem revertis.*

Fane sat back with a casual smile. He held out the paper to the secretary. "You are a Latin scholar, Mr. Tilley. How would you translate the phrase given here?"

Tilley frowned. "What makes you say that I am a Latin scholar?"

"A few moments ago you trotted out a Latin phrase. I presumed that you knew its meaning."

"My Latin is almost nonexistent. Mr. Gray was fond of Latin tags and phrases, so I tried to keep up by memorizing some of those he used frequently."

"I see. So you don't know what this one means?"

Tilley looked at the printed note. He shook his head. "*Memento* means 'remember,' doesn't it?"

"Have you ever heard the phrase *memento mori?* That would be a more popular version of what is written here."

Tilley shook his head. "Remember something, I suppose?"

"Why do you think the Latin word for 'man' has quotation marks around it?"

"I don't know what it means. I do not know Latin."

"What this says roughly is, 'Remember, man, that you are dust and to dust you will return.' It was obviously written on a computer, a word processor. Do you recognize the type?"

Tilley shook his head. "It could be any one of hundreds of company standards. I hope you are not implying that I wrote Mr. Gray a death threat?"

"How would this have made its way into his attaché case?" Fane said, ignoring the comment.

"I presume someone put it there."

"Who would have such access to it?"

"I suppose that you are still accusing me? I hated him. But not so that I would cut my own throat. He was a bastard, but he was the goose who laid the golden egg. There was no point in being rid of him."

"Just so," muttered Fane thoughtfully. His eye caught sight of a notepad in the case, and he flicked through its pages while Frank Tilley sat looking on in discomfort. Fane found a list of initials with the head, "immediate dismissal" and that day's date.

"A list of half a dozen people that he was about to sack?" Fane observed.

"I told you that he was going to enjoy a public purge of his executives and mentioned some names to me."

"The list contains only initials and starts with O. T. E." He glanced at Tilley with a raised eyebrow. "Oscar Elgee?"

"Hardly," Tilley replied with a patronizing smile. "It means Otis T. Elliott, the general manager of our U.S. database subsidiary."

"I see. Let's see if we can identify the others."

He ran through the other initials to which Tilley added names. The next four were also executives of Gray's companies. The last initials were written as Ft.

"F. T. is underscored three times with the words 'no payoff!' written against it. Who's F. T.?"

"You know that F. T. are my initials," Tilley observed quietly. His features were white and suddenly very grave. "I swear that he never said anything to me about sacking me when we discussed those he had on his list. He never mentioned it."

"Well, was there anyone else in the company that the initials F. T. could apply to?"

Tilley frowned, trying to recall, but finally shook his head and gave a resigned shrug. "No. It could only be me. The bastard! He never told me what he was planning. Some nice little public humiliation, I suppose."

Hector Ross emerged from the curtained section and motioned Fane to join him. "I think I can tell you how it was done," he announced with satisfaction.

Fane grinned at his friend. "So can I. Tell me if I am wrong. Gray went into the toilet to use his inhaler to relieve an attack of asthma. He placed the inhaler in his mouth, depressed it in the normal way, and…" He ended with a shrug.

Ross looked shocked. "How did you—?" He glanced over Fane's shoulder to where Frank Tilley was still sitting, twitching nervously. "Did he confess that he set it up?"

Fane shook his head. "No. But was I right?"

"It is a good hypothesis but needs a laboratory to confirm it. I found tiny particles of aluminium in the mouth, and some plastic. Something certainly exploded with force, sending a tiny steel projectile into the back roof of the mouth with such force that it entered the brain and death was instantaneous, as you initially surmised. Whatever had triggered the projectile disintegrated with the force. Hence there were only small fragments embedded in his mouth and cheeks. There were some when I searched carefully, around the cubicle. Diabolical."

"This was arranged by someone who knew that friend Gray had a weakness and banked on it. Gray didn't like to take his inhaler in public and would find a quiet corner. The plan worked out very well and nearly presented an impossible crime, an almost insolvable crime. Initially it appeared that the victim had been shot in the mouth in a locked toilet."

Hector Ross smiled indulgently at his colleague. "You imply that you already have the solution?"

"Oh yes. Remember the song that we used to sing at school?

> Life is real! Life is earnest!
> And the grave is not its goal;
> Dust thou art, to dust returnest,
> Was not spoken of the soul."

Hector Ross nodded. "It's many a day since I last sang that, laddie. Something by Longfellow, wasn't it?"

Fane grinned. "It was, indeed. Based on some lines from the Book of Genesis—'terra es, terram ibis'—'dust thou art, to dust thou shalt return.' Get Captain Evans here, please." He made the request to the Chief Steward, Jeff Ryder, who had been waiting attendance on Ross. When he had departed, Fane glanced back to his friend. "There is something to be said for Latin scholarship."

"I don't follow, laddie."

"Our murderer was too fond of the Latin in-jokes he shared with his boss."

"You mean his secretary?" He glanced at Frank Tilley.

"Tilley claims that he couldn't even translate *memento mori*."

"Remember death?"

Fane regarded his friend in disapproval. "It actually means 'remember to die' and a *memento mori* is usually applied to a human skull or some other object that reminds us of our mortality."

Captain Evans arrived and looked from Fane to Ross in expectation. "Well, what news?"

"To save any unpleasant scene on the aircraft, Captain, I suggest you radio ahead and have the police waiting to arrest one of your passengers on a charge of murder. No need to make any move until we land. The man can't go far."

"Which man?" demanded Evans, his face grim.

"He is listed as Oscar Elgee in the tourist class."

"How could he—"

"Simple. Elgee was not only Gray's manservant but I think you'll find, from the broad hints Mr. Tilley gave me, that he was also his lover. Elgee seems to confirm it by a death note with a Latin phrase in which he emphasized the word *homo*, meaning 'man,' but, we also know it was often used as a slang term in my generation for 'homosexual.'"

"How would you know that Elgee was capable of understanding puns in Latin?" asked Ross.

"The moment he saw Gray's body, young Elgee muttered the very words. *Terra es, terram ibis*—dust you are, to dust you will return."

"A quarrel between lovers?" asked Ross. "Love to hatred turned—and all that, as Billy Shakespeare succinctly put it?"

Fane nodded. "Gray was giving Elgee the push, both as lover and employee, and so Elgee decided to end his lover's career in midflight, so to speak. There is a note in his attaché case that Elgee was to be sacked immediately without compensation."

Tilley, who had been sitting quietly, shook his head vehemently.

"No there isn't," he interrupted. "We went through the list. I told you that the initials O. T. E. referred to Otis Elliott. I had faxed that dismissal through before we boarded the plane."

Fane smiled softly. "'You have forgotten F. T.'"

"But that's my—"

"You didn't share your boss's passion for Latin tags, did you? It was the F. T. that confused me. I should have trusted that a person with

Gray's reputation would not have written F followed by a lower case t if he meant two initials F. T. I missed the point. It was not your initials at all, Mr. Tilley. It was *Ft* meant as an abbreviation. Specifically, *fac*, from *facere*: 'to do'; and *tatum*: 'all things.' *Factotum*. And who was Gray's factotum?"

There was a silence.

"I think we will find that this murder was planned for a week or two at least. Once I began to realize what the mechanism was that killed Gray, all I had to do was look for the person capable of devising that mechanism as well as having motive and opportunity. Hold out your hands, Mr. Tilley."

Reluctantly the secretary did so.

"You can't seriously see those hands constructing a delicate mechanism, can you?" Fane said. "No, Elgee, the model maker and handyman, doctored one of Gray's inhalers so that when it was depressed it would explode with an impact into the mouth, shooting a needle into the brain. Simple but effective. He knew that Gray did not like to be seen using the inhaler in public. The rest was left to chance, and it was a good chance. It almost turned out to be the ultimate impossible crime. It might have worked, had not our victim and his murderer been too fond of their Latin in-jokes."

THE TURBULENCE EXPERT

BY STEPHEN KING

Stephen King—that's me—has written at least two stories about airplane frights. One is called "The Langoliers," and was made into a TV miniseries. The other, "The Night Flier," is about a vampire who flies a private airplane instead of turning into a bat. That story was turned into a feature film. This one is brand new.

1

Craig Dixon was sitting in the living room of a Four Seasons junior suite, eating expensive room service chow and watching a movie on pay-per-view, when the phone rang. His previously calm heartbeat lost its mojo and sped up. Dixon was unattached, the perfect definition of a rolling stone, and only one person knew he was here in this fancy hotel across from Boston Common. He considered not answering, but the man he thought of as the facilitator would only call back, and keep calling until he answered. If he refused to answer, there would be consequences.

This isn't hell, he thought, the accommodations are too nice, but it's purgatory. And no prospect of retirement for a long time.

He muted the TV and picked up the phone. He didn't say hello. What he said was, "This isn't fair. I just got in from Seattle two days ago. I'm still in recovery mode."

"Understood and terribly sorry, but this has come up and you're the only one available." *Sorry* came out *thorry*.

The facilitator had the soothing, put-you-to-sleep voice of an FM disc jockey, spoiled only by an occasional light lisp. Dixon had never seen him, but imagined him as tall and slim, with blue eyes and an ageless, unlined face. In reality he was probably fat, bald, and swarthy, but Dixon felt confident his mental picture would never change, because he never expected to see the facilitator. He had known a number of turbulence experts over his years with the firm—if it *was* a firm—and none of them had ever seen the man. Certainly none of the experts who worked for him were unlined; even the ones in their twenties and thirties looked middle-aged. It wasn't the job, where there were sometimes late hours but no heavy lifting. It was what made them capable of *doing* the job.

"Tell me," Dixon said.

"Allied Airlines Flight 19. Nonstop Boston to Sarasota. Leaves at 8:10 tonight. You've just got time to make it."

"There's *nobody* else?" Dixon realized he was nearly bleating. "I'm tired, man. *Tired*. That run from Seattle was a bitch."

"Your usual seat," the facilitator said, pronouncing the last word *theat*. Then he hung up.

Dixon looked at swordfish he no longer wanted. He looked at the Kate Winslet movie he would never finish, at least not in Boston. He thought—and not for the first time!—of just packing up and renting a car and driving north, first to New Hampshire, then to Maine, then across the border to Canada. But they would catch him. This he knew. And the rumors of what happened to experts who ran included electrocution, evisceration, even being boiled alive. Dixon did not believe these rumors…except he sort of did.

He began to pack. There wasn't much. Turbulence experts traveled light.

2

HIS ticket was waiting for him at the counter. As always, his assignment placed him in coach, just aft of the starboard wing, in the middle seat. How that particular one could always be available was another mystery, like who the facilitator was, where he was calling from, or what sort of an organization he worked for. Like the ticket, the seat was just always waiting for him.

Dixon placed his bag in the overhead bin and looked at tonight's fellow travelers: a businessman with red eyes and gin breath on the aisle, a middle-aged lady who looked like a librarian next to the window. The businessman grunted something unintelligible when Dixon sidled past him with a murmured apology. The guy was reading a paperback charmingly titled *Don't Let the Boss F**k With You.* The elderly librarian type was looking out the window at the various pieces of equipment that were trundling back and forth, as if they were the most fascinating things she had ever seen. There was knitting in her lap. Looked to Dixon like a sweater.

She turned, gave him a smile, and held out her hand. "Hello, I'm Mary Worth. Just like the comic strip chick."

Dixon didn't know any comic strip chick named Mary Worth, but he shook her hand. "Craig Dixon. Nice to meet you."

The businessman grunted and turned a page in his book.

"I'm so looking forward to this," Mary Worth said. "I haven't had a real vacation in twelve years. I'm sharing the rent of a little place on Siesta Key with a couple of chums."

"Chums," the businessman grunted. The grunt seemed to be his default position.

"Yes!" Mary Worth twinkled. "We have it for three weeks. We've never actually met, but they are true chums. We're all widows. We met in a chat room on the Internet. It's so wonderful, the Internet. There was nothing like it when I was young."

"Pedophiles think it's wonderful, too," said the businessman, and turned another page.

Ms. Worth's smile faltered, then came on strong. "It's very nice to meet you, Mr. Dixon. Are you traveling for business or pleasure?"

"Business," he said.

The speakers went ding-dong. "Good evening, ladies and gentlemen, this is Captain Stuart speaking. You'll see that we are pulling away from the gate and beginning our taxi to Runway 3, where we're third in line for take-off. We estimate a two hour and forty-minute flight down to SRQ, which should put you in the land of palms and sandy beaches just before eleven o'clock. Skies are clear, and we're anticipating a smooth ride all the way. Now I'd like you to fasten your seatbelts, put away any tray tables you may have lowered—"

"Like we had anything to put *on* them," the businessman grunted.

"—and secure any personal possessions you may have been using. Thank you for flying Allied tonight. We know you have many choices."

"My ass," the businessman grunted.

"Read your book," Dixon said. The businessman shot him a startled look.

Dixon's heart was already beating hard, his stomach was clenched, his throat dry with anticipation. He could tell himself it was going to be all right, it was *always* all right, but that didn't help. He dreaded the depths that would soon open beneath him.

Allied 19 took off at 8:13 PM, just three minutes behind schedule.

3

SOMEWHERE over Maryland, a flight attendant pushed a drinks-and-snacks cart down the aisle. The businessman put his book aside, waiting impatiently for her to reach him. When she did, he took a can of Schweppes tonic, two little bottles of gin, and a bag of Fritos. His MasterCard didn't work when she ran it and he gave her his American Express card, glaring at her as if the failure of his first offering were her fault. Dixon wondered if the MasterCard was maxed out and Mr. Businessman saved the Amex for break-glass-in-case-of-emergency situations. It could be, his haircut was bad and he looked frayed around the edges. It didn't matter one way or the other to Dixon, but it was something to think about besides the constant low terror. The anticipation. They were cruising at 34,000 feet, and that was a long way down.

Mary Worth asked for some wine, and poured it neatly into her little plastic glass.

"You're not having anything, Mr. Dixon?"

"No. I don't eat or drink on airplanes."

Mr. Businessman grunted. He was already through his first gin and tonic, and starting on the second.

"You're a white-knuckle flier, aren't you?" Mary Worth asked sympathetically.

"Yes." There was no reason not to admit it. "I'm afraid I am."

"Needless," Mr. Businessman said. Refreshed by his drink, he was speaking actual words instead of grunting them out. "Safest form of travel ever invented. Hasn't been a commercial aircraft crash in donkey's years. At least not in this country."

"I don't mind," Mary Worth said. She had gotten outside half of her small bottle, and there were now roses in her cheeks. Her eyes sparkled. "I haven't been on a plane since my husband died five years ago, but the two of us used to fly together three or four times a year. I feel close to God up here."

As if on cue, a baby began to cry.

"If heaven is this crowded and noisy," Mr. Businessman observed, surveying the 737's coach cabin, "I don't want to go."

"They say it's fifty times safer than automobile travel," Mary Worth said. "Perhaps even more. It might have been a hundred."

"Try five hundred times safer." Mr. Businessman leaned past Dixon and held out a hand to Mary Worth. Gin had worked its temporary miracle, turning him from surly to affable. "Frank Freeman."

She shook with him, smiling. Craig Dixon sat between them, upright and miserable, but when Freeman offered his hand, he shook it.

"Wow," Freeman said, and actually laughed. "You *are* scared. But you know what they say, cold hands, warm heart." He tossed off the rest of his drink.

Dixon's own credit cards always worked. He stayed in first class hotels and ate first class meals. Sometimes he spent the night with a good-looking woman, paying extra to indulge in quirks that were not, at least judging by certain Internet sites Mary Worth probably did not visit, very quirky. He had friends among the other turbulence experts. They were a close-knit crew, bound together not only by their occupation but by their fears. The pay was far better than good, there were all those fringe benefits...but at times like this, none of that seemed to matter. At times like this there was only the fear.

It would be all right. It was *always* all right.

But at times like this, waiting for the shitstorm to happen, that thought had no power. Which was, of course, what made him good at the job.

34,000 feet. A long way down.

4

CAT, for clear air turbulence.

Dixon knew it well, but was never prepared for it. Allied 19 was somewhere above South Carolina when it hit this time. A woman was making her way to the toilet at the back of the plane. A young man wearing jeans and a fashionable scruff of beard was bending to talk to a woman in an aisle seat on the port side, the two of them laughing about something. Mary Worth was dozing with her head resting against the window. Frank Freeman was halfway through his third drink and his second bag of Fritos.

The jetliner suddenly canted to port and took a gigantic upward leap, thudding and creaking. The woman on her way to the can was flung across the last row of portside seats. The beard-scruffy young man flew into the overhead bulkhead, getting one hand up just in time to cushion the blow. Several people who had unfastened their seatbelts rose above their seatbacks as if levitated. There were screams.

The plane dropped like a stone down a well, thudded, then rose again, now tilting the other way. Freeman had been caught raising his drink, and he was now wearing it.

"Fuck!" he cried.

Dixon shut his eyes and waited to die. He knew he would not if he did his job, it was what he was there for, but it was always the same. He always waited to die.

The ding-dong went. "This is the captain speaking." Stuart's voice was—as some sportscaster had popularized the phrase—as cool as the other side of the pillow. "We seem to have run into some unexpected turbulence, folks. I have—"

The plane took another horrifying lift, sixty tons of metal thrown upward like a piece of charred paper in a chimney, then dropped with another of those creaking thuds. There were more screams. The bathroom-bound lady, who had picked herself up, staggered backward, flailed her arms, and fell into the seats on the starboard side. Mr. Beard Scruff was crouched in the aisle, holding onto the armrests on either side. Two or three of the overhead compartments popped open and luggage tumbled out.

"Fuck!" Freeman said again.

"So I have turned on the seatbelt sign," the pilot resumed. "Sorry about this, folks, we'll be back to smooth air—"

The plane began to rise and fall in a series of stuttering jerks, like a stone skipping across a pond.

"—in just a few, so hang in there."

The plane dropped, then booted upward again. The carry-on bags in the aisle rose and fell and tumbled. Dixon's eyes were crammed shut. His heart was now running so fast that there seemed to be no individual beats. His mouth was sour with adrenaline. He felt a hand creep into his and opened his eyes. Mary Worth was staring at him, her face parchment pale. Her eyes were huge.

"Are we going to die, Mr. Dixon?"

Yes, he thought. This time we are going to die.

"No," he said. "We're perfectly all r—"

The plane seemed to run into a brick wall, throwing them forward against their belts, and then heeled over to port: thirty degrees, forty, fifty. Just when Dixon was sure it was going to roll over completely, it righted itself. Dixon heard people yelling. The baby was wailing. A man was shouting, "It's okay, Julie, it's normal, it's okay!"

Dixon shut his eyes again and let the terror fully take him. It was horrible; it was the only way.

He saw them rolling back, this time not stopping but going all the way over. He saw the big jet losing its place in the thermodynamic mystery that had formerly held it up. He saw the nose rising fast, then slowing, then heeling downward like a rollercoaster car starting its first plunge. He saw the plane starting its ultimate dive, the passengers who had been unbelted now plastered to the ceiling, the yellow oxygen masks doing a final frantic tarantella in the air. He saw the baby flying forward and disappearing into business class, still wailing. He saw the plane hit, the nose and the first-class compartment nothing but a crumpled steel bouquet blooming its way into coach, sprouting wires and plastic and severed limbs even as fire exploded and Dixon drew a final breath that ignited his lungs like paper bags.

All of this in mere seconds—perhaps thirty, no more than forty—and so real it might actually have been happening. Then, after taking one more antic bounce, the plane steadied and Dixon opened his eyes. Mary Worth was staring at him, her eyes welling with tears.

"I thought we were going to die," she said. "I *knew* we were going to die. I *saw* it."

So did I, Dixon thought.

"Nonsense!" Although he sounded hearty, Freeman looked decidedly green around the gills. "These planes, the way they're built, they could fly into a hurricane. They—"

A liquid belch halted his disquisition. Freeman plucked an airsick bag from the pocket in the back of the seat ahead of him, opened it, and put it over his mouth. There followed a noise that reminded

Dixon of a small but efficient coffee grinder. It stopped, then started again.

The ding-dong went. "Sorry about that, folks," Captain Stuart said. Still sounding as cool as the other side of the pillow. "It happens from time to time, a little weather phenomenon we call clear air turbulence. The good news is I've called it in, and other aircraft will be vectored around that particular trouble spot. The better news is that we'll be landing in forty minutes, and I guarantee you a smooth ride the rest of the way."

Mary Worth laughed shakily. "That's what he said before."

Frank Freeman was folding down the top of his airsick bag, doing it like a man with experience. "That wasn't fear, don't get that idea, just plain old motion sickness. I can't even ride in the back seat of a car without getting nauseated."

"I'm going to take the train back to Boston," Mary Worth said. "No more of *that*, thank you very much."

Dixon watched as the flight attendants first made sure that the unbelted passengers were all right, then cleared the aisle of spilled luggage. The cabin was filled with chatter and nervous laughter. Dixon watched and listened, his heartbeat returning to normal. He was tired. He was always tired after saving an aircraft filled with passengers.

The rest of the flight was routine, just as the captain had promised.

5

MARY Worth hurried after her luggage, which would be arriving on Carousel 2 downstairs. Dixon, with just the one small bag, stopped for a drink in Dewar's Clubhouse. He invited Mr. Businessman to join him, but Freeman shook his head. "I puked up tomorrow's hangover somewhere over the South Carolina-Georgia line, and I think I'll quit while I'm ahead. Good luck with your business in Sarasota, Mr. Dixon."

Dixon, whose business had actually been transacted over that same South Carolina-Georgia line, nodded and thanked him. A text came in while he was finishing his whiskey and soda. It was from the facilitator, just two words: **Good job.**

He took the escalator down. A man in a dark suit and a chauffer's cap was standing at the bottom, holding a sign with his name on it. "That's me," Dixon said. "Where am I booked?"

"The Ritz-Carlton," the driver said. "Very nice."

Of course it was, and there would be a fine suite waiting for him, probably with a bay view. There would also be a rental car waiting for him in the hotel garage, should he care to visit a nearby beach or any of the local attractions. In the room he would find an envelope containing a list of various female services, which he had no interest in taking advantage of tonight. All he wanted tonight was sleep.

When he and the driver stepped out onto the curb, he saw Mary Worth standing by herself, looking a bit forlorn. She had a suitcase on either side of her (matching, of course, and tartan). Her phone was in her hand.

"Ms. Worth," Dixon said.

She looked up and smiled. "Hello, Mr. Dixon. We survived, didn't we?"

"We did. Is someone meeting you? One of your chums?"

"Mrs. Yeager—Claudette—was supposed to, but her car won't start. I was just about to call an Uber."

He thought of what she'd said when the turbulence—forty seconds that had seemed like four hours—finally eased: I *knew* we were going to die. I *saw* it.

"You don't need to do that. We can take you to Siesta Key." He pointed to the stretch limo a little way down the curb, then turned to the driver. "Can't we?"

"Of course, sir."

She looked at him doubtfully. "Are you sure? It's awfully late."

"My pleasure," he said. "Let's do this thing."

6

"OOH, this is nice," Mary Worth said, settling into the leather seat and stretching out her legs. "Whatever your business is, you must be very successful at it, Mr. Dixon."

"Call me Craig. You're Mary, I'm Craig. We should be on a first-name basis, because I want to talk to you." He pressed a button and the privacy glass went up.

Mary Worth watched this rather nervously, then turned to Dixon. "You aren't going to, as they say, put a move on me, are you?"

He smiled. "No, you're safe with me. You said you were going to take the train back. Did you mean that?"

"Absolutely. Do you remember me saying that flying made me feel close to God?"

"Yes."

"I didn't feel close to God while we were being tossed like a salad six or seven miles up in the air. Not at all. I only felt close to death."

"Would you *ever* fly again?"

She considered the question carefully, watching the palms and car dealerships and fast food franchises slide past as they rolled south on the Tamiami Trail. "I suppose I would. If someone was on his deathbed, say, and I had to get there fast. Only I don't know who that someone would be, because I don't have much in the way of family.

My husband and I never had children, my parents are dead, and that just leaves a few cousins that I rarely email with, let alone see."

Better and better, Dixon thought.

"But you'd be afraid."

"Yes." She looked back at him, eyes wide. "I really thought we were going to die. In the sky, if the plane came apart. On the ground if it didn't. Nothing left of us but charred little pieces."

"Let me spin you a hypothetical," Dixon said. "Don't laugh, think about it seriously."

"Okay..."

"Suppose there's an organization whose job is to keep airplanes safe."

"There is," Mary Worth said, smiling. "I believe it's called the FAA."

"Suppose it was an organization that could predict which airplanes would encounter severe and unexpected turbulence on any given flight."

Mary Worth clapped her hands in soft applause, smiling more widely now. Into it. "No doubt staffed by precognates! Those are people who—"

"People who see the future," Dixon said. And wasn't that possible? Likely, even? How else could the facilitator get his information? "But let's say their ability to see the future is limited to this one thing."

"Why would that be? Why wouldn't they be able to predict elections...football scores...the Kentucky Derby..."

"I don't know," Dixon said, thinking, maybe they can. Maybe they can predict all sorts of things, these hypothetical precognates in some hypothetical room. Maybe they do. He didn't care. "Now let's go a little further. Let's suppose Mr. Freeman was wrong, and turbulence of the sort we encountered tonight is a lot more serious than anyone—including the airlines—believes, or is willing to admit. Suppose that kind of turbulence can only be survived if there is at least one talented, terrified passenger on each plane that encounters it." He paused. "And suppose that on tonight's flight, that talented and terrified passenger was me."

She pealed merry laughter and only sobered when she saw he wasn't joining her.

"What about the planes that fly into hurricanes, Craig? I believe Mr. Freeman mentioned something about planes like that just before he needed to use the airsick bag. *Those* planes survive turbulence that's probably even worse than what we experienced this evening."

"But the people flying them know what they're getting into," Dixon said. "They are mentally prepared. The same is true of many commercial flights. The pilot will come on even before takeoff and say, 'Folks, I'm sorry, but we're in for a bit of a rough ride tonight, so keep those seatbelts buckled.'"

"I get it," she said. "Mentally prepared passengers could use...I guess you'd call it united telepathic strength to hold the plane up. It's only *unexpected* turbulence that would call for the presence of someone already prepared. A terrified...mmm...I don't know what you'd call a person like that."

"A turbulence expert," Dixon said quietly. "That's what you'd call them. What you'd call me."

"You're not serious."

"I am. And I'm sure you're thinking right now that you're riding with a man suffering a serious delusion, and you can't wait to get out of this car. But in fact it *is* my job. I'm well paid—"

"By whom?"

"I don't know. A man calls. I and the other turbulence experts—there are a few dozen of us—call him the facilitator. Sometimes weeks go by between calls. Once it was two months. This time it was only two days. I came to Boston from Seattle, and over the Rockies…" He wiped a hand over his mouth, not wanting to remember but remembering, anyway. "Let's just say it was bad. There were a couple of broken arms."

They turned. Dixon looked out the window and saw a sign reading SIESTA KEY, 2 MILES.

"If this was true," she said, "why in God's name would you do it?"

"The pay is good. The amenities are good. I like to travel…or did, anyway; after five or ten years, all places start to look the same. But mostly…" He leaned forward and took one of her hands in both of his. He thought she might pull away, but she didn't. She was looking at him, fascinated. "It's saving lives. There were over a hundred and fifty people on that airplane tonight. Only the airlines don't just call them people, they call them *souls*, and that's the right way to put it. I saved a hundred and fifty souls tonight. And since I've been doing this job I've saved thousands." He shook his head. "No, tens of thousands."

"But you're terrified each time. I saw you tonight, Craig. You were in mortal terror. So was I. Unlike Mr. Freeman, who only threw up because he was airsick."

"Mr. Freeman could never do this job," Dixon said. "You can't do the job unless you're convinced each time the turbulence starts that you are going to die. You're convinced of that even though you know you're the one making sure that won't happen."

The driver spoke quietly from the intercom. "Five minutes, Mr. Dixon."

"I must say this has been a fascinating discussion," Mary Worth said. "May I ask how you got this unique job in the first place?"

"I was recruited," Dixon said. "As I am recruiting you, right now."

She smiled, but this time she didn't laugh. "All right, I'll play. Suppose you did recruit me? What would you get out of it? A bonus?"

"Yes," Dixon said. Two years of his future service forgiven, that was the bonus. Two years closer to retirement. He had told the truth about having altruistic motives—saving lives, saving *souls*—but he had also told the truth about how travel eventually became wearying. The same was true of saving souls, when the price of doing so was endless moments of terror high above the earth.

Should he tell her that once you were in, you couldn't get out? That it was your basic deal with the devil? He should. But he wouldn't.

They swung into the circular drive of a beachfront condo. Two ladies—undoubtedly Mary Worth's chums—were waiting there.

"Would you give me your phone number?" Dixon asked.

"What? So you can call me? Or so you can pass it on to your boss? Your facilitator?"

"That," Dixon said. "Nice as it's been, Mary, you and I will probably never see each other again."

She paused, thinking. The chums-in-waiting were almost dancing with excitement. Then Mary opened her purse and took out a card. She handed it to Dixon. "This is my cell number. You can also reach me at the Boston Public Library."

Dixon laughed. "I *knew* you were a librarian."

"Everyone does," she said. "It's a bit boring, but it pays the rent, as they say." She opened the door. The chums squealed like rock show groupies when they saw her.

"There are more exciting occupations," Dixon said.

She looked at him gravely. "There's a big difference between temporary excitement and mortal fear, Craig. As I think we both know."

He couldn't argue with her on that score, but got out and helped the driver with her bags while Mary Worth hugged two of the widows she had met in an Internet chat room.

7

MARY was back in Boston, and had almost forgotten Craig Dixon, when her phone rang one night. Her caller was a man with a very slight lisp. They talked for quite awhile.

The following day, Mary Worth was on Jetway Flight 694, non-stop from Boston to Dallas, sitting in coach, just aft of the starboard wing. Middle seat. She refused anything to eat or drink.

The turbulence struck over Oklahoma.

FALLING

JAMES DICKEY

Before you groan, shake your head, and say "I don't read poetry," you should remember that James Dickey wasn't just a poet; he also wrote the classic novel of survival, *Deliverance*, and the less-read *To the White Sea*, about a B-29 gunner forced to parachute into enemy territory. Dickey wrote from experience; he was a combat flier in both World War II and Korea. "Falling" has the same narrative drive and gorgeously controlled language as *Deliverance*. Once read, it is impossible to forget. An interesting footnote: Dickey admitted in a self-interview that the poem's central conceit was unlikely (a woman falling from that height would be flash-frozen, he said), but in fact it did happen: in 1972, stewardess Vesna Vulovic fell 33,000 feet in a DC-9 that was probably blown apart by a bomb…and she survived. The text quoted at the beginning of the poem comes from an October 29, 1962, NYT article about an incident involving an Allegheny Airlines twin-engine Convair 440 approaching Bradley Field in Windsor Locks, Connecticut. Two other stewardesses had been killed in similar incidents the previous month.

> *A 29-year-old stewardess fell … to her death tonight when she was swept through an emergency door that suddenly sprang open … The body … was found … three hours after the accident.*
>
> —New York Times

The states when they black out and lie there rolling   when they turn
To something transcontinental   move by   drawing moonlight out of the grea
One-sided stone hung off the starboard wingtip   some sleeper next to
An engine is groaning for coffee   and there is faintly coming in
Somewhere the vast beast-whistle of space. In the galley with its racks
Of trays   she rummages for a blanket   and moves in her slim tailored
Uniform to pin it over the cry at the top of the door. As though she blew

The door down with a silent blast from her lungs   frozen   she is black
Out finding herself   with the plane nowhere and her body taken by the throa
The undying cry of the void   falling   living   beginning to be something
That no one has ever been and lived through   screaming without enough air
Still neat   lipsticked   stockinged   girdled by regulation   her hat
Still on   her arms and legs in no world   and yet spaced also strangely
With utter placid rightness on thin air   taking her time   she holds it
In many places   and now, still thousands of feet from her death she seems
To slow   she develops interest   she turns in her maneuverable body

To watch it. She is hung high up in the overwhelming middle of things in her
Self   in low body-whistling wrapped intensely   in all her dark dance-weight
Coming down from a marvellous leap   with the delaying, dumfounding ease
Of a dream of being drawn   like endless moonlight to the harvest soil
Of a central state of one's country   with a great gradual warmth coming
Over her   floating   finding more and more breath in what she has been using
For breath   as the levels become more human   seeing clouds placed honestly
Below her left and right   riding slowly toward them   she clasps it all
To her and can hang her hands and feet in it in peculiar ways   and
Her eyes opened wide by wind, can open her mouth as wide   wider and suck
All the heat from the cornfields   can go down on her back with a feeling
Of stupendous pillows stacked under her   and can turn   turn as to someone
In bed   smile, understood in darkness   can go away   slant   slide

FALLING

JAMES DICKEY

Off tumbling   into the emblem of a bird with its wings half-spread
Or whirl madly on herself   in endless gymnastics in the growing warmth
Of wheatfields rising toward the harvest moon.   There is time to live
In superhuman health   seeing mortal unreachable lights far down seeing
An ultimate highway with one late priceless car probing it   arriving
In a square town   and off her starboard arm the glitter of water catches
The moon by its one shaken side   scaled, roaming silver   My God it is good
And evil   lying in one after another of all the positions for love
Making   dancing   sleeping   and now cloud wisps at her no
Raincoat   no matter   all small towns brokenly brighter from inside
Cloud   she walks over them like rain   bursts out to behold a Greyhound
Bus shooting light through its sides   it is the signal to go straight
Down like a glorious diver   then feet first   her skirt stripped beautifully
Up   her face in fear-scented cloths   her legs deliriously bare   then
Arms out   she slow-rolls over   steadies out   waits for something great
To take control of her   trembles near feathers   planes head-down
The quick movements of bird-necks turning her head   gold eyes the insight-
eyesight of owls blazing into the hencoops   a taste for chicken overwhelming
Her   the long-range vision of hawks enlarging all human lights of cars
Freight trains   looped bridges   enlarging the moon racing slowly
Through all the curves of a river   all the darks of the midwest blazing
From above. A rabbit in a bush turns white   the smothering chickens
Huddle   for over them there is still time for something to live
With the streaming half-idea of a long stoop   a hurtling   a fall
That is controlled   that plummets as it wills   turns gravity
Into a new condition, showing its other side like a moon   shining
New Powers   there is still time to live on a breath made of nothing
But the whole night   time for her to remember to arrange her skirt
Like a diagram of a bat   tightly it guides her   she has this flying-skin
Made of garments   and there are also those sky-divers on tv   sailing
In sunlight   smiling under their goggles   swapping batons back and forth

➤ FLIGHT OR FRIGHT

And He who jumped without a chute and was handed one by a diving
Buddy. She looks for her grinning companion   white teeth   nowhere
She is screaming   singing hymns   her thin human wings spread out
From her neat shoulders   the air beast-crooning to her   warbling
And she can no longer behold the huge partial form of the world   now
She is watching her country lose its evoked master shape   watching it lose
And gain   get back its houses and peoples   watching it bring up
Its local lights   single homes   lamps on barn roofs   if she fell
Into water she might live   like a diver   cleaving   perfect   plunge

Into another   heavy silver   unbreathable   slowing   saving
Element: there is water   there is time to perfect all the fine
Points of diving   feet together   toes pointed   hands shaped right
To insert her into water like a needle   to come out healthily dripping
And be handed a Coca-Cola   there they are   there are the waters
Of life   the moon packed and coiled in a reservoir   so let me begin
To plane across the night air of Kansas   opening my eyes superhumanly
Bright   to the damned moon   opening the natural wings of my jacket
By Don Loper   moving like a hunting owl toward the glitter of water
One cannot just fall   just tumble screaming all that time   one must use
It she is now through with all   through all   clouds   damp   hair
Straightened   the last wisp of fog pulled apart on her face like wool revealing
New darks   new progressions of headlights along dirt roads from chaos

And night   a gradual warming   a new-made, inevitable world of one's own
Country   a great stone of light in its waiting waters   hold   hold out
For water: who knows when what correct young woman must take up her body
And fly   and head for the moon-crazed inner eye of midwest imprisoned
Water   stored up for her for years   the arms of her jacket slipping
Air up her sleeves to go   all over her? What final things can be said
Of one who starts her sheerly in her body in the high middle of night

314

FALLING

Air   to track down water like a rabbit where it lies like life itself
Off to the right in Kansas? She goes toward   the blazing-bare lake
Her skirts neat   her hands and face warmed more and more by the air
Rising from pastures of beans   and under her   under chenille bedspreads
The farm girls are feeling the goddess in them struggle and rise brooding
On the scratch-shining posts of the bed   dreaming of female signs
Of the moon   male blood like iron   of what is really said by the moan
Of airliners passing over them at dead of midwest midnight   passing
Over brush fires   burning out in silence on little hills   and will wake
To see the woman they should be   struggling on the rooftree to become
Stars: for her the ground is closer   water is nearer   she passes
It   then banks   turns   her sleeves fluttering differently as she rolls
Out to face the east, where the sun shall come up from wheatfields she must
Do something with water   fly to it   fall in it   drink it   rise
From it   but there is none left upon earth   the clouds have drunk it back
The plants have sucked it down   there are standing toward her only
The common fields of death   she comes back from flying to falling
Returns to a powerful cry   the silent scream with which she blew down
The coupled door of the airliner   nearly   nearly losing hold
Of what she has done   remembers   remembers the shape at the heart
Of cloud   fashionably swirling   remembers she still has time to die
Beyond explanation. Let her now take off her hat in summer air the contour
Of cornfields   and have enough time to kick off her one remaining
Shoe with the toes   of the other foot   to unhook her stockings
With calm fingers, noting how fatally easy it is to undress in midair
Near death   when the body will assume without effort any position
Except the one that will sustain it   enable it to rise   live
Not die   nine farms hover close   widen   eight of them separate, leaving
One in the middle   then the fields of that farm do the same   there is no
Way to back off   from her chosen ground   but she sheds the jacket
With its silver sad impotent wings   sheds the bat's guiding tailpiece

Of her skirt   the lightning-charged clinging of her blouse   the intimate
Inner flying-garment of her slip in which she rides like the holy ghost
Of a virgin   sheds the long windsocks of her stockings   absurd
Brassiere   then feels the girdle required by regulations squirming
Off her: no longer monobuttocked   she feels the girdle flutter   shake
In her hand   and float   upward   her clothes rising off her ascending
Into cloud   and fights away from her head the last sharp dangerous shoe
Like a dumb bird   and now will drop in   SOON   now will drop

In like this   the greatest thing that ever came to Kansas   down from all
Heights   all levels of American breath   layered in the lungs from the frail
Chill of space to the loam where extinction slumbers in corn tassels thickly
And breathes like rich farmers counting: will come along them after
Her last superhuman act   the last slow careful passing of her hands
All over her unharmed body   desired by every sleeper in his dream:
Boys finding for the first time their loins filled with heart's blood
Widowed farmers whose hands float under light covers to find themselves
Arisen at sunrise   the splendid position of blood unearthly drawn
Toward clouds   all feel something   pass over them as she passes
Her palms over *her* long legs   *her* small breasts   and deeply between
Her thighs   her hair shot loose from all pins   streaming in the wind
Of her body   let her come openly   trying at the last second to land
On her back   This is it   THIS

                   All those who find her impressed
In the soft loam   gone down   driven well into the image of her body
The furrows for miles flowing in upon her where she lies very deep
In her mortal outline   in the earth as it is in cloud   can tell nothing
But that she is there   inexplicable   unquestionable   and remember
That something broke in them as well   and began to live and die more
When they walked for no reason into their fields to where the whole earth
Caught her   interrupted her maiden flight   told her how to lie she cannot

FALLING

Turn   go away   cannot move   cannot slide off it and assume another
Position   no sky-diver with any grin could save her   hold her in his arms
Plummet with her   unfold above her his wedding silks   she can no longer
Mark the rain with whirling women that take the place of a dead wife
Or the goddess in Norwegian farm girls   or all the back-breaking whores
Of Wichita. All the known air above her is not giving up quite one
Breath   it is all gone   and yet not dead   not anywhere else
Quite   lying still in the field on her back   sensing the smells
Of incessant growth try to lift her   a little sight left in the corner
Of one eye   fading   seeing something wave   lies believing
That she could have made it   at the best part of her brief goddess
State   to water   gone in headfirst   come out smiling   invulnerable
Girl in a bathing-suit ad   but she is lying like a sunbather at the last
Of moonlight   half-buried in her impact on the earth   not far
From a railroad trestle   a water tank   she could see if she could
Raise her head from her modest hole   with her clothes beginning
To come down all over Kansas   into bushes   on the dewy sixth green
Of a golf course   one shoe   her girdle coming down fantastically
On a clothesline, where it belongs   her blouse on a lightning rod:

Lies in the fields   in *this* field   on her broken back as though on
A cloud she cannot drop through   while farmers sleepwalk without
Their women from houses   a walk like falling toward the far waters
Of life   in moonlight   toward the dreamed eternal meaning of their farms
Toward the flowering of the harvest in their hands   that tragic cost
Feels herself go   go toward   go outward   breathes at last fully
Not   and tries   less   once   tries   tries   AH, GOD—

AFTERWORD: AN IMPORTANT MESSAGE FROM THE FLIGHT DECK

BEV VINCENT

Although flying can be scary business, I've flown all over the planet and I can't recall having any scary experiences. While working on this anthology, I spent over 24 hours in the air, and it was all smooth sailing (except I couldn't stop thinking about all the things that *might* go wrong, thanks to the stories assembled here). An aborted landing in foggy weather is about as bad as it's been for me in my entire air travel history.

However, the first time I was ever on an airplane was in March 1978, on a high school spring break trip to Greece. Our Alitalia 747 landed at Leonardo da Vinci airport in Rome the day after the Red Brigade kidnapped former Prime Minister Aldo Moro. The airport was on high alert, filled with soldiers carrying Uzis. Tensions were elevated. When one of my classmates went through a metal detector with his camera slung around his neck, he almost caused an international incident.

Another time, while returning to the US from a business trip in Japan, my coworkers and I learned that the police officers accused of beating Rodney King had been acquitted, setting off riots in Los Angeles. We were supposed to change planes there, but we decided to reroute through San Francisco after hearing unconfirmed reports that people were shooting at airplanes landing at LAX.

In July 2017, prior to the Bangor premiere of *The Dark Tower*, Richard Chizmar and I were in a restaurant (across the street from Bangor International Airport, as it happens), when Stephen King approached us. "I just had an idea," he said. "An anthology of stories about all the bad things that can happen to you when you're flying. I'll introduce the stories." To Rich, he said, "You'll publish it." He suggested a couple of titles, then said, "Someone needs to help me find some more stories." He turned to me. "That'll be your job."

So that's how this anthology came about. I immediately thought of "Nightmare at 20,000 Feet," and I set to work looking for other examples of scary stories involving airplanes and flying.

There are plenty of novels and films with terrifying scenes on airplanes. The gold standard is probably Arthur Hailey's 1968 *Airport*. Hailey started his writing career with a script called *Flight into Danger*, which sounds like a good title for a companion to this anthology. I read the novelization, *Runway Zero-Eight*, as a teenager, and I'm pretty sure I also saw the TV movie based on it: *Terror in the Sky*. *Airport* was, of course, turned into a feature film that spawned several sequels during the 1970s, but the hilarious spoof version *Airplane!* is probably better known these days. And who could forget *Air Force One* or *Red Eye* or *Snakes on a Plane*? There's no end to the kinds of disasters that can occur when you're trapped in a metal tube five, six, seven miles up.

The sub-sub-genre of scary airplane short stories is much smaller, I discovered. Finding good candidates took some work. Google search results were dominated by real-life scary anecdotes about bad flying experiences—much like the one Steve relates in his introduction. I also sought suggestions from the "hive mind," posting a query on Facebook, and was rewarded with recommendations for stories I might not have found otherwise. So, hive mind, many thanks!

While searching for candidates for the anthology, I was working on an essay for the Poetry Foundation and was reminded that one of Steve's favorite poems—one he has mentioned several times in interviews—was inspired by the real-life story from 1962 of a flight attendant who was sucked out of an airplane when the emergency door popped open in flight. I asked Steve if he thought we should include it in the anthology. As it turns out, he was thinking the same thing. Thus we end with a real-life tragedy made poetic and metaphorical.

I was also reading Joe Hill's novella collection *Strange Weather* while working on this book. "Aloft" starts with an anxiety-ridden young man trying to impress a woman by going sky-diving. Nerves kick in and he tries to back out at the last minute, but he ends up having to bail out of the airplane when the engine quits. We were pleased when Joe told us that he had another—deeply disturbing— idea for a story that was a perfect match for this book. Owen King brought Tom Bissell's story to our attention.

Does this anthology cover everything that could possibly go wrong on a flight? Absolutely not. As I was writing these notes, an alert went out about a passenger who went through Chicago O'Hare while suffering from the measles. So even if your flight makes it safely to its final destination, what other passengers might you carry home with you? The possibilities are endless. Something to ponder as you pack for your next journey.

Although this anthology consists mostly of previously published stories, I suspect there aren't many people out there who've read more than a few of them before. I had only read four of the works before I embarked on this project. It has been a voyage of discovery and we are very pleased with the group of stories we've assembled.

Once we had a table of contents mostly established, I revisited "The Langoliers" for the first time in years, and found unexpected connections between this novella—novel, really; it's as long as this entire anthology—and the other tales we had selected. This is the Stephen King universe, of course, where a character named Jenkins in "The Langoliers" muses that "you can't appear in the Texas Book Depository on November 22, 1963, and put a stop to the Kennedy assassination," so such things shouldn't come as a surprise, but it did.

Consider, if you will, the self-same Jenkins, an author who at first describes their plight in terms of "locked room" mysteries. One of the stories I'd found was a locked room mystery that takes place in an airplane bathroom. Jenkins goes on to say that a real-world mystery wasn't an appropriate metaphor for their predicament. "It's too bad Larry Niven or John Varley isn't on board," he says. Wait...what? Who did we have in the table of contents other than Mr. Varley himself?

And then there's the discussion about how to get back through the wormhole. Their solution could conceivably "turn the plane into Jonestown," Jenkins says. And where does the cargo in the opening story in our anthology come from? Uh-huh. Jonestown.

It was like it was all meant to be. I love that kind of discovered symmetry.

✈

AND now, an important message from your two pilots up here in the cockpit. We would like to thank the passengers on this flight. We know you had a choice of carriers and we appreciate very much that you agreed to join us on board. We hope the flight wasn't *too* rough, but you knew what you were getting into when you boarded this plane. Maybe one of the passengers helped smooth out the rough patches. These things happen, you know.

Thank you, too, to their travel agents, who arranged their journeys and made sure they arrived at their final and intended destinations. Many of the passengers in these stories were not quite so fortunate.

We would also like to thank our cabin crew, led by Chuck Verrill, for helping ensure a smooth trip for everyone involved, and the ground crew at Cemetery Dance Publications, who maintained this airship and made sure it was in working condition—in particular CD's crew chief, Rich Chizmar, and operations agent Brian Freeman.

Now, if you'll please obey the lighted signs, return your seat backs and tray tables to their full, upright and locked positions, stow any items you may have brought out during flight, turn off any electronic devices you have been using, we're about to land. It might be bumpy, so brace yourself—this is your co-pilot's first flight. Remain seated until the aircraft is parked at the gate and the seat belt sign is extinguished. Be careful opening the luggage bins as items are guaran-damn-teed to have shifted during flight and those heavy bags are just waiting to conk you on the head.

Oh, and if you ever see someone reading this book at an airport or—better yet—on an airplane, please take a picture and send it to us. That would be awesome!

Bev Vincent
The Woodlands, Texas
March 8, 2018

ABOUT THE AUTHORS

Ambrose Bierce (1842-1914) is perhaps best known as the author of *The Devil's Dictionary* and the frequently anthologized short story "An Occurrence at Owl Creek Bridge." He worked as a printer's apprentice and enlisted during the American Civil War, an experience that informed much of his subsequent writing. For a quarter of a century, he wrote and worked for newspapers on both coasts. In search of further wartime experience, he disappeared while traveling to Mexico to observe the revolution led by Pancho Villa. His fate is unknown.

Tom Bissell (1974-) was born in Escanaba, Michigan. He is the author of nine books, including the *New York Times*-bestselling *The Disaster Artist* (written with Greg Sestero) and *Apostle*. His work has been awarded the Rome Prize and a Guggenheim Fellowship. He lives in Los Angeles with his family.

Ray Bradbury (1920-2012) was the author of more than three dozen books, including such classics as *Fahrenheit 451*, *The Martian Chronicles*, *The Illustrated Man*, *Dandelion Wine*, and *Something Wicked This Way Comes*, as well as hundreds of short stories. He wrote for theater, cinema, and TV, including the screenplay for John Huston's *Moby Dick* and the Emmy Award-winning teleplay *The Halloween Tree*, and adapted for television sixty-five of his stories for *The Ray Bradbury Theater*. He was the recipient of the 2000 National Book Foundation's Medal for Distinguished Contribution to American Letters, the 2007 Pulitzer Prize Special Citation, and numerous other honors.

Roald Dahl (1916-1990) was born in Cardiff of Norwegian descent. He joined the RAF at the age of twenty-three and began writing for adults after being injured in a plane crash during World War II. Sitting in a hut at the bottom of his garden, he went on to write some of the world's best-loved children's stories, including *Matilda, Charlie and the Chocolate Factory* and *The BFG*. Today, his stories have been translated into 60 languages and he has sold more than 250 million books. Many of these stories have also been adapted for stage and screen, including the 1971 film classic, *Willy Wonka and the Chocolate Factory*, Wes Anderson's acclaimed *Fantastic Mr Fox*, Steven Spielberg's *The BFG* and the multi-award-winning *Matilda The Musical* from the RSC with music by Tim Minchin. Dahl died in November 1990.

James L. Dickey (1923-1997) was an American poet and novelist best known as the author of *Deliverance*, which was adapted as a major motion picture in 1972. Dickey had a cameo in the movie as a sheriff. He served as a radar operator in a night flier squadron in the U.S. Army Air Corps during World War II and served again in the U.S. Air Force during the Korean War. After receiving a bachelor's degree in English and Philosophy from Vanderbilt, he returned to complete an M.A. in English at the same institution. He taught at the Rice Institute and the University of Florida, and spent several years writing advertising copy. He started publishing collections of his poetry in 1960, and was the recipient of a Guggenheim Fellowship and a National Book Award for Poetry, as well as being named poetry consultant for the Library of Congress. After serving as a visiting lecturer throughout most of the 1960s, he became a professor of English and writer-in-residence at the University of South Carolina in 1969. He was appointed the eighteenth United States Poet Laureate in 1966 and was invited to read at President Jimmy Carter's inauguration in 1977. His reading of his poem "The Moon Ground" was broadcast on television on the day of the Apollo 11 moon landing in July 1969.

Arthur Conan Doyle (1859-1930) was a physician who created Sherlock Holmes, a consulting detective who appeared in dozens of short stories and four novels. Doyle also wrote historical novels and adventure stories featuring Professor Challenger. He wrote about the Boer War and other issues related to the African continent, but became fascinated by spiritualism, an interest that put him into conflict with the likes of Harry Houdini and Joseph McCabe. His autobiography, *Memories and Adventures*, was published six years before his death.

Cody Goodfellow (1970-) has written seven solo novels and three with *NY Times*-bestselling author John Skipp, and two of his four collections of short fiction, *Silent Weapons for Quiet Wars* and *All-Monster Action*, received the Wonderland Book Award. He wrote, co-produced and scored the short Lovecraftian hygiene film *Stay-At-Home Dad*. As a hierophant of the Esoteric Order of Dagon, he presides over several Cthulhu Prayer Breakfasts each year. He recently played an Amish farmer in a Days Inn commercial, and has appeared in the background on numerous TV programs, including *Aquarius*, *American Horror Story: Roanoke*, *G.L.O.W.*, *You're The Worst*, *Kirby Buckets*, *Kevin Hart's Guide to Black History* and videos by Anthrax and Beck. He is also a cofounder of Perilous Press, an occasional micropublisher of modern cosmic horror. Despite what you may have read elsewhere, he actually lives in Portland, Oregon.

Joe Hill (1972-) is the #1 *New York Times*-bestselling author of *The Fireman, NOS4A2,* and, most recently, *Strange Weather.* As he lives part of his life in the United Kingdom and part of his life in the States, he spends quite a bit of the time in the air, musing about all the hideous things that could happen to a person at 30,000 feet.

Stephen King (1947-) made his first professional short story sale in 1967 to *Startling Mystery Stories.* In the fall of 1971, he began teaching high school English classes at Hampden Academy, the public high school in Hampden, Maine. Writing in the evenings and on the weekends, he continued to produce short stories and to work on novels. In the spring of 1973, Doubleday & Co., accepted the novel *Carrie* for publication, providing him the means to leave teaching and write full-time. He has since published over 50 books and has become one of the world's most successful writers. King is the recipient of the 2003 National Book Foundation Medal for Distinguished Contribution to American Letters, the 2014 National Medal of Arts and the 2018 PEN America Literary Service Award.

E. Michael Lewis (1972-) is an aviation and ghost story enthusiast who studied creative writing at the University of Puget Sound in Tacoma. His short stories appear in *The Horror Anthology of Horror Anthologies* (Megazanthus Press), *Exotic Gothic 4* (PS Publishing), and *Savage Beasts* (Grey Matter Press). He's also on Facebook and Twitter. He is a lifelong native of the Pacific Northwest, the father of two sons, and the chief attendant of two cats, who are also brothers.

Richard Matheson (1926-2013) is the author of many classic novels and short stories. He wrote in a variety of genres including terror, fantasy, horror, paranormal, suspense, science fiction and western. In addition to books, he wrote prolifically for television (including *The*

Twilight Zone, Night Gallery, Star Trek) and numerous feature films. Many of Matheson's novels and stories have been made into movies including *The Shrinking Man, I Am Legend, Somewhere in Time,* and *What Dreams May Come.* His many awards include the World Fantasy and Bram Stoker Awards for Lifetime Achievement, the Hugo Award, Edgar Award, Spur Award for Best Western Novel, multiple Writer's Guild awards, and in 2010 he was inducted into the Science Fiction Hall of Fame.

David J. Schow (1955-) has had his short stories selected for over 30 volumes of "Year's Best" anthologies across four decades and has won the World Fantasy Award, the ultra-rare Dimension Award from *Twilight Zone* magazine, plus an International Horror Guild Award for *Wild Hairs* (his compendium of "Raving & Drooling" columns written for *Fangoria*). His novels include *The Kill Riff, The Shaft, Rock Breaks Scissors Cut, Bullets of Rain, Gun Work, Hunt Among the Killers of Men, Internecine, Upgunned* and *The Big Crush* (forthcoming). His short stories are collected in *Seeing Red, Lost Angels, Black Leather Required, Crypt Orchids, Eye, Zombie Jam, Havoc Swims Jaded, DJSturbia,* and a career compendium, *DJStories.* He has written extensively for films (*The Crow, Leatherface: Texas Chainsaw Massacre III, The Hills Run Red*) and television (*Tales from the Crypt, Perversions of Science, The Hunger, Masters of Horror*). His other nonfiction work includes *The Art of Drew Struzan* and *The Outer Limits Companion.* A follow-up volume, *The Outer Limits at 50,* won the 2015 Rondo Hatton Classic Horror Award for Best Book. As expert witness you can see him talking and moving around on documentaries and DVDs for everything from *Creature from the Black Lagoon, Incubus* and *The Shawshank Redemption* to *Scream and Scream Again, Beast Wishes* and *The Psycho Legacy.* He is also the editor of the three-volume *Lost*

Bloch series for Subterranean Press and *Elvisland* by John Farris. He co-produced supplements for such DVDs as *Reservoir Dogs*, *From Hell*, *I, Robot*, *The Dirty Dozen* Special Edition and *Chronicles of Narnia: The Lion, the Witch & the Wardrobe*. He was the recipient of the very first J.F. Gonzalez Lifetime Achievement Award, and thanks to him the word "splatterpunk" has been in the Oxford English Dictionary since 2002. He lives and works in his beloved Los Angeles. Google him, by all means.

Dan Simmons (1948-) was born in Peoria, Illinois, and grew up in various cities and small towns in the Midwest, including Brimfield, Illinois, which was the source of his fictional "Elm Haven" in 1991's *Summer of Night* and 2002's *A Winter Haunting*. Dan received a B.A. in English from Wabash College in 1970, winning a national Phi Beta Kappa Award during his senior year for excellence in fiction, journalism and art. Dan received his Masters in Education from Washington University in St. Louis in 1971. He then worked in elementary education for 18 years—2 years in Missouri, 2 years in Buffalo, New York—one year as a specially trained BOCES "resource teacher" and another as a sixth-grade teacher—and 14 years in Colorado.

Peter Tremayne (1943-) now lives in London and first made a reputation writing supernatural thrillers before turning to crime fiction. As a former Celtic scholar he is internationally known for his long running historical crime series, The Sister Fidelma Mysteries. These are set mainly in Ireland in the 7th Century, of which the 29th title has just appeared (July, 2018). Having appeared in numerous languages, an International Sister Fidelma Society was formed in 2001 in the USA and from 2006, a three day international fan gathering has been held in Cashel, Co. Tipperary, the "hometown" of the Fidelma character. Opening the 2014 gathering, Irish Government

Minister for the Environment, Alan Kelly, described the series as "a national treasure." Peter has written only a few non-Fidelma crime stories and "Murder in the Air" shows his talent is not confined to the 7th Century.

E.C. Tubb (1919-2010) is a London-born writer whose work has been translated into more than a dozen languages. In a sixty-year writing career he published over 120 novels and 200 science fiction short stories. His output included historical adventure, detective, and westerns, but he remained best known for his numerous science fiction novels, of which *Alien Dust* (1955) and *The Space Born* (1956) were acknowledged classics. Tubb became famous for his long-running "Dumarest of Terra" series, the galaxy-spanning saga of Earl Dumarest and his search to find the legendary lost planet where he was born—Earth. They eventually spanned 33 titles, the final one, *Child of Earth*, appearing in 2009. Equally well known were his *Space 1999* TV novelizations and his "Cap Kennedy" novels (writing as Gregory Kern). Some of his finest sf short stories were collected in *The Best Science Fiction of E. C. Tubb*. Tubb continued to write up to his death in October, 2010; his final work, *Fires of Satan*, was published in 2013.

John Varley (1947-) was born in Austin and raised on the Gulf Coast. His ticket out of the petrochemical stinks and hellish humidity was a National Merit Scholarship to Michigan State University with plans to be a scientist. Science turned out to be boring. So did English and, shortly after that, school itself. He stopped going to classes except the one where they showed classic movies. He hit the road with a friend, ending up in San Francisco just in time for the Summer of Love, which neither of them knew was going on. The first day there he sang and chanted with Allen Ginsberg in a hippie crash pad. He decided he was a hippie. He lived in Tucson where he met Linda Ronstadt before she got famous. He got caught in a traffic jam in upstate New York that turned out to be the Woodstock Festival. He couldn't get out for three days. He dodged the draft. In 1973 he decided to become a Science Fiction writer. He was one of the first writers to be called "The New Heinlein." This flattered and troubled him, since the Old Heinlein was a major role model—and not yet dead. His work has been translated into 16 languages he can't read, including Esperanto. There was a ten-year hiatus in his career when he worked in Hollywood. He made good money and once had an office right at the Metro-Goldwyn-Mayer studio gate. He met Mel Gibson, Paul Newman, Sigourney Weaver, Charlton Heston, and many other stars. They were all shorter than he had imagined, except Weaver. (John Varley stands 6' 6" without his cowboy boots.) Varley lived for a while in Portland, Oregon, with Lee Emmett, who has become his first editor. She's good at it and full of useful suggestions. They shared a nineteen-year-old dog named Cirocco, who was the best Sheltie in Oregon. They lived for a few years in a motor home parked fifty yards from the beach on California's Central Coast. They spent four years living in Hollywood in a neighborhood called Thai Town. They currently live in Vancouver, Washington.

Bev Vincent (1961-) is the author of several books, most recently *The Dark Tower Companion*, and over eighty short stories, including appearances in *Alfred Hitchcock's Mystery Magazine*, *Ellery Queen's Mystery Magazine* and two MWA anthologies. His work has been translated into several languages and nominated for the Bram Stoker Award, the Edgar Award and the ITW Thriller Award. He is the 2010 winner of the Al Blanchard Award. For more, see bevvincent. com or follow him on Twitter @BevVincent.